WEATHER CHILD
by
Philippa Ballantine

WEATHER CHILD

by
Philippa Ballantine

Imagine That! Studios, Copyright 2014
All rights reserved.

Cover Art and Design by Alex White
Cover Titles by Renee C. White
Interior Layout by Imagine That! Studios

ISBN 978-0615953489

www.pjballantine.com

For Ruth, Jean and Dorothy
Formidable, kind, and dearly missed

ACKNOWLEDGEMENTS

Weather Child is my love song to my family and my birthplace, and I hope that is what you find in these words. It took flight as a podcast, and so a thank you to all those that listened and encouraged me, is highly overdue.

Thanks also to Tee Tate, my editor and Lori Holuta, my line editor for whipping this story into a more publishable state.

Alex and Renne White took my image of Faith and brought it to light, so huge thanks to them and their crew for the beautiful cover shot.

To our intern, Katie Bryski who helped lay this book out, and reminded me why this story matters.

And lastly, thank you to my husband, who always encourages me, challenges me, and makes me laugh— which is the stuff that keeps an author moving. That and a good cup of tea as Faith might well brew.

TABLE OF CONTENTS

PRELDE

Gallipoli, Turkey. August 15, 1915

Sergeant Jack Cunningham sat in the mud at the bottom of the trench and knew for certain his death was a mere five feet away. Captain Morrow—a pretty good sort as far as officers went—was trying his very best to encourage men who all knew the truth just as well as Jack did.

It was the end; no more grumbling, no more weevils in the bread, no more constant terror—but then again no more chances, no more jokes, and no possibility of seeing New Zealand ever again.

The seraphim should have made everything all right. They were the hope of the allies, those invisible creatures living inside the New Zealanders that made them magicians, and yet in this situation they were unreliable. For some reason the seraphim revolted at killing even when it meant endangering their host; the army had a boat full of gibbering and broken men to attest to that terrible fact.

This shame the New Zealanders felt most keenly—that they could have saved their fellow soldiers' lives if only they became more. The odd person tried to Awaken a seraph by cutting themselves severely enough to invoke their presence. If those poor sods somehow succeeded, they ended up drafted to the Corp. If they didn't, they could be shot as malingers, or die in agony when their wounds became infected. Gallipoli was hell for every soldier, but for the New Zealanders it was a particularly cruel kind.

Jack looked down at his hands, and he realised they weren't his any longer; they belonged to a soldier who'd hadn't seen soap in many weeks, who had slaughtered with his bayonet, and clawed his way through mud merely to stay alive.

His real hands were back in Wellington, where they'd played the piano, grasped the smooth surfaces of beer jugs, and touched the soft skin of his wife.

He and his hands had never meant to be here. Jack was a First Child, the special one of his country, the first offspring of parents who had sailed far to reach the green shores of New Zealand. So, in his blood pumped the special magic of the seraphim, which opened up only for the First Children.

At least Jack had felt that way until he came to the shores of this damned Turkish peninsula. Anything that was special had been washed away in mud, sweat and blood.

A seraph was an answer and a curse at the same time. They had no physical presence, but they were a voice in the head that gave their hosts powers that made them literally magicians. No one knew exactly where they came from, but when they were first encountered, many thought them a kind of angel; others thought them demon. The curse was once you were Awakened, you were immediately and forever different. Even old age affected them more slowly. Not that he expected to make it to old age.

Harry nudged Jack in the side, shaking him from his dreary thoughts. When he shot Jack a shaky grin, it was apparent he wasn't even listening to Morrow. Instead, he turned back to something far more important. He was rolling a cigarette with the carefulness of one who foolishly expected to come back from the offensive. It appeared to be the most important thing in the world to him.

Jack, by comparison, had smoked his plump cigarette in great puffs hours ago, and couldn't even remember what it had tasted like now. He watched with dull distraction as Harry tucked away the leftover tobacco in his pouch and then stuffed it into his jacket pocket. He shook free a match, struck it, and lit his creation. The cigarette was so thin it was nigh on invisible, and the wane light was barely a pinprick in the grey early morning.

"You might as well have given your ciggie a decent send off." Jack shot Harry a glance out of the corner of his eye. "I bet old Will Sharpe wishes he had."

Henry pressed his lips together while slowly shaking his head. They both knew the truth.

William had hung on the wire for five days, mere paces from the trenches that gave such scant protection to his friends. No Man's Land was carpeted with so many bodies—some even formed part of the defences. Arms and legs stuck out at angles from among the sandbags like macabre sticks of wood. Once such horrors would have been unimaginable to Jack—now they were an everyday reality.

Yet it was Will that made the biggest impression, simply because the wind brought the rotten scent wafting in their direction. William had been such a polite young lad that Jack was sure he would have been horrified at this discourtesy.

Yet these were the terrible truths that Jack had almost become immune to. He'd survived the last attempt to take the Turkish trenches, but maybe the next one would get him, as it had William.

The guns had been roaring overhead for an epic eight days, pounding away at the enemy's wire and bunkers in an attempt to soften them. That wire better be bloody down, Jack thought, or the whole company might as well hang themselves up next to William and not bother with the run at all.

The pale and tired sergeant was giving the final orders now. Pulling his helmet down so it at least sat properly on his head, Jack unshouldered his rifle, gave Henry a nod, and then quickly followed him up and over the top.

All was madness up there; a churned mass of mud, bodies, and barbed wire flying at him from all directions. Jack had only glimpses of the rest of his unit ducking and diving, and occasionally dropping for safety into crater holes. Yet it was all an illusion—there was no safety up here.

The whistling sound came from above, and for a second Jack thought of a steam train like the one that ran between Wellington and Auckland. Yet, there couldn't be a train here—

His brain couldn't process fast enough, and then the bomb fell from the sky, exploding not ten feet away. Jack should have died there, but by some strange miracle the shattered remains of a once-tree—the only thing standing for a mile—stood between him and most of the shrapnel.

Hundreds of pieces of metal imbedded themselves in the stout trunk of the dead tree, with a buzzing noise that reminded him of that angry beehive Jack had discovered once in the bush when he was a child. However, plenty of their friends found their target.

He was lifted clear off his feet in a cloud of dust and burning metal. Jack was still conscious and surprised by the lack of pain, even as he was thrown to the ground.

It felt odd to find himself there, lying in the sucking mud, his whole body distant, but his ears ringing. Jack blinked. The sky above was a mass of seething grey cloud, but there was one odd square of blue directly above him.

To his dazed mind it looked like a portal into heaven. It was so beautiful and intense a moment that he could have wept—even when the voice entered his head.

Welcome, Jack. I am Waingaio.

The voice was female, soothing and kind. Jack instantly realised what it was.

No death for him. For Jack Cunningham it was a new, second life. He had never wanted a seraph, never wanted magic—but here it was nevertheless.

As he felt Henry grab and carry him back to their trench, a tear leaked from Jack's eye. Realisation had him. After this, nothing would ever be the same. He was trapped forever in an Awakened life with a seraph.

PART ONE

The Spanish Lady

Wellington, New Zealand, 1918

CHAPTER ONE

Sounds of the pursuit—the shouts of armed men and the crash of horses through the undergrowth—echoed up to the hilltop farm. Faith dropped the final pieces of washing back down into the basket, unhitched her apron into the waist of her skirt, and paused a moment.

It was a surprisingly warm spring day, and she was glad for a moment to stop even if it was to listen to shouting. Below, as far as she could see, there was nothing but a cloth of deep green trees running down to the distant beach; only the narrow dirt track made any impression at all on the wilderness. With her back to their farm it looked almost as it would have when her family first came to these fierce Tararua foothills. The wind whipped flax bushes and dense pockets of forest were as mysterious as they had been before any human had dared this country right on the edge.

Their farm seldom had any visitors, so the sight of a man urging his horse up the narrow zigzag path was unusual—as unusual as the sounds coming from the forest.

Shielding her eyes against the sun, Faith realised with a lurch that she recognised the uniform the mounted man wore. In a country moulded by the power of the Awakened and their seraphim, there was only one authority that could control them. She'd never seen any of the Officers of Awakening, more commonly known as Eyes, on her family's remote farm, but in Wellington she had many times. Her father ran a hotel there, and the city was used to the deep brown uniformed men and women keeping the seraphim hosts under control. They were Awakened themselves, and a living example of "send a thief to catch a thief."

Seeing them here and now, made Faith's stomach lurch violently. She'd been taught to fear them for most of her life, so by rights she should have run for the house. Nevertheless she remained rooted to the spot.

The official on the horse didn't much look like he was in control of anything. As Faith watched, he wheeled about, urging his horse off the track, and into the thick bush without much heed of his own safety. New Zealand forests could swallow battalions of men—so a single one would be nothing at all.

Now Faith could hear equally angry replies from under the thick cloak of bush. Obviously there was more than one person involved in the pursuit. This could well be the most exciting event the farm had ever seen.

The main trunk railway line between Auckland and Wellington followed the curve of the beach nearer to the sea than the vast lonely hills that her family farm was on. Faith understood immediately that these Eyes were hunting an escaped Awakened. Mad seraphim and their hosts had wrecked havoc before, and they could not be allowed to about with civilized folk—she understood that too—but part of her was with her fellow Awakened, urging her on.

If she cared to, Faith could feel the chase in her mind with considerable accuracy—better than any of her normal senses. She tucked her annoyingly curly hair once again behind her ear, and gave into curiosity.

Who is down there?

She could use words. Her seraph in the manner of his kind, could not, but what he could do was open a small window to power. Faith was suddenly aware of the pursued. The prisoner was moving fast up the hill, her mind full of fierce determination, but her body was old and wracked with pain. Faith could feel the sweat on her face, her hair getting in her eyes, and the ache deep down in her bones. The pursuers were trailing well behind; one on horseback, and two more swearing and cursing as they pursued her through the undergrowth.

New Zealand bush was unlike any northern hemisphere forest. While Faith had seen pictures of glades and tall straight trees in books and magazines, bush was thick—almost jungle-like. Plants crowded together. It was dark, moist and slippery. Hunter and hunted were not having a pleasant time of it— especially after two days of heavy rain. Yet they were drawing relentlessly ever closer, panting up the hill towards the farmhouse.

Faith shot a look over her shoulder, but she was quite alone. Her uncles, Jim and Roger, were up in the backblocks moving the sheep down for shearing. Her mother and sister were getting the quarters ready for the shearers who would arrive in a couple of days, so even if Faith yelled, no one would hear.

A normal girl of eighteen would probably have been very afraid in such a situation. Faith was not—safe in the knowledge that with Hoa she was never alone or vulnerable. The pain it would cost was a secondary concern.

The pursued woman emerged from the bush, and for a moment stood on the edge of the farm garden, blinking in the sunlight while staring at Faith. The hunted woman was filthy, covered in mud up to her knees, and bleeding from cuts on her face.

She wasn't what Faith would have expected from a fugitive; a frightened woman of about fifty, slightly dumpy. Faith would have passed her on the street without a second look that was except for her bound hands, Government Issue yellow coveralls, and the press of a frightened seraph mind against mental restraints. They always bound the seraph at the hospitals, but they could still be heard by the Awakened, yammering in fear for release.

Before Faith could move in any direction, the woman had scrambled up the slight slope. She slipped in her haste and landed on the girl's feet like some ancient petitioner.

Living on the farm, Faith had little chance to meet other Awakened—let alone any of the older generation. Those that had lived for a long time with the whispering of a seraph in the back of their minds were unknown to her; a glimpse into her own future. Plenty didn't make it to middle age at all. Many succumbed to suicide, madness or death. The rest of the world might envy New Zealanders, but they didn't think overly on the price that purchased that power. Not every day was one you wanted to share with another being. Sometime loneliness was a treasure Faith missed.

Today, however, was not a day where she was apparently fated to be anywhere near alone. Without thinking, Faith helped the older woman to her feet. The escapee smelt of sweat and dirt, was completely sodden, and her eyes flickered with a hint of gold in the iris; a sign that her seraph was perilously near to taking over.

Faith flinched back as the older woman latched tight onto her hand. Inside the girl's head, Hoa squirmed in anger and fear, causing panic to rush through his host. Faith tried to calmly unlatch the tightening fingers to no success.

"Please," she gasped out, trying to sound as polite as possible.

The escapee's mouth worked though no words came out, and Faith saw that she had no tongue. Her mouth was an empty wound. The girl muffled a cry as the image of the woman slicing out her own tongue darted across the slight link between their two seraphim. Madness had caught up with this poor unfortunate, and it now wrapped its tentacles around Faith across the link.

Pushed beyond the limits of civility, the younger woman shoved the escapee hard. Finally, she broke the physical hold, and sent the other sprawling. Faith looked around wildly for assistance, but the Government's men were nowhere to be seen.

When the girl glanced down at their prey, the older woman made direct and incredibly blatant mind to mind contact. It was beyond bad manners among the Awakened.

Make a choice, girl for the shadows are coming with their pretty faces. They will devour you, suck away your magic, and spit out the bones.

Faith gasped. Her right hand went unconsciously to her left and rubbed the spot where her ring finger should have been but was not.

They will turn you inside out girl-thing—just as they did to me.

It was the gagging fear that constantly bought her screaming out of sleep. It was the nagging constant worry that could sneak up on her even in moments of happiness. It was the one thought that Faith had to practice keeping at bay when her mind wasn't occupied. She could go mad. Effortlessly.

The seraphim's constant desire to please meant that the temptation to use the power they offered was constant. Faith knew people who looked on their companions as the enemy had it the easiest, but for her, Hoa was a friend, and he never denied her anything. If Faith wanted, she could ask for the power and he would give it blindly— perhaps somehow thinking that she would know her own limits.

The terrible truth was Faith wasn't stronger than any other human. She didn't want to be turned inside out, but she also knew deep, deep down she craved that power. Was this what the woman meant? Could she see that weakness?

The plague is coming and he rides on its coat tails. Beware the storm, beware yourself!

Faith clenched her remaining fingers around the stump of the one that had been taken fourteen years before. The door that had been opened that day to allow the seraph in couldn't be closed, but she had to live in this world and abide by its rules. The authorities knew best. The Awakened needed to be watched. She knew intimately how weak and dangerous they could be.

So Faith pulled back from the woman and broke the mental contact she had thrust upon her.

"Up here," Faith called to the man on horseback. While the escapee watched in pale horror, the younger woman waved wildly to the Eyes below. In a few moments the man had galloped up the remainder of the path. His horse was sweating and snorting, but his quarry hadn't moved—trapped in blank dismay.

The Eye looked down at Faith with blatant distrust, while his seraph prodded at the edges of her awareness. She met his gaze steadily so that he could see no trace of gold was in her bright blue eyes. Faith was aware that she was not especially beautiful, but she was proud of being Awakened.

The officer seemed to catch that because he smiled and dropped down from his horse. "You've done us a great service, Miss. She's a dangerous madwoman, so you're lucky to be alive."

The woman in question was suddenly grubbing around in the dirt, as if she expected to be able to dig her way out of the situation. She didn't look dangerous, but Faith was prepared to take his word on the matter. He was after all the law. His two fellow Eyes finally emerged from the bush looking annoyed, relieved, and almost as woebegone as their fugitive. Faith could tell that only one of them was Awakened.

The older Māori man, with a weather beaten face and pale eyes, was a second generation. The seraphim within his bloodline had died with his ancestor, but they had left a thin thread of magic in the descendants. Those lesser powers though were still more than any foreigner could claim.

Hoa showed her that his powers were those of a tracker. It was a common talent among the Māori, the *Tangata Whenua* who had been living in New Zealand a thousand years before her own people,. They had paid the price to reignite the seraphim in their blood by welcoming settlers to their lands. New comers like Faith's parents had bought back the powers that had faded into Māori myth from their own time of arrival. Magicians were not common, but neither were they rare in New Zealand now.

The second Eye was younger, but more out of breath. He had a crop of wild red hair that was peppered with samples of the local vegetation, and he probably would have started the conversation with a choice word or two—but then he saw Faith. Brushing his hair vigorously, he shot her an abashed look.

Faith smiled at him in the general way young women did towards handsome young men met suddenly and in unexpected circumstances.

Distracted as the two of them were, the prisoner's sudden surge of life took them all by surprise. Lurching forward, she grabbed hold of Faith's four-fingered hand as if it could save her from drowning. The shock of the contact ran up the girl's arm and right into Hoa. Suddenly she and the prisoner were in that most terrible of things; direct seraphim contact.

The young girl and the old woman had similar experiences; the pain of the seraphim's arrival in their life, the distrust of the majority of their fellow New Zealanders, and above all the fear of madness. The world flared around both of them: the bright blue sky burned harsh against their eyes, the smell of the sea slammed into the soft cells of their brains, and the call of the gulls below was like a knife thrust in each ear.

Every one of the Awakened had their own gifts, mostly insignificant magics that barely disturbed the surface of their lives, yet a small portion could touch greater powers. The joy of these larger magics was bought with madness and pain.

This frightened creature who had Faith locked in a moment of utter closeness was one of those full with magic. It had driven her mad but now she turned that insanity in the younger woman's direction.

A curse on you, Faith Louden, for turning against your own. May you and yours draw the darkness to you. May it follow your spirit in every realm and never will you find rest or love while the Craven Man walks. Break his power or never know joy.

The connection snapped free, and Faith was left gaping as the three officers pulled the dead-eyed woman from her. It was too late. Whatever she could do had been done. Hoa thrashed within her; supplanting her terror with his own rage.

"Sorry miss," the younger Eye stammered. They wouldn't have noticed. A curse was an intimate thing between two people and two seraphim.

The elder touched the top of the now re-captured prisoner's head. A faint halo of light flared briefly around her hair before she subsided completely like a puppet with her strings cut. The man's face relaxed a little; the requirements of his magic had been satisfied.

Faith barely noticed as they swung the woman unceremoniously over the back of the horse.

"There might be a reward, you know," the mounted Eye said to Faith as the rest of his men set off down the hill.

She swallowed a swirl of foreboding in her stomach. Though her magic was not that of foretelling, she had no doubt that the woman's curse would not be easily shaken off or ignored.

"It was just my duty," she managed through a suddenly dry throat. "There's no need to bother yourself."

She didn't watch him leave. Only the sound of hoof beats and the sobbing of the prisoner's mind told Faith they had gone. Shorecliff was the best place for those incapable of controlling their magic, so she shouldn't feel guilty about anything she'd just done.

Faith wrapped her arms around herself, and tried to tell herself that until she might actually believe it.

CHAPTER TWO

To have magic one must first have pain—Lily knew that well enough. Her mother had plenty of pain yet absolutely no magic, and it was only magic that offered any kind of hope.

Lily knelt on trembling knees at her mother's bedside, mopping her sweat away as best she could, for she was the only nurse her mother had. Even though the one room house wasn't isolated, and they had plenty of neighbours, all of them were either sick or too terrified of getting sick to help.

We don't need anyone else, Lily thought grimly. *I am old enough to do this.*

And she was calm until her mother started screaming hysterically for Lily's father and for her own long dead parents. Eventually she lost her energy, and subsided into thrashing feebly in the bed. The girl held the hot sweaty hand of Barbara Louden and prayed she would be still. Helpless, she watched as those pale beautiful features dissolved into terrifying blueness.

As if on cue her mother gained a sudden burst of strength.

"Lily...they're coming, Lily! We have to get out!" Her voice came out as a harsh gasp as she flopped around like a half-gutted fish.

It was hard to tell if she meant the landlord or some other delusion that only existed inside her feverish brain.

"Lie down, Mum," Lily squeaked. Her mother had always been so hale and hearty, but the form struggling half-in and half-out of the bed was like a feral creature.

Finally, Lily dared to push her back hard into the bed. Immediately guilty, she tried to mop her mother's brow with a damp cloth. It had been supplied by Mrs Agnew from next door, along with a half-stub of candle, a loaf of bread, and a tin of beans. It was the best Lily could hope for, as the Agnews had eight children of their own to take care of, and were probably just as terrified.

Lily's mother eyes went wide in fear, and she battered at her daughter's hand. Eventually, Lily gave up and sunk down on her knees, her eyes pricking with tears.

Leaking in from outside on the streets of Te Aro were the sobs and cries of others. The influenza had cruelly arrived just before peace, and the ringing of the bells for the Armistice had also served to toll for the dead. It was killing those that had thought they'd survived the war; those who'd been looking forward to welcoming home their soldier brothers, sons and husbands.

Not even the envied New Zealand magic could save the sick, for all of the Awakened had been drafted into the army; the healers among those most prized for sending to the front.

Apart from the rattle of a horse drawn hearse, and the stifled sobs of the afflicted, the streets outside were silent. Children were usually playing on the street, mothers hanging their washing in the brisk Wellington wind and gossiping over scraggly fences. Now all was quiet. The Spanish Lady, as they called the epidemic, had cast her veil on the whole city.

Apparently now, the Lady was setting to visit Lily as well. The room and her mother's pain had a blurry quality, as if she was seeing everything through a distorted pane of glass. Every now and then a shiver ran through her, and the girl knew what would come. She might not have long herself. She'd long ago abandoned games and playing to help her mother with her laundry business, but she wasn't all grown up. She still needed someone to tell her it was all right, someone to lie to her, but there was no one. Mother had seen to that, pushing away the family she said had rejected her marriage with enough bitterness to keep them away permanently.

Her mother surged upright again with a shriek and clutched her daughter to her. Her dry lips pressed against Lily's neck, "Samuel? Samuel? Save us!"

The girl closed her eyes and held back a sob. Father should even now be on a troop ship. Like every other able bodied man in New Zealand, he'd answered the call of Mother England and sailed away three years before. By some miracle he'd survived when others had not. His letters, ragged and tired from so much re-reading, were folded up and tucked under the very bed they sat on. He'd fought in Gallipoli and France, and now he should be on a ship back home. If Mother could only hold on it'd be all right. The girl clutched to that thought as tightly as her mother did to her.

After a frightening few minutes, Mum sagged back with a sigh, and Lily slumped back onto the floor. Letting her head rest on the edge of the bed, she watched with drooping eyes as her mother's dry lips moved with words she no longer had enough breath to voice. It could have been a prayer or just fevered ramblings.

A tentative knock on the door made Lily start from her spiral into fever. Surely that was a figment of her imagination. Surely she couldn't have summoned up a doctor from thin air. It took a long moment for her eyes to focus enough for her to make it to the door. It seemed easier and far more sensible to crawl towards it.

"Lily...Lily dear?" Mrs Agnew's voice sounded very strange and far off.

The girl propped her cheek against the door. It felt reassuringly cool, while her own skin burned, and her throat felt like a clenched knot. She barely managed a soft mutter of acknowledgment through it.

Mrs Agnew was crying. It was very sweet of her. "Lily...Lily is your mother there?"

She didn't know? Could it only be yesterday afternoon that they'd both been outside hanging the clothes on the line? Mother had complained about feeling a little odd then. So strange, but a day was indeed all the time that had passed.

"She's ill," Lily whispered, careful not to breathe into the gap in the door least the Spanish Lady visit their one kind neighbour.

A chill silence crept up, and she could only hope that Mrs Agnew hadn't run off in terror. Lily slipped against the door, but it felt good to be somewhat closer to lying down.

"It's alright, Lily." Mrs Agnew was obviously made of sterner stuff than most, since she was still there. "Hang a cloth in the window, the red one your mother has on the table. I'll go down to Mr Breaden's shop, and use his telephone. We'll get you to hospital—hold on my dear."

Lily heard her footsteps rushing away. Mrs Agnew was always rushing, always doing something...

Somehow Lily found the strength to do as she said though; hanging the red square of fabric her mother had used as a tablecloth out of the window.

Mother began to cough again while Lily staggered to the bedside. The deep wrenching sound rocked her body, and when she finally stopped there was the shocking redness of blood in the handkerchief her daughter had held up for her. It was as scarlet as the cloth in the window. Lily wanted to scream in horror, but instead she just stared down mournfully at her mother.

The blue mottled appearance of her face made a strange contrast against her flyaway blonde hair. Her lips, also the same colour, were dry and stretched. Nothing beautiful remained of the woman who had laughed and set off for the inhalation chamber set up in the town hall. People had been recommending it; a trip to secure healthiness and fend off the influenza, they said.

Mum had wanted to remain healthy, to look after her daughter, and see her husband come home. Her friend from further up the road, Edith Morrison, had set off with her.

Lily feverishly recalled them waving cheerily from the street. Despite everything around them they'd smiled—confident that the terror couldn't possibly touch them. Lily held onto that image as best she could. It was the last time Mum had smiled because bending over the laundry even later that day she'd been feeling it. She'd looked up with horror in her eyes as sweat had beaded on her forehead, as realisation slowly spread across her features.

In the hospital, Lily thought dreamily, *Mum will get better. Father will come home and everything will be all right. Mum would be propped up in bed, looking lovely again, her arms spread wide for him to fall into.*

Lily, not quite deep enough in the fantasy, coughed into the corner of the bedclothes. She didn't want to disturb Mum. Yet as she turned her head, she realised that they weren't alone in the room—and it wasn't a doctor or a nurse. She could see nothing solid, only a shadow. She hadn't heard the door though. Lily's head dropped against her forearms, but she couldn't quite find the energy to look up. Under her elbows, the girl could see a form solidifying in the corner.

"Mrs Agnew?" she asked weakly. Though how could their neighbour possibly be inside, with the key in the door, and a dread fear of infection?

"Shhhh," the shadow whispered. "Don't make a sound, Awakened...beloved..."

Mum made a cry like a mewling kitten while wriggling through the bedclothes to huddle against the wall. It was cooler in the room—through the fever the girl could feel that. Surely it was death come to collect them both. Only then did Lily begin to cry. She felt so bad. It wasn't fair.

Scrambling up onto the bed with her mother, she tucked herself in behind her, and tried to take her hand. Her mother shook her off with half a scream, and Lily found herself dumped unceremoniously onto the wooden floor. Across the room, the shadow still lurked, but it was growing.

What about Dad? He'd be so sad to get off the boat and find them dead. Mrs Agnew would have to tell him. They'll put us in the ground and forget we ever existed.

In her head she could hear the echo of the hearse rattling up Aro Street heading for the Karori cemetery, taking them to join all the others.

"You do not belong to the dirt." A face began to resolve itself in the darkness. "You have a chance to reach the stars and undreamed of power. First Child..."

They called them that, Awakened. Mum had been born in the slums of Birmingham and Dad in Scotland. Her bloodline was fresh to New Zealand, so she could Awaken. Yet her parent's had always resisted following others' dark impulses; forcing pain deliberately to bring on the process. Parents had done horrible things on the chance that their child would Awaken.

"No one will miss you, Lily." Eyes, normal human eyes, were now in the shadow, and a human face emerging to go with it. She didn't know who this person was, or how he had gotten into their tiny room, but there was something deeply disturbing about how he looked at her. All her mother's tales, all the warnings of those who preyed on the First, suddenly bubbled to the top of her mind.

Lily though, had nowhere to go and no strength to move, in any case. The world was dissolving into nothingness before her eyes.

Mum let out a terrible wracking cough. It seemed to go on forever before coming to an unexpected horrible stop. Her last gasp evaporated into the air, and then the room was chillingly silent.

The man laughed. "That's it for her."

Lily stuttered denials under her breath, while she could actually watch Mum's hand on top of the coverlet turn black like mould stealing over bread. The sane, happy part of Lily abandoned reality, retreating inside her head, leaving the sobbing and terrified remainder to cope with the horror.

The man shook free the last of the shadows that clung to his shoulders and walked to the bed. His polished dark boots rang with military precision on the wooden floor, and he seemed to fill the whole room. Lily trembled, caught between the terror rolling from his direction, and the blackening corpse that had been her mother. Her feet tangled in the blankets as she struggled weakly to get free. When by some miracle she managed to get to the door, sweating and crying in equal measure, he followed. The stranger stood watching her rattle on the door in vain.

His eyes were golden and terrifyingly focused. A smile tugged at the corner of his mouth as though she were merely some interesting exhibit trapped in a jar—then he bent down to Lily.

"Don't you remember, silly girl? Mum locked the door. The key is in her pocket."

A wave of fear swallowed Lily. "I want to die…let me go to her, please!"

Pitiless eyes glinted over her. "Oh now dear First, you won't die. Where would be the fun in that? I will heal you and make you all mine."

His hand caressed her cheek, and it was colder than anything she had ever experienced. Lily could actually feel her skin parting under his fingers.

"There now," he whispered, "my first little gift; something to remember me by."

And then he pulled her to him—into the darkness. Lily didn't even have time to scream.

CHAPTER THREE

Jack Cunningham and Hemi Cooper stepped down off the troopship and took their first real, deep breath of Wellington air. It was—as always—fresh. While they smiled, other soldiers swore, and pulled their coats tighter about themselves.

Jack enjoyed the rugged blast of it; the southerly straight off Antarctica reminded him with its familiar sting that he was home.

When he'd last felt its vigorous assault he'd been only eighteen, standing on this very dock, anticipating the adventure of war with all the stupidity of the inexperienced. His wife, Alice had cried—the only time he'd seen her shed tears over anything.

He was spared any further introspection when he and Hemi were jostled by other soldiers, also eager to make their way to land. The relatively good-natured swearing crowd moved them on down the gangplank.

"Good to be home, eh Jack?" Hemi's handsome dark face split with a joyful smile.

It was, and it wasn't, but Jack wasn't going to spoil his friend's happiness. "Yeah, sure is! Can hardly wait to see the old place."

They let themselves be carried along in the rush of soldiers, part of a joyful, crazy mob. Other people's wives, mothers, sisters and daughters were all on the docks to welcome home their loved ones. They bounced on their toes while tears poured down their cheeks, cried out and waved frantically.

Jack realised though, that there were far less greeters then there should have been. The flu had whistled through his hometown, and carried off far too many—just like the rest of the world. Even if it hadn't, there would still be no one to scream his name and rush into his arms. Olive maybe, but he doubted any of his letters had got through to his sister.

Hemi was in the same unhappy company. His whanau, his extended family in the Māori tradition, were in the Waikato part of the country. His chief hadn't wanted any of the young men to volunteer for war and certainly not for the Royal New Zealand Corps of Magic.

The seraphim were perceived differently by Māori. When they sailed their way to New Zealand from the other Polynesian islands, the symbiotes had taken to those very first First Children, giving them powers enough to make them demi-gods. Those early Māori pioneers called them the toa.

However, after that first giddy rush, the seraphim took no more of their people and the magic in the bloodlines dwindled, so that Māori with lesser powers were what the first white man, Captain James Cook, had encountered. So when newcomers arrived, and with them the possibility of more Awakened, many Māori had turned away in disgust. Others, like Hemi's father, had deliberately sought out a non-Māori wife to bring the seraphim back to the native people.

Māori treasured the Awakened—unlike the rest of society—so Hemi's decision to join the Magic Corp had left him somewhat adrift within his own tribe. They did not appreciate him risking his life for a far off power, but Hemi was like Jack and had foolishly yearned for adventure.

The British Empire actively sought out any Awakened; Māori, white, or even Chinese. After his induction by pain and suffering at Gallipoli, the corps had demanded Jack join them. He would much rather have remained with his own troop but he really didn't have a choice. Besides, a barrier had gone up between them when the seraph arrived. Immediately, men who he'd thought of as brothers had grown cold out of fear and jealousy. He could understand the first but never the second.

Still, today was not a day to linger on old wounds; it was a day to celebrate the miracle of homecoming—even if his own was slightly muted.

Jack shouldered his rucksack and followed Hemi as they pushed through the crowd of jubilant people and away from the docks. The mobs of people were not just waiting for the ships, and they found themselves carried through the streets by the tide of cheering folk.

Pushed back and forwards among the laughing, crying people Jack had little time to take in the city. Everywhere seemed to be pools of soldiers; washed up in little drifts on the pavements, congregating with people they ran into on the street, or gathering around shop windows to stare at delicacies that hadn't had in years.

Women were everywhere too. Jack saw their smiles, their laughter, and their beauty as a kind of sweet dream.

Hemi nudged Jack from his reverie with a grin. "Come on. We'll drop our gear off at this boarding house Auntie wrote to me about and then hit the town." He pressed the ragged address torn from a letter into his friend's hand like it was a magic talisman.

Jack scuffed his boots and fervently wished he could oblige. "I should visit my parents..."

Hemi cocked his head. "Heck, I almost forgot you came from Wellington! I guess you won't be needing a place to kip then since you'll be staying with your folks..." He shot his friend a half-amused half-appraising look. Hemi knew Jack's history very well. Home was one of the few things men at war had to talk about in the grinding terror of the trenches.

Jack felt the edge of his joy nibbled away a little. "Well, I might just not rely on that, otherwise I could end up sleeping in the street." He tried to make his tone light, but it didn't work.

Hemi readjusted his pack. "You wouldn't be alone, mate. A lot of these fellas will be partying all night and not worrying about a bed to sleep in."

Jack glanced down at the address in his hand. The boarding house was a reasonable way up Aro Street, not the nicest part of town, but still better than a crowded ship or a trench. He flashed Hemi a grin that didn't go all the way through. "Let's just say you better book me a bed as well. I doubt that I will be getting much of a welcome. I'll see you later, alright?"

Then, before Hemi could try to offer some sort of comfort or advice, Jack took his chance and disappeared into the crowd. It was hard work getting through the press of people all huddled together, but he finally he managed to get down Featherston Street and across to Willis Street where the crowds thinned enough to allow the trams to be running. The tram looked a marvel of technology after his time in Gallipoli and he smiled as he paid his penny and climbed on board. The red tram rattled off south in the direction of Haitaitai.

Jack climbed up to sit on the top where the wind blew fierce enough to chase away the mounting unease in his stomach. From there he watched the city rattle and grind its way past him. It suddenly struck him; this was the very trip on which he'd first met Alice.

He'd tortured himself about her plenty while he was away, but it was now obvious that he hadn't considered what coming home would mean and the memories it would stir up.

Examining their history in the dire muddy trenches had been a way to escape reality. Now here, where it had all happened, where she had breathed her last, was another story. These were the streets they'd shared, and her ghost was waiting for him on every corner.

Jack leaned back in the seat and endeavoured to turn his mind in another direction; he wanted to know how much home had changed.

Not that much, it turned out. As they escaped the city itself and trundled out into the suburbs, the shops gave way to neat wooden houses. Most were beautifully kept and—apart from being wood rather than brick—the same as ones in England. Gardens were full of hollyhocks and roses while children played among them. It was good to see little ones enjoying themselves, because in Europe there had been scant examples of that. In Wellington was almost as if nothing had happened—as if he had stepped back in time.

Jack finally hopped down at the stop closest to his parents' house, but took his time walking up the street. On this row, the houses changed from simple structures to the elaborate dwellings of the more affluent of Wellington. The gardens became elegant, restrained, and not dedicated to anything as common as vegetables.

He kept his hands in his pockets, until he reached the most splendid one on the street. The old house looked the same; tall and imposing, but not as much as it once had. In his childhood it had loomed almost as large as his father, but since seeing a few grand family mansions in England he knew it for an antipodean pretension.

As Jack opened the gate and walked up the path, he could see that the fretwork around the windows needed paint, and the roses didn't appear as well tended as he remembered. His footsteps echoed on the veranda, and he half expected to hear the strains of Mozart coming out from the parlour.

Jack hesitated for a moment and then rang the doorbell.

Inside a clock chimed, he heard muffled footsteps, and then Edith answered the door. Immediately it was obvious that much like the outside of the house, she needed some repair work. Her expression showed no surprise at him being on the doorstep—but no delight either. Edith was as dour as a Yorkshire woman came, and she stared at him for a long minute while offering no welcome. She was his father's minion as always.

Jack smiled at her, feeling every inch of the stubble on his face and every speck of dirt on his uniform. "Good afternoon, Edith. I'm here to see my mother…"

Her eyes flickered away from him, down the silent corridor, but eventually she stepped back to let him in, and then closed the door brusquely behind him. "I'll tell your father you are here."

Before he could protest, she hurried off at remarkable speed for someone her age. Left at a loose end, Jack wandered into the parlour.

He was a stranger here—both in this particular room and the house itself. As a child, Jack had seldom been allowed in the front room that was his mother's domain, but everything looked just as it had when he'd last seen it. The gold framed landscape hung over the marble mantle showing the wilds of Surrey, where his father had been raised. The set of red velvet covered chairs waited next to the window, so that guests could enjoy the view down the hill. The swirling maze of wallpaper in purples and golds, which had been in fashion when he was young, but would have brought peals of laughter from a Londoner, was still the same. Mother's latest tapestry hung on a frame by the window, as if she had just stepped out of the room—and perhaps she had.

Jack's parents had always presented a united front, even at the last occasion of their meeting, when voices had been raised and he might have used the odd curse word. Mother's look had been devastated when his father pronounced his disinheritance—but she had not interjected.

Jack could forgive her that; she was, after all, from another generation of women who, despite having the vote, did not disagree with their husbands—even when they cast off their only son. Perhaps she'd been working to change the old bastard's mind in Jack's absence.

His reminiscences were cut short when the thick oak door opened, and his father strode into the room. Royal Cunningham was still a massive man. At six foot two inches, he stood a little taller than his son, who also hadn't inherited his blazing copper hair and beard. They did, however, share the same emerald green eyes and stubborn nature. Even at this hour Royal was dressed immaculately, as if he was about to enter parliament or dine at some exclusive club.

Jack frowned, determined not to let his own dusty appearance put him on the back foot. "I'm here to see Mother, not you," he said calmly.

His father glared at him with ferocity that would have sent his managers running. "You were told never to enter my house again."

"As far as I knew this house was never totally yours," Jack returned, his hands flexing only slightly into fists, "and Mother never asked me to stay away."

Royal shook his head like an angry circus bear. He didn't like being reminded that his wife's dowry had set him up in business in the first place, let alone by his own son.

"And Olive," Jack continued, finding he was on a roll now, "she would want to see me. I wrote to her, you know."

Royal Cunningham raised one hand, a great meaty block of strength that as a young boy Jack had lived in fear of. "She's dead."

"Olive?" Jack felt his insides run cold.

"No, your mother," his father said shortly, and then looked around at all the feminine things that she had treasured. Jack wasn't so blind that he didn't see pain there, but he was wrapped in his own, and cared too little what Royal thought to offer any sympathy.

Jack closed his eyes. Here in the parlour he could still smell a faint hint of lavender, as if Mother had just stepped out for a moment. He'd imagined this day so clearly. Seen in his mind's eye, her leaping up from her needlework and embracing him in that strangely powerful hug she always had. Now that possibility was gone.

In that moment of shock, his father flung open the parlour door and strode across the corridor into his study.

Jack stood there for a second. The awful thing was, he didn't have any tears left. He'd used them all in Europe and for Alice. He now realised he should have saved a few. That was the trouble; for him New Zealand had stopped still, trapped in amber, a time warp of happy memories. That was stupid. Things happened here, people aged, and obviously died as well.

Mother had always been hale and hearty, cycling, swimming—the polar opposite of an English genteel lady. She'd become a woman of the new world and been proud of it. He couldn't imagine any scenario where she would just up and die.

Jack had to find out what had happened. As much as he wanted to leave, and slam shut the door behind him forever—he had to know. Also, there was Olive to consider.

So, straightening his jacket, he went after his father—daring the bear in his den. Royal was seated behind his desk and already had a glass of whiskey in front of him. Here too, nothing had changed; the same heavy oak shelves lined with law books, and a couple of animals' heads trapped in snarls glared down from above the onyx mantle. The curtains were pulled shut against the day's brightness.

His father took a long drink. "Couldn't even make captain, I see," he muttered to his son standing in the doorway.

Jack wasn't going to be drawn on that matter. "What happened to Mother?"

"Suppose you think I drove her to it?" Royal said with a bitter laugh.

His son kept quiet.

His father glowered at him some more. "She always said you'd make a fine magician—but that she was afraid of it, too."

So the news had apparently reached his father's ears.

Much as Jack had never wanted the benefits of being Awakened—after all, who did—he wasn't about to defend himself to his estranged father either, so he waited for him to run out of words.

Royal smiled a little. "Learned some restraint in the army I see—not a total waste, then." He took a deep swig of whiskey. "You were always too clever by half."

"Not really, I've just learnt how to handle your sort in the last four years." Jack smiled back.

"Handle me, eh? I always expected a clever bastard like you wouldn't have mixed up those letters. It was deliberate."

How much of the confusion that caused the letter debacle was accidental, Jack still wasn't sure of himself. Strange how the mix-up of two letters, one placating his father by saying he would never marry

Alice and the other organising the time and place with the woman herself, had bought them to this point. Without that whole mess, father would probably have accepted the marriage eventually. It was just his pride that couldn't allow being lied to by his son.

"Just tell me about Mother—you owe me that much!" Jack ground out, his fists now clenched to the point of pain.

Royal's face darkened like a thundercloud about to spit forth lightning. "She got the flu off some ignorant slum dwellers. Stupidly, she was helping at the hospital—even though I'd forbidden it."

If there was one thing Jack's mother believed in, it was aiding those not as lucky as she. He recalled her bustling around the kitchen, gathering supplies for those who had none, and her voice had been so happy. "If it wasn't for someone like me, your own father would have died in England—think about that."

He had and did again. The yawning chasm of loss started to open up before him. "I would like to see her grave at least..."

"You shall not!" Royal roared, throwing back his chair. "Keep your foul magic ridden self away from it. Let her rest in peace!"

Jack felt rage and grief near to choking his throat. "Don't tell me then! I'll find out from Olive!"

"You're not to see your sister either," his father spat. "She's to keep away—or be disinherited just like you."

It was getting hot under his uniform. Jack tried to swallow his rage, and find that icy cool place he'd thought he'd mastered. "I could look after her, and better than you ever looked after Mother..."

He ducked on instinct. Royal's half-empty whiskey glass smashed spectacularly just where his head had been. Without his battle trained reflexes, Jack might have well been killed on his first day back in the country.

The lamp above their heads flared once, casting blinding light into the room for a brief instant before shattering. Royal was now the one forced back, his eyes wide.

A rumble echoed in the study. Jack's father's rows and rows of books, leather-bound and weighty, danced in the shelves in random patterns like Irish jiggers gone mad. The brass and oak desk twisted on itself as if it were made of Indian rubber and sent the decanter of whiskey flying. His father stepped back in horror—not at what was happening, but who was causing it.

"Demon!" he shouted one hand already searching about him for something else to hurl. "Thank God your mother is not alive to see this! Get out of this house!"

Jack stood there a moment, just to make sure the old man understood it was going to be his own decision to leave. He tried to quiet his magic, but it was unreliable as ever and took a while to obey. Finally, the books dropped back into place with a thump that made Royal jump, and the desk settled back into its spot. Only the broken light bulb and the spilled whiskey told that anything strange had just happened.

Father and son glared at each other in the half-light. Jack smiled and tucked both hands into his pockets, showing the old crook that he wasn't going to offer him physical violence. The shattered light fixture swung and creaked in the quiet.

"Ashamed of what I am now, Father?" Jack asked. "Afraid that the old boys down at the Club will think you did this somehow? It's awfully common to have a magician in the family isn't it?"

Jack found that immensely amusing; Royal wasn't afraid of his new powers as such, but he was certainly afraid that it would leak out that young Cunningham had come back from war a magician. To many of their social standing, a magician was lower than a tradesman. Having magic implied that they were weak, or that they needed others to solve their problems. A good son of the Empire, if he had it certainly wouldn't use magic.

Leverage. The word popped into Jack's mind. He leaned over and picked up the decanter and a glass off the floor, and without his father's permission poured the last remains. He raised a mock salute to Royal and downed it in one hit. It tasted wonderful, so much better than the rotgut alcohol they'd brewed in the trenches. His father had always had a taste for the best things in life—just not much for his own children.

"You'll let me see Olive," Jack said quietly, "or I'll turn up outside the Club and throw those self-righteous fools down on their rumps without ever touching them. In return, I'll lay low and you can tell all your friends that your unfortunate son died in the war. That way we'll both be happy."

Royal fingered the fob watch in his breast pocket and looked off into the distance. "You'll need money."

"Indeed—but I won't be taking any of yours."

His father cleared his throat. "Your mother left you a sum…"

Jack thought about that, but her money came from the Harrington fortune and had never been Royal's at any stage. He nodded slowly. "I'll take what she left me then," he said quietly as he carefully put down the glass. "Is Olive here now?"

His father shook his head, slower this time; the bear held at bay and knowing the end was near. "She's in Auckland, some sort of damn nursing thing…but she doesn't know that you're alive…"

The air hummed again, but this time Jack managed not to let the power slip its leash. "Then she'll be relieved that reports of my death were exaggerated. You're a good liar—make something up."

"Not got much of a choice, have I…" Royal shot him one last angry look.

"Not really." His son smiled back, fully aware that magic gave him a slightly white halo in the half-light.

His father didn't stop him, in fact didn't say a word. For a moment, out in the hallway and out of sight, Jack paused to catch his breath. He found he was shaking. The after effect of summoning was hitting him. The rush of facing off with his father had temporarily held off the agony, but now it tumbled back over him with a vengeance. His muscles were ceasing up, and his jaw locked tightly around a howl. It would be very unfortunate to come off so well against Royal, only to let him hear the ramifications of the magic.

Jack staggered down the hallway as lightning danced in the back of his eyeballs. He made it down to the streets and around the corner before he was forced to his knees in agony.

CHAPTER FOUR

Many people thought the seraphim were a wonderful idea. To have a friend always on hand, one that knew the dirty, intimate, and evil thoughts that no one ever shared with a real person, seemed like a wonderful idea. Emma though, knew differently. It was hell on earth.

Not the blind airy-fairy hell that the bible bashers shouted from the pulpit, but the very real hell of yourself reflected in an unavoidable, harsh mirror. No one had been able to prove it, but she knew in her heart of hearts that was what caused the pain and the madness; the inability to hide from the reality of yourself.

She stood watching the troops arrive home from the far off war and wondered how many of them had been irrevocably changed—how many had come back with one more conscience than they had left with? Not just the maimed, she was sure. The horrors of war would have carved out plenty of brain space for the seraphim, and it would mean more Awakened than ever in New Zealand. Just what she needed.

Emma tapped the tip of her long fingernail on her teeth. Among these new arrivals were undoubtedly plenty of candidates, and most of them would be more than interested in her.

As long as Emma kept her rose-coloured and very fashionable glasses on, they would never notice the gold in her eyes. She was tall and slim and liked to think she exuded the kind of class most often found in Europe, even though she was born and bred in the backblocks of New Zealand's South Island.

However, that heritage was something she'd left behind long ago. She turned and walked brusquely away in the direction of the town centre, because it wouldn't do to be seen at the docks talking to soldiers. Eyes could be about, and despite their ineptitude, even a blind cat could occasionally catch a mouse.

Hunger made her rash sometimes; a fault often pointed out by her master. Yet if the awareness of the seraphim around her made her mouth water, she could still control herself enough not to act on it.

Not far along Featherston Street, she turned into a smart looking office building, going against the flow of soldiers and delighted families. They parted around her, seemingly unaware of her existence. She trotted up two flights of stairs, past where accountants and office staff beavered away, providing a wonderful screen to her master's den.

As far as lairs went, it was not lavishly decorated. Behind a simple glass door was a plain oak desk; neat, and lacking in any ostentation. The man behind it, however, was not the simple kind of office worker that might be expected—nor was what he was working on.

The Craven Man's form was masked in dancing shadow, and the spread of work before him was a flickering mass of light. Each of the little burning two dimensional spinning globes he was moving about under his fingertips were resisting, but it was a futile gesture.

"So do we have many candidates?" Her master's voice always seemed to come from a long way off—perhaps it did.

"Plenty," she replied, putting her bag down by the door, taking off her cloche hat, and shaking her long dark curls free. "Just as you said—more Awakened than the country has ever seen are right this moment coming off the boats."

Emma glanced at him out of the corner of her eye. Even with her own peculiar gifts, she found it was easier to actually see him this way. "And your business?"

A chill breeze slid through the room. "An exceptionally good week. Along with the soldiers returned, we are lucky enough to have many Awakened with the arrival of the influenza—including a very promising girl."

"And her seraph?" Emma asked, daring to slide onto a corner of his desk.

"Contained." It was impossible to miss the dismissive tone in his voice. On the desk she was sitting on, one of the burning lights attempted to dart free, but he pinned it mercilessly before it got far. "In fact, I have already put her to use."

As always, the Craven Man's experiments were a mystery to Emma, but she never questioned. It was enough for her to know that he had picked her out from among them for greatness. He had taken her leech and turned it into something else, apart from a terrible mirror.

Still, the lights made her uncomfortable, and Emma gave up her seat on the desk, instead striding over to the cupboard against the far wall. Without thought or embarrassment, she stripped off her street clothes and hung them in the wardrobe. Inside were several beautiful dresses that would turn any soldier's head around.

"Which shall it be?" Spinning about, she held up a blue beaded dress, then a deep purple one with a plunging back, before her breasts.

The Craven Man didn't even look up. "It really doesn't matter, does it?"

Sometimes it was hard to believe he was a man at all. In this form of shadow he had only a tenuous physical presence, but when he wanted to, he could enjoy the pleasures of the flesh.

So, she sighed and chose the blue dress. It was often a mistake to antagonise Sleeper women with anything too daring. She slipped it over her head and pinned back her dark curls with a diamante clip. Putting on a little rouge on her lips, she examined her reflection in the mirror hanging by the window. It would do for this crowd of desperate men.

A glance outside showed that the parade of soldiers with families had dried up, leaving those who had none. Those were her type of males—the kind that wouldn't be missed.

Wellington was about to turn into a party town after months of fear and death, and she was ready to take advantage of that.

She would be much happier in such an environment, but her predatory nature would miss the easy killing of the plague time. Still, the taste of fresh young man was something she hadn't savoured for a very long time. Emma folded up her rose tinted glasses and tucked them into the coat pocket hanging in the wardrobe.

Looking in the mirror, she passed her hand in front of her face and watched as her glamour turned her gold eyes into boring brown ones. It was a necessarily deception, since no one wore glasses out for a night on the town.

"Sad, little one?" When Emma turned, the Craven Man had conjured his face from the shadows. It was his idea of a joke, since neither could recall any emotion except hunger and hatred.

Sorrow and many other feelings were impossible for her now. Hunger had driven most of them out of her head.

Emma reached out and attempted to touch the face he offered. Nothing was there, and all she connected with was chill air. Hiding her disappointment with a soft laugh, she stepped back quickly, and slipped her coat on over her dress. "Anything in particular you want me to bring back?"

"You know what I like," was the only reply he gave. Already he had turned back to his experiments.

Baring her teeth in frustration, Emma went out to see what the pickings were like.

CHAPTER FIVE

Just over a month after the tidal wave of influenza had passed over Wellington, Faith's father sent word that he needed her.

It was early January, and though he hadn't seen any of the family for Christmas, she didn't hold that fact against him; he'd wanted to be sure that they wouldn't get sick, after all.

Apparently, since then the town had gone from morgue to dancehall. Having only just staggered back from the brink of disaster, the city was now inundated with soldiers who all wanted a beer and a good time. Agnes, her father's barmaid of ten years, had returned to her family farm in Taranaki to welcome back her brother, so John Cunningham needed his girls to help him behind the bar.

Mother grumbled and complained, but she couldn't deny the request since though she and Faith's father were estranged, the pub was still partly hers too. She wouldn't want it to flounder.

Faith also knew there was another reason, one that Mother would never acknowledge; sometimes it was very convenient for the women to get a break from each other. While Jean was Mother's favourite, Faith suffered under her more exacting standards. When the sharp words started to fly inevitably, Jean would always leap to her sister's defence—and then there would be a real to-do. The resulting furore would involve the whole family, and Faith knew her two uncles abhorred living in a house of bickering women.

So, sending the two girls off to Wellington for a few weeks worked out well for everyone concerned. Mother was more than capable of doing all their work and—as she often pointed out—to a better standard.

Faith was, for her part, relieved—and not just to be free of her mother's critical eye. The escape attempt she had foiled in the spring had been weighing on her mind. The woman's expression, first terrified and then shocked, haunted her dreams, and Hoa would offer no comfort on what exactly the prisoner had done to her, or what her revenge might be. Faith didn't know if it was even possible for Awakened to really curse each other, because she had no other of her kind to confide in.

Perhaps in town she might be able to find someone to talk to about it, or indeed consult the Awakened Magic section in the Wellington Public Library—she'd been there before. So, there were many reasons to be going, not the least being it was good to be getting away from the scene of what she now felt was a crime.

It was not a long trip really, the farm was only just up the coast from Wellington, but it was buried in the back hills of Paraparaumu which might have been on another planet. So, in order to catch the Silver Fern train on its way south from Auckland, they needed to be up before dawn. Uncle Jim, used to early mornings even more than the girls were, was up and ready to escort the girls, at least as far as the station.

Their mother stood with her hands on her hips and examined their small suitcases before they were allowed out the door.

"You've stuffed too much in, Faith," she chided in her soft Scottish accent that somehow always managed to sound disapproving no matter the circumstance. "If its handle breaks before you get to the station I won't be held responsible..."

If it had been Jean, she would have spent another ten minutes re-packing, but Faith had her back up, and argued back. "The suitcase is old, Mother, and I need—"

Before it could turn into a full-scale argument of epic proportions, Jean fussed Faith out of the door. "Come on," she whispered under her breath, "we'll miss the train if you get started with her now."

In the end, Isabel Louden stood glaring at her daughters as they prepared to set off from the porch for only a moment before spinning on her heel, and heading off in the direction of the hen house.

Uncle Jim was mounted on his horse, while the two smaller ponies, Bonnet and Bluebell, waited patiently with their heads down.

Maggie, his rough coated sheep dog, had her head cocked in a curious expression that somehow reflected her master's.

"Ready then?" Jim, who always spoke quietly, dropped down and helped them secure the narrow suitcases onto the backs of the horses.

Faith gave him a short hug, knowing that he wouldn't want to be seen getting one later in the exposed station in front of everyone.

"Now then," he muttered, as he mounted Betty, his tough bay mare, with smooth practice bred from hours in the saddle.

Jean, who at fifteen was just starting to come into true beauty, loved to be on horseback. Her older sister did not.

Horses sensed Faith was different, and the seraph inside her made them jumpy. They shied at the smallest thing and always found the deepest potholes to wade through. She knew she was bound to be covered in mud less than a mile after leaving home. It didn't matter too much though, as she was dressed in traveling clothes, anticipating the mess the sooty train would make of anything decent.

They set off with very little fanfare; Jim leading, Jean grinning to herself next, and Faith taking up the rear.

It was not going to be an easy journey. Faith's finger began to throb dully as they descended the hill top. Below them, the broad coast spread out in the dawn light, moss green and lovely. Just off the coast, the hulking mass of Kapiti Island was shrouded in mist like a lurking dragon. It was so rarely still on these hilltops that the utter silence made Faith nervous. Her horse, sensing her rising uncertainty, took the opportunity to pause for a mouthful of parched grass.

Up ahead, Jean was chatting with their uncle, oblivious to the fact he wasn't really answering. Jim was tall and lanky even on horseback, but the horses, along with dogs, were his preferred company. Teenage girls were an alien species that he would rather have ignored.

Faith had always suspected that her uncle had a touch of magic about him, though he was not of the First generation, being rather a recent immigrant. Sometimes a bit of the seraphim magic rubbed off on people on the fringes of society; the lonely, the mad, or the suicidal could sometimes sense thing in this land. Jim spent enough time out in the backblocks of the farm to be considered at least the first of those. The rest Faith did not know about.

Still, she knew he cared for her and her sister, as otherwise he simply wouldn't have come down from the hills. His dog, Maggie, trailed at his horse's heels, every now and then glancing nervously up at Jean as she chattered on.

Neither man, girl, or dog took much notice of Faith lagging behind. She knew why; they were used to her doing so.

Being of the Awakened meant more than just magic, it also meant perception. Faith often found herself staring at the beauty of a flower or an insect, intrigued by the intricacy of its petal or wing, only to be bought back to reality by her mother's complaint that she'd been standing still for an hour or more. They called her mooncalf—or sometimes lazy.

It was no wonder of the natural world that caused her to hang back this morning, though. Something else had caught her attention. Through the mist Faith could see a light in the bay. She knew there was no wharf or jetty for many miles, and something about the innocent looking twinkle inexplicably set her teeth on edge. The country had only just finished a war, so it wasn't as it had been when the threat of invasion loomed. It could be a troop ship damaged or lost—so it was worth a little of her pain to find out.

Faith closed her eyes and tapped into the deep well of strength that suffering had given her. She wasn't a fool; she only called on the power when she or her family really needed it. The dangers were too imminent to be constantly using it.

Her missing finger began to hurt, as badly as if it were once more caught in the seed threshing machine, but as used to it as she was, she did not cry. Jim and Jean wouldn't understand and would think she was being silly, yet lights out there stirred something in the deep pit of her instinct.

A breeze, a slight one, grew stronger at her command, and whipped down from the hills. At its touch, slowly the mist began to clear.

Uncle Jim shot a curious look over his shoulder, while Jean pulled her shaggy pony up and circled it back to where her sister still waited. The younger girl's blonde hair was now leaping about in the wind, and only served to make Faith painfully aware of how truly beautiful she was.

The rule was generally that the First were beautiful. Taller, straighter and more handsome, they drew glances wherever they went—but to every rule there was an exception. She knew herself to be pretty enough, but next to Jean, her complexion was muddy and her features not nearly as fine. The power she had in full measure, but the physical gifts she lacked and consequently desired the most.

"What are you doing, Faith?" Jean's voice was almost lost in the wind. As with all summonings of magic, it was not predictable. Faith knew she might well have started a storm.

So she motioned down the hill to where the wind was clearing the mist away and the boats could finally be seen. "Look!"

Uncle Jim was staring fixedly at them, his shoulders tense. It would be a while before everyone relaxed from the sensitivities of being at war.

For Jean, it was already old news. "They're just some fishing boats."

She could be right. The three barges looked like some of the fishing vessels that sailed out of Wellington, but they were moored closely together, not far from shore.

"Well, I'm not going to miss the train!" Jean glared at her odd sister and uncle, before urging her horse once more on down the hill.

After a few minutes, Faith realised that the ships were not going to reveal any of their secrets to her. The dim shapes moving about on the boats looked very much like sailors with nets, and though the appearance of them disturbed her, there was going to be nothing she could do.

With a sigh she followed after Jean.

First the station, and then the train was crowded. Jim dropped them off with a nod of goodbye, and then led the horses away before too many people could bother him.

As the train puffed into Paraparaumu station, Faith and her sister could see that there would be problems. People were trying to get into town to meet the latest troop ship docking, and that meant there were very few seats, but two young lads stood up quickly so that the sisters could sit. They were rewarded for their gallantry with a dazzling smile from Jean.

Despite being annoyed with the way the men fawned over her sister, Faith couldn't hold it for long. Maybe it had been a bit silly to bring wind just to see some rusty ships, but the question lingered; why had they been so close to shore and unnerved her so?

Faith sat back and tried to enjoy the journey. The train pulled them along the coastline and through many tunnels on its way south.

It was certainly an exciting trip, with everyone around them jubilant to see the returned soldiers, and no young woman alive could fail to catch that mood.

The only problem was they were suddenly aware how unprepared they were. Jean complained that she hadn't got any lipstick or powder on her.

Faith giggled at that. "As if Mother would let you have such things!"

In the spirit of sisterhood, another woman leaned over the seat, and let Jean borrow some from her. Before her sister could complain, she had applied a liberal amount, but when she offered it to Faith, she gestured it away as if she didn't care.

With a sigh, the older sister turned back to the window for the view she always anticipated—that magical moment when Wellington revealed itself. They barrelled out of the tunnel at Kaiwharawhara, and Faith straightened unconsciously in her seat.

Wellington was a harbour town, and wrapped almost completely about itself like a fishhook, so that every view of it was different. Today the water was silvered-blue and as smooth as slate—one of those precious moments of utter calm in the windy city—and the two islands in the centre of the harbour were punctuation marks amongst the blue. The buildings clustered close to the shoreline on the only stretch of flat land against a backdrop of green trees.

Hoa purred contentedly in her head. Something about this place made both of them happy—far more than they could ever be at the farm. These hills, though they might be prone to shaking, felt like the spot that she belonged to more than anywhere else in the world.

In addition, Faith was looking forward to seeing her father. Faith could vividly recall the arguments between her parents when they had lived together—this arrangement might be odd, but was better than that previous awkward situation.

At last, the train pulled into the bustling station, and the girls leapt lightly off the train, with their suitcases swinging from their fingertips. Immediately they noticed the difference from last time they had visited—so many men!

Faith and Jean stood there in wonder and surprise. Since the beginning of the war, young men had been a terrible rarity—now they were surrounded by hordes. It was not only fathers and brothers, but sons too. The older sister suddenly wished she hadn't rejected the offer of a little makeup.

Jean clutched her sister's coat sleeve. "Tell me I'm not dreaming..."

The sheer tone of her voice said to Faith that Dad was going to have a real problem. Yet she knew exactly what was going on in her sister's head.

They were beautiful; striding around in their brown uniforms and talking to each other in loud, joyous voices. Even with scars and injuries, there was such a presence to them that she found herself on the verge of tears. Faith's senses were overloaded with the thrill of it.

As they walked in a rather stunned fashion into the station, she noted it even smelt different; the odour of damp wool, aftershave, and the musk of men. It was an odour that the girls were familiar with living with their uncles, but not in such concentration, not in Wellington—and certainly not from such young men.

Faith felt a strange tug deep within herself, and for a moment imagined that a couple of the men were looking in her direction.

Hoa murmured caution.

Yes I know, she whispered back.

"Come on," she said, tugging Jean rapidly out of the railway station and towards the tram stop. All the while, her sister was craning her neck in every direction. Jean was just learning the power she had on men and getting to the stage where she wanted to experiment using it. Faith made sure to keep a stern hand on her sister while they took the short journey on the rattling tram.

The Albert Hotel stood on the corner of Willis and Boulcott Street. It was a tidy two storey building with a balcony that ran around the street side, which was held up by iron pillars with curled fretwork, and it always made Faith think of a saloon from a Wild West picture show. One difference was the 'Old Identities heads'. The hotel was also known by that name because of those carved-wooden heads representing the great pioneer men of Wellington that watched proceedings from above each top floor window. Old Edward Gibbon Wakefield, the founding father of the city, in particular made her shudder. She didn't believe in ghosts, but the feeling she got from that head was never pleasant.

The Albert had seen better days, certainly. Built in 1879, her father was the last in a short line of owners. It always seemed to teeter on the edge of decrepitude but never quite fell into it.

It was not what most people would think was the ideal atmosphere to raise two girls, but their father's sisters in Lancashire had been bought up in a similar manner, and 'it hadn't never done them no harm'.

It was still early, so the two girls went around the back, and let themselves in via the family entrance. The smell of bacon and eggs emanated from the kitchen, though there was no sign of any dishes or pans, so Dad had obviously already had breakfast. He was always one for cleaning up after himself—came from being a former soldier.

"Dad!" Faith called, even as Jean clattered upstairs to her room. He appeared at the end of the corridor that came from behind the bar. Her father's form filled the narrow doorway. Though it had been before her time that he'd been a boxer, he never the less maintained the physique, not letting it run to fat as some had. In one burly hand was clutched several bottles of beer, evidence he'd been stocking up for tonight's onrush.

He was fast; before Faith knew it, she was being squeezed within an inch of her life, her nostrils full of the smell of ciggies and alcohol, his moustache rough against her cheek.

"Curly!" Her father's voice rumbled through her like an earthquake. She very much hated that nickname but would never say so.

Jean heard him and bounded down the stairs. Dad wouldn't let his eldest go, so squished his youngest in as well. For a good long while they hugged each other in the dimness of the corridor as if it had been years rather than months since they met.

Finally, their father released them and held them at arm's length. "Feeling alright are you? No sniffles or fever?"

"The flu didn't get to us." Faith pushed back her hat off her face and smiled up at him. "We're fine, Dad."

"All of you?" That was going to be the only way he was going to ask about his wife. Her health mattered to him, but the same could not be said of Isabel.

"Everyone on the farm got through it," Faith said, finding she couldn't meet his eyes. "Let's put the kettle on and have some tea. We're parched after the train ride."

Soon all three of them were settled in the small kitchen with a warm drink and a gingernut biscuit. Faith sighed with relief. She did still love the farm, but Mother could be very difficult sometimes. Anything any of her daughters did was never good enough; the coals hadn't been racked properly, the garden never weeded enough, or the washing hung out in the proper manner. Dad, by contrast, was only grateful to have someone do anything for him.

"So how bad was it?" Faith leaned across and touched his hand. Jean only watched, her eyes wide—she would never have dared question their father.

John Cunningham rubbed his salt and pepper hair and sighed through his fine moustache. "Well, there were pretty much no customers all, and the city was as quiet as…"—he paused to search for a word, but there was none better—"…the grave."

"They said in the paper," Jean whispered almost to herself, "that there were over seven hundred dead."

It was an inconceivable number. Faith sat back, absentmindedly rubbing the joint of her missing finger. The pain had subsided to a dull ache that seemed to settle in her bones for a few hours after using her magic. Rather than talk about it, she usually found herself slipping into silences.

Dad and Jean glanced at each other and their raw thoughts imposed on Faith's receptive seraph brain. *Damn lucky to have everyone safe. We're so lucky all of us made it through.*

Faith slid back her chair, and forced a grin on her face. "Let's get unpacked then, Jean—it's nearly opening time."

They had very little in their suitcases, but they put their clothes away in the room they shared upstairs in silence. Faith knew it was a muted homecoming, but told herself that it was better than no homecoming at all.

Soon enough it was time to open for business. Luckily, the government had declined to pass a proposed bill to close hotels at six in the evening, and Dad had apparently shouted everyone at the bar a drink when the news came through. Such a measure, he'd told Faith, would surely have led to people trying to down as much alcohol in a shorter time as possible. Ten o'clock was far more civilised, and he was glad to have Faith serving under those circumstances. Jean—being too young to be exposed to men and drink—was relegated to the back rooms and cleaning up.

Faith wondered if her father's acceptance of her doing a shift pulling beers had anything to do with her lesser attraction to men. She'd like to think it was because she was more responsible—but the suspicion lingered.

The doors were unlocked at noon and they soon had customers—all male. They smiled at her with every glance; not the teasing kind they might have given Jean, but the welcoming smile they would have given their sister. Still, she enjoyed the attention, the happiness she got from pouring them a pint of beer and the cheery atmosphere.

As the day drew to a close more women came in, but certainly not what her mother would have thought of as the reputable kind. These were young women who came seeking the company of men that they hadn't seen for years. Women who wanted to dance, to sing, and make merry.

Faith got them glasses of gin, but some joined in with the drinking of beer. Soon there were rounds of toasts to the troops, cheers to the homecoming, and salutes to those that would never come home again.

Hoa was intrigued by all this, because while sharing the life of an isolated farm girl he didn't get nearly as much exposure to others of his kind. Faith was the only Awakened and Hoa was the only seraph for miles when they were on the isolated farm, and it wasn't as if she could even talk about it round the dinner table. Mother was slightly embarrassed by her daughter's powers. She found it uncouth to mention such a thing. It was there. That was enough.

Yet here in the bar, Hoa was aware of other seraphim. Unlike when they were out at the farm, in Wellington there were enough seraphim and their Awakened hosts for such interaction to be almost everyday. Faith had read books on the subject while Mother wasn't looking. One in ten people were Awakened, and most seemed to gather in the cities for that sense of community—the one that Faith ached for, too. Now here she was, back in Wellington, and oh so very close to it.

Two sandy haired boys sat in the corner clutching their beers as if they expected to have them snatched away. They were twins, but one had the lower portion of his leg missing. She noticed how he tucked it away under the table and kept his crutches hidden from sight. He was Awakened.

He did not have her kind of power—she could taste that—but something far more subtle. Faith felt sorry for him, not because of his leg or his seraph, but because as twins they would always be separated now. The relationship with a seraph was the most important and the most intimate anyone could have.

It had taken her years to adjust to Hoa, and being a child, she'd been far more capable of it. It was no fault of the seraph; they needed the world too.

It was not as though the twins were alone, at least half a dozen Awakened were in the hotel tonight; most were lesser powers, but the young Māori lad over to her right near to the door drew Hoa's attention. He was sipping at his beer thoughtfully, yet he didn't seem sad or depressed. The taste of his Awakening was more mature than most of the soldiers around him. Such calmness could only be earned with time, and she suspected he'd been Awakened before the war. He could even be one of the Corp of Magicians that the British Army had so valued.

Faith was more than curious—she was intrigued. It must be wonderful to use the seraph powers on the battlefield; to really flex and test the full strength of them. She'd even heard that a few women had been allowed in during the final push towards victory. Unfortunately, by the time she was eligible, the war had been over. She'd never mentioned this desire to join up to her father.

Just when Faith had managed to gather enough courage to talk to the young solider, her attention snapped around to the door.

It banged open and a woman walked in that made every man's head turn. She was exactly what Faith would have hoped to be; tall, elegantly dressed and beautiful. Her dark hair was cut in a fashionable bob that framed a face with high cheekbones and full lips. A stunning dark red cloche hat was pulled down over her neatly arched eyebrows, but what really caught Faith's attention was the sudden arrival of seraph power in the room. It literally knocked her back a step.

Hoa churned inside her in its wake, as though caught in the tidal eddies of some unseen ocean, and Faith spun away to cover it, pretending to fetch more glasses. Once beyond the sight of the public, she pressed her hands to her forehead. It felt as though her skull was in a vice. Hoa swallowed the pain and eased her burden as best he could.

"Are you alright, Curly?" Father paused, just about to pass her with a tray of clean glasses from the back.

Her parents did have one thing in common—they never would directly mention her seraph. The closest Dad ever got was the occasional aside about her 'talent'. Faith could sense he was trying to figure out a way to ask if that was the matter now.

"Sure, Dad," she said plastering on a smile. "It's all just a bit hectic in there."

"Well, if you need a break from serving…"

"No, I just felt like a breather. Must be out of practice or something, but I'll be fine." She followed him back behind the bar.

In the meantime, the woman had found a place next to the young Māori soldier. She ordered a gin and tonic and smiled at him in a devastating fashion. Faith slid the drink over, taking care not to get herself noticed.

She could have sworn the woman locked eyes with her for a moment behind those strange pink glasses; a flicker of recognition of one power to another. Yet Faith also realised she'd just been assessed and found not to be a threat in that more primeval way that women had. *You're not ugly*, that gaze said, *but no competition for me.*

As Faith mopped up some spilled beer further down the bar, she knew that this assessment shouldn't have rankled her so.

The young man was laughing with the woman, obviously flattered to have been singled out for her attention. If he ever noticed Faith behind the bar it was as someone might notice the forget-me-nots beneath the rose bushes.

Hoa soothed her ego by saying how wonderful she was and beautiful to him. Being admired by the seraph that lived within one's own body was not the same thing as a man smiling that special smile— the one the young soldier was giving the woman at this very minute.

Yet there was something else too that niggled at the edge of her perception. Faith had little time to consider the matter; there were men clamouring for beer and attention. Her father rolled his eyes in her general direction, as if to say, *Wish we had more barmaids*. Perhaps he was actually thinking that. It was hard to tell; her telepathy was weak and unreliable. Faith was used to catching the odd tail end of a thought that Hoa didn't mean to let through.

Prey.

That thought was definitely not from her father. Somewhere in the hotel, someone was suddenly very pleased with themselves. Faith made a light comment to the man she was serving, but tried to scan the customers as covertly as she could.

The thought must have been very strong for her to hear, yet she couldn't identify the source. All the people looked suspect, but she couldn't be completely sure that wasn't just her imagination.

The sudden influx of men had turned her head. The rattle of emotions and thoughts had caught her unawares—on the farm there were none of these problems.

Sternly, Faith told Hoa to filter out the thoughts, and he promptly responded by shutting all of them down. By the time Faith had turned around she realised that the young Māori solider and the woman were gone.

She could only hope that the one savage thought she'd picked up was not from either of them. He had a nice smile, but it wasn't her place to judge what had just happened. She was only a barmaid.

CHAPTER SIX

After dropping off his rucksack at the boarding house, Jack went back into town to find Hemi. He wasn't in the mood for drinking and dancing, but neither did he like the idea of being stuck in a bare room, chased by grief and anger into the wee hours of the night.

Mother was dead and Royal had not even bothered to send a telegram. Like Alice, she was now beyond his reach. What really hurt was that no one had bothered to tell him. *When Father cuts someone off*, Jack thought angrily, *he makes damn sure that they stay that way.*

But what about Olive? Where was she now, and would she be glad to see him?

When Jack had left she'd been as outspoken as ever, but though she was older, their father seemed not to mind her language or her women's rights campaigning. Women had been voting in New Zealand since the last century, the first country in the world to do so, but Olive knew that there was still plenty of work to be done. As long as she didn't end up in the papers, Royal tolerated it. After all, she was just a daughter. Jack, as the son, was held to a higher standard.

Marrying Alice, who Royal described as 'that pale faced gold digger', had been the straw that broke the camel's back, as the saying went.

Jack had spent his whole life trying to be the model son, but falling in love had given him a real reason to stand up to his father. Unfortunately, it all turned out to be for nothing.

All these contemplations changed Jack's mind. He *did* need a drink. His father's whiskey was souring in his stomach and a good, honest beer might just do the trick. He wandered up Willis Street and observed that nothing much had changed. It was as if the whole world had paused when the war started.

Now, though, it had started again. Mother and Alice might be gone, but by God, he'd survived. The streets were bustling with trams, cars and even the odd horse and carriage. He saw babies in prams, lovers walking arm in arm, and women laden with parcels—all things he'd thought never to see again. Jack tried to soak as much in as possible.

First though, he stopped in at the barber's to get himself a decent haircut. Lots of people had done their own on the ship, wanting to appear their best for their loved ones. Jack, knowing there would be no one like that at the docks waiting for him, had held off. He wanted to enjoy the luxury of a proper cut in the hands of a skilled professional.

Mr Christeson was definitely one of those. His family had been barbers in Wellington since the first immigrant ship arrived, and when Jack left his little shop he not only had the closest most invigorating shave in years, he'd also caught up on pretty much all the rumours and scandal in town.

Feeling slightly more human, he made his way to the Albert hotel. A long boat ride from England had made him yearn for a well-pulled pint almost as much as a shave.

The Albert wasn't his usual watering hole—in fact he didn't really have a usual, having only been eighteen when he went to war. Jack almost stopped in his tracks at the realisation. This would be his first legal drink in his hometown. If that wasn't cause for celebration then he didn't know what was.

Before he got to the door, however, he saw Hemi. That lucky bugger was standing chatting to a woman under the veranda of the Albert, his hands stuffed in his pockets and a rapt grin on his face. She had her back to Jack, yet he got the impression of tall elegance, and the reflected interest in his friend's face told him that she was well worth looking at.

He should have stepped back and given Hemi room to chat and see where the women was going, yet he found himself drawn over to them. His friend would probably give him a clobber later on for his stupidity, but Jack was gripped with a sudden desire to turn the woman around and see the shape of her face.

He only got ten feet. The brush of power rippled along Waingaio and through Jack at the same time. He knew immediately that she was aware of them. The woman's head turned slightly, so that he got a glimpse of a fine profile and a very fashionable cloche hat, before she strode quickly away.

For a second Jack almost pursued her, but Hemi caught his arm, a frown on his brow. "Bloody hell, Jack, it was me she was chatting to."

Turning back to his friend, he felt the lure of the woman diminish. Common sense now told him running down a girl in Willis Street would probably end in a situation where he couldn't order a beer. He shook his head regretfully, unsure at his own reaction. "Sorry, I just really, really need a drink."

Hemi gave him an appraising look and tucked his hands back into his pockets. "You saw her though? Bloody knockout."

"Sorry if I chased her off." Jack did feel bad; neither of them had much female company of late.

"Did you?" Hemi shrugged. "Nah, she was a bit out of my league, I'm afraid."

Jack gave him a shove on the shoulder, feeling the curious tension dissipate. He must just be in dire need of some female companionship if he was starting to imagine every woman to be familiar.

Hemi shoved him back. "Fancy a drink in the Albert, then?"

Suddenly he didn't want to be in a bar with people who would just ask questions about the war. He wanted to be doing something they didn't get a chance to in the trenches.

Haunting memories gave him a nudge. "Nah—the Majestic is just across the road. Let's try that instead."

Hemi smiled— if there was one thing he loved doing it was dancing. Tipping his hat at a rakish angle, he laughed. "Now you're talking."

Jack was not so easily distracted. He'd been wrong; Wellington was not as he remembered—the mysterious chill running down his spine told him that, but for now he really didn't want to deal with it.

It was a long hard weekend in which Faith hardly had time to think about what had happened three days earlier. When she cracked her eyes open, and felt the warmth of her bed on Sunday morning, the sunlight was just sneaking between the curtains. Her feet still throbbed after being on them all of the previous day.

She wriggled her toes and sighed, contemplating the fact she would have to get up soon. It was not as though they had church to attend to; their parents had never made a point of taking them to anything but funerals and weddings.

With the bedspread wrapped around her, Jean rolled over in her bed and blinked at her sister through bleary eyes.

"Do we have to get up?" she mumbled.

Faith couldn't hear their father moving about, and Hoa whispered that he was downstairs cleaning. "Dad's up," she replied.

Jean wrinkled her pretty face. "I suppose you think we should go help?"

Then without waiting for an answer, she wriggled out of bed, the blankets still clutched about her, looking like a strange orange caterpillar. "Do you think we'll see Aunt Barbara and Lily while we are in town?"

The question came out of nowhere, but Faith knew her sister was not just asking a hypothetical question. Her arched look hinted she was querying Hoa as well. Faith wondered why on earth Jean was doing so, because they hadn't seen either of them for years. The truth was, some family arguments festered longer than wars, which was about how long ago they had last seen their cousin. Doing the arithmetic, Faith reckoned that Lily was probably thirteen or fourteen by now.

Faith gave a slight, bemused shrug. "I don't think that's very likely."

"But they could be…" Jean paused, biting her lip. "I mean you could…do you think you could do something to find out…"

Now Faith understood; her sister must have been lying there thinking about the fate of their estranged family for hours.

Jean was more thoughtful than Faith sometimes gave her credit for. The elder sister pushed herself up in her bed. "I guess so, but if they're alright we won't tell Dad we did this…he'd be mad."

Jean nodded her agreement and quickly held out her hands. She was a First Child, like Faith, but she had never Awakened. This latency meant she felt things, and they had learned as children that they could share a connection that helped lessen the pain backlash on Faith. When she asked for favours like this, Jean insisted that she take her share of the consequences.

She plonked herself down on Faith's bed, and leaned over. The sisters locked their fingers together; nineteen digits that symbolised the difference between them.

Having her sister's mind connected to her meant Hoa had greater power to draw from. It more than doubled his reach.

Faith's worry was that it would be a bit much in the city, but it was too late to go back now. The fear of all the Wellingtonians had already rushed into the empty spaces Faith had in her mind. These were not the normal day-to-day fears of failure, rejection or death—but the compound agony of a whole city; mothers afraid for their children, people dying alone and fevered, and everywhere despair.

Images flashed across Faith's inner eye. Most were blurs, soon displaced by another, but some stuck. A small child rushed to a window to see carriage after carriage rattling past. The dark horses and the carts clattered up the road on their way to the cemetery at Karori, with bodies bouncing in their hastily made coffins.

The memories raced on through Faith again, and this time suffocating panic claimed her. A dead and rotting corpse on a bed, the stench impossible to escape, and in the corner a Craven Man, untouched by the illness, but threatening so much worse. A scream was stilled in the terrified girl's throat.

Faith leapt up with a horrified howl. She recognised the girl—their cousin Lily.

Jean had seen it too, and both sisters stared at each other with numb dread. They knew immediately Aunt Barbara was dead, and their cousin was in mortal pain.

"We can't *not* tell him," Jean said. Her eyes were filling with tears, and Faith nodded in mute agreement.

Both of them dressed quickly, and Faith was shaking as she did. Hoa was mumbling warnings against drawing on her power because he knew what she was contemplating. If Lily had been touched by this Craven Man and her seraph twisted, then the officials would only lock her up.

Her response to Hoa was very curt. *If I don't do something Lily will die or become an insane asylum inmate. She's too young for that!*

When their father saw his daughters standing at the base of the stairs, their expressions sombre so early in the morning, John Louden stopped abruptly in the corridor.

"What is it?"

Faith's mouth worked around words she couldn't quite voice. Once she did, everything would change.

"Curly, what is it?" He darted forward and took her hands. As always, his own fingers unerringly found her missing one, and his face flickered with guilt. Even through the pain of her awareness, his daughter saw that and wished it away.

Lily's situation was far more urgent.

Feeling gingerly behind her, Faith sat on the stairs, but did not reclaim her hand from his. "Have you heard from Aunty Babs lately?"

Guilt once more creased his face, and again it was foolish; her father had no reason to blame himself for his sister's choice. It was she that had spurned his offers of help, even though she and Lily were struggling. Pride was a sin their family was intimate with.

Dad looked at Faith askance. "I didn't think she was in Wellington anymore…are you saying…has something happened to her?"

Faith nodded, but spared him any further details. In the hubbub of the outbreak, it was obvious that no one had looked into one more poor woman, or tried to find out her next of kin.

"What about Lily?" Her father stared at a distant point over their heads.

"She's alive," Faith said, her tone as measured and calm as she could manage, "but someone is holding her against her will." He did not need the full details and horror of what was being done to her.

Her father's expression darkened as he got to his feet, went straight to the door, and grabbed his coat off the back of it. Then from underneath the kitchen sink he pulled out his billy club—just like the one he kept in the bar. In far Lancashire he'd been a bare fisted boxer, a rebel, and not afraid to fight his way out of any situation.

Faith knew that he would need more than brawn. Whoever this Craven Man was that had her cousin, he had power.

So she hastily put on her own coat, and turned to her sister. "You better stay here and mind the pub." She took Jean by the shoulders. "If we don't get back by opening time send word to our uncles. They'll know what to do."

"Now hang on," her father growled, taking Faith by the arm, "we'll be going into a right seedy part of town, I'm not putting you at risk..."

She smiled at him, and tilted her head. "Dad, don't you think I'm capable of looking after myself—just as much as you are? In some ways more so?"

John looked bemusedly between his two daughters, but as always they presented a united front. Jean was already clearing away the tea things and pretending things were already settled. "Heck," he said with an aggravated sigh, "ever since you lot got the vote, it's as if you've been running things."

"Didn't you know Dad?" Faith replied, opening the door, "We already are."

CHAPTER SEVEN

One of the main reasons people found magicians disreputable was the unspoken word that hung around them—possession. It was a nasty word, and a nasty concept. No one could avoid thinking of the consequences of it, yet no one really wanted to talk about it.

As Jack sat waiting for his sister in the tearooms, every one of the well dressed patrons were watching him out of the corner of their eyes. No one gave First Children a second glance, except to admire their beauty, or enjoy that special light that hung around them—however once Awakened, and even if nothing physically had changed about them, somehow the Sleepers still knew.

Jack took a long sip of his tea, and wished it were something stronger. He tolled that word around in his head. Sleepers—that's what the Awakened called everyone else.

He'd become a member of a whole sub group with a whole new language for things normal folk couldn't understand. He knew many of them looked down on what they had once been, but for himself he could only wish to go back to slumber.

For one thing, Jack had the strangest impression that those normal people could smell him, like a hen house full of chooks could smell the ferret or polecat. He wasn't a predator though—he didn't mean to use the power he had for anything like murder. Except he had—when the Empire called he had done so in Europe. Those dark memories reached up to wind their tentacles around him, pulling him down into a fearful pit of remembrance.

Luckily, Olive appeared at the moment, holding one hand over her eyes to peer inside before entering. She was as beautiful as their mother had been; dark green eyes, and a thick mane of black hair barely held in check by a silver clasp. She was smartly dressed in a dark maroon suit, with a broad, elegant hat and a matching purse. She was the vision of what every soldier in the trenches would have dreamed of coming back to. Suddenly Jack wondered if one had already claimed her affections.

Olive opened the door with great gusto, sending the bell above it ringing madly. Everyone in the tearoom looked up. Several of the men kept their eyes on her, watching as she rushed over to Jack with a radiant smile on her lips. He didn't need magic to know what they were thinking; *lucky devil!*

He *was* lucky; lucky to be alive and lucky that Olive was still speaking to him. After all, from her perspective she might have thought he had abandoned them all for Alice, and then Mother had died.

Perhaps he wasn't giving her enough credit, for she hugged him, pressing her warmth against his neck. She smelt of lavender. They stood clutching each other for a long moment, Olive hugging very tightly onto him, and Jack wondered if she would ever let him go. He also wondered if he was still in the trenches, dreaming sweetly this moment. She rocked him back and forth, and he could feel her tears against his neck.

"I never thought I'd see you again," she whispered into his ears. "Thank God, I was wrong."

When they finally parted, they both hastily brushed away their tears, and smiled at each other like fools. Jack was grateful Waingaio had not intruded on this one precious moment.

Olive wasn't one to mince words though. "God, Jack, you look a shock!" Several of the nearby ladies looked up in horror at her language. His sister paid them no mind, plonking herself down opposite and grinning. That was the amusing thing; she was incredibly blunt, and incredibly beautiful. It made for an uncomfortable mix— just like their mother. Undoubtedly, there would be someone in the world who could tolerate the first because of the second.

"Now that's charming," he said smiling back, "and I was going to bring you a present too..."

"Luckily I don't believe you," she said, pulling out the hatpin, taking off the hat, and setting it on the table next to them, "but then I get enough presents from my soldiers."

For a moment Jack was confused, until he noted the nurses' emblem on her lapel and recalled Royal's brief mention of training. Indeed she was just like Mother. "I'm sure you have them all wrapped around your little finger."

"Oh, most of them," she replied airily, then her brow furrowed, and leaning across, she grabbed his hand. "How are you, Jacky, really?"

He didn't like being touched and it showed. The teacups in their rack behind the waitress rattled. A small wind even started up in the middle of the room, unnervingly lifted a lady's skirt a little. She squeaked and leapt up.

The hens were now certain there was a predator in the house. Jack looked down at his cup, as most of the customers paid their bills and practically burst through the door on the way out. The waitress stood by the door, her hands veritably shaking, as if she too might abandon ship.

"Oh for goodness sake," Olive exclaimed, beckoning her over, "he's just back from the war is all. He won't hurt you, so bring us scones with some jam."

If anything, his sister's brusqueness only compounded the matter. The finger food arrived rattling on the plate, and it had nothing to do with Jack's lack of control.

He forced himself to take one, and focused on putting jam on it for a good few minutes. Finally when he was finished, he looked up into Olive's green eyes. "That's how I really am, Ollie—you asked and I answered."

She sighed, leaned back and fixed him with a steady look. "So what's its name then?"

Jack stirred his tea thoughtfully before replying. "She calls herself Waingaio."

"Her name is 'Unwelcome'?" Olive raised an eyebrow looking very calm, even though her hand trembled around her cup. "A bit of a worrying name. Do the seraphim name themselves, or do you?"

Early missionaries believed at first that the voices appearing in their heads after an accident or terrible loss were God's messengers. While later that had been proven false, they still didn't understand the seraphim completely.

What Jack knew was they were alien and demanding, and being the house they occupied was not a pleasant feeling. Madness could easily be the end of the tale.

"That's a mystery," he replied evenly, before getting out a cigarette and lighting it. He got in three quick puffs before being forced to stub it out in the little tin astray.

"You've given up?" Olive asked with an arched brow that communicated elegantly her surprise.

Jack snorted. "Not by choice, unfortunately—but at least it means I have more money in my pocket."

His sister made a half-hearted attempt at a smile. "I've heard the same thing from some of my soldiers. The seraphim won't let them, something about them thinking it's bad for you."

Jack laughed shortly. "Not very sporting of them considering how they get in by trauma and all."

"But you're still you." Olive's voice made the statement sound like a half-question.

"Father wouldn't agree with you," Jack said, toying with the ashtray, "and I have to say, it's bloody uncomfortable having another being living inside your head."

"I guess he told you about Mother, though?" He was glad it was Olive that finally broached the subject.

"He said she caught the influenza at the hospital." His throat felt tight around those words, as if saying them himself somehow made them more real than when Royal had said them.

Olive nodded slowly, her fingers playing with the napkin on the table in front of her. "It was…well it was quick at least." She glanced up, fixing him with a soft look, more tears threatening to breach her defences. "She thought of you up until the last moment. She loved you so much, Jacky. I hope you remember that."

Jack couldn't do it; he couldn't talk about Mother like this, in a little tea shop in front of strangers. For Olive it was old news, but for him it was too fresh yet. He looked away from his sister. "I wonder what she would have thought of me…a magician…"

Now Olive smiled, "Oh she would have coped marvellously. She saw plenty of them in the hospitals, just like me."

"How is that going?" Jack asked, eager to find a new path of conversation away from his mother's death.

Olive shrugged. "I'm coping. There are plenty like you in the wards—some with not a scratch on them, but deeply wounded and full of a seraph. Then there are others with limbs blown off, horribly mangled, but smiling and talking to themselves."

"Well," Jack said with a chuckle, "they're just talking to someone you can't see, Ollie."

"You're right. But they don't seem…happy." Olive stopped, and he could see her brow furrowing as she wrestled with something. "I hate to do this…you just back and all…but I am at a loss. I fear I need a favour from you, Jacky."

"Anything but money," he said with a wry smile, while leaning back in his chair.

Her lips twisted in a half smile before she went on. "There was this young man…"

"Not surprising," Jack said.

"Oh stop!" Olive downed the last of her tea, and leaned forward in her chair. "His name's Harry Belton—Awakened just like you, but…well…not taking it the best. When he was lucid he was quite lovely, but lately we've had to restrain him. His seraph gave him such terrible nightmares. So, I spent a lot of time taking care of him, because he seemed to have no one, but when I went in to see him this morning he was gone."

Jack swallowed a sudden surge of bitterness in his throat. "Dragged him off to the loony bin I gather…"

Olive shook her head. "Definitely not; the whole place was in an uproar. He'd just vanished."

Jack sighed. Sometimes it was very difficult for Sleepers to understand the true magnitude of a seraph. "He could have used any number of magics to undo those straps."

"But that's the thing—an official from the Awakenings Board had been in two days before and categorised him as a pure telepath, with no other physical magics. He just said poor Harry was sensitive." Olive looked away, and her brother realised with some shock tears had sprung to her eyes again.

His hand was halfway across the table to catch her hand before he remembered; he dare not risk more physical contact.

By the time his sister turned back to him, dabbing at her eyes, it was safely back around his cigarette packet.

"And that's the thing Jacky, I just know that Harry is in trouble… real trouble. The kind money and a place in society won't be able to fix." Her direct gaze left no doubt about what sort of mess she was really talking about; the seraphim sort. Latent awareness was not unknown among First Children, and he believed Olive. She wasn't the kind of person to jump at shadows, or lie to get her own way.

It wasn't as if she could go to the police with this. It would be passed on to the Eyes, and then Olive's Harry would most likely end up in an asylum.

He suddenly very much wished that they were in a pub—his seraph didn't interfere with drinking in most cases. He could have done with a shot of whiskey—and thank God they didn't have prohibition like the Americans.

"You're not listening, are you?" Olive snapped at him—her fingers tight on the edge of the table.

"Really, I am," he assured her. "It's just I don't quite know what you expect me to do about it."

His sister's gaze tightened on him, in that way he recognised from their childhood. "Find him."

This wasn't exactly what Jack had been expecting when he'd got his sister's call in the boarding house. He'd imagined a lively chat, ending perhaps with Olive inviting him to a party, not to a wild chase around the sordid dens of Wellington. But it was obvious that he either give into her, or be bullied for half an hour…and then give in. Jack decided to take the easiest option.

"Alright then." He stood up, paid the bill, and accepted his coat from an overeager waitress. "I'll see what I can do."

Olive rose, and replaced her hat neatly on her head. "Actually, Jacky, I'll come with you. If Harry needs medical help then you'll be next to useless. I remember how you are when you see blood."

Jack sighed, but didn't correct her. He'd prefer that his sister kept her somewhat naïve version of himself in her head. It was nice to imagine a time where he was allowed the luxury of squeamishness—even though Europe had beaten that out of him.

"Come on then," he said offering her his arm, "but if I faint you have to promise to catch me in your practised nurse arms."

CHAPTER EIGHT

Faith and her father had no difficulty finding where Barbara had taken her last breath. Following the call of the seraph like it was a beacon, Faith led them to the area of Te Aro, and there everyone seemed to know who Barbara was.

Even among all the ramshackle wooden buildings, where despair and opium seemed in equal measure, her aunt had made an impression. People mentioned her smile, her sweetness, and her determination. With every tale, Faith could feel her father's guilt begin to swell.

He had abandoned her, but she had still been the same. Yet, look at this place...

She slipped her hand into his. "This is what she chose, Dad. You tried your best, but she wouldn't let you get close."

His grip, still powerful after all those years between him and boxing, tightened on hers. "Makes no difference—family is family, and I could have done something. I *should* have done something."

"Knocked her husband down in the gutter, perhaps?" Faith pointed out tartly. "You know that would have just got you locked up."

Dad looked away. Faith still remembered a time when she was small, before he and Mum went their separate ways, that he had indeed ended up in jail for letting those great hands of his do the talking.

They were now in streets far different from the wide, tram-lined ones of Willis and Boulcott. It wasn't that far in distance really, as nothing could be in a small city like Wellington, but it might as well have been another island altogether. Little one-room houses, with pointed corrugated iron roofs crowded together with barely a foot between them to call their own. Long lines of washing could be seen flapping in many backyards, while flocks of young children chased each other through them. Hollow-eyed women watched them from doorways with unnatural stillness.

So many conflicting emotions rushed over Faith; behind some doors joy at the return of menfolk many had not expected to see again, yet hidden by others such terrible grief, mothers with lost children, children with no parents.

Several times Faith had to stop, catch her breath, and remind herself that these were not her feelings.

"Is it Hoa?" her father asked somewhat nervously.

He usually avoided mentioning Faith's seraph by name, and now it sat uneasily on his tongue.

It was impossible, really for a Sleeper to understand the joy of a seraph, but Faith knew they always assumed that it was a trial.

"No, Dad." She took his big hand in hers. "It's just there's so much raw emotion around here."

He rubbed his moustache, with a guilty twitch of his lips. "Hardly surprising, I suppose..."

"We're close to the last impression I have of Aunt Barbara." Faith tilted her head, twining her thoughts deeper with Hoa's, and reaching out among the houses for the imprint that belonged to her aunt. "This way," she said, tugging on her father's arm.

Faith led him to a bare-board house at the end of a row of others just like it. No children played outside this building, and the front door was ajar, with a little red scrap of cloth fluttering mournfully at the window.

"Just like a plague house," Dad whispered, his hand clenching and unclenching at his side as if he didn't know what to do.

Faith's connection with Hoa rang out in alarm. He was twisting in her head, maddened by something he could not communicate fully.

"You'd think someone would have taken in the linen, at least," her father commented.

Faith stayed silent, fighting back her seraph's rising panic, so father and daughter stood outside on the dusty street for quite a long time, until they attracted the attention of a bundled mop of a woman. She came racing out of the next-door shack, and stared at them belligerently from what passed as a porch.

"Blimmin' vultures," she said with a growl. "Why don't you just clear off?"

Dad used his best publican tone, the one that could calm an angry drunk. "Good afternoon, ma'am."

She sniffed, but her gaze drifted away from openly hostile towards wary.

"I was just wondering if you knew a Barbara Louden..." he said.

Faith left them to talk, because her attention was now able to focus solely on the house. She didn't want to go in there with her father, and definitely not until she had gone in alone first. Her Theta class telepathy needed quiet and concentration—especially if she was to read imprints rather than a living person.

Faith was afraid but resolute. After all, she had Hoa and the power of a storm inside her if need be. The Awakenings Board had never detected that in her, and she prayed she never had to use it in defence—but it was nevertheless there. Hers.

So while her father chatted, Faith drifted towards the door. The first board she stepped on in the house creaked like a tortured soul, and was so loud that she leapt. After a few moments, Faith's hammering heart subsided, and she was able to open her senses wide.

Her aunt's death had been weeks ago, and any physical smell had long drifted away, but the building still hummed with the horror of it. It had not been an easy passing.

While Faith steeled herself, Hoa hid himself deep in her subconscious. His gentle presence couldn't stand conflict or danger—so as a human, she faced it.

Faith did not believe in ghosts, but the fact that great horror could be imprinted on a place, she was well aware of. This house had recorded all the pain and fear of Barbara's death and Lily's abduction as well as any phonograph could.

Get away!

The cry was so intense, that Faith actually took a step back, her heart racing. No one was there, but the young woman's voice echoed in her head.

What happened here? Faith asked, feeling overwhelmed by so much pain and panic.

Hoa made no reply.

She sighed. Seraphim were not without their quirks.

So Faith closed her eyes and marshalled her own power. A series of images flashed under her eyelids—very similar to an incredibly rapid night at the cinema. She saw Barbara, along with a man in the room. The Craven Man, as Lily had already named him.

It remained a mystery how he had got there, but the impression of seraph power lingered all over him. Lily's face, white and terrified, burned in her mind's eye, and the psychic scream that followed after left her head ringing. Then all was silence.

Dad was suddenly at the door, peering in as if waiting for Faith to give him permission to enter. He'd been father to an Awakened child for many years, and knew that sometimes even the slightest disturbance could break her concentration.

"I'm alright, Dad," Faith said, wrapping her right hand around her left, and the space where her finger used to be— as always it was the seat of the after effects of using her power. The pain shooting up her arm made it harder to focus on finding Lily's trail.

Wordlessly her father rubbed her left shoulder, knowing this eased the agony slightly.

"Did she suffer?" he finally asked. "Did my sister suffer?"

Faith didn't think he needed to know the truth. "No Dad," she lied. "It was quick. But Lily…" she paused, thinking to find some way to sugar coat this more necessary reality, but there was none. "There was a man in the room. He took Lily away—he is definitely an Awakened, and now I think she is, too."

Dad's hand clenched on her shoulder. He was ready to make fists and smash someone's face. "Can you find her, Curly? Can you find them?"

"I'll try, but I think he has hidden her somehow or I would have already. It would be easier if I had something of hers…"

And suddenly her father was tearing the place apart—but there was not much to search through. He opened all the cupboards and kicked over piles of debris. It seemed to give him something to do.

Faith's eye was drawn to the sad remnant hanging in the window, flapping to a friendless breeze. Ignoring the numbness that felt like it was penetrating her bones, she stumbled towards the red scrap.

The girl was definitely Awakened, Faith knew that as soon as she laid hand on it. Whatever the mystery man had done to her in this room, he had begun the process whereby the seraph in her blood would break from their slumber. It was not just a physically violent act, but also a mental one.

Lily had just seen her mother die mere moments before—so it was a double ordeal.

Faith wiped her own tears away with the red cloth. "I have what I need, Dad. I don't know how much of her there will be to save. The things that happened…"

"She's still our family, Curly—and we have to get her back. Can you do it or not?" His voice was unexpectedly harsh, but wracked with guilt and grief.

Faith nodded, feeling the stirring of rage in Hoa now, but she had to ask. "Do we get the police involved?"

They shared a look. If Lily had indeed been driven mad, they both knew that the authorities would take her away. Places in the countryside, isolated and dreadful places, existed to house the mad Awakened. It was rumoured that the government used them in experiments to find out ways of removing seraphim.

"No," Faith's father finally said. "Keep them out of it. This is a family matter. We'll deal with it." His look was as chilled as stone.

It fired two things in her; pride and fear. Pride that he would trust her and her power so implicitly, and fear that she would disappoint him.

Yet under his jacket, she noticed his fingers strayed to his billy club. Maybe both her power and his fists would be needed before the end of the day.

Faith stuffed the pain away, to be dealt with later. After seeing and feeling her cousin's agony, she was very motivated. "She's somewhere on Haining Street."

A flicker of a nod, and then her father pulled her in tight, giving her a hug that for a moment took away fear. He whispered into her hair. "Then let's go get her back."

Together they left the house where his sister had died and set off for the most infamous street in Wellington.

It wasn't far, but it was a whole other world. San Francisco and Melbourne had their own Chinatowns, and the little district near Haining Street could hardly compare with these, but none the less this was the street where the 'Orientals' had been tucked away. Here Chinese families tried to live as normal a life as possible, among grocery stores, opium dens and bigotry. Standing at the entrance of the quiet looking street, untouched by trams or cars, Faith put out her senses.

It certainly didn't look dangerous, but most white children were admonished to stay away from this street. It was whispered that Chinamen would chop children up, and turn them into pickled ginger. Others said white slave trading went on, or that Chinese gangs, the tong, had taken over the area.

Yet it looked like any other street, just with different faces at the windows, and signs written in unfamiliar letters. "It isn't really as I imagined," she murmured to her father, while slowly becoming aware that several of the Chinese were looking at her oddly.

"They're just normal folk," Dad replied, patting her on the back. "Struggling to make a living like the rest of us—but don't be thinking there aren't opium and gambling dens here."

They walked down the road, knowing that Faith's femininity was drawing stares. No normal white woman would dare be seen here or risk the destruction of that all important reputation. Faith didn't care for such things, since mostly as an Awakened, her chances of marriage were slim. Her reputation, if she had ever possessed such a thing, was already long destroyed.

A few small horse drawn carts pulled loads of vegetables and piles of laundry up the street, to be deposited at various shops. It made for an interesting mélange of smells. A group of older Chinese men sitting outside a grocery shop played a strange board game made of little white pieces, with delicate cups of tea at their elbows. Behind them were floor to ceiling shelves, packed with glass jars full of interesting things she couldn't identify. Now the smells were suitably exotic.

A horde of children ran past, calling to each other in a foreign tongue, their shiny black hair gleaming in the sun. First Children came in all races, and Faith could sense their latency.

As she began to relax, she sent out her thoughts into the houses, searching for Lily. It was as her father had said in the most part; people trying to make the best life they could in a strange land. Their thoughts in a different language took her a moment to study and understand. Standing in the shadow of a guest house, the red fabric clutched in her hand, she found a hint of the girl Lily had once been. She was so scared that Faith didn't dare examine her too closely. Instead, she mutely pointed across the road and into a narrow back alley formed by a huddle of houses leaning against each other.

Her Dad's face settled into dark determination, and giving his billy club a tap under his jacket, he strode across the street. He didn't look back to see if she followed—he just knew she would. Pride surged up once again in her, and she had to fight it down. She had no right yet to feel that—not until Lily was safe.

The little alley reeked of alcohol and a strange nutty odour that Faith had never smelt, it made concentration difficult, but ahead burned the sensation of Lily's presence. Her thoughts though were impossible to discern past a muddle of panic and despair.

Dad had found a doorway, the only one in the alleyway. He made to touch the handle, but leapt back with a cry.

Faith screamed, feeling the flare of power go through her head like a spear. Father and daughter clutched each other, while Hoa wailed in the depths of her soul.

After a minute, the mental pain subsided and Faith was able to recognise a Delta class barrier, layered specifically to keep out Awakened, and people not Chinese. She began to hazard a guess what Lily was being used for.

Her father looked at her speculatively, and smoothed his moustache. He was waiting for her to come up with an answer.

It was hard to think with Lily's torment battering at her mental barriers, and Hoa squirming, trying to get her to turn about and leave. She had several choices; blow the hinges off, smash the whole place with lightning, or perhaps attempt something more subtle.

Lily, after all, was new to her power, and her older cousin had had many years to perfect her control. Faith placed her hand against the rough surface of the house, and projected her mind through to where Lily was wrapped in confusion. A cleverly placed impression, a hint of deception, and she and her father suddenly appeared to be old Chinese men ready to gamble and smoke.

Faith gestured to her father, choking back the prickle of pain, and he opened the door. Inside was another world unlike anything she had seen before. Low bunk beds lined all the walls of the first room, several of which were occupied by Chinese men, many smoking from wide bowled metal pipes. Some were muttering to themselves in their own language, while on a table in the middle of the room, another dark brown lump of opium was burning. The smell was sweet and nutty. Faith tried her best not to inhale, but if they stayed here long she and Dad might well end up on the long beds, too.

The room was full of far more than smoke. Terribly sad emotions crashed over Faith as she stood in the doorway. The men inside were trying to hide. Even though their bodies were present, their minds were traveling distant paths to their motherland. So much sadness, so much loss—tears ran down her cheeks at the combined weight of unhappiness.

Hoa tried to soothe her; laying its spiritual arms around her, spreading warmth through her being.

Truthfully, there was nothing she could do for these men, so she tried to focus once more on the taste of Lily, which was near, but could not be seen. They walked further into the small house, which seemed to be only two rooms, but the other was just like the first. The men here, though, were not solely Chinese— two white men, their ties undone and their faces lost in the distance, occupied the beds furthest from the door. One was Awakened, but his power was dimmed to a low ebb, his seraph broken and ill. He was using opium to cope, but he couldn't last long either way.

Putting aside that sadness as best she could, Faith looked around.

"Where's Lily?" her father asked, as if she could produce her cousin from the air itself.

The trouble was that while Faith could feel Lily near, she couldn't pinpoint exactly where; the smoke was starting to reach her blood, and while Hoa might not be affected, she could be.

Her father's boot made a strange noise on the dirt floor, and she got a mental shout of alarm from Lily. Faith took hold of her father's arm, and with a slight squeeze indicated down. Her father pulled aside a moth eaten rug to reveal a strange wooden door with a narrow slot in it, buried in the floor. It was secured by a large padlock.

"Pak poo," Dad whispered, as if afraid of disturbing the opium addicts, "Chinese gambling. It's illegal… not like our games of chance." Pulling out his billy club, he gave the door a couple of heavy whacks, but it had obviously been constructed to thwart such attempts.

"Stand back, Dad." The time for subtlety was over. Faith got up, dusted off her skirt, and touched Hoa. His power welled up through her so that every fibre swelled with it. The world bloomed suddenly beautiful, even this sad corner of it. Every scent, every sound made her smile. And she was the whirling centre of it; powerful, kind and aware.

This was the reason so many Awakened burned out— it was just as addictive as opium, but even more dangerous. So Faith reigned in her needs, asking for only a fraction of the power that Hoa could tap into.

Lightning cracked and sizzled behind her eyes, burning the inside of the little shack. The sound of thunder rolled from Faith, making her father jerk away, covering his ears. None of the addicts even moved. She held out her hand very carefully, as if balancing on a highwire, and lightning snarled from her fingertips. It blew the door apart, sending it clattering away like a discarded tin can.

Shaking his head to clear the din of noise from it, her father crawled down into the pit. Underneath a pile of sheets of marked papers, which Faith presumed had something to do with the gambling, he found Lily.

So changed was she that her cousin only recognised her by touching her mind. Lily was barely fourteen, and beautiful in the same way her mother had been; pale, with almost white gold hair.

Those things remained, but everything else was gone. She was dirty, covered in soil, blood and tears, and her blue eyes were fixed on a distant point. When Faith spoke her name, there was no visible reaction.

Father took off his coat and wrapped it around the girl. It was warm this summer, but she was shivering to the bone.

All this time, as her uncle rubbed her shoulders, and spoke her name, she made no sound, and no expression flitted across her face. Faith couldn't help making the mistake of looking down into Lily's mind.

It was like teetering on an abrupt void, like a dream of falling. The abuse had been unremitting; physical, mental, and most of all, upon the newly Awakened seraph within her. The man, who Lily only recalled as a mass of shadow and menace, had needed a guard on his opium den. Lily was a tool, and he had used her. Violating her body and the new born seraph within had been a game to him. He had broken her open, and poured his will into her.

The cruelness of that stirred Hoa inside Faith. He sprang up, roaring in her mind. The alien thoughts were suddenly wrapped around hers, a tangle of rage and unremitting panic, that someone had deliberately done this to one of its own. Faith struggled with the seraph's emotions, which were usually buried deep. Hoa had never demanded anything of her before, but when he touched his compatriot inside Lily, his outrage knew no bounds.

Slowly Faith straightened up, and saw white-faced fear dawn on her father's face. "Your eyes, Curly," he clutched Lily to him, "They're golden."

Everyone knew what that meant, and she would have panicked—should have panicked, but she felt nothing. Only Hoa mattered now. Seraph possession was something she'd feared all her life—but now that it was on her, she couldn't find the will to be afraid. Hoa cared little for the bonds of human society; what was right, or what was proper—he wanted to punish the transgressor. Nothing would stand between him and that.

So Faith ignored her father, instead reaching out once more to Lily's mind. *Who did this?*

Unexpectedly her cousin jerked upright, grasping her hand. "He has more, he has so many more!"

The Trocadero Hotel. Hoa had snapped up the information. Somewhere in one of those gilded rooms, someone was melding the Awakened to their needs; bending those recent dreamers to their own devices.

It couldn't be allowed to continue.

"Faith, don't!" Dad's cry of alarm was a very long way off, for she was enmeshed in the seraph's power. Its cause was now her cause.

The shamble of a building began to vibrate, its wood boards shaking against the restraint of their nails, the tin roof warping and buckling as the weather demanded in.

Even the opium addicts noticed now, but fear was beyond them. They simply stared in mute appreciation at the undisguised display of real seraph magic. Through the glaze of the drug it must have been glorious and mystifying.

Her dad threw himself over Lily, as his eldest daughter became the centre of a storm.

Outside, she could hear people began to scream as the mild weather turned instantly to wild. It didn't matter to her.

"They'll notice, Curly!" Dad yelled once more, desperately, into the teeth of the wind that was circling and battering the house.

She knew who he was talking of. The Ministry, the Eyes, families standing gape mouthed on the street corner, but she didn't care about that either. Why should she care what the Sleepers noticed? It was by far more important that her people be saved.

The house moaned once, and then came apart. The iron roof peeled off and flew away like the wing of a great grey gull, while the walls blew flat in an instant. What this meant to the people in it, Faith didn't see, for she was already flying. The wind scooped her up as she raised her arms to it. It was the gale from the south; harsh, bitter, and more powerful than anything the young woman had ever felt. It whipped her hair and body, but each touch was magnificent. It filled her lungs with strength and laughter. Let the foolish creature that had turned on her people tremble. She was coming for them. The city's Weather Witch was free.

CHAPTER NINE

Jack knew a bad situation when he smelled one—and this one smelt rank. Standing outside the Trocadero Hotel in the early afternoon, he pulled his hat down against a sudden threat of summer rain. The accommodations didn't look frightening, but his fledgling talents ran ahead and told him this was not a good place to be. It might not be a trench in France, but it was potentially as dangerous.

He spared a glance back across the street to where Olive was standing, her bag nervously clenched in both hands despite her feigned cool. Trams trundled past, and the usual buzz of traffic on the Terrace separated them. For sure it was a strange name for a street, but it did resemble something of a terrace; the bottom end of the slope was full of hotels and small offices, while further up the hill where the best views were to be had, was occupied by the homes of the wealthy. Added to that, it was also a hotbed of seraphim activity.

Oddly enough, Government departments were housed only a street away. Jack fingered his cigarette packet in his trouser pocket, and glanced up and down the road a second time. He knew full well that there could be Eyes watching him even now.

Jack stuck out like a sore thumb, but he couldn't quite bring himself to enter the Trocadero Hotel. It made no sense that a place oozing with power, enough for anyone like him to see for miles, was so close to the Ministry of Awakenings.

This was either a trap, or a conspiracy, and he couldn't decide which option he preferred.

Olive, seeing that he wasn't moving, took a step forward as if to cross over and join him. He waved her back, mouthing a 'don't you dare'. As soon as he had tasted the power oozing out of the Trocadero he was certain he wasn't going to take his sister in there. Still, Jack had better do something, or she'd take matters into her own hands.

Looking down at the picture of Harry she'd given him one last time, Jack took a deep breath and strode into the lobby of the Trocadero Hotel with as much confidence as he could muster.

It was a nice enough looking establishment inside; clean, busy, and to normal eyes the same as every other hotel on the street. Jack wasn't fooled though; somewhere above, someone was using their seraph's power, and didn't give a damn who could feel it.

A snappily dressed icy-blonde was behind the counter, and she studied Jack from the corner of her eye in a way that made him bristle. He wasn't too shabby, and he'd never considered himself disreputable, but when she turned her full attention on him he might as well have had no shoes on and be panning for pennies.

"May I be of assistance?" she spoke politely enough, but the gaze suggested that assistance might lead in the direction of the door.

In the war Jack had acquired a trick or two, since the fine art of negotiation was necessary if you wanted to live on anything apart from rations.

In his time as a solider he'd managed to wheedle, bully and charm his way into the possession of a case of good Scotch, a lovely French girl who'd been his commandeering officer's bit, and more than his fair share of cigarettes. So he wasn't going to turn tail and run at the sight of one aggressive blonde.

The trick when confronted by a beautiful woman was not to appear too ingratiating. They already suspected what a man wanted, and if it involved them doing anything they didn't want to, he invariably came off worse. So Jack's method was to fall back on the female of the species desire to improve or help the male. He had never been too proud to appear foolish or ignorant.

When Jack smiled at the woman behind the desk it wasn't an oozing leer, or a smarmy smirk, it was one of genuine bafflement.

"Perhaps...I hope so...I'm supposed to be meeting my friend Harry," he said, sliding the photo across the counter to her. "We were in the war together. He told me which room it was but..."—here Jack paused to touch his head lightly, almost apologetically—"I don't remember things so well these days. Since the gas it's all a bit fuzzy." He gave her another smile, this one embarrassed.

Her wary stare lasted only an instant, melting away to an understanding lift of her lovely lips. She even reached across the desk to lightly touch his arm. "He's in room 206, that's up two flights of stairs." They were obvious, a shining mahogany monstrosity—but maybe she thought he was blind as well as stupid.

Once Jack might have turned the embers of comfort he'd stirred in her into something more personal, but since Awakening he'd found it very uncomfortable to be near anyone. He'd enjoyed sex once; the smell and touch of a woman, the smooth skin, the feeling of long hair in his hands....

Jack leapt back from the counter as quickly as possible, and he caught the tail end of the woman's gaze. It was disappointed. He knew it was Waingaio's fault—plenty of other Awakened could stand skin-to-skin contact. Just his luck to draw the wrong leech, he guessed.

To avoid further thoughts that might heat him up beyond his endurance, Jack ran up the stairs two at a time, because suddenly Olive's task was more worthy of concentration than things he could not change. He passed no others on his way up, which was strange because there had been lots of people milling about in the lobby. The silence felt like the one before going over the top in Flanders, and so he paused on the last flight of stairs trying to reach Waingaio.

The seraph was a slippery creature. In fact, in his mind's eye he imagined it as one of the native eels; long, muscular and slimy. Every time he grabbed for it, it slipped from his fingers for deeper waters. It was what had made him a very hit and miss sort of magician.

His last commanding officer—a native Londoner with not an ounce of magic himself—had been driven to distraction by his newest recruit. Neither of them understood why in blue blazes Jack could sometimes blow the hell out of the practice targets, yet fail to set off an enemy ammunition dump on the front lines. If the Brits had got their heads around how to word a regulation, to encompass failure, to produce magic, he would have got it. Waingaio was really the most irritating seraph.

All Jack was getting were the flickers of the thoughts of those in the hotel; a returned service man used it as a place to meet his mistress, one tired government official pored over paperwork, and a door-to-door salesman rested in a bathroom, with very sore feet.

That all seemed to be below him—the floor above was quiet, both physically and psychically. Not a good sign in a place this busy.

Somehow he wished he'd bought a gun. At least then if Waingaio failed him, he'd have had something to fall back on. Jack's feet made far too much noise going up the last stairs for his liking. The hallway seemed innocent enough; a strip of maroon carpet on polished wooden floors, with about twelve doors leading off it. Yet it was the silence that disturbed him; even the wind outside seemed not to dare to disturb this level.

With a shake of his head, Jack realised he should have known better. Olive had been getting him into trouble since birth, and this felt no different. Experience in the trenches told him that he was better off not going down that corridor. Sticking one's neck out usually involved getting it blown off, but he'd made a promise to his sister.

So, he left what felt like the safety of the stairs and set foot on the carpet. Waingaio hissed and moaned in the depths, so Jack was left in no doubt what the seraph's thoughts on the matter were. He tried to make as little noise as possible getting to room 206, but every breath, or movement of his clothes sounded very loud.

As he stood outside the door for another moment trying to read what was on the other side, he got nothing. Better magicians could read even empty rooms, something like psionic sight, but he usually only got impressions if there were people there and he read their thoughts. Strangely, Jack could hear that there were breathing folk in there, because there were sounds of slight movement, but with her seraph senses he got nothing.

He had no choice, then. Cautiously he tried the door, once more wishing for a gun. Instead, he found the metal of the knob curiously warm. Jack swallowed back his annoyance, and put his hands against the oak while addressing Waingaio.

I just need enough power to open the lock. He whispered to the leech. *Not a big bang, don't blow the door off or anything.*

Nothing at all happened, seraph silence, and in fact perhaps a slight retreat deeper inside.

Anger welled inside Jack, the kind of pissed off, kick something variety that tended to strike when dealing with the damn leech. He hated talking to the thing like it was in control— because it reminded him it probably was. Yet, dammit, he'd never asked for the little bugger to take up residence.

In the moment where he might have turned tail and walked, Olive's little look across the table to him in the teashop came back to him. It had revealed how much this Harry meant to her. Now was not the time to get into a slanging match with Waingaio, because without a gun, he was going to be the only weapon he had. Trouble was, the seraph was inside him so always knew what its host was thinking. So Jack laid his cards out as best he could.

We have to do this for Olive. I promised, and you know how much she means to me. It's a good thing to keep your promises.

Maybe it was him not thinking of the blighter as a leech, or maybe seraph had the same view on keeping one's word, but Jack found he had just the right amount of power at his disposal.

His tiny explosion within the chamber of the door lock made only the slightest sound. Grinning, Jack eased the door open and peered in. The curtains were pulled against the day, and no lights were on. Music was playing softly, yet he hadn't heard it at all from outside.

Jack straightened and went in. The tune sounded awfully familiar. He wandered over to the gramophone that he could just make out in the half-dark and listened. The woman's voice was beautiful and singing in a language that sounded similar to Italian, yet he was sure it was not, somehow. She sang with such longing and loss that he was cast back to the trenches. The music seemed to remind him of the cries of the dying, and the sobs of those that would never see home again.

It was like a physical blow. Waingaio's mental punch jerked Jack out of his reverie and around on his feet as if he'd been slugged. When he shook his head to regain his bearings, Jack realised some sort of magic had prevented him seeing the rest of the room. Now, however, in the gloom he could make out five people sitting on chairs, or rather tied to chairs, facing the gramophone. Nearby, a brazier on a low table was burning, and he immediately recognised the scent of opium.

Waingaio flared in his mind, and with a short grunt of annoyance, Jack grabbed the brazier, and levering open the window, threw it out onto the fire escape. In short order he'd ripped open the curtains.

Somehow, light filtering into the room made it now possible for Jack to turn off the gramophone. The gap where the music had been was almost painful.

None of the other occupants of the room seemed bothered by it, though. Three women and two men sat with their heads dropped down on their chests, with their arms and legs tied to the chairs by bright green cord. But these bindings didn't seem thick enough to actually restrain them.

Carefully lifting up their hanging heads one by one, he checked to make sure they were alive. Though their faces were pale and still, he was relieved to find them still breathing. One as he had already guessed, was Olive's Harry.

Jack reached out to pull that green cord off him and see what would happen.

"Do you really think that is a wise idea?"

He stopped in his tracks. The door hadn't opened, there had been no footsteps in the room, but the voice was right behind Jack's left ear. Now he *urgently* wished he'd got hold of a gun. Waingaio, for once appreciating the danger they were both in, filled him with power—but he didn't use it just yet.

Carefully, with his hands in plain sight, Jack turned around to find the other end of the room wasn't there. He was staring into a pit of darkness which had swallowed the door, the fireplace, and the gramophone as well. If he cared to take two steps he would be in whatever that void was. He certainly had no plans to do so, but the nearness of it chilled both him and Waingaio.

It had a smell, that darkness, one that he found familiar; it was the smell of ripe death, the kind he'd become chums with in the trenches. The recollection made his stomach churn, and his body flood with the desire to flee or punch someone in the nose. A sensible person would have bolted for the door, which was free of the clinging darkness, but Jack Cunningham was still a soldier deep down, and soldiers knew that flight wasn't always the best option.

The candelabra above them slowly began to swing back and forth. The pictures on the wall abruptly all slid left with a shriek. It was all the usual poltergeist activity that Jack still hadn't learned to control. Curiously, this display of his own abilities made him feel better.

Fishing in his left hand pocket for his army knife, he smiled hopefully at the darkness. "These people don't really look like they want to be here, and some are being missed, you know."

"I know more than you can imagine…" The shadows were resolving, and now he could make out a human shape in among them. The voice was all too human, with the faintest of accents to it. None he could quite place, but it wasn't a New Zealander in the darkness.

He managed to back up a bit, and get the edge of his knife to the green cord holding Harry to the chair. That was when the shape stepped out of the darkness, totally resolving into human form, but shifting still so that he couldn't get a good look at the man's features.

Waingaio was howling about something; a warning, an admonishment, it was hard to tell. The kaleidoscope man turned his featureless face to the window, like a cat hearing a bird in a far off tree, and then the wind, which neither of them had noticed, was upon them.

Jack threw up his arm just in time as the two large windows smashed into thousands of sharp diamonds, and the portion of brick wall they had occupied fell away like a broken sandcastle. Then the infamous southerly wind of Wellington poured into the room, screaming with nature's power. Jack's ears rang, he tried to keep his feet, but he was he was hopelessly buffeted back. Then rain came with the wind, stinging his face with its icy presence, and making his fingers lose their feeling altogether.

Turning his head, Jack saw that the darkness was gone, and that the far end of the room once more was visible. Obviously his unwelcome guest had chosen flight in those moments before bedlam.

Staggering to his feet, fighting all the time against the wind, Jack saw something that certainly didn't happen in the city every day. Hanging in the swirling centre of the mini tornado, only ten feet away in mid-air two stories up, was a girl. In an instant he had summed her up; not beautiful, but striking, with strong cheekbones, and full determined lips. Her hair was long, brown angry curls, and her dress was in danger of being ripped apart by the force of the powers she commanded.

He had no doubt that she was holding the reins of this tumult. Even as Waingaio told him that, Jack had confirmation; the young woman's eyes were clear orbs of gold. It was the one sure sign that the human was no longer in control, but had surrendered to the leech.

Those terrifying eyes flickered over the scene; taking in the tied forms, the dropped heads, and the man standing in the midst of it all with a bared blade.

"Oh dammit…" Jack said, realising the instant her eyes turned back to him exactly what this looked like. This was one woman that he didn't want to have angry with him. A pity he comprehended that a moment too late.

Her mouth parted in a soft exclamation while her brow furrowed, and then she let him have it. The wind picked him up and smashed him against the wall two feet from the top of the ceiling before he could even blink. Pain was another reality, something that Waingaio mercifully cushioned him from.

He fell to the floor dazed and bruised—but surprisingly alive and whole. Jack managed to get to his feet and out of the way as a bolt of lightning leapt from the homicidal woman to where he had been sprawled.

The snap and blinding light made him stumble and fall in a heap behind the bed. Something caught fire as the lightning snapped—he thought it was the remains of the curtains. It flared up so quickly that even the whirling rain couldn't hold it back.

All the time her thoughts, angry and fractured, hammered against his, and he had no way of protecting himself from them.

Get away from them—horrible, evil creature!

Images of a hurt and crying beautiful girl exploded in his head, making it difficult for him to get out of the way of the physical attacks. Waingaio, finally coming to the defence of its transportation, pushed back with a surge of its own anger. Seraphim did not usually fight amongst themselves, but they wouldn't allow their hosts to be killed either.

The fire was spreading rapidly so Jack took his chance. Leaping over the bed, knife in hand, he cut Harry free of the chair. "Let's get you out of here, mate," he yelled over the roar of the woman and the wind.

Only then did he realise that he was holding a carcass. In France there had been plenty of corpses; friends, enemies and allies. By comparison this man's body was unblemished, just cold and pale.

Jack couldn't understand how he'd looked alive enough when bound to the chair, but quite patently he'd been dead for awhile. Someone had been using these people, but for what Jack had no idea.

The wind in the room died suddenly, and he looked across to where the brown-haired woman hung in the air.

Across flame, through wind and rain, their eyes locked, and comprehension flashed between them as the two seraphim whispered to each other. She understood her mistake—that Jack had only been trying to help, and was not the enemy. Terror now rushed into the space where the power had been only moments before.

This woman had the kind of magic that the Brits would have killed to have on their side at the Somme. Yet she was hollow like he was, the only filling inside being a seraph leech.

The gold was fading from her eyes as her seraph retreated—not giving any aid to the human that had done its bidding.

In that instant Jack felt deeply sorry for her—the leech had taken control, but now it was going to be this girl that shouldered the burden of responsibility. No government Eye could have failed to see her harnessing the wind, and ripping the Trocadero apart. It was unlikely that she'd ever see the sky again once they caught her. A special prison awaited.

She knew it too. As the gold seeped out of her eyes, and ran in rivulets down her cheeks, comprehension took its place. Perhaps if she had been a man they might have found a use for such power, but as a woman…well, the old fear of witchcraft had not died in the Middle Ages.

"Run if you can," he whispered to the girl. Then, holding the sagging body of Harry, Jack made for the door, as the flames rushed to engulf the remains of the room. Waingaio had filled his body with enough strength so that running down the stairs carrying a dead weight didn't even leave him panting.

From the next floor down he was engulfed in a tide of screaming, terrified hotel occupants. They all struggled downstairs together, then streamed out the front doors, and onto the pavement.

The wind had vanished as quickly as it had been summoned. Jack looked up the street, and saw something that every Awakened feared; the girl was surrounded by police and broad-shouldered men wearing the dark brown uniform of the Eyes. They were the police ordered to watch his kind.

Once Jack had passed them on the street without a backwards glance—indeed he had enjoyed the comfort of their presence, at least when he had been nothing more than a blessed First Child. Now they featured in his nightmares. The Weather Witch would be bound for some nightmare of a 'facility' where all delinquents of the system were tucked away from mundane eyes. Yet that was the fate of his kind that went beyond what society called tolerable.

Even though her attack had been aimed somewhat in his direction, Jack didn't want her to suffer that fate.

He watched her hands being bound behind her back, and with a lurch realised it was with a knotted green cord like that he had seen in use upstairs. It must have been spelled, for her head dropped, and if they hadn't caught her she would have fallen.

Above, the Trocadero had well and truly caught alight, and inside there were explosions, along with the crackle of expensive things burning. The crowd, which should have probably moved, was primitively entranced by the leap of flame.

"Filthy demon." A woman, wrapped in a mink stood next to him, commenting on events in her deeply English accent. "They should put them on leashes like dogs."

"It's thanks to demons like her risking life and sanity, that thousands of your boys got home in one piece." Jack snapped, finding himself welling with an odd patriotic fervour. "You might want to remember that."

He walked off, turning his back on the woman, and the girl being led away. An ambulance man took Harry from him, just as Olive came running over. She'd seen too much death to cry right there, but her face settled into emotionless pallor. Later, like their mother had, Jack was sure she would weep on her own.

So he'd failed her too. Just like Mother, and Father, and most of his friends in France.

"I'm sorry, Ollie," he said patting her on the back, before melting into the crowd.

If the girl was a demon, then so was he, and demons only hurt those they loved. Better if he had never come home at all.

CHAPTER TEN

Lily didn't cry—even when her uncle and Jean finally left her alone. They'd cleaned her up as best they could and finally—not really knowing what else to do with her—wrapped her up in Faith's bed.

Lily didn't tell them that her elder cousin wouldn't be needing it, because they'd work that out soon enough. She also didn't close her eyes. She wondered if she ever would again.

The room was quiet enough that Lily could hear the trams rumbling by outside, and the murmur of people passing in front of the hotel. Underneath everything, however, was the whisper of the Craven Man. He had stolen her seraph's name before she'd even had the chance to learn it, and that she knew should make her angry.

She'd heard Awakened talking about their symbiotes before—even in the poorer parts of town there were some. It had seemed a nice idea to her even as young as she was; to have someone always with you, like an invisible friend.

The Craven Man had prevented all that by taking the name, and now the seraph within her was impossible to reach. Instead of the warmth of a friend, it felt like a confused, cold stranger rolled up in the pit of her stomach. It had no voice, but filled her with power that terrified her.

Lily would rather have had the creature and not the magic. Yet as she lay there in a huddled ball, the seraph's memories began to rise up and wrap themselves around her.

Images, scents and sounds assailed her, even as she lay there perfectly still on Faith's bed. Lily's mouth opened in a scream she could not give voice to. Terror had a tight grip on her, but she did not cry. The Craven Man had laughed and enjoyed her tears through many days, as he did things to her body and mind. As he raped both her and seraph within, he had filled them both with his poison.

Her hand traced the twin scars on her face where he had first touched her. Even now they ached. Trapped in the tiny cellar space under the opium den, she'd been relieved to be somewhere silent, even if she was a slave. Now, having being rescued, she was going to have to cope with the outside world, and Lily didn't know how she was going to do that.

The one person that might have helped had been taken away. The Eyes had ripped Faith from her, and now, across town as she was, Lily could hear her cousin crying, feel the pain of the magic restraints on her skin. Silly, really, because they should be taking her away instead.

It was as the Craven Man had planned all along, and Lily knew for sure he wasn't done with either her or her name-stripped seraph.

Blue lights, like a tangle of wool, flashed in front of her eyes. Perhaps it was trying to communicate with her, or perhaps it was madness lapping up towards her again.

Outside the closed door, she could hear suddenly raised voices, people running and yelling. They'd caught the tail end of the wind and the storm—Faith's power as it dragged her under. One final lash of the storm she had brought into being.

Someone was banging on the door of the hotel, and Lily knew what it would be; an official come to tell her uncle that his daughter was 'in custody'.

Sure enough, Jean came running in, and Lily watched her out of the corner of one eye, not bringing her head up off the pillow. Her cousin was trying to pretend to be calm, but she was not much older than Lily, and wasn't doing a very good job. She went to the window to watch people running by, eager to catch the scandal and watch the Trocadero burning up on the hill.

Silly people.

Lily pressed her fingertips to her eyes, making weird and wonderful swirling images dance there. "All around the cobbler's bench, the monkey chased the weasel," she gasped out.

"What was that, Lily?" Jean started from the window, her face folded in confusion and fear.

Her cousin was really not worth talking to. She was even more mute and blind than Lily knew herself to be, but at least she had a seraph to fill out her insides. Jean was really just a hollow shell without one.

Folding her hands over her eyes, she listened to the fears mount in her cousin's mind. She finally sat down on the end of the bed and touched Lily's feet. "Can you...can you hear anything?"

In the dark under the opium den, when her power was harnessed for the Craven Man's purposes, he'd demanded everything from her, so she had nothing to share with anyone else now.

Pulling her hands away from her eyes, she enjoyed the world swimming, but then stared at Jean seriously. "The monkey thought it all was fun. Pop goes the weasel!"

Her cousin jumped nearly right out of her skin when Lily leaned close and yelled the last bit in her ear. She liked her reflected image in Jean's eyes, it was terrifying, just like the Craven Man was.

Yet anyone who knew wouldn't ask, so Lily closed her eyes and ignored her. The world was an evil, dangerous place, and she was cut adrift in it, so what was the point of reaching out to any of those other castaways? If only she had her seraph's name.

If only...if only...

It was a useless hope.

PART TWO

The Strange Crop

Wellington, New Zealand, 1925

CHAPTER ELEVEN

Faith was knitting; a little act of defiance to the pain in her fingers. At Shorecliff it had been more than that, it was one of the few activities allowed by the inmates.

Still, she enjoyed the fact it was something creative that let her blend into her surroundings. It was nice to imagine herself as invisible as the spider in her web in the corner of the room. The snick of the needles sliding over each other, and the warm rub of wool between her fingers was pleasant and deeply normal.

The rest of the inside of the farmhouse was quiet, but then again it was Sunday. Mum, Uncle Jim, and Uncle Ken were at church, leaving only Faith and Lily behind. Faith had only been taken to church when she'd been a child—before she'd Awakened and become something of an embarrassment.

Lily, however, could never have been taken to church. She could never pretend to be anything but what she was. In the seven years since her rescue, she hadn't changed at all; she still spoke whatever came into her mind, and that was usually something frightening or inexplicable.

Faith sighed and looked down at her hands as they repeated the calming dance of knitting needles. She knew she still wasn't the same as she had been when she was sent away. Shorecliff had made her thin, and painfully, awfully frail. She'd only been out three months, and though her family plied her with every food they could spare, she was still recovering. Her body might make it back eventually, but her spirit was another matter.

The facility was not a good place to think of because if she did, she might start to wonder why they had let her go. She might start to doubt the whole event and imagine it was all a dream, only to wake up gasping in the solitary confinement cell.

No, much better to concentrate on the needles and the wool.

Faith spared a glance outside. Lily was standing under the rimu tree, staring at the stream gushing over the rocks as if it were the most beautiful thing in the world. Her entranced mind tangled with Faith's because it recognised no propriety. It blended into all the thoughts around. It was another reason Lily couldn't leave the farm—she didn't even have the good sense to hide from the Eyes.

Yet, every Awakened should fear them. Faith swore softly as she dropped her stitch. She missed her sister, who would have remonstrated with her for even a quiet 'damn', but Jean was in town for several reasons. Lily's presence disturbed her. Her thoughts were harder to shield from their cousin. As a latent, Jean simply didn't have the shields to protect herself. So she had started staying at the Albert with Dad, and there she had met the young storeman, Len. Their engagement had been announced on the heels of Faith's recent release.

So, her sister had moved on. It was a sad fact, but Faith could barely expect it after so many years. It wasn't as if she was going to demand Jean stay in the quiet of the farm merely for her, but she really did find her days empty without her sister's unconscious happiness. Joy was definitely lacking around the farm these days.

Then again, Faith thought as she got up and looked out the window, *perhaps we wouldn't know how to handle joy if any of us found it.*

The dogs tied up by the gate signalled the arrival of someone with a low volley of barks and yelps, and Faith actually leapt. They were farm dogs not used to many people, but it was stranger still that Faith had got no warning. Her seraph powers hadn't warned her of anyone's approach.

Fear clenched her stomach—there could be only one kind of person able to sneak below her awareness. Her eyes darted to the corner of the room where Uncle Jim had left his gun propped up. She'd hunted rabbits plenty of times and was a fair shot.

It was only a brief temptation. Calmly she put away her knitting and took a moment to soothe her breathing, then she went through the front door and out onto the veranda.

Faith had to shield her eyes against the sharp rays of the summer sun. A man was walking towards her and from his attire she took him for a city man—yet she could see no sign of a horse. Surely he couldn't have walked all the way from town and remained so clean…

He was Māori but dressed fashionably like any other urban man; an expensive looking suit, clean cravat, and a bowler hat. It was as if he had stepped off one of those fashion plates in the newspaper, but then government officials always gave the impression of being well paid.

He was an Eye—most likely one of their detectives since he wore civilian clothes rather than the dreaded brown uniform. She'd seen enough of both kinds in the last few years to last her a lifetime.

Hoa moaned softly, and curled tightly in her, expecting the worst. But strangely Faith did not, for she sensed no danger coming from him. In the Shorecliff, privacy was not something the Eyes there believed in. They thrust rudely into her mind, trying to reach the bottom, and winkle out all her secrets. This man did not. So she waited on the top step, and looked down at him with what she hoped was calm.

He paused at the edge of the path, and admired her mother's dahlias and roses. Though he looked at them rather than her, she knew which direction his seraph was aimed. Finally, after giving her more than enough time to size him up, the Eye turned to her.

He was beautiful; like most of the First Children, nature had been kind to him. A strong face, with full lips turned slightly at the corners, and thick, dark hair. His skin was a beautiful creamy brown, with eyes curiously bright blue in such a dark face, and Faith wondered if his mother or his father had been new to this country.

Mother.

His inner voice was not pushed into her mind as she would have expected from an Eye, but rather insinuated itself against her outer barriers.

"Wirimu MacAlpine," he said but didn't hold out his hand, so perhaps he thought she was one of the Awakened who didn't like to be touched.

Rebelliously she offered hers, just in case he was one himself. He took it, and the flash of warmth and erotic sensation put Hoa into a whirl.

Faith bit the inside of her lip, but didn't smile. "You must already know who I am," she said softly.

He stood below her on the path, and waited to be invited up onto the veranda, but for the moment she was happier with him not in the house proper. Eyes were tricky, they knew ways to insinuate themselves into people's lives and heads, and she'd had enough of them at the facility. She had a momentary panic that perhaps this was all a seraph-induced dream, and she was in fact still there.

Wirimu smiled, and tucked his hands into his pockets. "No, you're really at home, Faith."

"Stop reading my mind!" she demanded, her hands clenching at her sides.

"You may be a wonderful Weather Witch," he said in a quiet tone, "but I'm afraid you have little control on your wayward thoughts. You should have your seraph keep a better watch on that."

She glared at him, hating to know he was right. "He used to be, but since…since Shorecliff it's harder somehow."

His brows drew together. "And now you're afraid I've come to take you there again?"

Faith unconsciously took a step back and nodded.

"That would be risky…" The Eye raised the corner of his mouth in a crooked smile. "I would need considerable power to stop you if you summoned a storm."

Faith believed him, because with that he opened his mind to hers, and Hoa touched his seraph. It was an intimate and surprising gesture. If she had wanted to, she could have known his symbiote's name, and used that to gain the advantage in an attack.

Reserving a little caution, she stepped back and did what every good woman of the land would do. "Would you like some tea, Mr MacAlpine?"

Wirimu took off his hat and followed her into the kitchen. She noticed he scanned the room with his eyes and those of the seraph. Lily, out in the backyard, was thankfully hidden from both. Ever since her rescue she had shown the ability to mask herself from even the most powerful symbiote probe. It usually happened when she was engrossed in something; luckily right now the stream outside probably had her attention.

Faith carefully guided her own mind away from her cousin, lest she give her away to this man whom she was beginning to suspect was far too observant.

Instead, she busied herself around the kitchen; stoking up the wood stove, setting the kettle on it, and ferreting out some of her mother's cake from the back of the cupboard. Faith tried to take as long as possible to finish, but he didn't rush her and soon enough she was forced to sit opposite him. Her hands she kept tucked under the table, lest they give away her nervousness.

Neither spoke for a minute. The Eye watched her and she could feel he was trying to figure the best way to win her trust.

"I want to say I am sorry for what happened to you, Miss Louden," his said, his voice sincere enough.

Years in the facility had taught her more control of her emotions than she'd ever wanted to have. "I was arrested legally," Faith replied evenly, hoping that the kettle would come to the boil soon so she could have something to do.

He sighed and leaned back in his chair. "That is not what I meant. Once the Amendment to the Awakened Act happened last year you should have been released immediately. That's why I'm sorry."

"Not many of us come back when the seraphim rise like that, so it was hard to believe. I understand." The lie slipped out easily since she'd had so much practice. Deception was a required skill at the Shorecliff.

Those remarkable blue eyes caught and held hers. "They wanted to understand how it was done, but you should have been released once your sentence was up and not kept like some lab rat. It was wrong to have cut you up and experimented on you."

A flash of recollection made her jump a little, and she knew that he noticed. Faith's fingernails were making half-moons in her palms. "I'd rather not talk about this, if you don't mind."

"I'm sure it's a painful subject." He put his spread hands on the table between them, and she wondered if he was going to reach across. "I want you to know that as soon as we heard that the Wellington Weather Witch was still in custody, we set the wheels in motion to get you out."

She wanted to believe that. His beautiful dark face seemed honest enough, and Hoa found no malice in him. Yet years in the darkness of the government facility had warped the trust in her own senses. Back there anything could be an illusion—even this conversation.

The whistle of the kettle interrupted whatever she should have said. The little ritual of making the tea occupied Faith until she regained her calm. Placing the cups on the table, she carefully poured, and was proud how stable her hand was. She cut a slice of the plum cake and slid it on a plate across to him. Those few minutes had steadied Faith's nerves until she felt quite brave.

"That's very nice, Mr MacAlpine," she said, "but you didn't need to come all the way out here to apologise."

The Eye smiled at that. "I didn't. The Ministry is not big on begging forgiveness." He opened his mind to her again, letting her pick out the information directly, rather than with words which sometimes Awakened found far too slow.

They were very interested in Faith Louden, but she might have guessed that after so many years in their care. Weather Witchery was not a common talent in the Awakened, and those that they knew of, had blown their powers quickly. Most had been 'put down', or were dribbling wrecks buried in asylums, the talent burned out of them.

Finally, Faith was angry beyond her control. She clanged her teacup down into the saucer and glared across at him. "I assure you that it wasn't just the wasted time that irks me—the 'treatments' wasn't much fun either!"

His eyes never wavered, and since his mind was still open against hers she let him in to the corner of her mind where those memories were locked away.

The long dark nights, with only a terrified Hoa to comfort her. The constant fear that today would be the day they gave up on her uncontrollable nature. The deep anguish of separation from her family. Worst of all, was the knowledge that the staff at Shorecliff honestly thought they were doing the best for her; they believed the ice baths, and the spells in solitary were helping her. Given enough time, they would have thought a lobotomy would be just the thing.

Faith had seen the shambling wrecks wandering the corridors; their seraphim silenced forever. She'd known that would have been her eventual fate. All this blazed into the government Eye in an instant, so that he gasped in shock and pushed his chair back in horror.

Faith flinched—sure that she had gone too far. Instead, he reached across and lightly touched the back of her hand, just for an instant.

His expression was earnest. "I can't ever give those years back, or make up for your suffering, but I can tell you that things are different now." His eyes never left hers. "The government changed while you were away, and we're hoping to change people's thoughts on the Awakened, too."

She recalled the frightened citizens outside the Trocadero hotel and wished him luck erasing those memories. They shared a smile, acknowledging that was the one thing their kind couldn't do.

"I am the Eye assigned to your case, Miss Louden," he said. "I'm your liaison with the Ministry. We left you these last three months to...well to recover from the facility—but now we need you."

Faith looked into the dregs of her tea. "So, not a social call then?"

Getting to his feet, Mr MacAlpine went to the window, and she had no way of stopping him. Lily was barely a few feet out of sight, round the back of the house, but he only seemed to be admiring the dahlias and veggie garden. Finally, he spoke. "I know she's there."

"Who?" Faith went to his side as her heart began to race, and power tingled in her fingertips. Hoa growled inside and shot her images of what he thought they should do about this dangerous Eye.

"Your cousin, Lily," the agent said conversationally.

"You're mistaken...I don't..."

"You don't remember then?" He turned and fixed her with those deep blue eyes. "They said you wouldn't. You finally broke at the facility—after you cracked you told them all about Lily and what happened to her."

Faith took a step back and didn't care if horror showed on her face.

She'd worked so hard to keep her walls up. Hoa had held everything safe, she'd thought. Together they had managed to hold a shield up against the facilitator's intrusion. Yet the days had seemed to run together, and Faith knew she'd lost some time somewhere in there. Still, to be told she'd revealed Lily and her secret was horrifying.

"I...I don't understand. Are you here to take her away?" she asked, her heart racing like a jack rabbit's.

"No more than I am to cart you off."

Faith stared at him for a moment before slowly realising that he was being truthful.

"You did your job, Miss Louden," he continued. "You held out long enough that the rules changed. We've decided that as long as you are around Lily to control her, then she may remain free. In fact we want both of you to go to come back to Wellington."

"Pardon me?" Now she knew she had to be imagining things.

"I should say…I would like you to come with me—help me, rather." He looked very earnest and serious. "Some strange things have been happening, and it seems as if it may have something to do with what Lily went through."

Faith projected her refusal. She wouldn't put her cousin in danger again; she was too frail, too damaged, and yes, far too vulnerable. Much as she wanted to see her father and sister again she wouldn't risk Lily. MacAlpine's thoughts made it plain that he thought they were the only ones that could help.

He wouldn't give away details, but she caught a glimpse in an unguarded corner of his brain; a child's face contorted with rage while her eyes stared back as dead as a doll's. The child's eyes were shining gold.

Faith covered her mouth to jam in a yelp of horror as Hoa whimpered. It was not that Awakened children were unknown. She had been only four herself, and occasionally even the trauma of being born could allow a seraph in. Yet it was something to be avoided. Even the craziest adult seeking to bring on their child's power would hesitate at doing it before five. A young mind was more malleable and ran the risk of the seraph overcoming it completely.

She knew it was not the seraph's fault. They only came when the door was opened by pain. It was as in their nature as a dog barking or a cat chasing a mouse. They wanted to be together with a person in the real world. They might prefer an adult body to live in, but they couldn't retreat once they came out.

Children were dangerous and precious. Hoa was practically yelling that she had to find out what was going on. His demands only backed up her own determination to snatch that image from Mr MacAlpine.

At least if they went back to Wellington, she would be able to rely on her father and Jean to help with Lily.

The Eye was watching her carefully. "We fear it has something to do with the man who tormented your cousin. She is the only one that we know of that survived after being influenced by him." The Eye realised he was making a convincing argument, but pressed his point. "We have nine dead people in Wellington we know of. Perhaps even more that we don't. Your cousin is a witness, and frankly you are the most powerful Weather Witch so far recorded. Do you think you can't control her or yourself?"

Faith considered. Hoa, whose primitive emotions had been the cause of her incarceration, obviously still wanted vengeance for his people—and if she thought about it, she wanted the same. The Trocadero was a blur, as the seraph's control had masked most of the memories, but she recalled a man. He'd been beautiful—storm tossed and frightened, but there had been an instant between them that was branded into her mind. He'd been holding one of the dead after cutting him loose, and he'd looked up, with terrible sadness written on his face.

"I can't answer for Lily," Faith finally spoke. "You will have to ask her yourself, but for me I will help…if you do one thing."

"As long as it doesn't break any laws," he replied leaning back against the windowsill and fixing her with what Faith assumed was an appraising look.

"What is your gift?"

She knew before he had even uttered the words, because there was another flash of memory that had been lost before. "I am a healer."

He'd been at the facility in those final weeks, Faith was suddenly sure. Hoa murmured confirmation. It had been Mr Wirimu MacAlpine that had fixed the wounds in her mind and body. Faith believed, because he hadn't told her himself, despite the leverage he would have gained from it. This was a man that instinct and seraph agreed could be trusted.

Brusquely, she cleared away the plates and cups and opened the back door onto the garden. "Let's go find Lily and see what she has to say on the matter."

The words of her thoughts echoed between them, *no more children will suffer*.

CHAPTER TWELVE

With an open mouthed gasp Jack woke from his terrible dream. His money had run out before his thirst had—that's what must have happened. The bar of the Central Hotel was silent and deserted. Mavis had wiped up the beer he had spilled, but left his head in sticky puddle all its own.

On cue, she appeared at the far end of the bar, wiping a glass clean, and giving him what was locally referred to as 'the Evil Eye'. She was a busty, feisty copper-haired daughter of Ireland, and thus had no touch of seraph. At that moment, Jack was glad of that.

He smiled, levering himself off the countertop, and pushing his hair back out of his eyes. "Did I miss anything?"

"Depends on what you mean, Jack; you playing the piano until everyone stopped dancing, or perhaps you mean buying the whole damn place a drink?"

He groaned, realising why the glass at his elbow was empty and his pockets turned out. She'd probably left the dry glass there just to emphasise the point. "Well Mavis, perhaps you'll take pity on a fella and find me a bed to sleep in?"

Her pursed lips and deepening frown didn't bode well. "Not ever again. Mine is not open for your sort of business."

It was a fine line that he was taking; too much alcohol and he couldn't bear to be touched, too little, and the whisper of Waingaio would begin again. He'd only managed to find the happy medium a couple of times, and then he hadn't sought the company of the professional ladies of Wellington—it had been the brightly burning Mavis.

He must have done something terrible if the usually accommodating red head was denying him entry. "Come now, my sweetie—surely you remember how much you like me?"

"You're a handsome devil," Mavis said, putting down the glass with a clunk as she strode across to him, "but that's not making up for the fact that you have got your head in the bottle from dawn 'til dusk."

She couldn't understand, and he wasn't about to explain it to a Sleeper. Instead, Jack pushed back out of the chair with only a slight wobble, and waved at his hand at Mavis.

Staggering out of the Central Hotel, he looked about blearily. It must be sometime after eleven in the evening, because the streets were mostly empty. The population of Wellington were likely to be either back happy in their beds or painting the town red in the dancehalls.

Looking further up Cuba Street, he could hear that was where the party was—and a party was just what he needed right now…even without money.

"Hey Jack!" He turned around, to see Skint O'Brian examining the last of his bottle, leaning against a slightly suspect fence, and grinning. "I'm going up to Café de France—wanna come? I hear they got a couple of new girls from Melbourne in…"

Skint—who was named for his forever lack of money—was Jack's most frequent companion in the town. Hemi had long since returned to the embrace of his tribe, and there was not much of a choice for company in Wellington for a drunk Awakened.

Skint was not exactly known for his wonderful personality, yet as long as Jack had coins in his pocket Skint would always be within shouting distance. Unfortunately, the money that his mother had left him was nearly gone—poured down his throat, and lost at the gambling table, so he imagined that Skint would soon be as scarce as the money was.

Still, it had bought Jack peace for those years it lasted. Constant drinking had kept Waingaio's voice muffled in his head.

Tonight he would muffle it once more, however he wavered at the thought of all the people at the Café— had he had enough booze to still their voices in his head?

"Aww come on," Jack's companion said, and began jostling him up the street. "Everyone would love a tinkle on the old ivories!"

The thing about this town was that they were always short of musicians, so anyone who could play a tin pipe, or the piano was an instant favourite of the rough characters who inhabited the town.

Jack's inherited money had really only lasted this long because his playing often earned him many shots of rotgut whiskey. His mother wouldn't have appreciated him using his talents in such a way, but that was of no consequence now.

Skint kicked open the door to the dancing hall, and led his friend in. "Appleseed's here—so get off that damned piano, Bodger!"

The unfortunate scarecrow-shape who was playing a hesitant tune on the shambles of an instrument gladly gave up his spot, and Jack took his place.

As he decided which song to begin with, he looked out over the dance hall. It was full of brightly painted women of varying ages, and as many roughened men as they could handle—perhaps a few more than that, actually.

Miss Flora O'Reilly ran a legitimate business, which meant that she didn't have to pay off any city officials, and more importantly it meant it wouldn't become tawdry. Men paid to dance with her girls, and whatever happened after was none of her concern.

The woman herself appeared from the backrooms on hearing Jack's name called, and promptly poured him a large whiskey, placing on the top of the upright.

She patted her jet-black hair, which was most definitely a wig, and adjusted her cobalt-blue dress. "Nice to see you back, lad."

Once she must have been the handsomest woman in Wellington, but now she was an overblown rose. Her chest had grown thin under the old-fashioned corsets she still insisted on wearing, just like her hair. Those brown eyes were watery and the lips narrowed to slits.

Life might not have been easy for her, yet she could be kind when it suited. A piano player that worked for booze was just the sort of person she was willing to smile on.

Jack took a quick shot of the rotgut she supplied, to still the voice of Waingaio a little longer and then began to play. The hall had plenty of sheet music, but Jack played from memory. That was the trouble—his memory was far too good.

He began with 'April Showers' without much thinking about it, and watched out the corner of one eye as the girls were whipped around the dance-floor by the men. It didn't matter the tempo, they just enjoyed the feeling of a woman pressed against them, and the sway of the music. Most were only passable dancers, but the women were paid to put up with trodden toes and bad breath.

Jack was having a worse time of it, though. Skint might have left his side to find his own sorry partner, but Waingaio was still with him. The ugly truth was, lately it had taken more and more alcohol to silence her in his head. Shooting a glance to the top of the piano, Jack realised he had already knocked back the whole glass, and Miss Flora was busy 'talking up the custom', so he ploughed on through the song.

He caught flashes of repressed disgust, lust and longing. His body ran alternatively hot and cold. Muscles burned and ached, others began to hurt. The cursed leech just wouldn't leave him alone. Then abruptly, all voices in the bar but one died out. Jack's head turned, even as his fingers kept dancing.

A young girl, a cloche hat pulled down low over her eyes, stood trembling in the doorway. He recognised her immediately as one of Miss Flora's regular girls. On the outside she was smiling, smoothing down her lilac dress, but inside she was awash with panic.

Drink and disgust kept Jack from identifying why this Awakened girl was so terrified, but one thing was certain; she knew he was inside her mind. Her green eyes locked with his, but Jack played on.

Miss Flora bustled over to the girl and thrust her onto the dance floor without even talking to her. Lanky Joe, whose lack of personal hygiene was almost legendary, gathered her up, but she smiled, and she danced.

At the piano Jack started 'Baby Face', while trying to untangle his mind from the girl's. Waingaio, for some reason, fought back, reacting by pushing him even deeper into her subconscious.

What he felt there reminded him of the trenches of the Somme; wretched despair so abiding that it drove out everything else. This girl, like the men at the Front, truly wished she would die.

Her name was Chloe, and in the deepest part of her mind, a child was crying. Why this sound would so occupy her Jack couldn't tell, but it was starting to drive him to the edge. He looked around wildly for Flora so he could get another shot—that might help.

She was nowhere to be seen, and Chloe's panic drew him back to her relentlessly. Waingaio, whose voice he had worked so long to quell, demanded that he take notice the only way she could.

Jack couldn't help it now, while he played on, his eyes followed her. She was tiny, with her dark hair cut in a fashionable bob, but she smiled kindly at the ridiculously smelly Lanky Joe.

Jack tried to concentrate on his fingers, but the bitter sweetness of the girl intruded. He could have wept, they were entwined so deeply. She was enjoying the music, and the movement, and even the closeness of Joe because, for a moment, it distracted her from her own troubles. It was easy to offer the man some comfort and enjoyment.

How such a sweet girl would think so many dark thoughts, and still be able to smile enough to melt her dance partner, Jack couldn't fathom.

Before the war he would have thumped down the cover of the piano and gone to dance with her himself, now he was numbed by his own fears. Besides, that was the very thing Waingaio wanted him to do—the damn leech was putting ideas into his head. However, there was no doubting that she was beautiful.

Jack played for an hour non-stop, hoping that time would lessen the seraph's hold, but whatever strange pact there was between hers and his, they did not release each other.

Damnably, Miss Flora did not return to refill his glass—despite his blatant gestures. Every time he made to get up and fill his own damn glass, the room would erupt in cheers and whoops, and he'd be forced to sit back down.

Finally, the unfortunate Bodger he'd replaced appeared at his shoulder and demanded a break. Bodger was from the motherland, seraph free, and obviously too deep in the bottle to be influenced by them.

Jack gladly gave up his seat at the piano, and made his way to the bar so that he was finally able to get paid. The tall shot of whiskey went down very well, but he couldn't help his gaze seeking out Chloe.

The booze started to work its magic, and he was finally able to disentangle his thoughts from hers—that was when Chloe decided to leave the dance hall. Jack by rights should have been relieved, but the misery she carried was impossible to ignore. Booze fuelled his legs while Waingaio disengaged his resistance, so soon he found himself outside the dance hall.

It was quiet on the street, and moving relentlessly towards dawn. Cuba Street was dark apart from the pools of light from the other dance halls, and the odd kindly landlady who had left a porch light on for her guests.

Up ahead, Chloe was walking slowly, head bent. They had shared a deep moment thanks to their seraphim, so as she rounded the corner and turned on Dixon Street, he found himself running to catch up.

Despite his loathing of human touch, Jack caught hold of her arm before she could disappear completely. Chloe spun about, blinking up at him as if coming out of a fog.

"Why so sad?" Jack blurted out, feeling her emotion bleeding into his own head once more.

Yet she wouldn't let him in; though Waingaio and her seraph were wrapped tightly around each other, she managed to resist his intrusion.

Chloe jerked her arm away from him and stared at him—not afraid, but surprised. In the wane light, streaks of tears gleamed like silver on her face. "Let me go or I'll scream," she said coldly.

"Who is the child?" Jack stumbled out the ridiculous question, struggling to find normalcy in a very abnormal situation.

Everything melted at once; her coldness, her tightly held control. Suddenly she was just a very young woman—not far from girlhood really—sobbing.

Jack swore, abruptly embarrassed that he had caused this. Chloe was crying as if she was trying to dissolve, and knowing his luck, a cop could turn up any minute. Since Jack didn't fancy a night in the cells, he guided her into the shadows of a narrow alley. Chloe went with him, her body still shaking with a storm of tears.

Jack stood opposite her, nervously rocking from one foot to another, not really sure what to do next. Finally when she showed no sign of subsiding, he gently touched her shoulder—that was a very wrong choice.

Next thing he knew, she had grabbed hold of him and was crying into his chest. Somewhere their seraphim were whispering to each other, making them more than just two strangers clutching each other in an alleyway.

After a moment, Chloe managed to get control of her emotions. "You heard him then?"

"The boy?" he asked hesitantly.

She nodded and producing a handkerchief from inside her coat pocket, began to dab at her eyes. "Billy…my son." She glanced at him as if she half expected him to say something—she was very young, he supposed. But, Jack had long ago given up on judging others.

Chloe's story tumbled out of her like a torment. It wasn't that unusual. Poor young woman with illegitimate child that the world condemns is forced to ship her child to one of the so-called baby farmers. By sending money each month, Chloe was paying someone else to look after the child that she longed to keep, but knew she couldn't.

After a few months when the 'farmer' wouldn't let her see Billy, Chloe began to worry. They claimed he was sick and had to be kept isolated.

"But I know it's something else!" Chloe's hands were tightened into fists. "I know!" She looked up at Jack, and he understood. Whatever seraph power the girl had it was a minor one, but it had linked her with her child. Maternal connections were already powerful bonds but magic made them even more so.

Jack sighed, leaned back against the filthy alley wall, and closed his eyes. Here he was again, faced with another woman who needed his help. Last time had not been a success.

Though Olive said she'd forgiven him for not saving the man she loved, the scar of it still came between them. He'd reached the conclusion that any help he offered anyone would only be poisoned chalice.

Chloe leaned forward and touched his hand. "I felt your strength in the dancehall. Whare, my seraph, he says that you could help us. I…I don't have much money, but…"

"*Tai ho*," Jack said holding up his hand, "I don't need your money, but I'm not who you think I am, either. Why don't you go to the police with this instead?"

Chloe bit her lip. "I…I tried that, but I couldn't tell them who my Billy is really—so they wouldn't believe me. They…they were judging me, and so they didn't believe me when the farmer told them I was lying…"

The ciggies in Jack's pocket were begging to be smoked at this point, and Waingaio for once was silent. It liked to do this sort of thing; drop him right in it, then retreat to allow him to wrestle with the moral dilemmas. Jack knew it would mean tapping those seraph powers he'd managed to avoid touching for years.

Yet some part of him thrilled at the chance to do something after all this time. Maybe it was time to prove that the boozing piano player was more than just that.

He looked across at Chloe and held out his hand. "The name's Jack Cunningham, and it would be my pleasure, pretty lady, to help you get your child back."

CHAPTER THIRTEEN

Wirimu was a magnet. Lily felt it sitting on the train being shaken like leaves on a tree. It looked like Faith felt it too. She was unconsciously leaning towards the agent, and her skin was slightly brighter, like a shiny apple gleaming in the sun. Lily almost had to shield her eyes from it. She squinted instead.

Wirimu's mind was silence. A warm blanket silence. He didn't yell in her face. He didn't stare at her for so long she had to look away. While he talked to Faith, it was his mind that was quiet.

In that pool of silence, Lily was able to relax even though they were on a train with other humans. While soaking it in, her fractured thoughts seemed to hold together. Wirimu shot her a smile. His seraph was in control—totally unlike the one residing in her. The old wound peeled open just a little and she had to look away from his face. Lily stared out the window as reality flew past her.

People and seraphim were always trying to fix her and her nameless being. They poked at her with unseen fingers, trying to work out how to stitch the two of them back together. It never worked. She was broken.

Wirimu was smart. He had told her about the darkness and the children that were in danger, but he also said he needed her. It was an odd piece of the puzzle; someone needed her.

Usually she was the bit out of place; always in the wrong place, always saying the wrong thing. Once, she'd been a sensible, normal girl. Nothing special.

However, she wasn't sensible anymore—that girl had died with Mum. All she had now was the battered and quiet seraph who had found his way in. She didn't know his name. He didn't speak to her, and because of that, she had no control over anything.

It was not his fault. It was the Craven Man. Lily squeezed shut her eyes and leaned her head against the cool window of the train as she realised her mistake. She shouldn't have thought of him. Now he was there, a shadow in the corner of her mind. He had taken the name of her passenger, and he would take her too if he could.

She ground her teeth and squeezed her hands into tight fists, until the pain of her nails in her skin made sharp spikes in her mind. Sometimes that got rid of the man.

"Lily?" Wirimu's hand lightly pressed on her shoulder. It was not skin to skin contact, but it was enough to chase away the Craven Man—at least for this moment.

Lily opened her eyes to his smile like a crack of sunshine in an abandoned room. Things were different now; she could see that. Taking her head off the window, she realised that the rattling engine dragging the tin carriage ride was actually terrible fun.

The world tumbled by in flashes of brown and green. Faith and Wirimu were talking quietly again. They were keeping their voices low, probably for her benefit, but if she'd wanted to hear, all she had to do was probe a little. She and her nameless seraph had ears.

Lily wasn't interested. The puzzle piece world mattered little to her or her unnamed friend. The images and smells of that place were interesting, but not valuable.

What she did hang onto was Wirimu's hope. The idea that perhaps she could be healed was attractive, more so than the danger that might be involved. Lily wanted to know the name of her seraph, and the only way she was going to get it was to find the Craven Man that had taken it. Not just see his form in her mind, but stand before him and take back her seraph's name.

That meant courage and determination. She thought she might recall what those were.

"Picnic time for teddy bears," Lily whispered into the glass as Wellington's harbour appeared. They barrelled out of the tunnel with a whoosh, and she bounced up and down in excitement.

"Lily," Faith said, her breath ruffling the top of her head, "calm down."

So, she tucked her feet under her and tried her best to slap on the façade of being normal. It was hard to do, and it couldn't last, but her cousin had asked.

They got down off the train and into the bustle of the station itself. People streamed past them in little groups like fish in a pond. Lily wondered what sort of sea life she was. Maybe a crab.

She trailed behind Wirimu and her cousin, her head tilted upwards at all the big buildings. It seemed impossible such inconsequential things as humans could have made them.

Her unnamed seraph smacked her between the eyes, made her look up at the building that they were all going into. It had the words "Ministry of Awakened" worked over its door in thick, gold letters. The world blurred again, leaping ahead like she was flickering through a book.

They were inside the building now, and Faith was yelling at Wirimu. Sharp and angry words slashed the air. People had stopped around them to observe. Lily stood swaying in the corner, but eventually the words calmed down. Lily caught the phrase "trust me," and she smiled.

The men and women were dressed in the brown uniform Faith had spent so long telling her to run from. She could hear the murmuring of their seraphim, but their thoughts were locked down tightly, so she couldn't hear precisely what they were thinking.

Some did stop and look over their shoulder in her direction. She waved cheerily at the first few, until Faith grabbed her arm. Lily giggled and whispered up to her, "The dish ran away with the spoon."

Faith didn't understand. She led her into a room where there was a pretty young man, two old rather grumpy soldiers in the brown uniform, and a long flat, metal table.

Lily clambered up onto the examination table without thinking. Faith sat opposite, her hands clenched nervously around her handbag, while her eyes darted from man to man as if she expected them to bite. Shorecliff had put twisted thoughts into her cousin's mind—almost as if she had met the Craven Man herself.

Lily held still as the men probed her mind lightly. She could feel their mental fingers tracing the places where her seraph merged with her, and their curiosity at what they didn't find there. They peered into her eyes deeply, searching for gold, but she could have told them not to bother. With no name, her seraph was certainly not going to be taking over.

The men were very clear explaining what they had found to Faith.

"She's been broken in rather deliberate ways," the older man said, tapping his fingers on the edge of the metal table. "The link between her and her seraph is stunted. It makes her vulnerable and powerfully dangerous at the same time."

Lily was glad to have someone else say the things she couldn't find the words for. She swung her legs happily on the table and grinned.

"Dangerous?" Faith leaned forward on her chair. Some of her curled brown hair had broken loose from under her cloche hat, the light illuminating the strands of red in it. Lily thought it looked very pretty.

The slightly younger looking man pulled up a chair and tried to explain. "She's vulnerable in that with the right cues—which were probably induced at the moment of Awakening—she can be controlled."

Lily noticed how her cousin's face turned a strange shade of white when she asked, "Like at the opium den?"

"Exactly," the older one said, sharing glance with his colleague. "But she's dangerous because she has none of the seraph limits that a complete symbiotic relationship brings."

A proper link? Lily stopped swinging her legs. That would be nice. She imagined a rainbow bridge with her seraph waiting on the other side. "All the king's horses and all the kings men couldn't put Humpty together again," Lily told them in what she hoped was a helpful way.

Faith was squeezing her eyes hard against frightened tears leaking out, while her mind screamed in horror. The image of Shorecliff burned in her mind. *Are they going to take Lily there?*

They considered it. Lily watched them out of the corner of her eye and smiled. They wouldn't. They were afraid of Faith. They wanted her to help them. They *needed* her to help them.

Another blink and now they were in Wirimu's small office with no windows at all. She wandered off to where they should have been and started describing the shape of one against the wall. She let Faith and the Eye think she wasn't listening. That was the best way to learn things, she'd found.

They were talking about children—killed and lost children. Lily closed her eyes as she sucked in what they were saying. Pale haunted faces began to inhabit the backs of her eyes.

This was why they needed Faith…and her too. They couldn't know it yet, but it was the Craven Man. The beast still hunted the streets of Wellington—seeking out children like she had once been.

Faith was frowning, and Lily knew she was going to say no. *It is simply too much danger.*

Lily had to do something—for her and her unknown seraph. It was going to be too late in a minute. Spinning around, her mouth popped open. "We have to do this. We have to help!"

For a moment all three of them stared at each other. The waves of unreality, which had momentarily ebbed away out of real necessity, rushed back. She turned her face to the wall abruptly.

Faith cleared her throat. "If there are children in danger we wouldn't be doing our civic duty to simply walk away. If we can stop what happened to my cousin happening to anyone else…"

The poor, unnamed seraph within Lily twisted with what she hoped was satisfaction. Impossible to tell but maybe, just maybe… just maybe…they could put Humpty back together again.

CHAPTER FOURTEEN

Lily.

Emma sat on the little farmhouse steps and felt the presence of the broken girl glance by. The only little fly to make it from her master's web.

The fleeting touch vanished, and she guessed it was on a train because the main trunk line ran near to Newlands. The farming area was just remote enough from the city to give them all the privacy they needed, but close esnough so that if she needed to hunt, she could.

Yet she was careful these days—far more careful than she had been. The Craven Man had left her in charge of the farm while he pursued his own nebulous aims. All Emma knew was that if he came back and his farm wasn't running as he'd left it, there would be consequences—consequences she didn't want to experience.

Getting up from the bench on the front veranda with a sigh, Emma opened the door and went in. The children were quiet, sleeping after their long night of work. Looking down at the twin boys who were the pride of the project, Emma felt a moment of sadness.

He called them his golden-eyed darlings, broken and waiting for the puppet master to jerk the strings. Sleeping, the children seemed normal. Their soulless eyes were hooded, and the terrible side effects on their personality masked. Emma was relieved. Being in charge of these children was not something she enjoyed. In fact, when awake, all they inspired in her was fear.

Her master was not a person to defy. He had said she would watch the children, so that was what she would do. The Craven Man had recalled her from Auckland, where she'd spent the last few years, hunting, all unnoticed. It also meant there had been no repeat of her close call with Jack outside the hotel.

He was probably still there; Wellington was his home and he loved the place. For sure he wouldn't have gone anywhere else in the last few years.

With a soft sigh, Emma pressed her face close to the window. The hills of Newlands shielded her from actually seeing the city, but its presence whispered at the edge of her conciseness. If she stretched out just a little she would be able to sense him, yet equally he would know immediately that she still lived.

She'd thought he wouldn't come back from the war. In those years, Emma had been born and Alice buried. She didn't even look the same, so perhaps it was ridiculous to be afraid of Jack recognising her. Yet that instant outside the Albert where she had been just about to strike and feed, Jack had seemed to sense something in her—some small portion of Alice that he found familiar.

It was foolish. She shouldn't be afraid of anything. It wasn't as if Alice's husband could do anything to her. But…but…

"You should be full of more faith, my angel." The voice arose from the shadows and, despite the nature of her new form, Emma jumped.

The children on their beds shook like eggs in a tray, but thankfully their eyes remained closed. The darkness coalesced into their master's shape, but she knew it was harder and harder for him to do so. She averted her eyes until he had completed the transformation.

"I heard your prayers," he rasped. "You are afraid."

To tell him about Jack would probably mean his death. Despite everything Emma had become, she didn't want him to die. It would be too cruel to have him survive Europe to perish in his own hometown. She tucked her thoughts away in the small part of herself that was still private, and shoved the realisation about Lily to the fore.

The man's eyes blazed with yellow light. "That creature? Surely you could not be afraid of that?"

"She was an experiment. I don't know what sort of threat she is…" She was, in truth, curious.

"The methods I used were complicated, yet even I do not know their real effect." Admitting such weakness was not her master's usual behaviour. He paused. "It would be interesting to see the results."

The Craven Man stood next to the bed, looking down at the children. The closest girl, about five years old, Emma guessed, twitched, and her fingers flickered as if she was playing an unseen piano.

Then he said the words Emma had anticipated already. "I need you to find her. Take the cart into town and bring her back."

Emma didn't reply, but her thoughts must have given her away.

He started towards her, enveloping her in his chill shadow. His icy hand brushed her skin, and she managed not to flinch. Once his touch had been all she craved and worth sacrificing her very existence for; now it conjured up far different feelings.

"You have not eaten for so long, pretty Emma," he said, pressing her against his equally frozen body. "I would think you would welcome the chance to stalk through the town like the lion you are."

His words conjured images in her head that moistened her mouth and opened a pit of craving in her gut. Every reality fled before that need.

"Yes," Emma replied with a stiff nod, "I do have hunger. I will find your flower and bring her back. Hope you don't mind if I stop for a snack first."

The Craven Man's laughter was brittle and painful enough to draw blood. It thrilled her to the core.

CHAPTER FIFTEEN

The Albert looked nearly the same as Faith remembered. It was perhaps a little smaller and the paint a little more faded than six years ago, or maybe that was just her perception.

The streets outside had changed though; they were far more crowded. Faith wasn't sure that she liked that.

"Are we going in?" Mr MacAlpine asked in a gentle tone.

Lily clutched her right hand tight, so with a slight smile, Faith led them across the road, and around to the back door.

Jean was silhouetted against the side window, head bent, intent on washing dishes. For a second, her sister didn't see her, and Faith held her breath—then Jean turned. With a squeal she grabbed her cousin and her sister against her. Lily made a slight giggle as she was squeezed against her Jean's chest.

Faith tugged away a little. "Jean, this is Wirimu MacAlpine."

Her sister, though, didn't have time to answer, because their father came in just then. His face was set in a scowl, and she knew behind his back his trusty billy club was at the ready.

Faith cleared her throat. "Dad, this is Mr MacAlpine, who is responsible for my release…"

"Oh…" He tucked his weapon behind the door before coming in properly, and shaking the other man's hand energetically. "Then let me buy you a drink, young man."

Wirimu's smile seemed genuine. "Thanks Mr Louden, but I'm on duty."

Faith could feel the atmosphere in the kitchen become suddenly chill, so she filled in the silence. "He says that Lily and I could be in danger, and insists we need protection."

Her father bristled at the implication. "Thanks for your concern lad, but I can take care of all my girls."

Wirimu shifted from foot to foot just a little. "I'm sure against normal enemies, that is very true—however the persons who assaulted Lily are far from normal. I'm sure you'll agree that you could use an extra set of eyes."

Dad snorted at the pun, but after a moment nodded. "We have a few rooms vacant upstairs."

"Why don't you settle Mr MacAlpine in, then," Jean hinted, "and Lily too while you are at it?"

John Louden grumbled through his moustache, but led the way. The two sisters waited until they were alone before taking the chance for another hug. It had been a long time since they had seen each other. When Faith had been released she'd been taken straight to the farm, and while Jean had visited, the sheer bedlam of family activity hadn't allowed them to really discuss anything.

Faith sat at the small kitchen table, and waited while Jean set the kettle on the stove. She chatted while they waited; nothing of consequence, but the small gems of her life that her sister had missed. Jean was engaged and now of an age to work in the hotel. She was happy with her life, but Faith read that she was very disturbed at the same time.

It was only once that they both had tea in front of them that they were able to talk about what was actually on their minds.

Jean leaned across and took her sister's hand. "How are you... really?"

To anyone else she would have lied, made some offhand remark, demurred in any way she could, but this was her sister; the person she had whispered confidences too since before time had any real meaning. "Shaky still. I can't seem to escape the nightmares, and Hoa doesn't speak to me like he used to."

"I'm sure that will come back," Jean said, wrapping her fingers around her cup. "He must need as much recovery as you."

"I suppose."

Jean leaned back in her chair, and fixed Faith with an observant look. "You know I always envied you; carrying your own best friend around with you all the time."

Faith snorted at this revelation. "It hasn't improved my life any. I would much rather have been like you…" She wasn't sure how much truth was in that.

Jean was silent a moment as she turned her head to the window once again. Faith waited for her sister's thoughts to coalesce, and finally Jean turned back. "Do you remember my accident?"

"Accident?" Faith frowned.

"The one when I was ten and fell down the stairs."

It was a vague memory. She hadn't been at the hotel that time since Mother had needed her help on the farm for shearing, but Faith nodded.

"Well, it wasn't an accident," Jean said with a sigh. "I wanted to Awaken like you. I wanted to have what you have—so I tried to get it."

Faith for a moment simply couldn't think what to say. The words took a time to make sense. "Why?" was all she could manage to croak out.

"Everyone is alone, Faith," she replied, her eyes gleaming with held back tears. "Everyone wants not to be, and you had something that I couldn't understand. I thought that if we shared that we'd be even closer."

Jean grabbed her hand across the table, and Faith didn't want to let go. Jean was touching the spot where her finger had bought her the Awakening.

"Anyway," Jean went on, "I wasn't brave enough to try again. I just wanted you to know that it could have been me at Shorecliff. I wish it had been…"

Faith squeezed her fingers. "And I am glad it wasn't. That, I couldn't have borne. Let's not tell Dad about this, though."

They both agreed on that. By the time both sisters had recovered themselves the kettle had been filled twice, and both had drunk three more cups each in companionable silence. Upstairs they could hear their father walking about, and the vague rumble of his speech.

"He's putting your Mr MacAlpine in the paying part, by the sound of it," Jean commented.

"Well he's hardly likely to put him near me."

Her sister laughed at that. "He certainly is more attractive than most Eyes."

Faith blushed, and traced the pattern of the tablecloth. "I hadn't noticed."

"Oh...of course you haven't," Jean replied archly. "Come on, let's go upstairs and get you sorted out."

Lily had already staked a claim to Faith's old room and would not be shifted. Jean speculated it was because it was the first place she recalled after 'the incident'

"Mary, Mary quite contrary," Lily chirped, swinging her legs in a similar way to that she had used at the Ministry.

"Yes, you are," Faith replied sharply, before settling on bunking with Jean, though it would mean sharing a bed as they hadn't since childhood. She placed her small suitcase on the edge of the bed and sighed. Indeed, it felt like she was reverting back to childhood.

She was bounced out of her reverie by a knock on the open door. When she looked up, Mr MacAlpine was standing there looking slightly ashamed.

She slapped on a smile. "Did Dad find a good room for you?"

"It's nice, but I'm all the way down the corridor," he said gesturing to the connecting door beyond which lay the public accommodations. "I suggested something on this side, but perhaps that was too...well... too close for his comfort."

The conversation was also too embarrassing for her comfort. Faith turned away and made a show of fussing with her clothes. "I'm sure we'll be fine. You really don't need to be here. I can take care of myself."

"I know that," he replied, but she felt his seraph brush the edges of hers. Hoa was concerned, and though he didn't completely trust the Eye, he was glad to have him in the hotel.

Since there was no support to be taken from Hoa, Faith knew she would just have to put up with having a government agent under the same roof. If she could survive her mother's exacting standards and constant arguing, she should be able to outwait one man.

"So what are we doing tomorrow?" The sooner she found out exactly what he wanted, the sooner he could be on his way.

"I've arranged a visit to the morgue," he said, leaning against the doorframe.

"Charming," Faith replied evenly, though her throat had gone dry. "I've never been to one of those before."

"Actually, we will need Lily there, too."

Carefully, Faith placed her clothes on the bed and smoothed them out, all the while considering what exactly she could say to change his mind. Her power was unfortunately not mind manipulation, or she would have tried it.

"We have no choice…" Faith murmured.

"Not really," he muttered actually sounded sorry, "but I'll do everything to make sure it is painless for you."

It was impossible to say how Lily would react in any situation, let alone at a morgue. Her fragile connection to reality might be tested to its limits. Beyond that, even Faith didn't know what would happen.

Her shoulders slumped. "I hope whatever you hope to gain from all this is worth it, Mr MacAlpine."

She didn't need to look to hear him close the door as he retreated into the hallway. As she heard him walk away his seraph's voice whispered in her head.

A child's life is worth the risk. I think you know that.

CHAPTER SIXTEEN

As Jack rode his hired bay mare out of town and up towards the northern farm land, Waingaio was silent in his head, yet he could feel her smugness radiating through him. Jack might call her a leech, but if he was going to help Chloe, he would have to make his peace with her.

The ramshackle mare snorted and tap-danced sideways—perhaps after a little dig from Waingaio. Clenching his teeth, Jack pulled his mount in tightly and guided her to the side of the road as trucks and cars spluttered along.

The narrow strip of land between the Wellington hills and the harbour edge was busy. When he reached the gap that was the Ngaranga gorge, he turned to the winding road that led up into the foothills. His nag slowed down as the incline increased, and he was able to sit back to appreciate the view.

Wellington was made of hills. He'd always liked that about the city, but now, looking up, he might have wished for the flat plains of Canterbury. Together, horse and man joined flagging carts and stuttering cars, so Jack had plenty of time to consider Chloe's story.

Many old women in Wellington offered dangerous back-street abortions, but Chloe had found another way. A man called Hooper and his wife took in bastard children as long as the monthly payments kept coming, but Chloe only got to make two visits. After that, the Hoopers had claimed the boy had died of the flu, but a mother—an Awakened Mother especially—knew better.

Jack guessed he would be following the suspicions when he reached Newlands. The little township was tucked in a high valley near the top of the main road. It was a place where wind ran up the hills and whipped the houses without mercy.

Jack rode up to the local hotel called *The Curly Cat*, and slid down from the saddle. It was early in the day still, but the bar was being propped up by two gangly men. Soon he had bought them both a drink, and found a shot of whiskey for himself that he managed not to down in one go.

The afternoon wore on, and soon enough he was alone with the rotund bartender. Jack wasn't used to this sort of situation. He'd just been in the army—not the secret service—so he had no idea how to pump anyone for information.

In the dark distant corner he saw salvation; a battered upright piano. Knocking back the last of his drink, Jack brushed off the dust from the stool and sat down. This was where he was more comfortable.

As he played and the barman eyed him suspiciously, Jack felt Waingaio uncurl inside him. Years of denial had kept her folded and sullen. Yet while the music flowed through him and his mind was occupied, the seraph ventured out.

She might be a leech, but the sensation of joy the she flooded Jack with was refreshing. He'd had little happiness since coming home. Not that he'd done that really…home had been merely an illusion. He'd only seen Royal once distantly on the street, and Olive had retreated to Auckland to finish her nursing. Perhaps Waingaio was all that was left to him.

Only a moment's acceptance, only the briefest of weakenings in his hatred for the seraph, and she flooded through him. It had been so many years since they had worked as one that Waingaio was perhaps awkward at it. Jack flinched upright, his hands jangling on the keys.

The power washed through every fibre of him. After so long a time it made every sense leap to life; bright lights flashed in his retinas, he could smell the smoke on the bartender's breath, he caught the conversation of the farmers outside talking of their latest crop, the ivory under his fingertips was like the slip of satin, and the taste of the whiskey burned like fire. He recalled now the danger of the seraphim. To believe in their power and beauty was to fall under their control.

"Just give me the strength," he whispered under his breath to the dreaded creature.

She twisted up with annoyance, but the desire to stretch her power was too much to resist. Jack's mental vision shot from the hotel and back along the road, so that now he could sense every tremulous life in each house along the way. There was one that burned far brighter than the rest.

The farmhouse nestled in tight against the hills blazed in his seraph sight with a power that drew him near. It was the place that Chloe had described. Within, were many presences, some small, all terrified. Waingaio and he reached out…

Only to fall back with a scream. The barman was staring at him, one hand reaching under the bar for something—most likely a weapon. Jack was too busy holding his head together to really care.

Someone had cut his mental sight off as effectively as slamming a door. Using seraph power always demanded a price, but this backlash was more than that.

Whoever was up at the farm had sensed his intrusion and thrown down the barriers. With a gulp, Jack gestured the barman over. He approached with some caution, but put the bottle of whiskey in his hand. After Jack slipped him some money, he left it behind.

Jack waited until he'd retreated before addressing Waingaio. "Do they know who we are?"

His seraph seemed to be enjoying his reliance on her, yet she was also a proud creature, and assured him that there was no chance that anyone could follow her probe. All of this was communicated without words, just flashes of emotion. It was confusing, and he was out of practice. It took almost the whole shot of whiskey to work it out.

He had confirmed Chloe's fears. Someone with significant seraph power was indeed at the Hooper farm, and there were children alive inside.

Jack had learned some things as a soldier—most of which he wished to forget. He'd learned that mad dashes across no man's land were for the mad, and if you were going to do something foolish like that, better to do it with the cover of night.

Jack sighed and once more gestured to the tavern owner. "I wonder if you have some rooms available in your fine establishment. Newlands seems to need me for a night or two."

CHAPTER SEVENTEEN

Lily sat on the benches inside the dim Albert, kicking her legs back and forth. Faith was barking at Wirimu. "The queen was in the counting house," she muttered while her cousin burned furiously at the Eye.

He wanted Lily to go to the place with the dead people...dead children rather. Faith didn't want her to. It was silly really, they were dead, and the dead didn't hurt people. It was the living that were the real problem.

Uncle John was lingering in the background, shuffling around like a hedgehog out in the morning. Lily wondered if Faith would pop soon. Wirimu stood firm and weathered the storm. Lily liked that.

Finally the storm all blew over. Faith was sagging from the loss, and the Eye was in control. Lily giggled under her breath. Soon they would be off.

"If you are uncomfortable, we can go home," Faith said as she plopped down next to her.

Jerking away, Lily sidled closer to Wirimu. "And one for the little boy who lives down the lane."

The Eye tilted his head, the lightest brush of his seraph ruffling against her consciousness like a warm breeze. "I think that means that she is fine with it."

Faith's lip tightened as if she was chewing on her arguments. "Well then, let's get it over and done with."

Leaving Uncle John in the shadows, they exited the Albert. When they got on the tram, Lily sat next to Wirimu. She counted the three tram stops to the building under her breath. It was the same one they'd visited the day before. It looked no smaller, its head still in the clouds.

"Agent MacAlpine, good to see you." A tall, man with hair the colour of sand met them at the door. He looked as pleased to see Wirimu as he should be. He herded them deeper into the cool stone interior.

They went past rooms full of people with odd faces. Lily grinned and waved at those that stared back. Streamers of interest trailed after them, like smoke traces, and Lily heard their thoughts rattle in her own head.

Who are they?

Do they have clearance to be here?

What is wrong with that girl?

Lily wrapped her hands on each other, whispering to herself and her unnamed seraph. "I skipped over the water, I danced over the sea and all the birds in the air couldn't catch me." The cry of unseen gulls echoed in her head.

The sand haired man introduced himself as Seth Adamson, and guided them into his office. He had a pretty face and somewhere deep down were a lot of smiles. Lily beamed at him.

Under her concentrated gaze he turned into the red of a beetroot. It was magic. "We didn't get any word you were bringing your family with you."

"These are not my family, Captain Adamson," Wirimu replied, taking a seat, "these two women are going to help you find your murderer."

Adamson leaned on his desk. His face was calm, but Lily could taste his doubt behind it. "I don't know how two young girls can possibly assist, Agent MacAlpine. Unless you're planning to use them as bait…"

Wirimu's brows drew together in a thunderous expression. "These ladies are Awakened and more capable than you at finding the killer. In fact, Lily here is the sole survivor of something very similar a few years ago. Now I presume you got the files from Shorecliff?"

The young agent flinched, but he pulled out a thick folder relatively quickly. Lily got a glimpse of Faith's picture; sad, drawn, and taken in the facility. Dark shadows flickered at the edge of her vision that reminded her of nothingness.

Seth's eyes skidded over Faith, and the word *lightning* bloomed in his mind. Lily could taste his sudden fear in her mouth. They knew about Faith. They feared Faith. They should, though.

Deep down, her own seraph yearned for such respect, like the distant peal of trumpets.

"Look these over." Wirimu leaned forward, took the folder from his colleagues hands and handed it to the shocked Faith. "They will tell you what happened in those days you lost. Then return the file to us."

Lily's cousin's fist tightened on the folder, white as flour. She was not far away from shaking.

Wirimu nodded as if everything was as he wanted it to be, but he had a smile for the man named Seth. "Now, we would like to see this latest victim."

"With due respect Agent, I don't believe young ladies, Awakened or not, should see something so... unpleasant. Especially..." he coughed and looked in her direction. Was he being funny?

"Enough!" Wirimu stood up, and took the Lily's hand. "She has made up her mind, and she is an adult despite everything. You aren't as soft as everyone thinks, are you, Lily?"

Everyone's eyes were on her abruptly. This was even stranger than everything that had happened today. Most people went out of their way to avoid looking in her direction. It might be odd, but it was also good; when she had her seraph's name this would be hers all the time. It would be just like this.

Smiling. Lily tried to unearth the right words to assure them of her sanity. Images flickered through her; birds, waterfalls, the clouds in the sky, but unfortunately not the right thing to say. As always, silly children's rhymes bubbled to the surface, yet this time she managed to keep them locked away tightly. Lily merely nodded her head slightly. That should hold them.

Adamson sighed, straightened up his pile of papers, and ushered them once more out into the corridor. This time he took them on a different path, one where there were considerably fewer people. The smell of antiseptic grew stronger the deeper they went into the building. It burned Lily's nose, but she held still as it invaded.

"We've tried to keep a lid on the whole thing," Adamson said, clearing his throat as if he didn't like the smell either, "but a local woman found this latest body and now the press is onto it."

Wirimu clapped him on the back. "I have some excellent media handlers in my unit. By the time they're finished the story will be buried somewhere on page ten."

His mind whispered how useful some of the smaller seraph powers could be. Lily was suddenly glad that her gifts were as yet unknown—otherwise she might have to end up working in this building. With the smell and the odd faces.

Adamson led them silently through the corridors. The inside of the morgue was small, and crowded with yet more people. The doctor, young and somewhat pale, stood in front of the sheet-covered body. The antiseptic up this close was still not enough to cover the smell of burnt flesh. Lily couldn't decide which was worse.

"Dear Lord!" Faith staggered back, her hand over her mouth as if to prevent something flying out.

Lily pressed her fingers to her lips, mimicking her cousin. "We all fall down."

Wirimu nodded, and the captain pulled back the sheet like he was ripping off a bandage.

A mangled sob made it out of Faith's throat. A small breeze stirred in the corners of the room, twitching the edge of sheet, and scuttling between the agent's ankles. It tickled Lily's skin before her cousin gained control of herself.

Faith took a step back, not risking a second glance.

Lily leaned forward, feeling her own brow furrow and the tickle of curiosity start.

The seraph was gone. That was strange, since the remains of the symbiote always lingered, even once the person had gone. This little body, twisted and crusted, had the aura of power still clinging to it, but the centre of the magic was gone. No hint remained of the seraph. It had been sucked out.

"Empty," Lily whispered. "Tapping at the window and crying through the lock, Are all the children in their beds, it's past eight o'clock."

Wirimu MacAlpine stared at her, and for a moment she hoped he might have seen through her window. "Where did you find this one, Captain?"

"On the South Coast. Some old lady gathering firewood stumbled on her two days ago. We asked about, but no one is owning up to missing a child."

The Eye rubbed his forehead. "Maybe she's not from Wellington. Check the reports from the other branches. I hope that we haven't gone so wrong in this world so that people don't miss their own children."

"Unless they have but are too frightened to tell the officials," Faith interrupted. "Illegal immigrants, or people in some other type of trouble."

The images of the Chinese children in Haining Street were dancing in her cousin's mind. Lily would not think of that place.

She rubbed her stomach as her poor symbiote twisted. He was scared too— well as much as she could guess.

While Faith turned away from the dead child, Wirimu ran his hand through his thick hair and turned to Lily. "Can you tell me anything?" he asked softly. For a second she stood twisting her fingers together trying to find the words to explain herself out of the room.

Finally, unable to dredge up any, she took two strides towards the contorted figure on the gurney. The smell was like one of Aunt Isbelle's roasts too long in the oven; it made her nose wrinkle, but in her jumbled world it was hard to judge if that was a good thing or not. She put her fingers squarely on the burned eyelids and pulled them back. They cracked and broke under her touch.

"Oh dear Lord!" Faith's scream echoed in the tiny bleak room, and hurt Lily's ears.

Underneath, the eyes, which some alert part of her brain realised should have been boiled away, were a chill gold colour.

"Why did no one tell me about this?" Wirimu spun on the doctor.

Everyone knew that a child with gold eyes wore the mark of a seraph possession. Lily leaned forward, inhaling the smell of meat and victory. She almost envied the little girl.

"We...we never thought," Adamson stumbled.

"Who would?" Faith chimed in softly.

Raising a hand to her own face, Lily wondered what colour they were. It was a long time since a mirror had meant anything.

Faith caught her fingertips. "They are blue," she whispered.

Wirimu took hold of Lily's shoulder, pinning her between them. "Is this the work of the same man that attacked you?"

It was the inevitable question. She shivered. The Craven Man who had taken so much from her and her poor seraph. Did she dare to cross over into his world again?

Quickly, before anyone could scream or stop her, Lily touched the dead child again. Reaching down, she rested the first and index finger of her left hand on the curved and quiet spheres, like two still marbles under her touch. Then, with her right hand she repeated the gesture against her own eyes. Faith's cry of dismay faded with the arrival of shadow.

It was foolish to fear the dark; but this was not merely the absence of light, it was the corrupted vision of another—a man who thought nothing of warping children to his plans. In his world they only existed to serve.

Ruby had wanted to live. She wanted to see her mother and get out of this nightmare of a farm. Other children cried and sniffled in the darkness, harnessed in a similar way. Their fear filled the small room with a rank, thick smell that drove them onto the brink of madness. Occasionally a splutter of power would illuminate the room like a glow worm's faint light. Ruby caught nightmarish glimpses of her fellow captives; none could have been any older than she. Some had indeed barely learned to walk.

Then a burly man came and pulled her out of the tight bundle of children. Hope flared in her at that; maybe Mummy had come to get her. Perhaps there would be sweets and cuddles. On the other side of the tall door, though was only the Craven Man and a woman she didn't recognise—she wore funny coloured glasses. Outside the wind howled, just as when her Mummy had bought her to this place. Ruby couldn't understand why she'd been left here all alone, but she remembered how her mother had cried. The memory was faded; she could only remember her as a warm, kind sensation that she missed.

On the bed near the window, four children were asleep—except their eyes weren't closed. Ruby began to cry when she saw how still and pale they were. Her frantic sobs faded when the Craven Man, in his envelope of shadow, approached. Her throat was suddenly too dry for anything except a rattle of terrified horror. He had a blade; it looked so big.

"Now," he said from within darkness, "It is time you Awoke, my dear."

The blade descended, and Lily was thrown free. She came back to her fractured world on the floor with Faith, Adamson and Wirimu bending over her. She couldn't recall tripping.

"Are you hurt?" her cousin asked as she helped Lily to her feet.

Wirimu's seraph was testing that very possibility. Lily glared at the agent, and he withdrew it with a slight grin. "She's alright, Miss Louden."

Faith gave her a short and fierce hug. "That was very foolish."

"And very brave." Adamson blinked, as if he hadn't expected her capable of such a thing.

"The question is," Wirimu said, "Was it worth it? Did you see what happened?"

Lily's mouth worked, but again words failed to materialise; the best she could manage was, "Old McDonald had a farm."

The three of them blinked.

So she tried harder, until sweat popped out on her forehead, "And on this farm he had some...." She pushed through the veil of misunderstanding, "Babies."

"My goodness!" Lily's brow furrowed. "I don't..."

"Baby farming." Wirimu worked it out before any of the others. "My Lord, she means a baby farm!"

Lily couldn't help making a giggle, imagining the little children growing from the ground like turnips, but then the darkness of Ruby's rememberings clouded over her laughter. Such a place wasn't a joke.

"Where?" her cousin's face had gone from concerned to rage in a matter of moments. Lily knew she wasn't angry with her, instead with those that would hurt children. A flicker of gold stirred in Faith's eyes.

Cocking her head, Lily considered the unbridling of the Weather Witch. In her head she could see the winds beginning to stir and lightning dance around the hills. She smiled, and pointed northwards to where the dim echo of Ruby still ran.

Faith helped her to her feet and turned to the two government agents. "You have what you need—now I hope you will do as you promised and leave my family alone."

Wirimu raised one eyebrow. "North is a big direction. Perhaps we can get Lily to go with us...try and narrow it down a bit for us."

They wanted her to face the Craven Man—that was what he was thinking deep down. Lily might be crazy, but she knew that was a step too far. Without a proper name for her seraph she would be in mortal danger. Once more she could feel the Craven Man's chain around her neck and his hands on her body, while he bore into her soul.

Jamming her fists into her eye sockets, the words poured from her lips, "Jack fell down and broke his crown…Jack be nimble Jack be quick…Little Jack Horner sat in the corner…"

Dimly she felt Faith's arms around her, but it took a long time of wailing for her to recognise what she was saying. "You can't make her do that! I won't let you do that to her. I'll go instead."

"That's no good, Miss Louden; she was the one touched by the perpetrator, not you."

"But I tasted his power in Haining Street and I am properly Awakened." Faith protested, placing herself between the agents and Lily, like a bristling cat before a looming dog.

Wirimu nodded slowly. "Alright, if you are willing to do that… then we can probably spare Lily any further trauma."

At her name she launched forward to grasp Faith's hand. There were no rhymes for her to express her fears for her. Yet when her cousin turned her bright blue eyes to her, some part of Faith's seraph latched on to Lily's broken one.

"It'll be fine, dear," Faith said without a shadow of fear. "This man cannot get away with what he did to you and that poor girl. Hoa and I won't let that happen to anyone else."

She would not be shaken, and Lily's pride swelled for her kind and brave cousin. For a second she imagined that the Craven Man himself would burn out against this bright and true woman.

Lily sagged back as the shadows retreated to the corners of her mind. Faith would go into those dark places she couldn't dare…yet. If only she had the ability to warn her of the dangers, to prepare her for the challenges that lay there. Yet her cousin had her seraph's name and the true power of the weather at her back. Perhaps the Craven Man would bow down before that. Perhaps the world would turn out to be a better place than she imagined.

CHAPTER EIGHTEEN

Spring in Wellington was all about wind. Daffodils and the yellow kowhai trees bent to its power, and perhaps, if Jack was not forcing himself out into it, he would have quite enjoyed watching everything whip around from the comfort of a warm pub.

Alcohol, usually his numbing friend, had left him feeling decidedly melancholy. He wanted to crawl into the bottle and fade away, but the uncomfortable truth was that he needed Waingaio and her power. The connection he'd spent the last years trying to ignore was now his best chance of helping Chloe.

He waited until dark, looked regretfully at the half-full bottle of booze sitting on his hotel room windowsill, before wrapping a scarf around his neck. Outside, the chill weather of early spring blasted him full in the face as soon as he eased the rear door shut. It was obvious that he wasn't going to get any breaks in this endeavour.

"Well, Waingaio this is for a child, so I hope you're feeling soft hearted," Jack addressed his seraphim.

The dim shapes of the night-scattered farmland suddenly grew brighter. Surely this was how a cat must see life under the stars. Still, his seraph didn't communicate anything else with him, so perhaps she was still holding a grudge.

"Fine, old girl. Hopefully won't need you for this anyway."

Sticking close to the fence line, he retraced his earlier progress to the Hooper spread. The farmhouse hunched on the slight hill up from the road. To Jack's enhanced vision, it appeared like any other, surrounded by a stout but not tall fence. No lights showed at the windows and in this weather he couldn't blame them for retreating to their beds early. It also made his job that much easier.

Hunched over, Jack checked for signs of dogs before making his way up on the edge of the path. He didn't want any pernickety gravel spoiling his sneaky approach.

Waingaio might have enjoyed it when he ran straight into the magical barrier just inside the fence line. The power smacked him between the eyeballs, making his vision flare white-hot.

Jack paused, breath caught in his throat, but there was no sudden eruption of light from the farmhouse, no running feet, or sound of hounds released. So he cautiously reached out, until his fingers tingled against the barrier. It was similar to one he'd seen in basic training, but nothing he'd be able to create himself.

His old sergeant, the drill instructor in Magic Corp, had a particular amusement in placing one in front of the door on their first morning of muster. It was a lesson in how to listen to a seraph, because those that had a proper connection saw and let the others out first. They enjoyed it even more than the sergeant when those not so well acquainted with their symbiote bounced off the barrier. Jack had been among them then, too. Apparently a little age didn't really give any wisdom.

Rubbing his chin, Jack stood back and considered. Removing of barriers had only been lightly covered as the New Zealand Magic Corp were the only magicians on the field. He hadn't been any good at it then, so was unlikely to have got any better.

So it was time to come at the problem from a different angle.

He traced the circumference of the barrier hoping to find a gap or a weakness. Nothing. But there was one possibility that made him grit his teeth; a tall pine tree, slightly leaning thanks to the predations of the wind. In a strange way it reminded him of the warped tree that had sacrificed itself in Gallipoli.

Waingaio shot pain into the back of his head; the closest approximation to a kick in the backside. "Fair enough," Jack grumbled. "Stick to the problem at hand— I get it."

Sometimes it was like living with his mother again. Waingaio, just like her, seldom let him get away with anything. The wind kicked up the sharp scent of the pine, and under Jack's hand the bark was thickly textured. Against the thin sliver of the moon he could just make out a likely looking branch.

It had been many years since he'd climbed a tree—just how many years in fact he soon realised. The pain in his hip where the piece of Turkish shrapnel still lurked made the ascent somewhat difficult, and Jack also came to another sad conclusion. Far too long hanging out with Skint and his brethren had left him weaker and less fit than he'd been; even in the trenches of France. Thirty was just around the corner and all he had to show for it was a fine collection of scars and a liver that would probably give up on him one day.

Jack would have resolved right there and then to sharpen up if he could only be sure that it was Waingaio's doing. Yet a part of him also recognised that she'd been protecting him all the time. The sheer miracle that he hadn't killed himself with his lifestyle yet was most likely down to his leech.

A curl of satisfaction wafted into the back of his brain. She certainly did like to be appreciated.

"Well," he muttered, pulling himself up the last feet near the top of the pine, "maybe we can discuss things after all this is over."

She didn't reply.

From this vantage point, Jack couldn't even see the ground. The clouds were racing past at an alarming pace over his head while the wind threatened his precarious position. But this wasn't a fit of madness, for from this vantage he was probably only six feet from the edge of the barrier. Jack's limited knowledge of barriers told him that it was unlikely to be high. Such a creation would take a lot of power and most wouldn't bother with anything over eleven feet or so.

This tree, though not close enough for him to just drop over the rim, was tall enough to take him more like twenty into the air. The branch he was currently hanging onto stretched out in the general direction of the farmhouse.

After a moment's hesitation, in which he considered how this particular venture was smarter than getting himself royally drunk, he lay flat against the rough bark and worked along it. Waingaio had taken care of any paunch alcohol might have wanted to develop on his waist line, so he was able to do that reasonably well.

Still, he was nowhere near being able to struggle along the last six feet of branch. He wasn't able to actually see the barrier, but he could feel the hairs on his outstretched arm twitch, so it couldn't be far.

"So now we're here," Jack said, feeling slightly stupid talking to the sulking seraph out loud, "I'll need you to help me over the barrier."

Nothing. The leech liked to leave him hanging, literally. The branch shifted under his legs with a slight creak, so it was unlikely he could stay there in mid-air for long.

"It's for Chloe's baby, you daft creature."

If there was one thing that seraph had always shown a particular interest in, it was children. Waingaio flooded him with her suspended power. Everything grew brighter and more beautiful. He could smell the spring flowers as strongly as if they were directly beneath him, and back by the road he could hear the furtive rustle of a hedgehog in the verge.

Putting aside the temptations of the leech, Jack flexed his fingers. It was a silly physical gesture that nonetheless prepared him. He hadn't used this magic for many years and even back in basic, his command of it had been less than perfect. Scrambling to his feet, he held onto the branch until he'd got his weight balanced enough to stand. The branch was going to give way with all his weight concentrated on one spot, so he'd knew he best be quick about it.

The explosion of power directly beneath his feet made only the most muted of thumps, but the force of it catapulted him from the tree and a good distance into the air. For a long impressive moment, Jack was ecstatic. If it were not for the risk of discovery he would have whooped with the joy of the sensation. Then, gravity angrily reinstated its dominance over him. He'd overestimated how much power he'd need to get up and across the barrier.

The plummeting sensation was not nearly as fun. Waingaio, perhaps fearing for her own survival, set off a series of smaller releases of power on their descent. These little pauses, which required more control than Jack had, slowed their descent enough that he wasn't killed.

Instead, he fell to the ground in amongst a convenient patch of scrub. Waingaio might have had something to do with that too. Nevertheless, Jack lay there for a moment, stunned, staring up at the night sky. He should have known better than to use magic. It always ended badly.

Yet, if he let go now, the backlash of consequence might well incapacitate them both. So, clinging resolutely to the reinstated connection with his seraph, Jack crawled out from the bushes. Under his feet the ground was still wet from the rain two days before. It squished and sucked at his boots, making silence almost impossible, but then, no one had heard his crash into the undergrowth.

A hot trickle of fear ran down his backbone, and Jack didn't find that unreasonable. The place oozed unfriendliness and the house still lurked dark and somehow unwholesome up ahead. As quietly as he could manage, he worked his way up the slight rise.

He would really have liked to have a gun, or at least a knife. Even though with Waingaio for company he was more armed than anyone with either of those things, the weight in his pocket would have been reassuring.

An especially deep hole, one that even his enhanced sight had missed, grabbed at his foot. He twisted but couldn't get his other around quickly enough. Only his outstretched arms prevented him from falling directly into the mud. This close to the earth, his leech shot him a terrible image of what was only inches from his face. Not far below the surface, Waingaio informed him, was the body of a small child. The flash of brutalised flesh and tiny fingers wrapped in mud made Jack grunt in horror.

A normal person would have leapt up and run screaming, but the unfortunate truth was, he wasn't a stranger to death in the mud. That unbidden thought set off a torrent of memories he'd been fighting off for years. Holding himself only a whisker above the sucking dirt, Jack waited until he had shoved those images back into the recesses of his brain. It took a while and Waingaio was no help.

Yet, those boys who had died in front of him in Europe had at least a gasp of real life. The poor mite under this earth was so tiny. A little boy who would never get to grow any bigger, to make the mistakes of childhood, and the unfettered recklessness of a teenager, let alone the murky advantages of adulthood. Those moments had been stolen before they'd even begun.

The boy was not alone in sleeping under this cloying earth. More little graves lay about him, and Waingaio spared him no detail.

A cool fury began inside Jack's head—his hot rage having been burnt all away in the trenches of the Gallipoli peninsula. Levering himself out of the mud in short calculated gestures, he looked up at the house. The stretch of distance between where he was and the front door looked remarkably like No Man's Land. It might not have any machine guns and grenade throwing Turks, but he wasn't under any illusions that it was probably just as dangerous.

"You better get off your behind, Waingaio," Jack muttered, "because we're going in."

He circled around the side of the house, senses still attuned for dogs or people, but it was only the silence pressing down on him. Creeping through the long grass around the edge of the farmhouse, he dared approaching the window. It was thick with grime and covered with layers of spider webs.

Jack paused with his hand mere inches from clearing a spot. He had the sudden feeling if he did, he wouldn't like what he would see, and he had the abrupt desire to turn about and go back to his stiff hotel bed and an even stiffer drink.

So, it was rather unfortunate that just then, a child cried. The thin reedy sound pierced the silence as if like an arrow.

Could it be Chloe's Billy? Even if it wasn't, he certainly couldn't leave any child in there. Ripping off one of the loose panels of wood from the veranda, he used it to lever the window open without disturbing any spiders. Waingaio joined her senses with his and though he appreciated it, he wished she hadn't.

Inside smelt of cold and dust and fear, but thanks to her added awareness he could also taste the bitterness of true terror around him. Jack could taste tears and sweat and hear the retreating echoes of childish screams. Chloe surely could never have been in here, because no mother would ever leave her child in such a place.

He eased himself deeper into the main room. A small table stood alone in the centre of the room, two chairs lay tipped on the floor. Nothing of this place seemed capable of sustaining life. Two cupboards looked bare of anything except crumbs and the memory of better times.

Every part of Jack wanted to find not only Billy, but any other children and get them out of this place immediately or preferably sooner. Waingaio didn't disagree.

God, he didn't want to open that door. The sound of a child crying rattled on Jack's eardrums and set his nerves off. Resting his hand on the cool iron door handle, Waingaio flooded his body with more power than he'd ever felt. He could have blown the whole sorry house apart.

The silly leech had too much trust in his control. Years of neglect and booze had whittled away what he'd once had.

Jack clenched his teeth, grinding his molars painfully to distract him from the possibility he would fail. Waingaio didn't speak but waited behind his eyes, perhaps to see what he would make of what she had given.

Finally gathering his nerve, Jack kicked open the door; the sound echoed like a gunshot in the silence and the utter blackness beyond. Breath freezing in his chest, Jack peered into it. Waingaio coiled in concern, urging him to flee. The crying continued, emerging out of the darkness as if it were down a very deep well. The little boy must be terrified to howl like that, a wild hiccupping scream that signalled the child was beyond hope that anyone would respond.

As Jack slid forward into the room, he recognised the feeling, abruptly and terribly. This was as dangerous as that room at the Trocadero hotel. The yawning possibilities nearly swallowed him. Could the same person who had killed those people somehow be here in this farmhouse?

How unlucky could one person be? Jack would have sworn, would have cursed his damn foolishness, but the chill in the chamber froze his tongue.

Moving forward, with his hands slightly held out into the blackness, Jack inched forward. He could make out no details in the room, not even the floor. Only the child's crying lead him on, while his heart pounded in his head and Waingaio urged caution. As if he needed to be reminded.

Finally, he reached a spot where the sound seemed to be all around him. Though Jack cocked his head and turned about, it surrounded him. He could have sworn that the farmhouse had been tiny, so surely he had somehow walked beyond the bounds of the walls. Whatever terrible magic had created this he couldn't fathom, nor where he was. Waingaio blared in his head to turn back and find the door, but where that was exactly, she didn't offer.

His body, flooded with power, moved fast—unfortunately not fast enough. Three children, they couldn't have been more than eight, emerged out of the darkness.

"Dammit!" Jack stumbled back, his dry throat finally managing a strangled explicative. He'd seen immediately the familiar knotted green cord, binding each of them together around the neck, like an unholy leash. They might have become visible, but the blackness was still with them. It flooded their eyes, reflecting back the void. Such emptiness clawed at the edges his consciousness, and Jack could feel them burrowing into his mind, finding every pain and weakness.

In that space was the place Waingaio lived. She wailed and thrashed as their perception drew nearer to her seat of power, and in a few more moments they would overcome both Jack and his seraph. God only knew what would happen then. Dimly, he heard the cries of the child echo on.

Blindly, he released the power he'd been given; flinging it into the young faces that loomed from the darkness. The sound of the explosion never came. It too was swallowed by the emptiness as if it had never been.

For the first time since Awakening, Waingaio spoke inside his head. Words, which had always been beyond their relationship up until now, boomed in his head. *Run you fool!*

Jack fervently wished that he was able to. Every muscle strove to do that very thing, but the void had grabbed hold of him from within the dark eyes of those creatures who had once been children. The whole thing was a trap. The child's cry dropped away and became laughter of the nothingness. He and Waingaio were caught as securely as a blundering fly in its web.

His seraph, in a desperate bid to save them both, summoned up a reserve of power that threatened to destroy her. It was the last shred of herself—and she gave it all to Jack without hesitation.

Yet in the end, that too wasn't enough. Though he cast it with all of his meagre talent at the bound children, they were ready for him. They caught it and took it from them both and then threw them down into the darkness.

CHAPTER NINETEEN

Emma waited outside the Albert Hotel until darkness came, then she melted in amongst the sleeping masses and watched the comings and goings with narrowed eyes. Humanity didn't even notice the predator walking in their shadow. Like the sheep they were, they lived in ignorance of the wolf.

She could sense the other woman known as Faith and her active seraph, but Emma could only feel pity for her. She recalled her own days before her master found her, with a shudder. He had destroyed the seraph within her, and while it had been a painful trial, it had been worth it. The Craven Man had never been able to replicate that success—though he'd tried many times.

That was why Lily was so important; a halfway point to perhaps success. So, the Craven Man had sent her off to bring him this curiosity, and she knew it wouldn't be an easy thing. The Weather Witch wouldn't be easy to overcome. No, Emma had to be subtle and clever and use every advantage that magic had given her.

The hotel closed up at eleven o'clock. Emma observed the doors being closed, then shortly after the lights flicked off downstairs, following the progress of the family into the top storey. A little while later those, too, were extinguished.

After giving them enough time to snuggle into their beds, Emma dipped into her magic to conceal her. The Sleepers and the mundane, engrossed in their own petty desires and fears, wandered blindly past her. They didn't know how lucky they were not to have her full attention.

The hotel was tightly locked and barred but such things did not concern Emma; she simply held out her hand and pushed her magic into the spaces between things. Even she didn't know how she did this.

A seraph could have told her perhaps, or her master, but he hoarded his knowledge jealously. The fact was though, all that mattered was that no solid object was a barrier to her.

Emma stood in the dark and silent bar with her head cocked upward. Two men and three women were sleeping above. One of the males would be the father—the other, a guest with a seraph of his own. The three girls were very different. One was not Awakened at all but full of tasty potential, this would be the younger sister of Faith.

The Weather Witch, even when she slept, sang with power, yet it was the tangled mess of the Awakened. Her seraph still coiled within her, rank with its own machinations. Then there was Lily.

Emma considered. If she went up there, the Weather Witch's seraph would wake her, then there would certainly be trouble.

Fortunately, her master had taught her how to deal with troublesome Awakened, and conveniently this would be made easier with them both asleep. Into the darkness Emma whispered a word, a word that he had given her. The pale light of it lit the bar with a pearly glow. Holding out her hand, Emma cupped it, and then tossed it into the air.

It flew off, a sparkling net rising towards the Weather Witch and her seraph upstairs. With a slight smile, Emma followed it, and when the stairs creaked, she was no longer terribly concerned with being silent. The Sleepers she had control on, the witch she no longer worried about, and Lily was helpless. She strode confidentially up the corridor and pushed open the girls' bedroom door.

In the reflected light from the street that the curtains did not fully block out, Emma could see that Lily was now more than a girl. Her master had caught her right on the cusp of womanhood, perhaps that timing had caused the unusual effect, or maybe it had been the reason she'd been driven mad. That insanity could be used, though.

Emma began to whisper the words to make another net, but this one had a different purpose; this one would carry Lily back to the farmhouse.

The pearl light danced between her fingers, the strands of it leaping from tip to tip. This physical manifestation of magic she'd stolen from the seraph entranced her for a moment. Turning, she made to cast the spell down upon the sleeping girl.

All the warning Emma had was a momentary fluttering in the corner of her vision. It shouldn't have been possible for a mere human to catch her out. Emma had put thoughts of Faith out of her mind once the seraph had been tied down. She simply hadn't considered that she could wake up from it.

She was without her seraph, but she could still move. When Faith launched herself from the darkness in the doorway, Emma turned reflexively, the net of the spell still in her hands. They rolled to the floor as the magic wrapped around them and obeyed its nature, throwing them to the destination she had chosen. Emma screamed angrily as they disappeared from the Albert Hotel with Faith's hands on her throat, and her target still in her bed.

CHAPTER TWENTY

Faith woke in the dark, hearing nothing at first above her own panicked breathing. Everything was close and smelt of the soil. It was a suffocating nightmare. It had to be a nightmare because she was buried alive.

Horror flooded through her, and Faith did what came naturally, she reached for Hoa. He was there, deep down, but strangely somnolent.

Panic receded slightly as she realised she was not alone. In this terrible situation, in the most frightening position a human could imagine, Faith clung to Hoa. Once when she was a child, before the accident that had bought her seraph to life inside her, she had woken screaming. Running to her father, she had sobbed that she didn't want to die. The reality of the terrible end, all alone, had come to her very early, and the gaping maw of aloneness had nearly swallowed her. That haunting fear had followed her until that shattering day when blood and terror had woken her seraph.

In Shorecliff she'd actually confessed to a doctor that she would gladly go through that again to have her seraph. The warmth of Hoa had chased away her night terrors.

Yet it was obvious that terrible woman had done something to Hoa that still lingered. So, she had to get them out of this situation, and began to feel around with her fingers. A strangled squawk escaped her when she realised that it wasn't just her and Hoa in here. Her fingers had brushed a human arm.

Faith suddenly feared she was buried with a dead person. Her throat clenched shut, and it took a long time for her to gather the frayed remains of her sanity.

Trembling, Faith reached out again and touched the arm. By feel she could tell it was a man's arm and still warm…so most definitely alive. As if on cue, Hoa was finally able to give her enough power to see.

As her sight began to resolve into a pattern of greys, Faith was at least able to make out her fellow captive. It was a man, slightly older than herself, his face cast in stark planes with a ragged moustache and beard. It was the kind of facial hair of a man not given to much thought of his appearance.

Something of familiarity lingered about him, even though she couldn't immediately put her finger on it. Thrusting aside that feeling for the moment, Faith managed to wriggle closer to the man. Putting one hand against his throat, she felt his pulse leaping. His eyes were flickering rapidly, and this near to him, Faith could feel his muscles twitching.

She recognised the signs of seraph Shock, and having suffered it herself after the Trocadero, she could only feel sympathy. Whoever this man was, he was hovering on very edge of madness—it could go either way.

"Hoa, can you help him?" she whispered. Her voice sounded small and deadened by the earth.

Her seraph was still restricted, tied down by whatever spell that dark-haired intruder had cast at him while Faith slept. So, she took a ragged breath. If Hoa couldn't help him, maybe he could instead reach the other's seraph.

But working together was not in a seraph's nature. People had puzzled and tried to get past this for many years, but it was a simple fact.

Faith had no wish to harness her magic to another's, let alone a stranger. Yet if she could get Hoa to communicate with the other seraph, perhaps this man could be pulled back from the brink of madness.

It took some persuading, but finally Faith was able to convince Hoa that if they were going to get out of this situation, then it had to be done. It was a strange sensation for her seraph; he had never attempted unity with another of his kind. Faith and her seraph shared nervousness.

Eventually, Hoa did obey, linking himself with the man's seraph, though it was a shock when the connection was suddenly made. Faith started, banging her head on the wood above. Now inside, she could feel not only Hoa, but also the distinctly feminine emotions of the man's seraph.

This new presence was terrified, almost incoherently so. Since Hoa didn't really know how to deal with one of his own kind, Faith had to try and soothe the strange seraph's panic as best she could.

She wouldn't tell the human her name, that would give Faith power, but she seemed relieved to have someone nearby ready to take control.

The man had been tumbled into the Shock, not as badly as she'd suffered after the Trocadero, but still enough to probably to knock him down for hours. And time was something they didn't have because there could only be so much air in here.

Instead of panicking, she took a shallow breath, and rolled onto her right side. This close, the smell of man overcame the smell of dirt, which was a blessed relief. Without question this was the closest Faith had been to any man, let alone one whose name she didn't know. He smelt slightly of beer and sweat and Faith, with some embarrassment, realised that her body was flushed with enjoyment of that masculine odour.

Behave, she told Hoa, though why her seraph would send on such a reaction was unknown. He found his own kind attractive...that was what it had to be. Faith wasn't a virgin, but her understanding of physical intimacy was limited to a couple of unsatisfactory couplings with farm boys. It was another advantage of being Awakened; the seraph controlled her body enough that they didn't have to worry about unwanted children.

It was why some overseas visitors thought of New Zealand women as 'loose' and perhaps after experiencing that dizzying sensation, they could be right.

Stuffing down the sheer ridiculousness of her body's reaction, Faith laid her palm against the man's eyes. Physical contact closed the gap between the seraphim, and from there she was able to get the man to pass some of the agony across to her.

Faith had a lot of experience with the Shock, but even so, it was a surprise to take on another's. The world tilted and became even more insane. Light flashed in her eyes and her stomach churned, but Faith managed to bury the Shock in her body. By changing the symptoms to pain she'd at least be able to concentrate.

The man's eyes popped open, and Faith recognised the panic she must have faced when she awoke.

"It's alright," she whispered.

"God dammit!" The man tried to lurch upright and cracked his head against the wood. Faith winced as he slumped back and turned his head to her. Their gazes locked, so his seraph was obviously giving him enough power to enhance his sight.

He coughed slightly. "I'm sorry, Miss. Didn't mean to curse…"

Faith smiled. "Under the circumstances, I accept your apology. What's your name?"

"Jack Cunningham." He gave away his name easily, but then there was not much power to a human name any more.

Faith found herself smiling, but as she did so insight hit and she recognised him. Turning her face up away, Faith tried to keep her expression neutral. It couldn't be possible that she was trapped in a box in the earth with the man she'd almost killed in a seraph fuelled rage years before.

Hoa felt the shame as well but was—and always had been—unapologetic for it. A seraph's rage was a rare thing, but they always had their reasons.

This Jack didn't seem to have made the connection as she had, possibly because the receding effects of Shock probably still clouded his brain. Whatever the reason might be, Faith was not about to bring the subject up.

So she muttered, "Faith Louden, your fellow prisoner."

He managed to get his hand up to his mouth and rubbed it with a pinched, nervous gesture. She imagined he was trying to gain control of his primitive fears like she'd had to. It wasn't easy, and without their seraph it would have been that much more difficult.

"So," Jack's voice sounded a little steadier, "how do we get ourselves out of this?"

She knew he could feel her seraph as well as she could feel his, but it was most impolite to mention it—yet if she didn't…

It felt like every ounce of her blood was rushing into her face, but she managed to force the words out. "My seraph has had his powers tied, but yours hasn't."

He didn't answer for a long time, so long in fact that Faith began to fear he had slipped back into Shock. Finally, he let out a long sigh "My...seraph and I aren't really on very good speaking terms. I fear if I tried, I would kill us both."

His unspoken word *leech* disturbed her deeply. The symbiotic relationship could be a very fragile one; some fought it, some loved it, and some did both. This man Jack had enough magic—more than enough—but his lack of a connection with his symbiote could kill them, just a lot faster than if they stayed.

It didn't seem that this situation could get any worse. Faith lay back with a sigh, clenching her fingers into her palms with thoughts of what might be happening back at the Albert haunting her. Neither did she want to suffocate.

There was only one choice.

She rolled over onto her side and looked straight at Jack, though her skin trembled. Hoa and the other seraph had not withdrawn their tangled edges, but what she was about to suggest would bring them even closer.

Amazed at her own terrible daring, Faith touched the man's hand. "You have the magic and I have the control. It will not be easy, but if you want to live then you must do as I say."

CHAPTER TWENTY-ONE

Wirimu MacAlpine looked very handsome standing in the early morning light yelling at Uncle John. Lily liked the way his eyes flashed like they had lamps in them.

Faith was gone, and the shadows inside whispered that the Dark Queen had stolen her away. This had made Wirimu very angry and Uncle very upset.

Lily had woken from a dream of falling cards and dancing rabbits in which she had tasted the presence of the Dark Queen. It meant bad things that couldn't be explained in nursery rhymes, so when she went and shook Jean awake, she didn't say anything, simply dragging her to Faith's room.

After that, everything went higglety pigglety. Uncle John was woken up and then he was barking at Wirimu. Now the Albert was full of men in uniform and a number that weren't. Those were the ones that caught Lily's attention. Each of them was full of a seraph, all knew their name, all were everything she wanted to be.

Finally, pushing through the crowd of buzzing people, Wirimu managed to get through to her. Lily looked up and smiled. He took the seat next to her and rubbed his eyes like he hadn't had enough sleep. Perhaps his dreams were of the Dark Queen too.

"Are you sure that you didn't see anything, Lily?" he asked in a quiet tone.

She shook her head, struggling to find words in her limited lexicon. "The Queen was in the...house."

Wirimu treated her like an adult most of the time, but as soon as she mentioned her dream and the Dark Queen, she saw that expression. It was the look most adults got when they were around her; like they'd been expecting a tiger and found a sleeping kitten instead. It was a shame that Wirimu used it now.

The Eye stretched back on the bench seat. "We've found no evidence of forced entry, Lily. Your uncle is adamant that he locks up very securely every night."

Explanations fired in the back of her head, but all that came out was the surprising phrase, "Jack fell down and broke his crown."

"Who's Jack?" Now his tone verged on a snap.

She didn't know. Sometimes the connection with her sad, unnamed seraph had flashes where normalcy seemed possible. The symbiote within her knew so much more than she was able to access. A normal woman might have screamed or broken something in frustration. Lily had none of those options.

Uncle John said some very bad words, very loud, pushing away from the two stern-faced Eyes he'd been talking with. Turning his head sharply, he spotted Wirimu and strode over to him, with Jean trailing in his wake. Lily's cousin had dressed in a hurry. Her clothes, which were usually so well matched, were all topsy turvey, and her hair was astray in all sorts of odd angles. In such desperate circumstances, Lily knew it was bad to laugh. She still did…just a little.

Uncle John was certainly in no mood to be jovial. "So, when are you going to get off your arse and get my girl back?" He glared at Mr MacAlpine.

Lily's eyes were locked on his billy club, once more hanging from his belt. She hadn't seen that since the day of her rescue. It's appearance now couldn't be good.

The Eye rose to his feet, hands out as if her uncle was an enraged bull. "We are assembling a team, Mr Cunningham. The Central Region Trackers are unfortunately in New Plymouth working on a homicide, but I have put the call in and they should be on a train in the next hour or so."

"That would mean midday before anything gets done!" John swung about and gestured to the pub full of agents. "How about using some of this lot? Anything could be happening to Faith while we sit on our thumbs here!"

Wirimu MacAlpine sighed and rubbed his eyes. It was a good few hours until dawn, and Lily could sense he'd not slept much that night. "These are all good agents, I'll give you that, but their magics are not Tracking, and without any other clues as to what has happened to Faith…"

An expression of despair fluttered across Uncle John's face; the look of someone used to control who can feel it slipping from their grasp. At his shoulder Jean gave a tremulous little sigh as reality settled on her, too.

Faith had offered to face the Craven Man for her, and Lily now knew she should never have accepted. It was her fate, hers alone, to face him. By allowing Faith to take it from her, she'd bought this whole thing down.

She touched Wirimu MacAlpine's hand lightly. "Old McDonald has a farm…"

He didn't pull away from her touch. Was it her imagination or did it tighten on her fingers? Without words, he knew what she meant.

"You know the way, Lily," he whispered so that the others in the room couldn't have overheard. He didn't ask her to reconsider, didn't remind her it was dangerous.

She nodded fiercely. Let the Craven Man beware of her for a change. She was coming to claim her seraph name.

CHAPTER TWENTY-TWO

In the years Jack Cunningham had spent in a trench with a company of terrified, hungry men, he could only have dreamed of being locked in a box with a woman. Perhaps he was asleep or mad. Maybe he was still in that trench.

"Whatever you're thinking, you've got to realise that you are really here. This is happening. You just have to trust me." Faith's words came out of the darkness.

He imagined her beautiful, with bright blue eyes, but the confines of their prison had stolen any chance of telling if that was true. She was merely a grey shape against the darkness. Carefully he raised his hands and traced the roof of the prison again. The wood was rough under his fingers, more real than even his worst nightmares.

"Can you read my mind?" he asked under his breath.

Her chuckle was deadened by their limited surroundings. "I'm afraid not, or I might not have ended up in this predicament. It's just that I can see your expression."

Her seraph was obviously more kindly disposed to her. "So you have no idea why we are here?"

Her silence told him much. Jack reached across and unerringly found her hand. "If you want me to trust you, to get out of here, then you have to tell me what is really going on."

Her laugh was strained and muted. "You'd trust someone you can't see?"

Outside, under a wonderful open sky, he would have made an off the cuff comment, smiled his little smile and flirted. Somehow it didn't seem appropriate under the circumstances.

"I guess I will have to go with my instincts," he admitted, "even if they are what landed me here in the first place."

"Very well then," she said, "I believe this is an attempt to drive us mad."

Jack swallowed hard. "Feels perilously close to working."

He wasn't imagining it; a faint warmth began to build between their hands. He could feel her shift in what he presumed was uncomfortable awareness.

Faith cleared her throat. "If they do that, if they break the bond between us and our seraphim, they can perhaps…harness us."

The image of the slain people in the Trocadero, tied together by that green cord, flashed in front of Jack's eyes. "So, how do you propose we stop them?"

"We must get behind the barriers," she whispered, and the heat between their joined hands flared. The seraphim were pushing aside the thin veneer that separated them, reaching out towards each other like long separated lovers. Jack had never felt such longing for togetherness.

He had a brief moment of deep and utter panic. No symbiote had survived working together more than in the shallowest of manners. It was impossible. It would be the end of them. Letting the terror take control, Jack thrashed about in the tight confines of the box, while his mind twisted to memories of mud and blood. He had to get out—now!

Dimly, he heard Faith call his name, but his wildly swinging arm came roughly into contact with her side. Her exclamation of pain became merely another sound in the terror that was overcoming him. He was, after all, buried alive.

Then she was holding him, and for a tiny woman, she had real strength. Her arms around him snapped Jack back from the brink, but the intrusion of her seraph in his head went on.

It was too much. It was bad enough having one of those leeches in his head— he wasn't about to allow a damn colony in. He fought the invasion while the woman shook him and demanded he stop, but he had gone beyond caring.

Jack suddenly didn't worry if they both died in the box; he wasn't going to let another creature in his head. Slamming down all the barriers he'd cultivated over years of possession, the invading leech was stopped in its tracks.

"You idiot!" Faith's voice in his ear made him jump, but when she grabbed his head and turned it to hers, he was shocked rigid. Her lips broke through the mental walls he'd thrown up with brute physical contact. Terror fought an abrupt losing battle with arousal as Faith pressed against him.

The panic dissolved away from his concerns as he kissed the woman he had yet to see. Darkness whittled the sensation down to sound and touch; her leg over his, her breasts pressed against his chest, while her hands locked around the side of his head. Jack could not move far, while his body wished for more space to turn and hold her. They struggled against each other and with their clothes which seemed to get in the way of what they both wanted.

Then suddenly, it was much more than physical. The seraphim slithered across the barriers and met in that small space between their two hosts. Jack, even as he drew Faith tighter against his body, felt the awareness between them spring into life. It was a thoroughly strange feeling, but not necessarily an unpleasant one.

Running a hand up her neck and into her hair, his skin felt the ghost echo of his own touch, but beyond that was the pleasure of the two seraphim, writhing with the unexpected joy of being together in a synthesis. The combined excitement and arousal of four beings in one head was explosive. It was like drowning in honey and for a time Jack let it wash them all away.

His entire world was Faith's skin under his hands and her lips against his. They were jammed so tightly against each other—with their minds just as close—that nothing else mattered.

She was the Weather Witch at the Trocadero all those years ago. Her recollection lay over his own of that moment. He snatched her memory of the window exploding outwards and saw himself standing over the prone victims.

"Godamnit!" Jack swore and pulled back as far as the box would allow.

"Now then, what are the odds of that?" Faith's breathing was coming in gasps like his own. The humans might have broken apart, but the seraphim certainly hadn't; their erotic twining made it very difficult to think or speak properly.

Jack remembered her face and the halo of red-brown hair—he reached out and touched it.

"I'm sorry I hurt you." Faith's voice was tinged with embarrassment, and he could feel it was more for what they had nearly done.

It was too late now—the damage had been done when the seraphim were allowed to contact each other. The effects of Shock might have dazed him, but Faith's control on her magic was more than enough to get past that.

"Just get us out of here," he snapped, aware that if he was remotely civil he'd be kissing her again in moments. That didn't fool Faith; Jack presumed she could feel his emotions as he could feel hers. Bloody impolite leeches…

"Please don't call them that. Hoa doesn't like it."

Her words were surplus to requirements. Jack could feel the disapproval like a knot in his stomach. He was also aware of Faith within his head. She might have her power tied down, but her mental fingers were sure on his.

"So much power," she muttered, wriggling around until her back was to him. The gentle curve of her rear was distracting in the extreme. "You really don't understand that, do you?"

Jack chose to believe that was a rhetorical question. The fact that she was ferreting around in his head was bad enough; the sharp-tongued questioning was just too much. And dammit, she knew all of these things.

"Cover your ears," Faith whispered. Remembering what she was capable of, Jack obeyed.

Then everything blew apart. Earth and wood flew around them while his ears popped, but the explosion never touched either of them. Jack could feel his mouth drop open at the sheer impressive nature of the power that she'd unleashed. He couldn't believe that the magic had been drawn from him.

The hiss of earth and the sudden influx of cool night air felt as though it was bringing him back to life. Faith was up before him. The eerie image of her against the sky full of moon and stars made him catch his breath. Her hair, just like that time at the Trocadero, was standing around her. He desperately wanted her to touch him again and ease his arousal. To touch and possess such fire seemed terribly necessary.

Jack surged to his feet, ready to take her against him no matter what. Yet when he did, the looming presence of the Hooper farm broke that intense feeling. In it he'd almost forgotten the horror of it, and the burial. Faith clutched his arm so he was prepared to see what he did when he turned. The children bound with the cord were standing on the front porch, looking down to the erupted earth where he and Faith stood.

Yet it was the woman standing at their side who grabbed his attention, so much so that the rest of the world faded into greyness— even Faith, who he had only moments ago desired so intensely. It was Alice; the wife he'd thought dead many years. She was just as beautiful as he recalled, though her hair was different. She inclined her head and smiled at him. "Hello, Jack. I imagine this is quite a surprise."

After that, nothing else mattered.

CHAPTER TWENTY-THREE

Faith's head was scrambled. Her magic and Jack's were so muddled that his thoughts were bleeding into hers.

The name Alice bloomed in the silence after they exploded out of the ground. The woman, standing calm and confident beside the bound children, brought with her such a rush of emotion that she felt a sob rising up the back of her throat.

Jack's beloved—the one he had thought dead while he was in France—was standing there before him. Faith might be raging with the horror of seeing those children enslaved, but he was struck with the impossibility of seeing Alice standing there in the shadow of the house.

Overlaid however, was her own dawning realisation that she too recognised the woman. It was with a horrible chill in the pit of her stomach that she identified her as the figure that had been hovering over Lily; the one that had taken her and tied her powers. Rage, almost equal to the one that had consumed her at the Trocadero, rose up inside her. Hoa and Jack's seraph were roaring in the back of her head to strike and avenge the children with their soul-sucked eyes.

Luckily Faith didn't need Jack, because she already had his power. He might be stricken by the sight of the woman he'd been married to standing all unexpected before him, but she wasn't.

Faith channelled Jack's vast untapped reservoir of magic, and it was a wonderfully heady sensation. Her power was a vast whirling cloud of chaos, like riding a wild horse, all unfettered and joyous. Jack's magic was deep and vast as a cavern of ice. Standing on the precipice of it, Faith felt very small. How could he not have made better use of his power?

Hoa revelled in it even more than she did, because the chance to work with new magics was one a seraph seldom got.

Brimming with magic so that her eyes burned and her nerves sang, Faith smiled back at the woman. Between them, Jack had dropped to his knees. His dirty hair sat up in strange spikes, while his fingers clenched in the dirt.

"Alice?" His voice also sounded as though it had only just been dug up. "I thought you died…they…they told me you died."

Her eyes, still seeped in shadow, flickered only briefly to the man. "They were right enough. Alice is dead."

Faith had enough of this. She raised her hand, and the air grew heavy with power. It was only the oppressive warmth that got the attention of whoever the woman was. Jack and his incredulity ceased to matter as the women concentrated on each other.

As full of magic as she had ever been, Faith once again felt the heady arrogance from all those years ago. "It matters little what your name is. If you don't release those children immediately, you will be deeply and truly dead."

"These creatures are no longer children," came the chilling reply, "and you have overstepped your boundary, little girl."

It was a comment designed to enflame her, Faith knew that, yet she couldn't resist. Jack's power begged to be used. Hoa howled with delight as she released the flood of magic. Faith's body faded into white, a mere conduit to magic of such depth and strength.

The air around Alice folded before exploding with a bang. The house rattled and shifted, buffeted by the explosion. The children staggered back to shelter in the veranda. Jack howled when Faith grabbed hold of him, sheltering him with her own body.

The explosion might have blinded her for a second, but Hoa saw more than her, even at times like this. Alice had moved.

In that split second when Faith had made the decision to open the flood gates to power, Alice must have seen it. Having never battled another Awakened, the publican's daughter wasn't prepared to have her opponent blur and step away like that. It was just what had happened at the Albert.

When the air finally cleared, Jack and Faith were left gasping, with only the taste of dirt in their mouths and strange tang in their nostrils.

The children, their necks still bound with the odd knotted green cord, stepped forward out of the shadows. Their guardian might have vanished, but they didn't seem to care.

Hoa howled a warning to do something, but Faith couldn't strike at children.

The air around them grew cold enough to cut to the bone, so that Jack and Faith's suddenly exhaled breath condensed in front of their eyes.

She contemplated her own Weather Witchery; a quick blast of ice might have rendered the trio at least incapable of movement. Yet all she had was the vast incendiary power of Jack, a power that she had no experience of wielding.

The bound magic of the children opened up in front of them, and it was a yawning pit made to swallow all those that stood against their unseen master. The howling frozen void screamed at them while the winds tore at Jack and Faith.

He was yelling something that she couldn't make out, not only because of the chaos around them, but also the chaos that came with two seraphim struggling to get her attention.

They were trying to tell her something that required words, and words were the one thing that no seraph had ever been able to project into a human brain.

Jack clutched her hand, trying to pull her back from the void which now flared white, and together they fruitlessly struggled to run away. Faith could feel it; behind the white was nothing but emptiness and death waiting.

It was going to end like this. Faith felt that deep in the calm part of her separate from the desperate struggle. They would be killed by these children while the masters who had turned them into weapons got away.

Hoa finally penetrated her terror with the only solution, and it was as mad and as dangerous as it got. The Shock could kill her, but indeed the only way to unleash her power was to break whatever bond Alice had placed upon her.

The wind ripped at her hair as she clutched Jack to her. They gripped onto each other even as the hungry void pulled them backwards.

"Hold on to me," she yelled into his ear. "The Shock will take me immediately, so don't let go!"

Jack looked at her blankly, but wrapped her tighter in an embrace she couldn't recall ever having had from a man. No time at this point to enjoy the sensation. Instead, Faith plummeted into the midst of magic, down into the tangle of power made from two seraphim. It was a place that no other Awakened had ever gone and the only possibility that she could save both of them.

Both of the seraphim welcomed her into their world. Opening her eyes, she threw all that she could touch into the void. Thunder roared and the air imploded with terrible vigour.

CHAPTER TWENTY-FOUR

Lily tugged on Wirimu's arm. She had felt the magic building up since they left the Albert, but as the trail of government cars climbed the narrow road to Newlands, her senses caught on fire.

Her seraph wailed, jealous perhaps of such unconstrained power—it was impossible to tell. Lily felt herself flailing in the unknown.

Wirimu had his arm over the back of the front seat and was talking to the Māori woman in the back. The magic of this agent ran deep in the earth, and though Lily was curious about that, what she was more concerned with was what was up ahead, waiting in the darkness.

She patted Wirimu's arm more urgently and pointed over his shoulder. No one needed seraph magic to be aware of what was happening. Light blazed from behind the hill, lighting up the night sky as if a star was burning on the earth. The darkness rippled and pulsed as if it had life of its own.

Wirimu's breath whistled over his teeth, and he leaned over to their driver. "Step on it, Aaron. Looks like hell's just broken loose!"

The passengers held on as best they could as the line of cars accelerated up the hill, bumping and rattling. Lily felt that some little magic was being used just to keep them on the road.

She grinned and finally let out a little whoop of delight as they rocked around the corners. The shocked looks from the other occupants made her laugh all the harder.

Lily wasn't needed for navigation anymore, yet they couldn't stop and leave her by the side of the road. Her chance, and that of her seraph was coming—she could feel it like she felt the rush of wind on her skin.

The convoy of cars shrieked to a stop just short of the light. It blared over the rise like the sun was imprisoned there by Maui, or some other demi-god.

The agents, ten in all, bolted out of the cars. They unloaded their guns from the rear of the car, though only four took them. The rest of them didn't need anything as demeaning as firearms, they had plenty of other, more concealed weapons.

The sandy haired Seth Adamson took a pair of pistols while shooting a concerned look up to the ridge. "You sure we can't find some nice farmer's house and call for some backup?"

"It would be too late," the dark-eyed Māori woman said sharply, tucking her hair under her hat. Lily noted she didn't take a gun.

Wirimu seemed to consider the situation before him. His eyes raked over Lily before settling on the lean, young man who'd been in the other car. "Tipene, drive back and see if you can find a phone in one of those houses we passed."

She heard his thoughts, *One less won't make much of a difference.*

It was as obvious as the fire on the hill that Tipene was vastly relieved. He leapt into the front seat and drove off at a fair clip.

Wirimu—whose healing gifts even Lily knew were highly unsuited for attack—took the long lean barrel of a rifle and tugged her aside. "Now you are definitely staying here."

She might be muddled, but she wasn't stupid. He wouldn't be swayed, so she would just have to go around him. Biting her lip, Lily nodded and clambered back into the car. Luckily, they couldn't afford to leave any of their number behind to babysit.

That was the joy of being considered an idiot, most people expected her to obey the basic commands a dog might. However, Lily simply waited until they had spread out and disappeared over the rise, before getting out of the car.

She ran circular to where the agents had gone, all the time singing softly under her breath. She sneaked through the brush, watching the agents, with a slight smile on her lips. There was a barrier, beyond which was the farmhouse, though she had to shield her eyes to make out even that much. The agents made swift work of bringing it down, though once it was they seemed to hesitate to enter the light.

Lily had no such compunction. She ran down the slope and towards the house, while the sound of darkness drew her on. She saw Faith. Lily called her name, but her cousin didn't turn. She was fending off a great void that threatened to suck her and the man at her feet down.

The power she was channelling was responsible for the brightness. Faith was very beautiful in that moment, however it was too much. Lily could see it with the eyes the Craven Man had forced wide open, but her cousin couldn't.

Tied together as the seraphim were, they knew no boundaries, and were drawing on the man's power rather than Faith's. Again, Lily's lack of words stymied any warning she might have given. She could only cry out, "Humpty Dumpty!"

Her cousin glanced up, mystified, but it was too late. The man tried to struggle to his feet like a sick horse, but then collapsed into Shock, felled like one that had been offered a mercy blow.

Faith howled, forced to drop the hold on his power. The lines of linkage evaporated between them and the void surged forward.

It was now or never. Lily wouldn't be condemned to a half-life. Her seraph, needing a name as much as she needed to know it, seemed in agreement. Gathering up her skirts, she darted towards the hollow-eyed and tied children.

Behind her, the agents were running up to Faith. Maybe they knew how to put Humpty together again. It didn't matter—they couldn't stop Lily now.

The children didn't even acknowledge her. She picked up the dangling end of the cord that was bound about their necks. The knotted rope was made of some dense plant material, and she could feel the tingle of magic running through it. It was His work, and yet the only chance she had to regain what had been stolen.

Locking the cord around her neck, she was plunged into darkness. All was confusion. The children who on the outside had seemed so calm, in here were screaming. Trapped in the web of the Craven Man's making, their powers were bound to his plan.

Lily was falling, spiralling down into it as well. Her seraph could offer no stability or help in all this, since he was as lost as she was.

Terrified of losing herself, Lily cried out for her cousin as any trapped creature would have. It seemed like an age before Faith followed her down into the darkness. Lost and with her own Weather

Witchery still constrained, she without hesitation threw the remains of the man's magic to her kin.

It was not hers to give, but it was also Lily's only hope. Dropping down into the shadow with her cousin's borrowed power tethering her to reality, she risked it all. Below, amongst all the maze of magic and pain, she called the name of her seraph to her. She demanded it from the darkness as her right, and eventually it came back.

His name was Tau.

With a cry of sheer relief, Lily sprang back from the brink. Looking over, she saw Faith with her head thrown back, lost in the midst of the power. The look of utter ecstasy on her face had erased the vaguely worried look her cousin usually wore. Light danced around her fingers, and it was immediately obvious that this was power she couldn't bear to let go. At her feet the man sagged as it was draining him.

Tearing off the green cord, Lily dashed across the short distance and shook Faith. Her now-known seraph reached down deep and touched Faith, telling her what she was doing to another human being.

With a shuddering howl, Faith released the magic that had surrounded her. "Foolish, foolish girl," she sobbed, though if she meant herself or Lily was hard to tell.

Lily only looked up into her eyes. "I know his name. It is Tau. Isn't it beautiful…"

She enjoyed Faith's gape of amazement. "You…you can talk?" she stammered.

"I can do anything now," she replied with a grin. It faded when she looked over her kin's shoulder. The man was lying silent on the ground, but his eyes were open wide and were very gold. By saving her, Faith had plunged the man down into Possession and Shock. "You did that for me," she whispered.

Her cousin's gaze dropped away while her hand rubbed her forehead. "I didn't mean to, but you were going down...there was nothing else to be done."

The agents were clustering around the fallen man, all except Wirimu who was striding towards them, the rifle draped under one arm. Lily smiled at him. Looking at him made her feel like the puzzle pieces were all falling together.

"I thought I told you to stay in the car," he said with the hint of a growl in his voice. He bristled while he took in the battered house and the still quiet row of children.

"If I'd listened to you, then I wouldn't have gotten his Name at all." Lily rather liked the sound of her own sassy reply.

His expression was nearly as priceless at Faith's.

"His name is Tau," Lily repeated. She'd never get tired of saying that, nor of the intense feeling of contentment her seraph was blazing forth.

Wirimu smiled, a beautiful expression that made him even more handsome. "You got it back then, girl. Good for you!"

"I'm not a girl anymore," she said in turn with a slight dip of her eyes.

Faith stepped between them. "We can examine all that later. For now I need you to help Jack…if you can…"

She hurried over to the downed man while Wirimu and Lily followed.

"Don't get too close," one of the agents said, tugging Faith. "He's in deep possession."

Tau told Lily how bad that was.

"Well," Wirimu said with a frown, "we'll get him up to Shorecliff at once, see what they can do. For now, secure the area."

Lily stayed with Faith as all but one agent hurried to obey the superior officer's commands.

Her elder cousin bent down and looked into Jack's eyes, her face folded with guilt and concern. "Shorecliff," she murmured under her breath. "Of all places for me to put him in."

Despite being overwhelmed by her own delight, Lily could see how deeply her cousin was affected.

With a sigh, Faith got up and hugged her briefly. She pulled back and gave her kin a long hard look. "Do you know who did this, Lily?"

Dare she explain the Craven Man, now that she could? Looking into Faith's eyes she knew she couldn't. Let her think that she had won a victory.

"I don't know…but you beat them."

She wanted to believe the lie, to pretend that the world was that simple and easy. The vast expanse of the Craven Man's power, she had only tasted a tiny morsel of. Lily recognised that she'd already suffered a lot of guilt and panic, but all that really mattered was Tau had his name back.

That was enough victory for now.

PART THREE

Burning Shores

New Zealand, October 1929

CHAPTER TWENTY-FIVE

Faith Awakened because her Mother was ill that day. Father piggybacked Jean out of the house, while Faith trotted at his side, grinning at the joy of a whole day of freedom.

The day was a warm summer one, and though she would have loved to be out in the backblocks of the farm with her uncles, sharing her dad's day was even more exciting. At seven years old Faith considered herself to be much more helpful than Jean, who, since she didn't even go to school yet, was too young to be of any real use.

It would be a busy day. Dad had many chores, yet they would be like a game since they were together.

"Now," he said, swinging Jean down from his back, "you two girls just have to be quiet and still—can you do that?"

It was an insulting question, but Faith decided it was really directed at Jean. Her little sister still sucked her thumb, after all.

So Faith nodded solemnly. "I'll be good, Dad."

"I'm sure you will, Curly." He tossed Jean up in the air, making her giggle.

They went into the barn, and he tucked the girls under the hulk of the seed sorting machine. Faith could dimly remember other times when she'd been here. The smell of the great mass of the iron machine mixed with the smell of dry grass, making her wrinkle her nose and rub her eyes.

Still, Faith didn't mind. Mother was stern, and Father, by contrast, treated her kindly. He tickled her and didn't shout; all important things at seven.

Still, he had to do important things; the seed needed to be sorted, and the machine wouldn't run itself. The barn was full of things little girls shouldn't get into, so despite her protestations, they had to stay under the machine out of the way. Jean had her collection of pegdolls, loved and chewed on, to keep her amused, while Faith, spurning such childish things, had a dog-eared alphabet primer. She'd preciously learnt to read when she was four, but the book was the first thing Dad had grabbed, so she wasn't going to complain.

The machine whirred and spun around Faith, and hidden under it, with her father's feet close by, she felt deeply happy. It was so much better than being stuck in the house with Mother. It felt like Father trusted her, and that she was somehow helping.

Shaking and rattling, the machine let out a hiss as the seeds scattered into the right sack bags pinned to its outside edge. The whole operation sounded like rain on the tin roof. Father had explained how the ones that would grow were shaken out from those that wouldn't, and it was an expensive machine that they shared out with all the other farmers in the area.

From underneath, the workings were fascinating. Faith watched as complicated mechanical things happened right above her head, and that was how she noticed that one of the seed bags wasn't properly attached at the back.

From where he stood, Dad couldn't see it. She yelled out once, but the rattle-bang voice of the sorter drowned anything out. He'd said not to make a fuss, and Faith took her Dad's instructions very seriously.

It wasn't that much of a gap, and it wouldn't take but a moment to fix for him. With a smile of satisfaction at being of use to her beloved Father, Faith reached up to help him.

With barely a change in its shambling tempo, the machine ate her fingers hungrily. Time seemed to snag on that instant. She could see the sliding pieces of metal coming back together as they shook against the bag, but couldn't seem to quite move fast enough to pull back her hand from the jaws of the machine. It didn't matter how much she considered herself a big girl, Faith screamed as much as her lungs would allow.

Everything went blurry after that. She heard Dad's exclamation of horror, and Jean's howls. They silenced the hungry machine, and he carried her inside, calling for her mother in a terrified voice. Faith could concentrate on nothing much more than the pain. Her *fingers—no, her whole arm—felt as if they had been bathed in fire, while the rest of her body shuddered in sympathy.*

They put her on the kitchen table just as her screams failed in her throat. She found it hard to breathe. Agony wrapped itself around her, so that she didn't even feel the passage of time. It hurt, she knew that, yet somehow she was disconnected from her body as well.

Something was finding a place within her. It was the only other sensation apart from pain. Her parent's words couldn't reach her, but Faith could feel the dawning presence of someone else within her head.

By the time the doctor was summoned and said that he could save the hand but not all of the fingers, she'd subsided into a wide-eyed state of terror. He amputated the ring finger on her left hand without anaesthetic, as he had none to give. This second pain travelled through flesh and bone like a dagger into her brain. The once ajar door flung open, and the presence hovering nearby swooped down to cover her with its soothing magic.

On the table Faith turned her head to her Dad and said, "He says his name is Hoa."

Mother gasped, her hands flew to her mouth, and her gaze quickly turned to Dad, an accusation in a fleeting moment that Faith saw very clearly.

He looked so alone and guilty.

His daughter tried to comfort, even though it was her hand that the doctor was bandaging. "Don't worry, Daddy I'm alright...I'm alright..."

It was the truth. Hoa insulated her from the agony and comforted her. She'd always have a friend and never be lonely again. It was a magnificent gift.

It was the memory Hoa always calmed her with, and somehow Faith knew he found it soothing, too. Still, recalling her Awakening distracted her from what was going on in the room. Maybe that, too, was the seraph's plan.

"Agent Louden!" The captain's voice snapped her out of her reverie very effectively, even though he was standing at the end a very long briefing table. The other agents, who had been watching with rapt attention, flicked their heads in her direction, no doubt grateful not to be her. Her commanding officer had lately taken a dislike to her, and she knew full well why. It was the very same reason Hoa disliked him so intensely. Then again, her seraph and she were in complete agreement on that matter.

"Dreaming away the day, are we?" Captain Lane rapped his cane down on the table, which made the nearest agents jump.

Faith had been expecting it, so she met his gaze levelly. "No sir, sorry sir." She wasn't about to give him a reason to go on more. Dealing with her mother had taught her when irascible people explode, silence is the best defence unless you have ammunition to take the battle to them. At this moment Faith had none.

"Well then," the captain said, retrieving his cane and tucking it under his armpit, "as I was saying, it has always been assumed that the seraphim have no concerns or agenda of their own...until now."

Faith shifted uncomfortably in her chair, but the storm of her commanding officer's temper seemed to have passed by. The rest of the half a dozen Eyes also in the meeting seemed to be rapt by his words, but a deep fear was beginning to unsettle Faith. The others would say it was Hoa influencing her. Within the government, admitting that a seraph could offer its own opinion on matters was a big no no. The trouble was, the authorities relied on the Agency to police the other Awakened, yet they couldn't shake the fear that they didn't truly control them.

"You have something to say on the matter, Agent Louden?" Captain Lane could be cunning. She'd thought his attention had drifted away from her, but obviously it hadn't.

Now that he had asked her directly, something that had happened seldom since she'd joined the agency two years before, Faith wouldn't lie. She dropped her pen down onto the open notepad in front of her.

"No, sir. I was just wondering if you were referring to research done by Doctor Masters at Shorecliff, because I have almost finished my report on that and there are several inconsistencies..."

Lane's gaze narrowed. "I thought we had agreed that your time at the facility was on a purely voluntary basis, especially after your... experience there."

She didn't rise to that bait. "Certainly sir, but I've been talking to some of the doctors the last time I was there, and they are..."

"But you haven't spoken to the good Doctor himself, have you?" The slight hint of a smile on the captain's lips said that he already knew the answer to that pointed question.

"Unfortunately not. Masters won't meet with me unless I am on official business, and as you've said…"

He cut her off. "Well, I can't waste time in this meeting discussing your… interests."

One person couldn't quite hold in their snigger, and she caught the whiff of how the rest of her fellow agents thoughts were leaning. Thompson, the most junior member of the team, and by chance the most recent Awakened, couldn't be bothered, or didn't know how to wall up his thoughts.

Visiting her mad lover.

It wasn't a surprise. Agency gossip had quickly gotten hold of the facts and turned them into something else. Let them think what they liked. She'd much rather have them think it was love rather than guilt that took her to Shorecliff every month.

Lane, seeing that she had retreated into silence, smiled in victory. "Very well then. Doctor Masters has indeed been working on understanding what the seraphim are working towards." Scientists were forever trying to find a basis for the seraphim, but so far not even autopsies had ever revealed any physical symptoms of the symbiotes. They labelled it endosymbiosis—living within the cells of the host, but even that was conjecture.

Hilary Chen, Faith's partner, leaned forward. "But, sir if you don't mind me saying, how can he find that out? No seraph can actually talk to their host."

It was a reasonable question, one of the hundreds Faith would have asked the good doctor if she'd ever had the chance. She suspected she wouldn't necessarily like the answer.

Captain Lane would have loved to find a way to cut Hilary down as he'd done to Faith, but the willowy Chinese woman was smarter than that; she covered her intelligence with a smile and good manners.

The captain rocked backwards and forwards on his feet, and Faith realised that he had no idea how to answer her partner's question. Like most of middle management, Lane had no clue what was going on above him, and unfortunately no better comprehension of what was happening in the ranks below him.

"I can't answer that, Agent Chen. Doctor Masters' work is highly classified," he replied chewing nervously on the corner of his moustache. "His results do, however, suggest that the seraphim are working together towards some sort of goal they refuse to share with us."

Looking around the table, Faith saw that the rest of the agents were not buying this any more than she was.

"Well then," Lane said, picking up his papers from the table, "if you have any inkling from your seraph that would assist Masters' research, please let me know."

Faith and Hilary waited until everyone had filed out of the meeting room before leaving themselves. Both wore civilian clothes, being detectives rather than sworn officers in the Agency. Faith would somehow have preferred the simplicity of the uniform. Hilary's slender form always looked immaculate, with her ribbon of black hair swept up and tucked under a neat little hat. She, by comparison, always felt dowdy, and somehow there was always a stain on her front. The only time Faith felt as confident and assured as her partner was when she summoned the witchery that was Hoa's gift. With training she had managed far better control—that at least was one thing that had improved.

Hilary shot her an oblique look as they went back to their tiny office space. "What do you think Lane was trying to do? Get us to dob on our own seraph?"

"I'm not sure," Faith found she was whispering, though there were certainly plenty of otherworldly ways they could be overheard, "but who would? The seraphim give so much, and even if you did, both of you would be punished for any indiscretion."

Hilary sighed. It was not the time to be rocking the boat. Everywhere workers lived in daily fear of losing their job. Businesses were closing down all over the country, and though the Ministry was a government department, it didn't make it immune to cutbacks. Her income was the only cash her mother and uncles received. They could survive off the land, but they still needed money now and then. She also helped out Jean. Her husband's tile making business had been an early victim of the economic crisis.

So, Faith was in no position to challenge Captain Lane, and she knew pretty much everyone in the building was the same; grateful just to be pulling a wage.

They reached their office; her desk cluttered with paper, Hilary's uniformed and organised. Both had the same amount of work, it was just Faith believed in keeping things where she could see them and jog her thoughts.

"Have you ever wondered how this doctor is getting information from his patients?" Hilary sat down and pulled open her drawer, then drew out their latest bunch of case files.

They shared a look. As partners, even if it was only for the last year, they had shared much. Working in concert, their two complimentary magics could be linked. Unlike the normal police, the Agency created teams through compatibility between seraphim rather than people. Faith knew that she was lucky in that she and Hilary were also on good terms. Sometimes agents could clash even if their seraphim were comfortable with each other.

"Since my time, things have changed," Faith said with near conviction.

"And you believe that?"

"My cousin's husband assured me that on the first day I met him." Thinking about Lily and Wirimu still gave her a twinge of jealousy, even though she'd long ago made peace with the fact that the handsome agent had preferred her repaired cousin to herself.

Hilary didn't meet her eyes. It was an Awakened politeness that Faith appreciated. "You're going up to Shorecliff again this weekend, correct?"

Faith frowned. "Yes. I'm not going to let Lane put me off."

"You shouldn't, but if there is no change in him…"

Faith cleared her desk by the simple method of pushing the paper back with one forearm. Hoa was sad and didn't know what to do about it. She sighed, and folded her hands together. "You know that's not why I go."

Hilary was not one to offer words of platitudes, but a sensation of comfort ran across from one seraphim to another. She'd tried only once, suggesting that Faith not go, when that had failed she'd simply allowed her partner to do what she needed to.

"You have no need to be guilty, Faith," Hilary assured her.

Faith could have lied and said she wasn't, or that she didn't know what Hilary was talking about, but their connection made a mockery of regular human lies. The truth was that she was haunted by what had happened in Newlands; not just by casting Jack Cunningham down into possession, but more deeply by the fact it had felt very good. The magic running through her had been heady and addictive. If it hadn't been for Lily, she might have gone on and on until both of them were drawn down into darkness. As it was, only Jack had been sacrificed.

So, she fixed Hilary with an unbending look. "I have more reason than any I know of to feel guilt."

Her partner nodded. "Then I suppose you will be heading north again this weekend."

"Actually I have the day off Friday, so I'll be going up then instead."

Hilary raised an eyebrow. "Maybe you can catch this mysterious Doctor Masters off guard."

"That is the general idea."

They'd usually discuss Captain Lane and his theatrics until afternoon tea, but mentioning the doctor had somehow taken the shine off that activity. Instead, they spent the afternoon tackling the relentless paperwork on their just completed case.

The Dannevirke case had mostly been handled by the Northern regional office, but Hilary and Faith had been called in when it appeared the young boy might be showing signs of Weather Witchery. His concerned parents, part of a large group that had emigrated from Germany after the end of the war, were not capably of looking after the young magician that had suddenly appeared in their family. Faith, running purely on instinct, had tried to find any sign of them pushing him into early Awakening.

Such acts of violence had always been illegal, but since the change in the Act, the Ministry had been far more vigorous enforcing it. However, she'd not been able to prove anything, and the local office had taken over responsibility, promising to keep an eye on the lad. His Awakening feat of creating a small waterspout off the beach had never been repeated, and she'd sensed no power of a kin to her own lurking in him.

Still, there were always many miles of forms to be filed with these inter-regional cases. It occupied her mind for the rest of the day, which was a good thing because otherwise it was a quiet day.

The time seemed to drag by. A couple of runners came in with half a dozen more case files for them to examine. Faith found herself glancing up at the clock and realising it was nearly seven in the evening. Their office phone rang, and Hilary answered. With a raise of her eyebrows she beckoned Faith over. "Yes, she's here."

The tone in Hilary's voice made her partner's pulse kick up a fraction, and she took the receiver with some trepidation. The voice at the end of the line was cool, calculated and familiar. "Miss Louden, it's Doctor Hastings from Shorecliff."

"Yes?" she said, feeling a chill run through her.

"You asked me to ring if there was any change in Patient Cunningham's status."

Faith's hand tightened around the receiver. "Is there a problem, Doctor?"

"Not a problem exactly, but he does seem to have regained some level of consciousness." In all the years since the farm, that had never happened.

Her brain was spinning faster and faster. "Thank you, Doctor. I'll be up on the first train." She carefully replaced the receiver and took a deep breath. "He's awake."

Hilary glanced over her shoulder, and whispered, "But you're not due to go north until Friday…"

Faith was packing her brown leather satchel as swiftly as she could. "I have to get there immediately. I don't suppose…"

Hilary moved to the coat rack and threw her partner's battered felt cap across Faith's desk. "I'll cover you. Family emergency— something like that."

She nodded. "Well, the emergency part is right."

With that, Faith made herself scarce, darting out of the office by the back door. Her mind was already directed northwards, to where the man she felt terribly responsible for might be opening his eyes for the first time into the world of Shorecliff.

CHAPTER TWENTY-SIX

Jack lay very still, looking up at the ceiling. The white light of the full moon bounced off the uneven surface, making shadows that looked like faces stretched in screams. He knew they weren't there, which was the most frightening bit, but whatever medication they were giving him gave them an eerie other-life.

Apart from their screaming, his head was quiet. Waingaio, who he had once despised, was silent. That, too, was from the drugs. The seraph's screaming was what drove him away from his own body.

Something, he couldn't recall what, had upset the delicate symbiosis between Waingaio and himself. If he could only remember.

Turning his head sideways, Jack could just make out the door, though what lay beyond he couldn't recall. Dimly, there came the sound of a set of squeaky wheels going past.

A hospital. He tensed his arms, willing himself to rise. That was when he realised that he was restrained, in fact tied to the bed. So, not the type of hospital they let you out of and probably not the type of hospital where they fixed afflictions of the body.

It was certain; Jack was living every Awakened's nightmare. Without Waingaio, he had no way of getting out, either.

The squeaky set of wheels suddenly became very important, a link to an outside world he might never see. Until this point he had never really considered how much Waingaio's senses had heightened his own. He could have smelt the sex of the trolley pusher, heard by their breathing if it was hard work or not, and maybe had a touch of the emotion they were feeling.

Jack was just contemplating the delicious irony of that when the squeak of the trolley halted and the sound of running feet replaced it. Voices, at least three, rattled along the corridor in a jumble of aggressive panic. At first it was hard to make out what they were saying, but they seemed to be right outside his door.

With mounting panic Jack tugged at the restraints. Even without his seraph magic he should have been able to get loose, but something had happened to his muscles. How long had he been strapped to the bed?

Long ago nightmares from the trenches rose up from the great unknown to chew on the fragile cords of his sanity. Just as the door creaked open, Jack slammed shut his eyes and tried to control his ragged breathing.

In the silence, the urge to turn and look at the people at the door almost overwhelmed him. He concentrated, instead, on making his chest rise slowly and evenly, rather than take the shuddering gasps his racing heart demanded.

"So, he's finally ready." The voice was light, with a slight burr to it and totally unfamiliar.

"Recovery from Possession can take years, so we're lucky he made it at all. Let's get this over with." The second voice was thick with an accent he immediately recognised as German. It made him think strangely, not of the enemies he'd faced in Flanders, but of his uncle Herman; a man with a thick blonde moustache, a bright white smile, and a talent for the piano that had stirred a kindred feeling between him and his nephew. Herman had been interred on Somes Island along with all other immigrants during the war, and had died there, far from his beloved parlour Schimmel. He'd left it to Jack.

The sound of footsteps came closer, and his mind raced further ahead. What he wouldn't give to feel Waingaio's presence right now.

"If only that bloody Eye would leave him alone." The first sounded angry in the way harassed workers did when their routine was interrupted.

"Blame the doctor for ringing her." Jack's sensitive ears picked up what sounded like a bag being opened, followed by a metallic or glass noise.

He couldn't help it then. With a start, he threw himself upright against the restraints.

"*Die Kacke!*" The German, who didn't look anything like his uncle, dropped the syringe he was preparing.

The other man, whose voice also seemed to have little relevance to his form, was swifter. His muscular frame landed atop Jack's with enough force to crush his primitive howl of rage. What emerged was probably nothing special for this madhouse, but it made Jack feel at least that he was causing his two assailants some distress.

"Shut the hell up," the man yelled back into Jack's ear, but he bucked and strained and fought hard to stop whatever they were planning to do to him.

The image of the syringe filled his body with adrenaline until his muscles felt like they were going to snap. It was no use. The sting of the needle in his arm made the world suddenly tilt.

The man who had been holding him down slid off with a smile. "Don't know why you're fighting it, mate. Where you're going, it's every man's fantasy..."

Jack's head sagged back, far too heavy, and his body was drifting away from him. He struggled to hang on to consciousness.

"Not until Agent Louden's been and gone." The German looked a long way off.

The name seemed familiar, he could almost see a face, but the more he tried to grasp it, the further it slipped out of his reach. Damn unfair to be getting a visitor and not be conscious to appreciate. The world was still unfair, apparently.

CHAPTER TWENTY-SEVEN

Shorecliff was a beautiful building in a beautiful place. Every time she drove up the final stretch of the hill, Faith was impressed by the view. The wild Tasman Ocean battered the rocky cliffs, filling the air with the sting of salt. Clumps of tortured plants clung where they could while seabirds wheeled overhead. It was the kind of place a wealthy man would have built a great castle in the old world. In this new one, it was not that different.

The place of her nightmares rose like a great gothic mausoleum of brick. She didn't recall arriving here the first time, she'd been heavily sedated and wrapped in Geas, but still each visit was unpleasant.

The taxi pulled up at the front, and after paying the driver, Faith got out and looked up. The building had an overhanging portico that looked very much like a glowering brow. If it were not for Jack Cunningham, she never would have come back here after her own experience.

But with the change of the Act controlling the Awakened, the so-called treatment she'd received here was a thing of the past. She had to remind herself of that every time she went in.

Walking up the path, her feet crunching on the gravel, she tucked her loose hair under her hat. Each time she returned, Faith did her level best to appear the efficient agent, anything so that they would not be reminded she had once been a patient.

Inside the cool interior, the smell of antiseptic hit the back of her throat as roughly as always. It had taken several visits before she'd been free of the desire to choke. Policy might have changed, but hospitals were still hospitals.

Nurse Maureen Horomia's warm smile was something that made the entrance bearable. Her large efficient frame was tucked behind the front desk. Checking the upside down watch pinned to her chest, she smiled a little. "Doctor Hastings wasn't thinking you would make it up here before lunch."

"I left first thing this morning," Faith informed her, unclenching her hands from her purse and trying her best to appear relaxed. "Is he available?"

"He's in a meeting until eleven, but you can go ahead and see Mr Cunningham without him."

It was worth a try. Faith put her bag down on the counter and carefully removed her kid gloves. "I don't suppose Doctor Masters is around instead?"

The nurse's face hardened a little. Faith had never actually met the elusive Masters, but she could tell a lot about him from the reaction he engendered in his support staff. Because of what he was saying about seraphim, Faith could only feel a certain grim satisfaction at that.

"I can check if you like, Agent Louden…" her voice trailed off.

Faith shrugged. "I understand that he is busy. I'll go up and see Mr Cunningham, and maybe if he could drop in…"

Maureen's expression managed to be non-committal and disapproving at the same time.

Climbing the green linoleum stairs to the second floor, Faith made sure not to run. Doctor Hastings had said there was a change in Jack. Could it be that perhaps after all this time he and his seraph had come back into equilibrium? It had happened that suddenly in her case. Unfortunately, it had only been the change in legislation that had secured her release. Those unrecalled months under Possession had not been the problem—it had been the years of unnecessary experimentation and needless torment.

She would make certain that Jack didn't have to suffer from such a trial. If he was conscious, then Faith would move all earth to make sure she left today with him. Hoa flooded her with his agreement. So maybe it wouldn't be earth she would move, maybe it would be the sky itself.

Once again the temptation of power tickled at the edge of her conscience. It was too easy to be arrogant and imagine flattening the whole place, but that would be very unprofessional. Faith poised on the landing just below the final set of stairs and took a few deep breaths.

Upstairs, she checked in with the ward nurse and was let into the small padded room where Jack Cunningham was confined—thanks to her.

If Shorecliff was nightmares, then Jack was something much nicer. Faith found it funny that men thought they were the only ones moved by beauty. A male eye might follow a fine form, but always, somehow, imagined that a woman could not. Jack, even after years in Shorecliff, drew her in. His handsome face had a burr of stubble, while his blonde hair was spiky with sweat. It was strange to think that she, for all intents and purposes, a fully-grown woman, could still be capable of a silly infatuation.

Hoa wasn't happy. He sensed nothing different about Jack, so Faith hurried to his side and pushed his hair out of his eyes. They were wide, blue and distant just as always.

A choked-back sob and a rush of rage made Faith shake. She'd been promised some change. She'd driven through the early morning hours, imagining him back to his old self. He was still tied to the bed and still a patient of this loathed place.

Yet it wasn't his fault. Carefully she felt behind her, found the chair they always left for her and sat down.

Over the years the memory of Jack had not faded. Their brief moment trapped together had burned as one of her brightest moments. She'd been changed forever when their seraphim had joined together, and she could not bury the feeling of touching the well of his power. Part of Faith now cried out to regain that feeling.

A wave of such longing and despair washed through her. She could feel it rushing through her feet and legs and leaping all the way up. It was as if Shorecliff had infected her once again with its horror.

"Agent Louden?"

The voice was soft, yet full of derision. Faith glanced over her shoulder, caught out in a moment of naked emotion. The man who spoke the words was not what she expected; a round little fruitcake of a man, with blank, dark eyes peering through window-thick glasses. The white coat implied he was one of the medical team, yet he was totally unfamiliar to her. Her logic made the leap.

Before getting up and facing him properly, she brushed those squeezed out tears from the corners of her own eyes. She held out her hand. "Doctor Masters, I'm glad to finally meet you."

His grasp on her hand was firm and icy. Suddenly Faith realised that she was lying; she was very unhappy to be face to face with the doctor. Fighting the urge to snatch back her hand, she tried instead to reclaim her calm.

He smiled—at least it was a baring of teeth she assumed was a smile. "I hear you have some issues with my recent research, Agent Louden."

It was said blandly enough, but Faith tensed at it. Her murmured comment in a Ministry briefing had only been the previous day and she couldn't imagine how Masters had been made aware of it. He might be a senior researcher in the field, but he was not a sworn agent. Faith bristled at the implication that he knew more than she did about her own workplace.

She wasn't as good as Hilary at concealing her emotions, but still better than she had been. A few years previous, maybe she would have done something drastic. This time Faith simply retrieved her hand and snapped, "Indeed I have, Doctor. I must say that many people in the office are wondering how you have come to such conclusions about the seraphim. Not since the bad old days of illicit experimentation have such assertions been made so boldly."

Faith's attempt to provoke a reaction fell on barren ground. He merely took a breath and stepped around Faith to stand hovering over Jack. "I understand you come up every month to see how this case is progressing."

"He has a name. Jack Cunningham."

"No need to be defensive, Agent Louden, I am merely making an observation." Masters peered over the rim of his glasses and down into the patient's face.

A tickle ran across Faith's scalp, like invisible fingers, making her instantly aware that this doctor was using seraph magic. Even an untrained, newly hatched Awakened knew this was the height of impropriety. These unwritten rules were all that stood between the Awakened and the possibility of clashes, yet here was this doctor blatantly doing so. Faith had very seldom felt so inconsequential.

"Yes, well," Masters said pushing his glasses back up his nose with a finger, "I cannot see why you bother with this particular patient. He is too deep into Possession for us to do anything about. If we didn't have him drugged appropriately who knows what mayhem he'd wreck."

Having once been the object of such assessment, Faith could feel her hackles rise. "So you won't be enrolling him in your program then, Doctor?"

"Certainly not. I required my subjects to be at least conscious, and a seraph locked into Possession tells me nothing." The thin smile he gave her was as clinical as the antiseptic they used to clean the floors.

"And what exactly do you find out from them?" Faith glanced up out of the corner of her eye, not wanting to see that smile again. Hoa uncurled angrily in her belly like a dragon roused. It was a reflection of the feeling that she'd experienced outside the Trocadero. Her seraph might not speak to her, but he managed to let her know exactly what he was thinking. He wanted to smash the chill doctor with lightning, or hammer him with the tornado. The cruel man did not know how close he came to destruction or how much it cost Faith to hold back her symbiote's fury.

Or, then again, maybe he did. Straightening, he fixed her with a sharp gaze. "I find out what they want, Agent Louden, and believe me, if you'd heard what I had, you would not be nearly so defensive."

"I have read your research," she replied evenly, "and you seem to think that the seraphim have some sort of agenda. I'd like to know how you've managed to reach that conclusion when no one else, no Awakened, has ever suggested anything similar."

Masters cleared his throat. "I wouldn't expect you to understand, Agent. The Awakened are often so influenced by their symbiote that they find it difficult to hear anything negative about them. I fear we have nothing more to say to each other." With that, the little man turned on his heel and left the room.

Faith was left staring at the door. She'd heard that Masters was cold and intensely combative over his research, but it was eye opening to see just how brazen he was in the face of a Ministry official. He must have some support within the government to have so much confidence in bluntly ignoring her.

By the time Doctor Hastings came in and told her the bad news, that Jack had slipped back from the reality of the world very quickly, she'd put Masters out of her mind.

Hastings touched her shoulder lightly, imagining he knew how she felt. Looking up into his rugged but kindly old face, Faith tried to find the words to explain it wasn't just guilt that brought her here month after month. It was far more primal than that.

Instead, she just nodded. "I understand. Could I have some time with him?"

"My apologies, Faith. I'm very sorry to have dragged you up here. He showed promise yesterday." His eyes drifted to the window. They might be on a first name basis, but they were not close enough to share real emotions.

Faith waited until he had excused himself before perching herself on the edge of Jack's bed. It was a familiar gesture she would have never have dared if his eyes had been open. She touched the smallest part of her fingertips to his temple. It was warm and reminded her of darkness and drawn breaths.

"Hoa," she whispered, "try again."

Her seraph wanted it as much as she did, so he reached out along the connection, diving deep into the dim waves of the hidden mind— the place where Jack Cunningham had sunk. Hoa opened Faith's mind, exposing every surface of her psyche to the cruel emptiness of the patient's. Words in such a place are worse than useless. Calling names into the void was a dangerous activity; no one could tell what might come. The power of naming was legendary, and certainly nothing that Faith with her agent training would have been stupid enough to do.

Instead, she sent out recalled sensation and memory—all that she had of their one short moment together. Recollection ran through her body as she broadcasted it into the space where Jack and Waingaio should have been.

Then she waited, open and listening for any reply. Wirimu had healed her in a similar way. He'd been at least kind enough to tell her that. But, because of the ill feeling that now lay between them over Lily, he would not offer her any more help than that. It did have its own dangers.

Something spoke to her in those shadows. *Remember the curse, child.*

And her mind darted back, along those dusty paths of memory to when a wide-eyed Awakened had expected her help, and she had turned her away.

You were a seraph child and you denied your own kind.

Faith struggled to get free of the hold it had on her. She'd been young and unwise, that was true, yet in those days she'd believed in things far more strongly than she did now. The world back then had been all black and white and centred around herself, so surely she couldn't be held accountable for what that naïve young woman had done.

It was this place. That prisoner had, like Faith, been imprisoned here. She had died behind these locked doors. Faith gagged on her own fear even though her body was distant.

Remember the Craven Man. Break him or there will be no rest for you.

Under her skin, the Geas, slumbering as it had been, was awakened. It rushed from the corners of Shorecliff to fill her. Wailing, Hoa broke the connection to that other place.

Faith came back to her senses with a howl, and there was no one to comfort her in the world. Jack still stared at the ceiling. She wanted his arms around her, but he was even more distant than before.

It seemed a cruel thing to be condemned for a choice a long ago version of herself had made, yet a curse was a curse. She hadn't believed in them even though magic surrounded her. But belief wasn't required. Thinking of all that had happened since that day, Faith now recognised the hand of it.

All those years in Shorecliff, Lily's affliction, and then the destruction of the one man she'd found herself attracted to. The one man that had seen deep down into her.

"The Craven Man," she whispered to herself. The title seemed ridiculous but it was the very same wording that Lily had told her of.

Lily. Faith's fingers twisted against the worsted wool of her skirt. If she was to track down this man, then her cousin would have been the sensible place to start. Yet she could not bring herself to do that—not when there could be other avenues of investigation.

Until she had satisfied the curse, Faith knew to be careful. Ill fortune on herself she could bear, but to be responsible for the condemnation of another was unacceptable.

Picking up her bag, she allowed herself one last kiss on Jack's cold cheek. She wouldn't return to Shorecliff for a visit—not with an active curse hanging around her neck like a millstone.

"Forgive me Jack, please." It was some comfort to think he wasn't capable enough to know she wouldn't be there next month. That was a blessing.

CHAPTER TWENTY-EIGHT

Lily had just finished darning the second hole in Maggie's tiny sock when the falling sun captured her attention. From the little house on the hill, she could see the churning seas of the Strait. The southerly wind rattled the ill fitted windows and she thought of her cousin, the Weather Witch that had somehow lost herself.

Tau reminded her that she wasn't the same. She had succeeded.

"Dreaming away," Wirimu whispered in her ear and touched her shoulder.

She turned her face to her husband with a smile. He was still as handsome as ever, perhaps more so with their daughter in his arms. Maggie, who at two years old was usually unhappy to be carried anywhere, giggled in her father's embrace.

Their daughter seemed to Lily to have nothing from her. She was Wirimu's image; deep brown eyes, and thick curling dark hair. Only her slightly paler skin colour hinted at the other blood running through her veins.

As one of the Second Children she had no seraph, but whatever minor gifts she had inherited from her parents would need no pain to Awaken, and for that Lily was very glad.

They made a tiny but happy family in the cosy house Wirimu had managed to buy when he left the Ministry. Lily still felt guilty about that. He'd soured every important relationship he'd ever had in the government in an effort to keep Lily out of the testing facilities.

In the end, the fact that they hadn't been able to figure out what had been wrong in the first place, had saved her from becoming a research subject. She, though, could never forgive Faith for her part in trying to get her examined. The strange haunted look she'd given

Lily wasn't easy to forget, as if she doubted that her cousin was restored. As if she imagined something else lurked behind her eyes.

Tau said it was simple jealousy of the power that Lily had been able to reclaim. The Weather Witch wanted it all. It was sad, but true. So, Wirimu and Maggie were her entire world.

Her husband had set up a small private investigation business of his own, dealing in the type of work that the Ministry didn't value enough to take on; wayward children, lost pets and such. It meant he couldn't really use his healing powers, but the chance to use his investigative training was what really mattered to him.

The pay could be sporadic, yet since there were growing numbers of unfortunates without any work at all, they knew they were lucky. Taking Maggie from Wirimu, Lily managed to get the repaired sock on her daughter's wriggling foot. Once that was done, she let the child loose onto the rather worn carpet.

Husband and wife watched her whirl off to the corner where a small collection of toys were kept. Tau felt the edges of the girl's curiosity, examining it like a something he didn't recognise. Lily twitched, hurriedly gathering up her wool and putting it away neatly in the leather bag where all her mending materials were kept.

It was good that Wirimu's magic was totally aimed at healing and his seraph not inquisitive. He didn't know how things were in her head. As far as he was concerned his wife had recovered completely after the baby farming incident.

She watched out of the corner of one eye as he went into the kitchen and laid out his case files on the narrow table. When he was settled, she went in and made them both a cup of tea. Wirimu wordlessly took the mug she offered and placed it down on the table, eyes scanning the report, mind wandering.

Lily frowned. It might not be the nicest table in Wellington, but it was all they had. She'd asked him time and time again not to put a damp cup on it. He always shrugged and said it didn't matter, but it did.

Tau reached in, meddling with that which disturbed his host. Wirimu's hand stretched out idly, and lifting the cup, put it atop his pile of files.

Lily bit her lip, managing not to let the squeak of horror out. She scampered back to the living room, clutching her own cup. *Don't do that.*

He wouldn't have listened. You were annoyed.

Tau hadn't stopped talking since they'd been reconnected. Lily had never told anyone that, least of all her husband. That was bad enough. Everyone knew that seraphim never talked. Never.

She could have borne that, but lately Tau was doing more than talking and his true power was revealed. Lily's seraph could make people do whatever pleased him.

The first time the grocer had popped two extra tins of beans into her bag it had been quite a scene. When she pointed it out he denied it, calming counting 'one, two' but incapable of seeing 'three, four.' She'd brushed it off as perhaps overwork, but the next day the butcher had doubled the amount of mince he gave her.

Now Lily found not only shopping terrifying, but any encounter outside the house. She'd avoided it as much as possible since Maggie's birth, yet now Tau was beginning to use compulsion on Wirimu. He, unlike Faith, didn't seem aware of it.

Lily couldn't decide if she was more afraid of him noticing or not. If he did, then she didn't really know what her husband would do. If it went on unremarked, then that would mean her seraph was capable of manipulating another Awakened without consequence.

We're capable of far more than that, darling.

With a shudder, Lily folded her arms. The terms of affection were frightening as well, though she had no one to talk to about that, either. If only she had enough bravery to discuss this with Faith.

She'd turn you in, send you to Shorecliff like that man.

Maggie squealed with delight in the corner. She'd managed to lever herself upright. Her mother jumped, jamming her fingertips into her mouth against her teeth.

Lost in confusion and feeling her pulse race, she wandered to the overstuffed chair to look out over the ocean. The stretch of sea between the North and South Islands was a wild and treacherous creature that had broken boats and wrecked lives. Yet, the danger it posed was far less than the unleashed power in her very core. Lily wondered if she had as much chance of controlling the Strait as she did Tau.

Such depressing thoughts were interrupted by a knock on the door, and glad of the interruption, she hastily went to answer it.

A woman was on the doorstep, immaculately dressed and smiling under a fashionable felt hat, but something about that grin unsettled Lily in ways she couldn't quite name.

"Mrs MacAlpine?" The woman's dark eyes told a different story than her lips. "We haven't met before, but I believe we share a common friend, your cousin Miss Faith Louden."

Lily glanced up the road. The tiny and sparsely housed street was quiet, though the wind was howling and the ocean smashing against the rocks. The little scrapings that humanity made barely dented the primeval nature of the wild coast, and yet the woman standing on her doorstep didn't seem to feel the ice in the air or the stinging spray that swirled around them.

Uncertain what this visitor could possibly want, Lily wished there was some mistake. "Yes, Faith is my cousin, but I hardly see…"

"We work together, you see." The woman, who had yet to reveal her own name, stepped closer.

Go away. Tau flicked a finger of his power out through the chill air, though Lily begged him not to.

The visitor's dark eyes narrowed, her perfectly arched brows furrowed with slight displeasure, but she did not go away. Somehow Tau's magic slid off her and she retained possession of the top step.

Lily's disquiet grew like a burning pit in her stomach, though she couldn't bring herself to challenge the woman. Her mouth had grown quite dry. "I see," was all she could manage through dry lips.

"Perhaps we could go inside?" The woman was now so close she could discern that her perfume was Lily of the Valley. It was a disturbing observation, as were her next words. "I'm sure your husband would like to hear what I have to say."

Only one hand on the door jamb was Lily's last defence.

Her visitor held out her hand. "I'm Emma Walton, Mrs MacAlpine, and I think you really would like to know what I know."

Her nearness broke through that remaining strength. "Certainly, come in." With a half-whisper half-sigh, Lily stood back and let the woman into her house. For once, Tau's behaviour and the worry it caused slipped from the front of her mind, and was instead replaced with the horrors of the creature that now stepped over her threshold.

CHAPTER TWENTY-NINE

Just as he'd been unable to say anything to Faith at his bedside, Jack was rendered incapable of defending himself when the men came through the door that night. Inside he was screaming, spitting and daring them to do their worst.

Unlike last time, they didn't even speak to him. Instead, they hauled him into a wheelchair. His head flopped forward, beyond his control, so he had very little view of where they were taking him. It was mostly a long strip of linoleum with the occasional puddle of light on it where they passed doors. As each approached, he imagined leaping up from the chair, smacking his captors in the jaw, and bolting through the entrance.

Unfortunately, this was only possible in his brain. Instead, they wheeled him into the elevator and shut it with a rattle that grated on his nerves.

"Down into heaven," the hulking brute to his left said with a chuckle before punching the button.

The elevator ground and shook as they descended rapidly. Jack had stared bleakly out of the windows at Shorecliff, he knew there were only two stories, but they were surely going down further than that. He had the sudden image of falling into the muddy pit, back in the darkness of the trench. Fear clutched him so that he wished for his own throat to give voice to it.

God, God not down into the earth!

They lurched to a stop and his heartless captors wheeled him out into another corridor, this one darkened with the only light far off into the distance. It was not as quiet down here as above in the decent part of the hospital.

Soft and persistent like rain on a tin roof, the rattle of women crying. As they wheeled him down this new, more disturbing corridor, Jack was able to strain his eyes to the side and dimly catch hold of sights he didn't want to see.

Rows of women caged like beasts, all young, no more than twenty. Some had their hands clenched in fists, restrained against walls. Jack could barely believe it, but the ugly truth was that many of them were pregnant.

"*Helfen Sie mir*," one cried out, the only one capable of more than sobs.

German. The words of the language he'd learned out of necessity in the trenches, and suddenly he started to put it all together. War had taught the world the true value of a New Zealand magician, and they were tricky things. Seraphim did not like to be away from their home for long, and what the symbiote wanted sooner or later, the host wanted too. So, there was only one solution if a country wanted their very own army of New Zealand magicians; breed them for themselves.

On the heels of that realisation came his part in this sordid affair. He was the New Blood, that of a powerful Awakened. He'd heard rumours that if one parent was such a creature while the other was new to the land, an even more powerful seraph could be born within the child.

Jack, for one, was not about to have fatherhood thrust upon him. They might be able to drug him into insensibility, but he was fairly sure being comatose might stymie any plans they had. If he could have smiled, he would have.

"Smarmy bastard, this one…" The burly captor was obviously more than he appeared.

The German was unlocking the end cell, a thick padded door with no way of seeing in. He glanced over his shoulder and smiled coldly. "This one is mine, I think."

"I'm sure it ain't."

"I am sure you will find I am correct."

Jack felt as though he had evaporated as the two argued over something he had no comprehension of.

Finally, in the face of the chill stare of the smaller man, the burly one backed down. "Fine," he muttered, shoving the wheelchair forward. "He's been lying in a bed for years. So, good luck with that."

The German pushed the door open and Jack could finally see inside. A woman, he'd been expecting that, but unlike the others. She was leaning back in the shadows, naked but not bound, while her long blonde hair curled under her breasts. The welcoming look she gave him suggested a conscript, not a prisoner.

She was young and beautiful, and so just the thing a soldier in the trenches would have fantasised about. Yet everything in Jack shrunk from her.

"You see, my friend," the German said leaning down and whispering to him conspiratorially, "your New Zealand magic means we can implant any number of suggestions into a broken mind."

Jack blinked. The world was coming into focus, a slight tightening of the background that signalled the drugs were ebbing away.

The smart thing to do would have been to stay quiet, but the woman was close now. Jack worked his mouth. "All...very nice... but nothing doing. Sorry boys," and glanced down.

The German snorted through his nose. Reaching into his pocket he pulled out a thin slice of greenstone. Pounamu, the Māori called it, and valued it above all things from the earth. The German, who couldn't possibly know the true spiritual meaning of the stone, turned it over in his fingers. "There are those," he said, shooting Jack a hard look, "who say that the seraphim come from the soil of this land. We tried several....uncomfortable experiments that proved that hypothesis wrong. However, it was not all in vain."

The greenstone glimmered with golden veins that hurt Jack's eyes. The light reminded him of that he'd seen in the eyes of the Possessed. The man, the light reflecting oddly off his face, snapped the thin stone, and while Jack watched horrified, swallowed the piece of stone no bigger than a fingernail.

Then, before he could marshal his slowly recovering strength, the two men shoved the remaining sliver into his own mouth. They pushed it so far back that he gagged, but couldn't stop them struggling to hold his jaw closed. For few minutes he managed not to swallow, but nature would not be denied. The piece of stone slid down his throat like a hot bullet. It dropped into his insides and his body came alive.

Unfortunately, it was not a good sensation.

A coldness rose back up the way the pounamu had come, solidifying in the core of his spine like something had been shoved up it—and just like that, control was gone. Jack found himself riding in the back of his own body. He could see out of his eyes, feel the cold air on his skin but he couldn't make them move.

The German man was staring at him with empty eyes. They were empty because, Jack realised, he was now no longer there. He was the one pulling the strings in Jack's body.

He struggled against it, but his seraph was buried, and he'd been lost in Shorecliff for too long. He had no weapons, nor any way of throwing the intruder out. Even the throat he would have howled out of was no longer his.

It was too cruel to watch from afar as the German moved Jack's body into the cell and pulled the naked woman against a body he'd stolen.

She tasted hot. Nerves and blood came to life, but Jack was trapped beyond a wall of glass. He could feel the sensations, but could not enjoy them as they were forced on him. It was a rape of the mind through a body no longer his.

CHAPTER THIRTY

Faith was standing in the rain. It was a pleasant sensation on her slightly tipped face. Hoa and she both knew that it could be changed if they wanted, but the price was too high merely for a rugby game. It was always a matter of evaluating the costs and the worth of them.

Certainly the players out on the drenched field would have appreciated a respite from the constant wet. The long, dark green pitch had been turned into a mud slide. The power of the men defied the elements. A slight wind from the south added to the difficulty of the day, yet the players' concentration was solely on the ball and their opposition. Faith envied them that clarity of focus.

She was one of the few women standing on the side lines. It was not considered completely proper for the fair sex to be there, so the only ones there were Awakened. Seraphim, much like the rest of New Zealand, had always shown an interest in rugby. As with everything symbiote related, they could not explain why, but Faith could guess.

It was power and communion. The mass of dark coated men, rain running off the brims of their hats, huddled close to the side lines urging their chosen team on; the weight and strength of such concentration in the air was heady and deeply male.

However, everything was tempered by the curse and there was only one person that she knew of that dealt in curses. Thanks to her work for the Ministry, Faith came into contact with all sorts of people; people that her parents would be horrified that she even knew existed.

Yet she did. Pulling her coat tighter around her, Faith slipped through the crowd as best she could. The men, smelling of wool and sweat, let her pass. The crowd milling around on the side lines eased once she got up into the stands. Under her feet, the wood creaked and whispered of years of hope and tears.

Most of the people up here were older; some were even scarred by war. The flicker of their thoughts was particularly hard to brush aside. Utter longing, so deep and sad, plunged through her. The young man tucked his one remaining leg out of her sight when their eyes locked. His desire to be out there on the pitch was so real that Faith could, for a moment at least, understand. She might have never played rugby, but she was no stranger to dreams dashed and promises unfulfilled.

If there was one person that might be able to set her on the right track, at least for today, it was Tom Moore. She'd run into him two years ago, having been the agent that cleared him from the facility and allowing him to return to as normal a life as he could manage.

Moore was a rarity among the Awakened—an old man. He'd been born to one of the first white women in Wellington, and despite his age he still had the red hair she'd given him. Its dimmed fire was easy to spot amongst the grey hats of the rest of the crowd. Tom didn't like hats.

He was also easy to find if there was a rugby match on. At all other times, he was pretty much a ghost in the town. His penchant for the game was what made him particularly useful to the Ministry, making him one of the few old timers that hadn't gone bush and disappeared into the wild country.

Having spotted the hair, Faith was able to quickly make her way up the incline of seats to reach her quarry. Tom's spare form was leaned at an acute angle towards the action below. Looking at him, it was impossible to believe he was in his eighties. Everything about his appearance would have suggested at least twenty years less than that, while his suppressed energy, evidenced in the barely contained jiggling on the seat, would have done a twenty year old proud. Despite the reason for her hunt, Faith smiled. Tom's joy in life always gave her hope; a sliver of optimism that said even an Awakened could make it, as he had.

He didn't acknowledge her, eyes firmly fixed on the action happening down on the field. Tom's bustling energy had already cleared a space on each side of him. Flicking her coat under her, she took the space to his right. Wellington was playing a strengthening side from Northland. The power and speed in evidence made her heart race and her fingers tingle.

"In trouble again, then?" Tom quickly shifted gears as the players trotted off the pitch for their water and slices of orange.

She didn't reply. They both knew that there was no other time the Ministry called on Tom. They were embarrassed about how one of their own had fallen so badly from grace, so only hunted Tom down when they needed his expertise. And there was only one thing that he was an expert on.

Leaning forward, he concentrated on the several inches around Faith's slightly hunched shoulders. He smelt of stale cigar smoke and beer. Growing up in a pub meant she didn't find it as repulsive as many would have.

After a moment's examination, he shot a glance up. "That's some Geas you have, Agent Louden. I didn't see it before, so I presume it's only now causing you a problem…" Retrieving his bottle of beer neatly tucked under the bench, he emptied the final dregs and waited for her to explain.

Certainly there was no way Faith was going to share her own foolishness with the old man. "I didn't believe in it, but after the fire it started to become more obvious."

Tom nodded, but as quick as a hare he'd changed tack on her. "How's that Lane fellow doing? Still managing to get in the way of those doing actual work?"

Tom had trained her captain, and for his good work Tom was rewarded when Lane arrested him. Faith didn't want to go down the path this particular conversation would open up.

"I need your help, Tom." A person more practiced at deception and manipulation would have put her hand on his knee, or plucked at his fatherly feelings for a young recruit. But Faith was smart enough to realise that such methods wouldn't work; Tom was too wilily and she was ill practiced. Truth, instead, would have to do.

"I can see that." He sat up straight in his seat, eager to see if the players would emerge from the changing rooms soon.

She couldn't blame him, not wanting to get involved. The Ministry had repaid his years of service very poorly. A reflective curse on a child killer; many would have thought that a small infringement. Unfortunately for Tom, the murderer had been the nephew of a very wealthy landholder in the South Island. The man had died after he attacked an eight-year-old boy. Shortly after that, an investigation had been launched. Tom had done two years in Shorecliff, lost his job, and his wife.

Yet he was still the foremost expert on curses that anyone had ever found. Even without his seraph, Tom was still a valuable resource.

With no warning, he lurched across and placed his hand across Faith's eyes, hard. She jerked backward, as his hand was feverishly hot, but then felt a wash of cool energy run through her body.

Then just as quickly, Tom pulled his palm back and wrapped it around his beer instead. He said nothing.

Faith rubbed her temples. "Will that help with the curse?"

He snorted. "Unlikely, but it might hold off some of the effects for a day or two." Tom took another swig and looked at her somewhat speculatively over the bottle as if expecting her to break into tears.

"Is it really that bad?"

Tom leaned forward. "Dear girl, it is quite the most deadly Geas I've seen. And consider…I lived through the gold rush. Imagine how many curses I have seen in my time…"

A dragging sensation of hopelessness descended over Faith.

The team ran back out onto the field so she had to sit through the remaining forty minutes of game. Wellington played hard and beat the contenders from the north comprehensively, but she couldn't find much enthusiasm for the win. Tom waited with her as the jubilant crowd filtered out past them, slapping each other on the back and getting ready to find a warm pub to begin the celebrations proper.

Faith turned back to the old man. "So what do you suggest I do—learn to live with this hanging over my head?"

"That sort of curse is not something you can live with, girl." Jiggling his leg up and down, Tom stared off into the distance. "Only really one way for sure of finding out how to rid yourself of it. Consult an expert."

Faith could feel her one shattered nerve about to give way entirely. "That's what I am doing," she snapped.

He reached over and placed one sharp index finger directly between her eyes. It was a gesture that was at the same time unnerving and relaxing. Her mouth shut with a snap. "Wrong," Tom whispered, "you need to talk to him. You need a dreamhunt."

A seraph might not be able to communicate directly, but there were ways that the Awakened had developed over the years. Emotion could not be accurately used to determine what seraph planned or thought. So the technique of dreamhunting had been formulated to allow the seraph to communicate in the real world. But relaxing the reins on the body enough for the symbiote to take over was not a technique that the Ministry favoured.

Faith shivered at both the possibilities and what Captain Lane would say. She sat back a little.

"Not the answer you wanted," Tom muttered. The words were almost dragged out of him. With the game over, his ability to talk was draining away, she watched as he retreated altogether. Through Hoa she could feel nothing but his hollowness. Loneliness deep and profound possessed him, all the worse for having known the completeness of the seraph. If he'd been whole, Hoa would have whispered comfort to his kin, but that was impossible, so they both had to watch as Tom shambled to his feet and away down the steep steps. He wouldn't come alive until the next game.

In an unfair world, the old agent's loss was terrible but not unique. So, through the rain, Faith found her own way back to the Ministry. The last thing she needed was Lane riding her case about tardiness.

As always, Hilary was there before her. They were working on yet another forced Awakening of a minor; Faith could tell that just by the set of her partner's shoulders. By the time Hilary looked up, their symbiotes had shared confidences; she knew about the dreamhunt. Sometimes being so close was useful—others it was just a little too much. Seraphim hardly seemed to know about keeping secrets. Once they became as close as Hoa and Tapiri had become over the years, there was virtually no stopping them.

Hilary already understood about the furore with Lily, so she didn't bother asking if things were really that bad that she couldn't just go directly to her cousin. Instead, she folded her hands and leaned towards Faith across her immaculate desk. "How are you going to explain this? A dreamhunt can take days."

As always, her partner went straight to the kernel of truth and left Faith feeling more than a little uncomfortable. She smiled uncertainly at Hilary.

"Oh no," her partner said waving her hands, "I can't possibly cover for you. We have a lot of work to do on this case."

Faith looked at the stack of depressing manila folders stacked in a tidy pile between them. "I know, I know. Believe me that I understand how important the work we do is." She leaned over and grabbed her partner's hand, it was chilled and rigid in her grasp. "However, with this Geas on my tail I will be worse than useless to the Ministry. Everything I touch will be in danger, including our cases."

A small frown lodged between Hilary's eyebrows, but she did not pull her hand away. Hoa and Tapiri murmured to each other, sharing truths that their hosts could only dream of.

"I do have some research to do." Hilary squeezed Faith's fingers, before grabbing up a fist full of folders. "I can keep myself occupied down in archives for a couple of days. Lane is unlikely to go down there."

"I'll take 'unlikely'." Faith grabbed her hat and made for the door.

"Be careful." Hilary's words made her stop in her tracks. Tapiri was consoling Hoa, communicating his own fears. Dreamhunting was not without its dangers.

Faith was deeply touched, knowing that her partner was putting herself in danger of losing her career merely by agreeing to such a hare-brained scheme, yet she was able to be concerned. Luckily, she hadn't completely shared the knowledge of the Craven Man. If Hilary suspected what she was dreamhunting, then she probably wouldn't let her go.

Faith knew that the Geas had been caused by her own naiveté. She was responsible for it, and for the bad blood between her and Lily. These things meant it was her place to fix it; face the Craven Man and make up for her own past.

CHAPTER THIRTY-ONE

Jean took Maggie into her arms and a smile broke over her face. All those years of marriage and Lily's cousin still had no child of her own. It was sad, yet it made her a reliable babysitter. Tau did not need to do any nudging to get her to take on the task.

The way Jean inhaled a little of the girl's hair while her smile wavered, said she was thinking sweet and bitter thoughts. Her eyes locked with Lily's and she recognised her elder cousin's demand not to be pitied. Lily knew a lot about being pitied.

"Just a couple of hours, Jean," she said softly, trying to keep her own emotions sealed out of sight. She would have turned away onto the street, but her cousin caught at her hand.

"Is everything alright, Lily?" Jean knew the answer to that question, so her asking it was meant to be a prelude to something more.

Lily paused and waited.

Jean's face, beautiful and faintly lined by her and the family's trials, was still open to the kindnesses and cruelties of the world. She took all the storms and remained unbeaten. Lily could never communicate to her how much she envied that quality. Because of it, she had far more patience with Jean than any other human.

"Have you spoken with Faith at all?" Jean asked, rocking Maggie on her hip.

Lily swallowed.

Traitor. Tau whispered angrily.

She clenched her fingers tight into fists, but managed to keep them behind her back. "Not for a long time."

"You have to forgive her sometime. She only wanted you to go to Shorecliff for a check-up—not to be locked up there."

"But I could have been," Lily replied as evenly as she could. Tau, though, was twisting in agitated circles, muttering to himself.

Jean lightly touched her shoulder. "It was just you were so…well, you must understand she just wanted to know how you…"

"Stopped being mad?" Lily couldn't stop herself her from snapping. "Funny how she wanted to hide me when I was all broken, yet when I get better she wanted to throw me in the asylum."

She could see that Jean didn't know how to respond. On one hand, she had real loyalty to her sister, but Lily also realised that she needed her little visits with Maggie. It was leverage. It was also disturbing to find she recognised that.

Go back inside. Tau pushed, and Jean's mind was so much easier to bend than Wirimu's. She smiled gently, her mouth forming a mindless goodbye, her hand already shutting the door as told. Lily heard Maggie's giggle through the frosted glass and resisted the urge to press her hand against it.

Turning on her heel, she walked back up the street. Unlike her own home, Jean favoured lots of close housing and neighbours that could see into her backyard. The mere thought made Lily shiver. So many minds so close, so many thoughts pressing on the back of her skull made her nervous. No telling if Tau might break loose and begin moving them around like chess pieces, either.

It was now very difficult to hold him back. This very morning Lily had that amply demonstrated to her. Wirimu was running late, flying about the house with his shirt half undone, looking for his papers. Lily tried to help him find them in the chaos, but Tau had other, more primal, ideas.

Tau didn't like sex purely for its own sake, though the seraph did seem to glory in the rough and tumble of skin-to-skin contact, but more for the opportunities for manipulation it presented.

When Wirimu lay sated and happy after a tumble with Lily, she had discovered to her horror that Tau was able to breach even his deepest barriers. The little nudges that her seraph gave to her husband were nothing compared to this rifling around in Wirimu's head. Everything was exposed to Tau and, consequently, to her as well.

She was frightened by what exactly her seraph could make him do once he got deep into his head. It had made their relationship as husband and wife. It was simply impossible for her to explain to her young, handsome and virile husband why she didn't want to make love. Months, it had been months, and not because she didn't ache to be naked with him. Fear kept her scooting out of his embrace, deflecting his attentions by using Maggie as an excuse.

Yet, neither could she bear to blame Tau. He still bore the scars of the Craven Man's attack. As a seraph, he'd been thrust into a world late. He simply didn't know, and Lily could only hope that he would eventually learn some restraint.

Lily sighed. It would have been nice to kiss Wirimu, run the palms of her hands against the smooth skin of his back, slip downwards into a pleasurable oblivion…

You should have. Tau's displeasure sizzled along her nerve endings.

Certainly there was no purpose in even trying to explain why she hadn't. The concept of right and wrong was one that was totally alien to her dear, fuddled seraphim.

At the end of the street, Lily turned right and headed up towards the tram stop. A slight wind skidded across the rooftops to ruffle her hair, brusque and chill. She paused.

That night in Newlands, in the burst of re-Awakening, Lily had sensed everything around her. Each of the Ministry's agents had flared in her awareness as two entities; the bright halo of a seraph around the dimmer, yet more substantial form of the human. Not Faith, though.

Faith burned fiercely and thoroughly in the ether, not as two, but as one. Such beautiful togetherness, such seamless joy Lily envied.

Fools. Tau did not share her admiration. He hated everything about her cousin. She could only imagine what dangerous thing her seraph might do were they to meet Faith now. Whatever disappointment she might have in her cousin, she used it as an excuse not to find what Tau's reaction might be.

A small collection of people were waiting for the next tram; an old lady wrapped in a faded and moth-eaten coat, and a young woman, barely a teenager, painfully thin with a whey-faced child at her side.

None were Awakened, and so did not merit Tau's attention. He was, however, surprised when Emma caught Lily's arm and turned her about. Perhaps it was a good thing that he was shaken, not to have sensed her.

"Are you ready now?" Emma said very conversationally, as if she hadn't just stepped out of thin air.

Lily looked about, but the Sleepers were busy looking up the street as if they couldn't hear or see either of the women. Impossible to judge if it was Tau's or Emma's unnamed seraph's doing.

The agent had convinced her that Faith was indeed once again plotting to have her committed, and she knew she had to find out more. When the tall woman held out her hand, Lily discovered she was loathe to take it. Some visceral part of her rebelled, entertaining thoughts of running back up the street, reclaiming Maggie and heading home. That, however, would not help her if Faith turned up with a straight jacket.

She can help. Tau hummed, sounding happier and more content than he had for months. So, Lily put her hand in Emma's naked one.

At first she didn't realise what the agent was doing. Lily watched in horror as Emma turned her given hand over and gently began to undo the delicate buttons on her glove. Then she stripped it off so their two hands rested skin to skin.

Magic. Real and powerful magic...finally. With a sigh of satisfaction, Tau relaxed as the other seraph, who did not give up his name, slid against him. To Lily it was a curious sensation; at first frightening and then satisfying.

Then she felt Emma's magic begin to assert itself; a totally terrifying pulling that seemed to be trying to stretch every fibre of her body. It was as if her arm was in a hole in the wall and something on the other side was trying to tug the rest of her through.

Horrified, Lily gave a little squeak of pain. Looking at Emma with tears in her eyes, she tugged backwards, both physically and magically. She was consumed by the desire to get herself free. Tau boomed in her head to stop, but a primal urge flooded her body and for once overrode his commands.

"Stop," Emma said clamping her other hand down on Lily's, pinning it. "If you want to learn," she continued raising one perfectly arched eyebrow, "if you want to avoid being locked up by your cousin, you will let me work."

Lily managed not to blurt out what she was thinking, but it made little difference. Emma smiled slowly, aware through their seraphim communion that the other woman was thinking how like Faith she appeared; all commanding power and calm assurance.

Suddenly the agent let go of Lily. The seraphim slipped apart a little more, and Tau wailed with frustration. Emma cocked her head, regarding her as if she were a stuffed exhibit in museum. "Naturally, it is up to you."

Lily didn't like her. The woman's cool exterior was enough to cement that, but it was the touch of her seraph that confirmed it. In all the years since her re-Awakening, no one had seemed to understand her real fear of being sent to Shorecliff. Faith had argued convincingly that, even though she'd had a terrible experience, things had changed there. Lily could never tell her the real reason for her fear was that they would discover Tau's unique abilities.

This woman, she too had magic that no one else understood—one brief touch of their seraphim had told Lily that. It was a dark, attractive fact.

A moment's hesitation, a deep breath, and she took Emma's hand. The world folded in, the tram stop shivered and disappeared into the light.

Keep calm, child. It was Tau, happy—giddy almost. *We are in the Void, traveling through the space between worlds. It is so beautiful, so bright.*

Lily didn't think that. It might be the last, but certainly not the first. The whiteness burned her eyes, and the cold was merciless as it cut into her bones. In the back of her head was the sound of Emma's laughter.

And then they were back in the real, kinder world. Wrenching her hand out of Emma's, Lily tried to rub warmth back into her frozen limbs. "What was that?"

The agent's eyes were wide, dark and, for a moment, as reflective as a cat's. She was quivering with barely held excitement. "The Void. The White. The Between Worlds. It has been called many things. I use it to travel from place to place, but even I can only dare a few heartbeats. Any longer there and our lungs would have frozen—it is not meant for humans to travel."

Yet she did not sound afraid. If anything, she sounded aroused.

217

Lily began to worry about the sanity of the person she had thrown her lot in with. The possibility of not getting back to her little girl began to grow in possibility. Considering her options, Lily looked about and was even more horrified by what she saw.

They were standing on a windblown ridge looking over the sea. Below, just between the waving fluffy flag heads of the toi toi grass, there was a driftwood scattered beach. The smell of salt was a shock to the senses after Wellington's urban scents. Even worse, the sprawling brick building hovering on the cliff top to her left, with a distinctive bell topped tower, could only be one thing. It screamed institution and her mind raced to make the connection.

"Shorecliff?" Lily spun on Emma, her hands clenching into fists while she prepared to run.

"You wanted to know," Emma replied. "You wanted proof of your cousin's intentions towards you."

Lily swallowed hard on her panic, urging it to submerge once more beneath need. From up here Shorecliff looked calm enough. It could have almost been a gentleman's country estate; some mad folly built on the edge of nowhere.

"She isn't here at the moment, you know." The other woman moved closer, so that Lily could feel her hand hovering just above her shoulder blade. "Once you see, you will know that Maggie has to be protected."

The instinctual panic swelled again, while recalled impressions of her daughter's smell and feel welled up inside her. Above all, Maggie had to be safe.

Trust her. Her seraph was just as worried, she could tell that. After all, they shared the body that had carried and nurtured the child. Tau, despite all his eccentricities, only wanted the best for her.

Lily straightened. "Then show me what you want and let me decide."

CHAPTER THIRTY-TWO

When a seraph Awakened in a person, the first instinctual act of the host was to reflexively make sure that they were still in control.

As Faith contemplated giving this over to Hoa, she tried to remember all the things her seraph had allowed her to do. He'd saved her in the dark cells of Shorecliff. He'd been a constant companion and friend to a lonely child on an isolated farm. And he had given her the greatest gift of all, allowing her to touch the power of Weather Witchery.

Holding tight to this understanding, Faith took the cable car up the hill to the Botanical Gardens. It was one of those mixed spring days, where the weather hadn't decided to be cruel or kind. It oscillated between beams of sunlight and patches of stinging rain. The gardens had been planned as mostly trees with sudden openings to clearings. She followed winding paths that ducked in and out of the trees, sure of where she was going and what she was looking for.

In a little clearing hidden up in the hills, away from the more popular areas like the rose gardens and the band rotunda, was an old kowhai tree.

This was her favourite place in Wellington—a solitary spot that few bothered with. Smoothing her skirt over her knees and getting as comfortable as possible, Faith tried to relax and let her mind open to nothing.

It was reassuring that her seraph did not immediately rush to take up her invitation. In fact, he seemed as hesitant to cross the divide as she was to open it. Faith whispered an invitation. *I trust you.*

He slipped across, shyly, and now Faith was reduced to a rider in her own body. She gave him her mouth but, Hoa couldn't seem to make any words come out. That frustrated him. It was the first time Faith had realised that lack of concrete communication annoyed him, too.

Faith did the best she could to soothe him as they got up. For a long time Hoa stood there, looking about, inhaling the crisp after rain scent, and finally touching the wrinkled bark of the kowhai tree. Second-hand sensation seemed to be different than the direct kind.

She whispered to him, and Hoa fished in her bag for the glasses she had packed for this moment. As their dark lenses slid over the now golden eyes, Faith relaxed in her place. Hoa was her friend, she had to trust him.

He walked Faith out of the gardens. Today the harbour had shaped itself to glass, reflecting the mountains to the east, some with a sprinkling of snow. Love of this land welled up in Hoa, so deep and profound that Faith couldn't, even with her own adoration, possibly match it.

So many theories of what seraphim were, and yet they remained unable, or unwilling, to communicate that. In that instant it didn't matter to Faith. She, feeling his love of this place, felt a corresponding love for him. Anything that loved so truly could not be evil.

In the city, among the bustle of the workers and shoppers, Hoa lapped up the energy. She felt him examining every face, every detail of dress. She warned him that it was not the quite the done thing, and he used the corner of her vision to satisfy his hunger for detail. Yet Hoa had purpose, for he was walking Faith quickly up Willis Street. And then, about a third of the way up, he stopped them and turned his attention across the road.

It was Wirimu. Faith blinked, but Hoa wouldn't let her turn tail and run. Willis Street was as busy as ever on a Monday morning; full of ranks of men pulling their wool coats against the early spring chill. Cars rattled past, honking irritably as the trams pushed their way through the throng. Like every other day, Wellingtonians darted across the street, ignoring shouts and imminent vehicular death. Still, between all this madness, Hoa craned her head and kept Wirimu MacAlpine in sight.

Her cousin's husband was seated by the window in the milk bar, reading a paper. From this angle he couldn't see her, while she could study him. Only three years had passed since she last saw his face, and she thought he was the most handsome man she'd ever seen. It was impossible to fault Lily her choice. Faith had long ago given over the feeling; it was one of the many attractions that she'd experienced but whose time had passed.

Wirimu was not as well dressed as he had been in his Ministerial days. The life of a private detective in this worsening economy couldn't be an easy one.

Because she was taking in his appearance so thoroughly, it took Faith a minute to realise that he wasn't merely reading. The cup of tea at his elbow had long ceased steaming, and his eyes, though directed in the general direction of his newspaper, were, in fact, fixed on the building up the street a little.

He was therefore on a stakeout of some sort; most likely following a straying husband or wife. Like most agents, Faith had a low opinion of private detectives. As far as she knew, once Wirimu had left the Ministry, most of his co-workers had given him a wide berth.

Hoa stopped her opposite the milk bar, and turned her towards a fashionable shop window. Inside were the latest dresses, influenced by American tastes; though the number of people who could afford much in the way of new outfits lately was dwindling. Her seraph was not focussing her eyes on dress, but on Wirimu's reflection. At this angle, opposite from where his attention was currently directed, even if he turned his head he would only see her back. With her red-brown hair tucked under a hat there was little to recognise. Hoa was more than strong enough to shield her from his seraph's attention.

Despite herself, Faith felt sorry for Wirimu. It mattered little that he had chosen to leave the Ministry. The truth was, he would probably have been pushed if he'd waited too long. The uproar over Lily's re-Awakening, or whatever it had been, had effectively ended his career. Faith was sure under most other circumstances he would have remained a Ministry man until his retirement.

If she was honest, Faith could admit that her resolute anger towards Lily had a something to do with this waste of potential.

She had nothing to be ashamed of—so why then this desire not to be noticed? Hoa felt as though he knew the answer but was not prepared to share. As Faith stood there pondering, Wirimu folded up his paper, knocked back the surely cold remains in his cup and moved quickly out of the milk bar. He was turning right, away from her, moving at a quick pace further up Willis Street, and away from the commercial heart of the city.

Hoa wouldn't allow her to relax though. Taking control of her legs, he sent her scuttling after him. Willis was one of the longest roads in Wellington, running from the fashionable end of Lambton Quay and heading toward the working class area of Te Aro. They passed the new Majestic Cinema just before the intersection with Manners Street, and for a minute Faith thought Wirimu spotted her when a workman, hanging precariously from scaffolding, took time out to whistle in her direction. She was sure the worker was probably very bored to bother with her, but Wirimu did look back. Hoa pushed her into a grocery shop alcove, where a frowning matron growled, "Well, excuse me, I'm sure!"

Her seraph didn't know enough of social niceties to be embarrassed. Instead, he made her chase after the ex-agent's retreating back in a most unseemly way. Faith was sure many of the good citizen types were eyeing her askance. It didn't get any better when Wirimu hurried into the YMCA near the middle of Willis Street.

Its young man's *association,* she reminded Hoa as sharply as she could, not sure if the seraphim understand social convention terribly well. With deceptive ease, he wove them a Geas. Illusion was not one of her seraph's great talents, and so Faith was rather surprised. Perhaps being closer to the surface of reality gave him added power. She considered what that might mean for Weather Witchery. Somewhere deep down, the old temptations rose up again.

They waited until Wirimu had entered the building before crossing over. Hoa did not take the staircase, instead guiding them around the side of the three-storey building. Here, he deftly flung out a Geas of ignore-me, before clambering atop a parked car and yanking down the fire escape ladder.

Faith was aghast. If someone discovered an agent doing this sort of thing and not on a case, there would be dire consequences. Hoa wasn't listening to her concerns. He hitched up her skirts, flicked off her shoes and got her to climb up as quietly as possible.

This was not what Faith had been expecting of her dreamhunt. The few that she had read about were deeply personal, spiritual experiences, so to find her naked feet on bare steel, and her skirt hitched above her knees was a bit of a shock. Hoa didn't care, though.

They crept up the full three stories, and then along past several windows. Now Hoa had her crouch down and slide up next to the very rearmost window. They dared a glance in. A man was sitting on one of the three beds in the small room. From this angle there was not much to see, but he was holding his head in his hands as he hunched over.

The door handle turned, and Hoa ducked back before Wirimu could enter the room. Her seraph was inordinately proud of the fact that his was not as good at these things as he was. Faith tried to tell him pride was a dangerous thing, but Hoa was too intent on the room to listen to her.

Extending his own magics, he enhanced Faith's senses to straining point. She could smell the tang of fear on the man waiting, and even hear his short rapid breathing as if he had been running.

"MacAlpine, don't you ever knock?" His voice was tight and shrill, so every word came out slightly punchy.

She could hear Wirimu moving about the room, but he didn't reply immediately. This only added to the other man's nervousness—but then that might well be the point. "You called me, Skint. Or don't you remember?"

"That was a mistake. I don't want any trouble."

A flurry of movement came from the room, the bed creaked alarmingly, and Faith judged that Wirimu probably had the guy by the collar. She'd never seen such quick anger from the ex-agent, but then she really had no idea what his life had been like outside the Ministry.

"You don't want to mess with me, Skint. I have two distraught parents who want to know where their son is, and you said you had information on him. Now talk!"

It sounded like he flung the other guy against the bed, because Faith heard it creak and then she caught a glimpse of Wirimu's back in the window. His clenched fists on the frame gave her plenty of hints about what was going on in his thoughts.

"You said they'd pay!" Skint's voice was now a strangled knot. Hoa could feel he was a Sleeper, so perhaps the mere suggestion of an Awakened's anger was enough to open his mouth. Faith had seen it many times in her work. Even if he knew Wirimu's magic was healing, he probably wouldn't believe that a seraph wouldn't hurt him. It seemed the ex-agent was playing that card for all that it was worth.

Still, he buttered up the proposition. "They will…five hundred when they have their son back."

"Is that all?" The sneer was obvious in Skint's voice. "Is that all their precious little boy is worth to them? Cheapskates get what they deserve."

Wirimu remained at the window. His years of training kept him relaxed in the face of defiance. Faith would have been the same in that position. She couldn't imagine being in his situation; without a partner or backup and teetering on the very edge of legality. She was just considering that when Hoa, in her body, darted forward.

The seraph moved much faster than she would have were she in control of those same muscles and reflexes. He heard and processed the sound of Skint yanking out a gun from his belt. Hoa recognised the sound of metal sliding over the top of his belt buckle, a noise so tiny she would never have been able to work out what it was.

The seraph threw her body across the creaky length of the fire escape, grabbed Wirimu around the waist, and pulled him forcibly out of the window. A bare second later Skint's shots flew over their head.

Both of them landed on the iron with a breath stealing thump.

"Faith!" Wirimu seemed more shocked to see her than the fact that he'd just been shot at.

Hoa, still incapable of speech, was moving however, because so was Skint. Hearing his rush to the window, Faith's seraph tugged Wirimu to his feet. They both scrambled down the stairs, leaping steps two at a time as Skint fired down at them. The bullets pinged and rattled off the fire escape. Faith knew Hoa would have liked to use some pithy phrases he'd heard from her lips, and was rather upset to miss the chance.

In a position to think calmly, since Hoa was taking care of her body better than she could, she wondered at the whole turn of events. This was even less like her imagined dreamhunt than before. They glanced up, and there was Skint, staring down at them.

Once again Hoa's knowledge and perception was far ahead of her own. In the eyes of their attacker he recognised something. It could not be. Her seraph didn't sense one of his own, yet he could see power building inside the thin man's frame. It was impossible.

And yet it was so. Hoa shot a warning across to Wirimu's seraph, but it was too late. Magic sparked across the distance, catching them just as they reached the bottom of the fire escape.

Faith had the briefest impression of a net of fire reaching out to them, and then they were caught by it. Even Hoa was surprised by that.

The magic wrapped around them all like amber, holding them suspended in the moment. The air was gradually sucked away from them, pulled out of their lungs and the bubble of space Skint had them in. Faith could feel her chest constricting, encased in lead. They were being killed by inches. Their body screamed out for oxygen—a primal demand for life. Wirimu was choking, caught in the same fight for survival as they were.

Hoa was horrified. The first-hand experience of being in the brain denied air, and a body flailing for it hit him harder because he'd never fully felt it.

Think! Faith called from the dimness as their vision began to waver. The distraction of the body could mean Hoa killed them both.

So he did the thing a seraphim did naturally; he reached for the magic that up until this moment, he had only been a conduit for. It came so easily that Faith could only feel envy.

Skint was coming down the fire escape slowly, smiling, confident that he was about to see the end of two Awakened. They would die like gaping fish denied water, and it was obvious that he would enjoy it.

Hoa called and the sky answered. Lightning sprang up to his command. Out of the corner of her eye, Faith observed as the clouds clashed together and then the electricity bloomed, glorious, bright and deadly. It struck Skint just as he leisurely reached the final flight of steps. For a dreadful moment he was outlined in the halo of white, and then he was thrown from the fire escape like a bundle of discarded clothes.

The world wavered. Faith felt as though everything was turned about, twisted and tumbled in grey. When she staggered free, it was to the realisation that Hoa had retreated to his usual place, ending the dreamhunt. She had no time to wonder at that, before she found Wirimu helping her up off the ground.

Once she was standing somewhat unsteadily, he went to where the smoking Skint lay. Playing the healer as was his nature, Wirimu bent to see if there was anything to be done. His silent seraph reached out, but there was only so much her magic could achieve. She could not bring back the dead.

Faith remained silent, her mouth dry, and full of a strange metallic tang. It was the only magical hangover effect. Hoa was so much better at handling the power, it seemed.

Wirimu turned slowly on his heel and looked at her with an expression that could have been disapproval or admiration. Hard to tell. The memory of their last, rather heated argument hung between them.

That was until he spoke. "Thank you for my life, Faith."

She gave a short nod, not quite sure if it was right to take credit for Hoa's swift actions. Also, she was unsure why exactly her seraph had bought her to this place on the dreamhunt. It was a good thing to save Wirimu's life, yet she couldn't see what this had to do with her Geas or the Craven Man.

Wirimu was gingerly picking through Skint's pockets. "I guess you heard the whole thing?"

Finally finding her voice, Faith went to his side, curious to see what he was looking for. "Yes." She didn't trust her newly reclaimed voice to say any more.

"And I don't suppose you want to tell me what you were accidentally doing outside that particular window just when I needed you?"

"Just passing," she said. "What exactly are you looking for?"

Wirimu had given up being cautious, instead he was turning out the pockets. Skint was not a pretty picture, and the smell of cooked flesh would have made an average member of the public gag. Being old hands at such scenes, neither of them did anything more than occasionally flinch.

He found a large bundle of cash, only slightly singed at the edges. He whistled, "Well, I sure didn't give him that."

"Could it have been you weren't the only one paying his way?" Faith said tartly. Snitches were notoriously unreliable and she'd had more than her share turn on her for a better offer.

The ex-agent shot her a half amused look. "The idea did cross my mind when he pulled out the gun." In his hand were a couple of crumpled pieces of paper. "Is this a train ticket?"

Just glad that he hadn't mentioned his wife, Faith took the fragile remains from him. "Looks like it."

Standing up, Wirimu claimed it back rather hastily. "I appreciate the bother of saving my life and all, Faith, but this is my investigation." He frowned at the remains of the paper. "It says Wellington to somewhere, but the destination is burnt right off."

"No need to have that." Faith put back on her gloves. "I can tell you. You see, I recognise the colour. That is a normal fare to Shorecliff."

They both looked at each other for a long minute. The unspoken history of that place filled in the silence, yet Faith came to the realisation that her dreamhunt had led here. Hoa knew more about that place than she had noticed—that much was obvious.

In these hard times, the amount of money in Skint's pocket was an even greater sum. With so many desperate people out of work, even Awakened could be bought. Seraphim had been known to do things to protect their host.

With a jolt, Faith remembered Hoa's shock. "But he's a Sleeper," she said touching Wirimu's shoulder, "so how did he..."

Wirimu frowned. "I have no idea. Another mystery among all those mysteries held by the Ministry, perhaps?"

Faith looked down at the burnt remains but she replied honestly. "We have many secrets indeed, but I am as surprised as you at this."

"Then perhaps we can find the answer at Shorecliff." He crumbled the ticket and let the remains fly away on her summoned breeze.

Outside of the Ministry he didn't need evidence, but Faith flinched none the less.

Faith tugged down her plain cloche hat. She could see the question in Wirimu's eyes, because even before he left she'd gotten a reputation for her visits there.

"I might know a bit about the place," she conceded.

"I could use the help. These parents tried the Ministry. Mysteriously their file got lost."

It wasn't the first time she'd heard of such things. The innocent part of her said it was simply because there were too many people going missing in these tough times; fathers running from responsibility, sons seeking work in distant parts of the country and all sort of other people who simply couldn't take the stress.

However, another part, the part Hoa lived in, had picked up a current at the Ministry; something Captain Lane personified.

"Alright. We will go together," Faith said, looking down one last time on the pathetic remains of their attacker, "and find what we can, but I'm going to call in backup on this one. Hilary is on the taskforce supervising Shorecliff. I'll tell her to meet us there."

Faith could only hope that she hadn't just finished off her own career.

CHAPTER THIRTY-THREE

To wake naked in a strange place, with a strange person, was not an unfamiliar situation for Jack to find himself in.

What was, though, were the bars on the window and the foul taste in his mouth. He examined it without opening his eyes, and realised it was a magical hangover. It was one of the minor consequences he'd experienced, but the worst part was that he hadn't been able to enjoy the use of power. He'd only been the conduit.

Glancing over at the woman in the corner of narrow bed, Jack could feel his anger begin to bubble through his system.

Her long, sleek back gave him a glorious and dreadful flashback, a memory from the brain of someone else. He'd been forced to act another man's fantasy, feel another man's desire.

As he lay there considering his options and trying not to bring back those memories, Jack's anger grew and grew. It'd been the same in the trenches; a hopeless rage, a burning hatred for this feeling and the people that had caused it.

It took an act of will to try and focus that anger in ways that would get him out of this place, rather than just uselessly smashing a wall or some other pointless act of violence. Violence did seem like a very good idea.

The real question, as he lay sweaty and simmering, was, where was Waingaio? Somehow his captors had managed to invade the space where his seraphim usually lived; so where was the original inhabitant?

Unable to answer that question, Jack turned his mind to his choices on how to get out of this madness. It might be some men's dream to be turned out to stud, but it wasn't his. Under the thin covering of the sheet, both his hands clenched to fists.

The woman next to him stirred, but he didn't open his eyes. In his occasional moments of clarity when he'd been upstairs, he'd tried to escape. All had been futile. So, his chances of getting out of here couldn't be much better than back then.

A slight murmur, then a yawn, and the woman was sliding out of bed. He heard her pad to the door, followed by a quiet conversation in German. The word that shot through him was one not that different to the English translation.

"*Ein Lobotomy würde dieses viel einfacher bilden.*" The guard was right, a lobotomy would make it easier—for them. Jack had heard in the bad old days people had found that it made a seraph far less likely to rise to the surface. He'd thought himself lucky not to be born in those times.

Those words spurred him to action. A logical person wouldn't have tried it, but Jack's anger had carried him long past that point.

Still, when he imagined leaping up off the bed and rushing the door, he hadn't really imagined the sluggish response of his body. He'd no way of knowing how long he'd been in this place, but from the drunken wobble his legs did instead of a determined dash, it must have been a while.

By the time he reached the prison door, the guard had yanked the woman onto the other side and locked it. They both laughed, which only served to bring Jack's rage to a boiling point. Leaving him to slump down onto the floor, they wandered up the corridor out of sight.

"Shit!" Jack punched the bars, but even that was a weak effort that only got him skinned knuckles. Looking down, he surveyed what this place had left him in the way of a body. God, it was thin and pale—the form of another man.

Jack had always known he was good looking; not movie star handsome, but well enough put together to draw a woman's stare, and he'd been used to it always doing what he needed. His body had got him through a War and years of dancing and playing music after. Now, through no fault of its own, it wasn't going to help him out of this situation.

Without being able to rely on his own muscle and sinew, he needed Waingaio, but whatever they had done to him had shoved his seraph so deep that he didn't know how to recall her.

Leaning his head back on the bars, Jack realised that wasn't quite true. Everyone knew there was one way to awake a seraph, one basic instinct that even they had to obey.

No. Surely it hadn't come to that. With a sigh, Jack looked across the corridor, and almost accidentally his eyes met the woman on the other side. Young again, but unlike his previous cellmate, obviously uncooperative. Her short mousy hair stuck out at odd angles where she'd rubbed it against the wall, for they'd chained her on a short leash to it. Her hands were bound together over a belly that was months gone with child.

"Do it..." She was a New Zealander, her voice said that, but it was cracked and emotionless.

For a second Jack wondered if her seraph was still active and she was reading his mind, but then she began to scream that phrase over and over, and her eyes were looking down the hall. No one came, and eventually the woman subsided into mournful sobs.

It was then he noticed the long thin tube and funnel hanging on the outside wall next to her cell. Jack was well enough experienced in the methods of torturers to recognise force feeding apparatus...

Jack's anger swept over him once more. These bastards were going to pay. Pushing himself up, he made it back to the bed, and hastily ripped the sheet into long strips. Twisting them into a narrow rope, he tied them to the bars of the door in a loop that ended in a noose.

He could only hope that the rumours of the lengths a seraph would go to save its host were correct. However, he had no other options. The woman across the hall was smiling at him enviously, tugging at her own bonds at the same time.

Jack put the loop around his head. It would have been easier to do this from a beam or some fixture, but the window bars were all he had. Memory told him they would do, as long as he could hold his nerve and go all the way and override his own body's desire for life. He recalled in boot camp a young man from Fielding had hung himself from the window fixture, bent down as if in prayer.

Yes, he'd rather die than stay here and be used. It wasn't the bravest thing perhaps, but he hoped…he really did hope that Waingaio would be forced up.

As he placed the noose around his neck and got ready, he thought of all the things he'd left unfinished. Too late now for false recantations, and he certainly wasn't about to deny all the foolish and wonderful things he'd done in his life.

Jack lunged forward and dropped to his knees. His self-constructed strap jerked tight around his throat, closing it with an audible snap. It was the last sensation from the outside he had, before everything concentrated on a lack of air. Reality was sucked into a vortex of grey while the sound reduced to his own strangled gasps. Everything in him screamed to get up, go back, get his feet under him—anything but keep leaning forward.

But rage, deep seated would not let him. We're going down, he thought as his body slid in mere minutes towards the end. *No, not we. I'm going down alone.*

That greatest of fears confronted, he felt himself passing away from awareness into a languid state where care and worry had no hold over him. Jack's body gave up the fight, and he wandered into the dark places alone.

Yet he was not. Since that moment in no man's land in France, he'd never truly been alone. His seraph, in that moment of death, rushed to him. Waingaio wrapped him in her warmth, leaping up from the dark places she'd been imprisoned. He felt her coming as a column of heat rising up his spine, flooding his muscles with euphoria. It was almost as if he could see her, a collared rainbow of light engulfing him. The body that he'd been long a stranger to suddenly sang with life and awareness. Waingaio swooped on him at the moment of death and brought him back. She was in him and he was glad.

Not needing his command, she blew the constructed noose apart. Jack caught himself on his hands as he was dropped free, laughing into the chill concrete like a madman. Only by losing Waingaio had he realised how much he needed her. So long gone, her presence filled in all the empty places every human has. Utter acceptance, devotion and trust; what more could any creature want from another?

For a good few minutes he lay still on the concrete, savouring the delicious sensation. The light tugging at his closed eyes seemed the most beautiful thing he'd ever witnessed. He hadn't truly understood the almost painful, wonderful awareness his seraphim made him see. He'd treated her badly, and if she were a human, he'd have probably gotten a slapped face and a turned back.

Waingaio had neither a front nor a back, but she could have retreated once he was free. Seraphim were as different as people, but his girl was kinder and better than he deserved.

Smugness, however, was still not beyond her. The shifting tides of her emotions ran over Jack; anger, sadness, horror, love and then more anger. It took him a moment to shuffle his way through all of those and realise that she was angry the second time, not with him, but with what had been done to him in her absence.

Magic would provide the vengeance. As Jack crawled to his feet he found the one flaw in his plan rage had helped him ignore. The price of using seraph to get out of this place would be immense. The truth of the matter was that he was in terrible physical condition, and the price for exerting magic could kill him. For a moment, Waingaio's indecision bled in with his own.

Jack used the bed to get back onto his feet. God damn it, he was so weak. He pushed himself upright by sheer will power. For once, Waingaio was stronger than he, and he didn't fight her urging him back to the bars of the door.

It was imperative someone come along. Jack, not faking weakness, leaned against the bars. "Water." His voice was so frail it took him a minute or so to realise it was even his own. Licking his lips, he managed a slightly stronger, "Please, water!"

Out of the corner of one eye he saw the door at the end of the corridor open and heard a muffled German explicative. The burly guard, the same one that had moved him last night, appeared. His collar was askew and Jack suddenly realised that the guard had been watching the show last night, as long as it had gone on. He probably hadn't had much sleep, either.

He was not in the mood to feel sorry for the bastard. Putting on entertainment for his pleasure had bought Jack to the edge of physical ruin.

The guard was carrying a basin of water, though he looked unhappy at being forced to be nursemaid. As he drew near, the woman in the opposite cell hissed at him like a cat, and strained against her bonds. That bought a smile to his lips, and Waingaio felt somewhat better about what was going to happen.

Jack reached out through the bars, as if to take the basin, but instead he grabbed the other man's hand. He didn't have a chance in hell of overcoming the guard; even if he was fully healthy, the man was twice his size and there was the small matter of the bars. Jack's seraph didn't have any such plan. All she needed was skin-to-skin contact.

Nowhere, not in a book or whispered in a dark corner, had Jack ever heard of a seraph doing what Waingaio did now. If anyone had an inkling that it was even possible, in the Ministry or out on the street, the Awakened would have hung them from the nearest tree.

Waingaio drew sustenance from the guard. As Jack stood by in shock, his seraph sucked the life from another human being to power their magic. He'd seen a lot of men die in France and Turkey, mostly in pain and screaming—that was almost preferable to the way the guard slowly faded, his life pouring out of him like water from a jug. He didn't even have time to make a sound. The ladle of water crashed to the floor just before he did.

The guy was a bastard, yet that didn't make it any more pleasant. It was always the way with revenge; anticipation better than the reality. It wouldn't do to look this particular gift horse in the mouth. The ramifications of it would have to wait until they were both safe. For now, Waingaio handed him all the stolen power they would need to get out of this place.

Strength had returned to his limbs, and his brain suddenly felt sharp and clear. He thrust his hand between the bars and searched the guard's pockets. Not finding a key anywhere, Jack instead place his finger against the lock. The magic came so easily; one muffled explosion and the lock was blown apart.

He'd never had so much control of it before. Waingaio soothed him, urging him to move before the guard came and they would have to kill again.

Jack shoved the door open, pushing the dead weight of the guard as hard as he could, to squeeze himself through. Once outside, he stripped off the man's pants and jacket with little compunction. He'd had to do far worse in the trenches than that, off bodies far less fresh.

Putting the official looking cap on his head, he dragged the corpse into his recently vacated cell, out of eye line.

Now there was the matter of the pregnant woman. The sensible thing to do would have been to leave her; she was at least eight months gone, as well as likely insane to boot, but the memory of young William dying on the wire in no man's land had never left him.

Another short explosion and then he was in her cell tugging at the leather straps that bound her. "What's your name?" he asked as gently as he could.

Her eyes were so wide and unblinking he hoped she hadn't gone into some sort attack, but after a minute, as her hands came free she whispered, "Evelyn."

He helped her up and supported her weight on one shoulder. The poor woman whimpered at the close proximity of a man, a creature that had caused her so much pain.

Jack wanted to swear, to lash out. Instead, he talked to her as calmly as possible. "Well, Evelyn, we're going to go for a walk, you and I. We're going to get out of this place and find some sun and maybe an ice cream cone." She was so young that it was the only thing he could think of to entice her. "Does that sound all right?"

Prisoners were never asked their opinion on anything, so it took a moment for his fellow inmate to nod her head.

"Good then," Jack said, sounding far more convinced than he actually felt. Together they made it to the door, but it was a struggle. "Do something, Waingaio."

She wasn't sulking as she once had, merely waiting for him to take control. Together they reached out to Evelyn's scared seraph, passing some of the power over to him.

Her face, once so distant, cleared a little as she felt her legs gain strength. Together, they got out of the cell and down the corridor. They passed more people, who shrank back from them as if they were unclean; after a while a prison could start to seem a safe place. Many of these prisoners were likely from the edge of society. In an economic slump such as the country was in, that meant a lot of people who could go missing easily.

Place that sort of strain on people and then imprison them in an asylum and their minds would bend in all sorts of strange ways. Jack and Evelyn would have to find somebody in authority to come back and clean this place out.

They reached the end of the corridor and the rattle bang elevator. There was no other way up. Jack helped Evelyn in, and she leaned in the corner, rubbing her belly as if it were a talisman.

After he pulled shut the double doors, Jack examined the buttons; only five. He had limited recollection of what floor he'd been bought down from the night before, and no idea how many stories there were in the facility. He didn't want to think about the possibility of them both of appearing in the middle of a secure wing or some such nightmare.

What Jack really wanted to do was appear in one of the service areas; a laundry or a kitchen. Waingaio was amused. Their shared senses were enough to help him out.

Through his enhanced smell he could actually make out the odour of burning porridge and frying bacon. It couldn't be more than one floor.

He pressed the button for that level with the conviction that he hoped Evelyn thought he had. They rattled up the shaft and it seemed to take an awfully long time and be incredibly noisy.

When they lurched to a halt, Jack slid back the doors and peered out. It was another featureless corridor. To his left, it made an abrupt turn and he could hear the crashing of pots and pans. It had to be the right, then. Keeping a hand behind Evelyn's swayed back, Jack guided her down that way, as he looked behind him somewhat nervously.

So far no one had spotted them, but there were several barred doors. Jack stopped at the first one and looked ahead; there were at least three more that he could see. He didn't know if he had enough magic in him to open them all. Waingaio assured him it would be alright, all he had to do was let go.

The old fears about his magic welled up again. Even in France he'd been unable to control them sufficiently. Jack had no desire to bring the whole facility down on their heads. Evelyn's hand, chilled and trembling, slipped into his. Within her he could hear the echoes of a battered seraph, and slightly further away, the murmur of a child stirring.

They would just have to trust Waingaio. Jack let go his fears and let his seraphim point the way. The power radiated, moved out of him, warm and delicious. Unlike his own self-conscious efforts, this felt as natural as breathing. The explosion did not fly off in all directions, or spiral out of his control. It pushed away from him down the corridor, lighting up the shadows. Jack, who had unconsciously closed his eyes and held his breath, opened them as the feeling of control awakened his curiosity. Either that or it was the sound; the faintest of hissing and crackling, like a distant fire.

The orb of light, flickering with blue incandescence, was moving slowly down the corridor, bobbing slightly and only about the size of a football. Reaching the first door, Jack flinched, ready for destruction to rain down, but when the globe hit the bars there was nothing but a flare of white light. When it had faded, the power had moved on, leaving a neatly shaped hole directly where the lock had been. It moved on silently to the next one.

Jack and Evelyn shared a shocked look. Slowly, a smile began to tug at his fellow escapee's mouth. They quickly pushed the unrestrained door open and followed the gleaming orb down the corridor, where it was making short work of the other two doors. Once that was done, it simply shrunk and disappeared with the slightest of pops.

This was, Jack realised, the formation his power had always been trying to take. All those mini explosions and uncontrollable movements of objects had been merely aborted attempts at this creation.

Whatever it was, Waingaio was feeling incredibly smug. Jack helped Evelyn to the end of the corridor, where they found a short flight of steps. Checking ahead, he was relieved to see through the quarter plane of glass in the door that beyond was some sort of yard. From this angle he could make out a white Rover van, the compact form of a red Austin Roadster convertible parked a little further away, and even further off by the gate, the stern lines of a Model T. The Roadster had to be one of the doctor's, he supposed.

Waingaio could sense no people in the immediate vicinity, but Jack knew that was no guarantee of anything. Some seraphim were very good at hiding their hosts from others of their kind. As far as the symbiotes reasoning went, their humans were more important than any loyalty to their own kind.

That had worked for Jack once, now he could have wished for a little more solidarity. He contemplated taking the van, but he imagined they must be a decent mileage away from civilisation, and the speed of an asylum van might not be enough in a pinch. The Tin Lizzie's could overheat without notice and could break a man's wrist with their crankshaft. So it would have to be the Roadster.

"Can you drive?" he asked Evelyn, concerned that he might have to pull more magic out of the proverbial bag to get them away.

She nodded.

"Right, then." The door wasn't locked, presumably people relied on all those bars to keep the prisoners locked in sections. No one was meant to get this far without restraints or an escort, he imagined.

It was hard going to make a dash for the Austin with a heavily pregnant woman. That was something that even the war hadn't taught Jack. He tried to hurry her, but the idea of delivering a baby in this sort of emergency situation wasn't a comforting one. He'd heard that stress could bring on labour and he didn't want to find out if that was true or not.

So, together they half waddled, half galloped towards the convertible. They had just about reached its dubious safety when their luck ran out. A shot rang out from above. Evelyn gave a strangled half scream as Jack pushed her towards the car and the bullets began to fly.

Up on the surrounding hillside, he could see three guards scrambling towards them, while a fourth shot down at them from the perimeter brick wall.

"She's pregnant!" he yelled to the man, but either he didn't hear or didn't care; whatever the reason, the shots kept coming. Evelyn climbed as quickly as she could into the two seater, but being a convertible there was absolutely no cover for her. Bullets made metallic thumps as they peppered the rear of the car, working their way towards the driver's side.

Jack saw immediately that she wouldn't make it without someone to cover her escape. "Get out of here," he bellowed, already trying to summon that cool control he'd had just minutes beforehand.

He caught a glimpse of Evelyn's pale, frightened face, frozen in spot, so he yelled again. "Go. Get help!"

Under her hand, the car bubbled to life, even though she had no key. Somewhere her seraph was shaking off the bonds and emerging into the light. She screamed, it almost sounded like delight. The Roadster skidded out of the yard with a patter of displaced gravel.

The guard fired again, but Jack held up his hand. Waingaio crowed with delight, and the power flowed through them both. The wall directly before the shooter exploded into a shower of brick dust and mortar. His shot went wild, but the others were coming down the hill quickly.

Jack dashed for the gate as Evelyn circled the yard, just realising that it was barred shut. This summoning was nearing the end of their stolen power, but it was truly spectacular. The circle of light was massive. Snapping into existence mere feet from the gate, Jack heard the guards swear loudly. It was definitely something worth swearing about. The iron gate burst apart with crackling blue electricity and left the sizzling remains buried in the earth on either side. The Roadster roared through the gap as the new guards also began to fire.

Jack was running now, very glad indeed of the strength in his legs. Escaping in the trail of the Roadster exhaust, he veered to the right towards a dark hill of ferns and low scrub. He was glad to see the convertible keep going down the dusty road, somehow managing to stick to it, but not slowing down.

The guards were calling out and following him, rather than the Roadster. Dimly, he could hear a lot of shouting and horses whinnying. The posse was on his trail and Waingaio's strength was starting to ebb. Feeling his breath catch in his throat, Jack began to scramble up the bank.

CHAPTER THIRTY-FOUR

The train from Wellington left on time, which was the first of many curious things to happen to Faith that day. She was very grateful, as it would have been even more uncomfortable sitting opposite Wirimu in a stationary car. The train swayed as the waiting staff came round with their tea trolley. Faith silently paid for one of the thick Temuka Railways cups and its tepid contents. Sipping at it at least meant that conversation between them was not called for.

Wirimu was looking at her with an intensity that hadn't really wavered since they left Wellington. Finally, after he obviously decided she was not going to break the silence, he spoke. "So, are you ever going to ask after Lily?"

Faith looked covertly up and down the car. The rest of the seats were nearly empty; only a grey-faced matron with children thin as twigs clutched near her shared it with them.

She really had no excuse. "How is my cousin?"

"We had a child…a girl called Maggie."

Faith smiled, remembering that was her aunt's middle name. "I'm glad."

"It would be nice," Wirimu said fixing her with an uncompromising look, "if you would ring her and let her know you were wrong. She hasn't gone mad or broken down."

Faith took a sip of her decidely insipid tea. "It's more complicated than that, Wirimu. I did contact her six months ago, but she wouldn't talk to me."

"She never said." He looked like he was genuinely taken aback.

"And do you wonder why that is?"

They stared at each other for a long time. He was first to break away, staring out the window. Hoa could feel his confusion, and it was not a new emotion. Whatever accusations he had levelled against Faith, they were made stronger by his own deep-seated, scarcely voiced fears.

"We were not," she said softly, "brought together by accident—I was on a dreamhunt, and that is why I was outside that window."

"A dreamhunt?" Wirimu's eyebrows shot up.

Faith opened her mouth to explain—but then both of them felt it. In the carriage the air was suddenly hot. It wasn't just the coal dust and steam from the engine, but something else. In the shadowy places in her brain, Hoa was screaming, howling that the curse was come.

Wirimu must have heard it too, because he growled, "Are you armed?"

She shook her head. The Ministry, like the rest of the enforcement agencies in New Zealand, did not carry weapons. In the case of Eyes, it was usually not required. Her cousin's husband, however, was not armed in any sense, conventional or otherwise.

Or, at least that was what Faith thought. When Wirimu bought out a long hunting knife from a strap against his calf, she was the surprised one. Then again, his magic was not the combative type. Watching him hold a weapon with ease, she was reminded that the Māori had been warriors of the finest order for generations. Hand to hand combat was still taught in the various tribes, and under normal circumstances she would have felt confident that he was more than enough protection.

However, the feeling of dread was palpable— so palpable in fact that the woman and children caught the edge of it, too. All were Sleepers, yet they looked up and towards the back of the train. Someone was drawing closer and one word sprang to Faith's mind: *Hunter*. Something was coming down towards them from the rear carriages.

She glanced out the window. They had passed over the Paekakariki hill and were now running on the track the slithered between hill and ocean. Outside, the white-capped waves were smashing out of the Tasman Ocean, while somewhere up on those hills her childhood home was still being worked by her mother and uncles. It seemed truly ironic that they would be in so much danger so close to home.

The train, having come down the hill, was moving swiftly, the pounding of the engine increasing in tempo like a mad drumbeat.

"They must have been watching Skint," Wirimu said getting to his feet, and twirling the knife between his fingertips.

Faith swallowed back the rising fear of dread as best she could. "Makes sense if they gave him that amount of money."

Together they made their way to the front of the carriage, swaying to the irregular beat of the train, imagining all the time their pursuer right behind them. They passed the wide-eyed woman and her children huddled in as far away from the aisle as they could.

Having reached the far end, they paused at the door.

"How much further to Shorecliff station?" Wirimu asked, bracing himself against the corridor and glancing backwards.

Faith ducked her head to look out the window. Outside they were nearing Paraparaumu station, the very one Uncle Roger usually picked her up from. "We'll be stopping for a while, but at least another hour once we set off again."

If they'd been working inside the Ministry, Faith would have suggested jumping off at the next stop. Her ID would have let them commandeer a car from the local police, but that wasn't an option.

"If we get off," Wirimu pointed out, "whoever is following will get to Shorecliff first, and I guarantee there won't be enough left of my client to hose into a bucket."

Hoa, searching the train behind, couldn't sense any other seraphim, which frightened him most of all. He itched to have Faith reach for the magic, but she reminded him that any incapacity at this point would be more than awkward.

Wirimu, while she was thinking, shoved open the door and balancing on the twisting walkway, held out his hand to her. With not much choice but to move on, Faith took it. They emerged gasping into the next carriage.

This one was first class, full of fur-coated women, and immaculately dressed men. Some shot needle glances over their shoulders—but if anything was amiss, the train guard would sort it out. These were the type of people who were far too well bred to ever be Awakened.

Which was fortunate, because if they sensed the thing that was working its way up the train towards them, there would have been pandemonium.

Faith was just about to comment on this very thing and lighten the mood, when there came a huge thump above on the roof of the carriage. They might not have seraphim, but their fellow passengers had ears. They looked up all together, and one woman clutched her hat and squealed as if she expected the roof to cave in.

Faith and Wirimu didn't have time to say anything, for suddenly their seraphim were howling. She'd never heard the like; a wailing gibbering that overloaded her senses with Hoa's panic. Their own thoughts were impossible to get past this wall of fear. Meanwhile, overhead, there came the distinct sound of claws on the roof. Impossible. There was nothing but birds in New Zealand. The country had no large predators that could possibly make such a noise. Yet, there it was.

Something primitive fired in the well-heeled inhabitants, and they suddenly became just a mob of terrified people.

"Quickly!" Wirimu grabbed Faith by the elbow and pushed her forward once more, against the flow of those fleeing back into the lower class carriages. Above, the claws screeched on the metallic roof as the train chugged around another corner.

The train raced into the final tunnel before Paraparaumu. Lights flickered overhead, casting the carriage into a weird altered state. Faith couldn't be sure that it wasn't something more than just electrical problems. They finally reached the front of the foremost carriage. Here they stood panting, heads tilted upward towards the strange grating sounds.

"Got any ideas?" Faith gasped, not because she was out of breath, but because keeping Hoa under control meant she was exhausted.

"How about a change in the weather?" Wirimu muttered.

Faith was used to this sort of attitude. Even in the Ministry everyone but Hilary expected her to be able to do the impossible at the drop of a hat. They'd heard the stories, but every time she reached for the power, it was a dice roll if she would lose herself to the madness.

Yet Hoa was urging her on, and something in the sheer volume of his demand told her that she might have to give into temptation.

"Not in here," she whispered to Hoa, afraid to fully voice her needs. Above, something was breathing, crouched low and only a few feet away.

"I don't know what the hell that is," Wirimu said, his dark eyes gleaming with fear and excitement, "but I intend to get home to see Lily and Maggie. Do what you need to make sure that happens."

Before she could answer, their purser did instead. With an unearthly groan the metal of the roof gave way to four large claws. Racing to the door, Faith threw it open and looked up—needing to know was now more important than denial.

Atop the roof of the train, a woman's face peered down at them; a young woman's face, perhaps only a teenager, but her eyes blazed with gold. Her two hands, clenched around the edge of the carriage, were stone grey and curved into impossible taloned claws.

Hoa was again screaming. This was the kind of sensation oil might have for water, or creation for destruction; it was that primal and base. Her seraph would have thrown himself upon the creature leering down at them if he had a body of his own to throw.

It was not seraph, though it oozed power and certain sameness. Everything in Faith's symbiote could not believe this creature above was there, though Hoa clearly recognised it. Wirimu, by the revolted look on his face was experiencing the very same thing. He voiced his seraph's rage in the fiery flow of a Māori war chant, the kind of incantation his ancestors would have given in the heat of battle.

The creature gave the most awful smile, as if something behind the eyes were pulling the strings and only had a vague idea how a smile should look. Faith saw that there was no child in that body, only an alien identity. This was unlike a seraph. It had not come as an ally or friend; it had come a possessor and thief. The girl was long dead.

This offended both Faith and Hoa. Opening up her arms, she prepared to call on her magic. The attacker above was swifter. It needed no time to find its power.

Something in the most infinitesimal gestures the creature gave triggered ancestral warrior instincts in Wirimu. He grabbed Faith and hauled her backwards as the inside of the carriage filled with flame.

The train squealed as they landed on the narrow walkway between the final car and the coal wagon. Faith managed to catch herself before rolling off, but her hat came loose and was lost into the dust.

Scrambling up, they could see over the pile of coal the pale and astonished face of the engineer. He was taking in the fire and the creature that he could obviously see. He disappeared back again. The train sped up and Wirimu and Faith were forced back into the ruined carriage by the swaying of the train.

"He's not going to risk stopping in Paraparaumu," Wirimu yelled over the screaming of the wheels. "He'll push on to Shorecliff where there is a police presence."

It made sense, and Faith was thankful for the quick thinking of government employees. Glancing behind her, Faith knew they couldn't be far from the tunnel.

"You go unhook the back carriages from this one," she instructed Wirimu. "I can't risk an all-out battle with so many civilians. I'll hold her off. Quick, there's a tunnel." Mid sentence she had already delved into her magic, Hoa leaping to aid her. The wind began to scream even louder than the train. It filled her with satisfaction and completeness just as always. When it was in her, she was more than just human; she was the living, breathing embodiment of nature's might.

Seeing the oncoming darkness and feeling the wind begin to batter at the sides of the train, Wirimu didn't ask any further questions. He dashed back along the now pitted and ruined first class carriage, just as the train plunged into the darkness of the tunnel.

Time slowed. It wasn't a trick of Faith's perception or magic; she sensed that immediately. The train was slowly shuddering, where as mere moments before it had been bucking like a wily rodeo horse. Only two remaining lights at the far end of the carriage gave any illumination, but it was enough.

Not even a small woman could have stood atop the roof of the train as it passed into the tunnel, so when the creature appeared in the window to one side of Faith, she was not surprised. The claws that had been twisted from the girl's once charming little hands were locked around the melding of the window without any apparent difficulty. The golden eyes peered in at Faith with burning fury, but she had the real impression it was not staring at her, so much as through her to the seraph within.

The moment, trapped in amber, passed. Faith heard an almighty clank as the back end of the train fell away. The engine, stoked to full capacity, leapt forward eagerly, but like the well-seasoned traveller she was, Faith managed to keep her feet.

While her attacker shot a glance back, distracted perhaps by losing its audience, she threw the wind at it. The glass exploded and the walls of the carriage bulged as the might of a Wellington southerly wind confined in a small space smashed at that which Hoa found hateful. It pummelled the creature with broken glass, and then, with the full force of a gale. The glaring gold eyes flared wide, but whatever dwelt inside was still beholden to the demands of the real world. The claws scrambled on the side, but couldn't hold forever.

The long dead girl's voice howled in anger, before the wind picked up the creature and smashed it against the last few feet of the tunnel.

Wirimu came racing up just as the creature was pulled from view and the train leapt out of the tunnel.

"You got her!" he shouted exuberantly, slapping Faith on the back.

She frowned, feeling behind them with her magic and sensing the worst. "Not even wounded, I am afraid. Hold on!"

The train rocked and squealed on its tracks, throwing them side-to-side like marbles shaken in a box. The carriage grew suddenly hot like a furnace and only Faith's healing winds stopped them being roasted where they stood.

"Shit!" Wirimu lost his footing as the train tilted to one side. It teetered, as if indecisive about if it should derail, before dropping back down with an ear-splitting crash. Faith, held slightly aloft by the wind, managed to stay on her feet, though loose bits of charred debris knocked her black and blue.

Helping Wirimu up again, they both flinched when the sound of something heavy smashed into the rear of the carriage.

"The train's for it," Wirimu yelled clasping her arm tightly, and his brown eyes locking on hers with all the intensity of a drowning man. It was always this way, even at the Ministry. Everyone looked to her to save them.

With a sigh so small it was lost in the confusion, Faith held out her other arm to him. He took it and their seraphim fused, sliding in so tightly there was no space between them. It wasn't quite as intimate as she had been with Jack or even Hilary, but still close enough to cause her embarrassment.

This close, he wouldn't be able to avoid reading her surface thoughts, and her thinking of him reading them brought all the ones she'd prefer hidden to the surface. Faith wasn't practiced enough at this skill to hide herself from him. Still, it was that or die.

The southerly blast grabbed them and pushed them up into the air, through the rent roof. It was not a gentle wind, but the easiest for her to summon in the prevailing weather conditions. She could read Wirimu's stunned look. Her magic had the same effect on everyone; at first delight, and then, as comprehension sunk in, fright.

Even as the wind battered them, their attacker raced up the remains of the carriage and leapt at them. Hoa howled a warning and Faith caught the movement out of the corner of her eye. So, she managed to bring the wind about to deflect the ball of flames and claws that came barrelling towards them.

She had to take one hand out of Wirimu's grasp to direct the power of the wind. Her attention, thus divided, struggled to hold them both aloft, half in, half out of the tattered carriage.

The possessed girl pressed down with the weight of flame against the strength of the wind. The fire flared and washed backwards and forwards in the currents of air. Faith felt it come searingly close to either side of her head.

It was hard to concentrate on Wirimu and defending them, but he wasn't stupid. He pried her remaining hand, the one with four fingers off his forearm, and dropped down to the floor with a grunt.

It made no difference to the creature; she was intent on Faith. Hoa opened some of his reserves into his host, flooding her with magic. It was not yet the same dangerous levels as had overcome them at the Trocadero, but it could quickly become that bad. Obviously, her golden-eyed attacker had no worries about going too far and losing herself to possession, but Faith was terrified.

They struggled back and forth. Faith managed to guide herself up onto the roof to stand at a level with the creature. The flame was now all around her. The heat and danger took up too much of her attention. Those mutated claws slashed at her face.

Ducking back a fraction too late, one caught her neatly above the collar. Even this glancing blow still ripped a jagged tear in her jacket and the top layers of her flesh. It stung and bled and made Hoa roar with outrage that his host had been hurt. Seraphim were such primal creatures that they didn't really understand such distractions could be more dangerous than remaining silent and vengeful.

Lightning began to build in the clouds above, but there were not naturally many about, and the extra summoning involved could open herself up, or plunge her into madness.

Before Faith could make up her mind, the possessed girl leapt once again on her augmented legs. The wind caught and whipped away her body, but her clawed hands managed to get past it. Faith caught hold of her wrists before the claws could land.

Now her attacker was within the sphere of the wind, snapping and screaming. She was incredibly strong. Faith's own muscles protested their weakness in comparison. Hoa offered more magic, but she would not take it. Not yet—not until it was the only option.

Together they tumbled in a ball of whipping wind and licking flame. Faith had no thought about where they would land, concentrating on keeping those claws from reaching her body. It was a terrible thing that they landed directly in the coal wagon.

Immediately, the fuel caught. Her attacker's eyes sparkled in the light as the creature behind them realised this was a significant advantage. Taking this break in concentration, Faith hurled the girl away from her.

The other tumbled away and would have gone over the edge if she hadn't caught herself with those damn claws again.

The wind shielded Faith from most of the fire, but she needed to raise herself above the bed of igniting coal. Her attacker stepped back, igniting her boots on the coal, yet her flesh did not catch. That terrible smile gathered in the corners of the attacker's mouth again.

Faith ran for the front edge, sure that the girl would catch her before the wind could lift her away. A gunshot rang out, sounding pitifully small against the moans of the train and the shrieks of the weather about them. Faith glanced back in time to see the possessed girl jerk. She hadn't expected that; too engrossed with destruction.

It gave Faith a moment to scrabble out of the coal truck and into the cab. The driver and his shoveler were pale beneath the grime that was the mark of their trade. The young boy had his shovel held at the ready as if a good whack over the head would make any difference.

Faith could see death in their future. Those Sleepers who got too close to the power of the seraphim never lasted long. The train was dying, spitting out gouts of steam and struggling forward like a huge stag bought to bay by hunters. The end was near.

"Jump," Faith yelled to them, "if you want to live, that is." One look at this virago of weather, her hair whipped backward and forth by the storm of her making, and they made their choice.

They leapt from their doomed engine, and Faith spared a finger of power to guide them safely to the ground. If anyone died today, it would not be innocent Sleepers. She'd just turned to Wirimu to get him to do the very same when the girl leaped down from the burning coal.

Faith saw nothing but flame. Her hair was singeing, sacrificed as Hoa fought to save her flesh. Strangely, as the animal part of Faith's brain screamed that they were burning, another calm part was able to direct the weather against their attacker. It was Hoa. Her seraph was aiding her directly rather than merely being the conduit.

Another curious fact she would have to deal with later.

For now there was only the thrashing train beneath, the fire all around, and the weather within; as close to chaos as a human brain could come.

She did not think. Her knowledge of engines was non-existent. It never crossed her mind that they were atop the boiler.

There was only the faintest rumbles—barely noticeable in the tumult, but Wirimu felt it and shouted a warning. All three of them looked at each other as something cracked below them deep in the boiler.

A moment, a split second, and the engine exploded upwards into a thousand splinters of iron.

CHAPTER THIRTY-FIVE

Lily was standing on the ridge, looking down at her feet. Emma, all smug and silent at her side, had the most beautiful red leather boots. It was an incongruous thing that she should feel envy at that particular moment.

It was all true. They'd heard the gun battle, the scream of a car barrelling down the hill, and seen the man running for his life into the bush. For a moment, Lily had been sure that she'd seen real distress on Emma's pale, cool face, but perhaps that had only been her imagination.

"This is the place your cousin wants to send you," the older woman had whispered, as if there were many about to hear her words. "Once you are locked up here, they will take your baby forever."

Tau tuned her senses down into the looming brick building, and she could see it was all true; there was nothing there but pain and misery. Lily could taste the minds of those enclosed there; some were indeed mad, turned on their head and lost in a seraphim daze, but she could see there were others, too. They were not there by choice, and terrible things were being done to them.

Her seraph turned her mind's eye away to protect her from those terrible thoughts, but she had a glimpse of rape and humiliation that would haunt her dreams forever.

"So now you have seen," Emma said, sweeping her arm out to encompass the whole sorry scene, beautiful and tragic. "What will you do about it?"

Barely had the words left her perfect mouth, when there came a terrific roar. The explosion rattled through the hills, and not far away in the foothills near the train tracks, there was the reflection of red light and a huge gush of smoke. In the aftermath of the ear-ringing noise, came gentler metallic sounds.

Lily tried to push her mind down the slope to see what was happening and if there were any poor unfortunates that needed help. All that she could sense was a confusing muddle of anger and pain. Emma pressed her hand to her forehead, and a look of profound shock came over her.

"There are...people in need of my assistance, but there are too many agents down there. Stay here just in case." Then just like that, she wavered and disappeared in the white.

Lily shuddered. Whatever was going on down there was surely terrible, yet Wirimu was the healer in the family, not her.

"What was that?" A man's voice, panting and strained behind Lily made her jump.

Tau was getting lax in letting her know when strangers were about. She supposed it was the strangeness of the situation. She immediately recognised on her own though, that this was the man she'd seen escaping from Shorecliff. Pale, his face was outlined in a series of sharp planes that would have made it handsome enough had he been fed. He was hanging onto the thin trunk of a young kowhai tree as if keeping a grip on it was all that kept him alive and upright. Perhaps it was.

In her head Tau flared angrily, flinging instructions at the man before she could stop him. *Go away!*

Yet he did not. Lily considered him more closely; there was something familiar about him, muddy and exhausted as he was. She took a step back, distracted by trying to dredge up recognition from her memory. The curious thing was, it was taking a while. She usually had an excellent memory for names and faces, but lately fog seemed to have descended on her brain.

Just as she was gathering her thoughts to frame an answer, another curious thing happened. A line of four black cars appeared over the hill. Lily didn't need to see inside to know who they were; she'd seen enough of those type of vehicles in her life.

"Agents," she whispered.

The man jerked as if shot, and staggered back a few steps into the bush. He eyed her warily.

"It's alright," Lily cried out. "The Ministry is no friend of mine. And I'm glad you've escaped from there."

His thin frame relaxed a little as he let out a little sigh. "So you are a fugitive like me, then?"

Barely were the words out of his mouth when the hills shook to a second explosion. This one was considerably closer. Lily and the stranger ran to the edge of the clearing where they could peer down among the swaying ferns to the asylum.

Shorecliff was burning. The distinctive tall brick tower in the middle had been knocked half off, as if some angry giant child had had enough, and flames were leaping out of the broken funnel and further along the structure. The whole place was on fire, and yet there was no one outside the building. Surely they couldn't all be dead already.

"The main entrance is blocked," the man yelled, "and the rest is bloody locked. Those poor sods have no way out."

It was utter insanity. Lily pressed her hands to her mouth and looked away. Had she somehow dropped back into madness without knowing it? The train, the cars, and now this. Maybe the whole thing was some fevered dream, and she was, in fact, down in Shorecliff right now. Or worse still, maybe she was still in the crawlspace under the opium den. She barely stifled a sob.

Broken and lost. Tau moaned, but offered no reassurance or denied her fears.

Below she could faintly hear the sound of cars pulling up and then, awfully, the sound of screaming.

The man was pulling on her arm. Dimly she realised he was talking to her with surprising firmness. "We've got to go down there and help!"

He doesn't know, Tau murmured. *He thinks we Sleep.*

Lily could only wish to be a Sleeper. The cries of the trapped and mad were beginning to filter past her own distress. She could feel their panic, taste the ash and smoke in their mouths. Her own lungs clenched in sympathy.

The man said something but it didn't make any sense in her scrambled brain. It had become impossible to tell her thoughts from those of the trapped patients below, as they ran backwards and forwards trying to find a way out. Many were locked in their cells with nowhere to go.

A few more tugs on her arm registered. He was gone, back down the hill to do what he could. Lily, trapped in the terrible deaths of others that Tau did not shield her from, could only curl up in a ball. Shoving her hands uselessly into her ears, she let her voice join those that burned. Her screams were lost in the hills.

CHAPTER THIRTY-SIX

Jack left the useless woman and ran back down the hill. She might well be an escapee just as he was, but a little more disserving of incarceration, perhaps.

It didn't matter now. He had to get down there and help those patients and nurses. All of his concern to get away was now lost. He was one of the few on the outside that could help.

As he ran, saplings and ferns slapped against his body, while Waingaio's fear reached him. Jack understood completely. Not much of their stolen magic remained. The amount needed to keep himself going at this speed was dangerously close to the limit, and if he drew any more he might just collapse.

Yet he was alive, which was more than those damned creatures in the asylum would be in very short order. Their screams, even filtered by the trees were powerful, and like everything terrible he'd encountered in life, it reminded him of the war. Every inhumanity had been there. He'd seen boys caught out in the open by flamethrowers. Their sergeant, as unmanned by their screams as the rest of the unit, had ordered several shot.

Being burned was not a primitive fear for nothing.

Breaking out into the low scrub he'd just spent good energy running through in the opposite direction only minutes before, Jack saw those cars again. Agents all right, but there wasn't much he could do about avoiding being seen.

At this moment they looked fairly occupied. A slim woman, dressed in man's pants, was using her government issue baton to smash windows on the ground floor. It wasn't much use, because everyone was barred. Hands from the inside reached out helplessly like the damned reaching out from hell.

Seeing that she was doing the most good, Jack ran up to her side. She looked askance at him once, but said nothing about his pyjamas or rail-thin state.

Instead, she turned to the other agents and called, "Rose, Wainui, Elder, give some support to Jenkins."

The three men huddled and Jack could feel them sharing magic between them. It was the way of lesser gifted people to mesh their powers in situations like this. Abruptly, the nearby trees and shrubs began to shift and grow, their long arms and vines struggling upward towards the bars.

Jack watched as the greenery began to tear at the bars, but the heat was shrivelling it. The woman at his side held out her hands, and the temperature began to drop. Her somewhat stern face began to twist in pain, and he knew the price that was obviously her payment to bear.

Waingaio would not give him anything. She was worried about him, cautious of the littler power they had to spare. Jack was furious and frustrated. To see others using their seraph gifts made him itch to show what he could do.

A freezing southerly blast straight off the sea made their small group stand back. It was strong enough to bend the hungry flames leaping above the brick building. Somewhere down deep, Waingaio crowed with delight, revelling in something that Jack had yet to grasp.

He looked up into one of the strangest sights any human, Sleeper or Awakened, could see. The weirdest thing was that it was familiar. A tug of déjà vu shot right through him.

It was the Weather Witch. Not the same one he'd seen outside the Trocadero. He could see she'd suffered, grown and become more than he could ever hope to be. The joining of seraph and human had never been so beautiful, and that was why his symbiote was so delighted, and why all of the Awakened below were looking on in awe.

She was in the middle of the maelstrom. Her hair was cut shorter in the style of the time, and somehow he missed the whirling mass of it. He hadn't forgotten the witch, and as she looked down at him, Jack realised that she hadn't forgotten him either.

Jack's memory, shattered and fractured, shot him back to the darkness and closeness of them under the ground. His body, just as broken as his mind, leaped to life like the weather had filled him. Somehow, he was right back there, next to her in the shadows.

Was that the ghost of a smile on her lips? It took Jack a long time to notice that she was holding up another man; a handsome Māori who had his arm over the witch's shoulder as if he were injured or exhausted.

Hell, it was almost amusing how quickly jealousy flared, even while they were in the middle of chaos. Feelings could be born and die in one breath. Everything immediately after their clinch in the darkness was fuzzy, but the intensity of his desire for her was just as crisp and real as then. He had no idea how long ago that had been.

The surge of flame behind them bought Jack back to reality. The Chinese agent screamed, "Faith!" and her voice reflected such relief that the Weather Witch might have been Jesus himself come to save them all.

The wind died away, and she and the man she was supporting touched the ground. As if the earth suddenly drained her, Faith staggered. Jack saw finally that she was no avenging angel or goddess from history. Her clothes were charred, she only had one shoe, and her mouth was held in an exhausted line.

The man at her side was nearly as badly off, but he had clenched in one hand a long knife. His face was grim. They both stared up at the towering flames that had roared back to life with the end of the wind.

Faith seemed to droop, and the other woman ran to her. Waingaio could sense that she was lending her some magic. In only a moment the new arrival had waved her friend away. Her eyes never left Jack.

Quickly, the agents returned to what they were doing, the other man joining in their efforts. The trees ripped the bars free.

Jack and the others helped the five staff members out of the smashed window. Two young orderlies and three nurses staggered out of the smoke, eyes pouring and desperate with panic. Jack, out of the corner of his vision, saw Faith talking with the Māori man. They appeared to be arguing about something and pointing back down the hill.

"We may need your help." The Chinese agent introduced herself as Hilary Chen. She wanted to know if he would assist. "My partner, Faith has power as you can see, but we need more."

Waingaio keened in despair that she had nothing left to offer. He shook his head, ashamed that he couldn't give anything. Would Faith forgive him that?

"I'll do what I can, but..."

She eyed him, one Awakened sizing up another, seeing how low his reserves really were.

With a curt nod, she turned away. Just like that, he was dismissed, as much use as a Sleeper. The connection between him and Faith was still there however, as taunt as a guitar string, but neither of them moved at all.

Above, something exploded, and now they could hear screaming. Faith raised her hands, reaching up into the clouds with fingers outspread and eyes closed. Around her the others formed a loose circle, heads bowed, pointed towards her like a congregation around a preacher.

God, he wanted to be in there, helping and feeling just a taste of their previous connection. Waingaio wanted it very badly too, but would not allow him to offer more than was safe for him.

They were engrossed. They couldn't see, but Jack could. The horizon was lit up like it was boiling with fire. The sun wasn't setting, yet from below he could see fire on the water. And it was moving up towards them, even as Faith called down the rain to save those inside.

Jack saw it move; a globe of flame that seemed to have been spat out by the hills. Faith's upturned face was cast in a curious light by it, but she did not follow after it. He imagined that the magic she was using to summon the rain was considerable—more than he could ever dream of controlling.

So, she had no concentration to spare. Only he stood outside the circle of those giving power, and only he saw the circle of fire smash down into the western wing of the asylum. Up until now, only the tower had been touched, but now the rest of the building burst to life as if it had only been waiting for the chance.

If only he could have a little magic, because those people needed some. Waingaio would not budge. She would release nothing.

Picking up one of the broken bars, Jack ran off toward the back of the building. What he couldn't do with magic, he would be able to manage with sheer brute force.

CHAPTER THIRTY-SEVEN

Up on the hill, Lily had crept down to the tree line. The sight of the building on fire conjured up nightmares she'd had since she'd re-Awakened. Pressing herself against the rough bark of the tree ferns, she considered running into the safety of the bush.

It was as Emma said; foul things were being done there.

Get away. Get away now before they find you.

She had half turned, ready to do as Tau urged her, when one of the figures down there with the agents caught her attention. It was her husband.

For a moment she couldn't believe what her eyes were seeing.

It's a lie, a trick.

She couldn't quite grasp what her husband was doing down there. He'd always said that he'd never go back to the Ministry, and yet there he was talking with the dark suited people.

Look who else is down there. Tau hissed to her, focusing her eyes on the other figure she should have recognised immediately.

It was hard to miss Faith in a crowd, especially when she was hatless. Her coppery-brown hair was sticking out at all angles, and she was gesturing wildly towards the burning asylum.

This is the place she wanted to send you. If she'd had her way you'd be down there, burning with everyone else.

Lily was torn; she wanted to join her husband, yet she was still cautious of her cousin.

Get out of here.

She'd never experienced Tau trying to influence her as he often did with others, so when she found her feet turning away from the asylum, it took her a moment or two to realise that was what he was doing.

With a lurch she stopped. "Tau!"

I am just trying to protect you, he whined in her ear.

"That may be so, but I choose what I do," she said, actually stomping her foot like she was a child again.

Lily turned around and walked determinedly down the hill towards the group. Magic was running over her skin and she could see the Eyes manipulating it to rip apart the front of the building. As she ran down the hill, a group of people, their tidy white coats covered in soot, emerged coughing from the rubble.

"Wirimu!" Lily couldn't help calling out to her husband.

He turned and her heart sank. His clothes, the ones she'd sent him out the door in that very morning, were in tatters, and blood was oozing from many tiny wounds in his chest.

"Lily?" He shot a glance over his shoulder to Faith. "What are you doing here?"

Luckily, she was saved from having to provide some sort of explanation because at that point the eastern wing, which until now had remained untouched by fire, erupted in heat and light. Flames could be seen leaping like angry sprites along the edge of the roofline.

"Get back!" the Chinese female Eye screamed. A wall was crumbling, and the agents scattered as best they could out of the way. The front façade of the asylum, wood on the ground floor with the next faced with brick, gave up to the flames with an almost human scream. Lily ducked at the roar of the flames and the explosion of glass as the windows blew out.

Everyone was running, yelling, and there she was, standing looking up at the scarlet chaos above her with an almost blinding fascination.

"Lily!" a woman's voice snapped her out of her reverie for an instant. It was Faith.

The world was certainly a curious place. Standing in the shadow of the asylum her cousin had once wanted her sent to, Lily now found herself being thrown to safety. Faith's magic was all around them, as powerful and heady as that time in Newlands when she'd dived into the midst of it.

They lay there staring at each other, seraphim jostling between them like ill-suited children. Faith was as battered as Wirimu; her hair singed, her clothing torn, but there was an incredible brightness in her eyes. Lily guessed that her cousin would say she was horrified by this whole situation, but deep down some darker part of her thrilled to it.

The moment of communion passed quickly when Wirimu gathered Lily up. He was hugging her, calling her name and wiping her face. Faith climbed to her feet. Then all three of them looked up in horror.

Something was pulling itself out of the rubble; a woman surrounded by an aura of flame. It was hard to see any features in amongst the fire, because what there was seemed blackened and tortured.

As if on cue, the screams in the still standing east wing increased in volume. Lily felt her whole body revolt at the sound of so many hands banging on locked doors and the smell of cooking flesh.

"What...what is that creature?" Lily asked her husband while clutching onto his arm, but it was her cousin that answered.

"An abomination," Faith screamed over the howl of the fire, waves of the truth of that washed over Lily. Tau could feel that Faith's seraph was twisted with hatred.

The fire woman on the roof raised her hands and the flames obeyed, wrapping themselves about the remaining windows where could be seen the shapes of the trapped inmates.

"We've got to do something." Wirimu muttered to himself as he clutched Lily tight, as if he expected her to rush into the flames.

She wouldn't have done any such thing, but she wanted to help. She knew her husband and his seraph were not strong enough to offer anything, and the other Eyes behind her, she could feel, were tapped out as well. The amount of energy that they used to free those in the east wing had left them as nothing more than hapless bystanders to the unfolding tragedy.

The only person Lily could feel that had enough power was Faith. Tau rebelled at what she was thinking, demanding she not do it.

Fool. Idiot. Cat's paw.

Yet if Lily listened to the seraph, she'd spend such a long time hoping, for all those people could be dead very soon. She couldn't allow that to happen under any circumstances.

So Lily held out her hand to Faith and looked up to where the woman of flame was staring down with such hatred. When her cousin did not immediately take what was offered, she instead looked at her.

"This is silly, Faith," she whispered so that only the two of them could hear. "We are the only two who can do anything about this. Isn't other peoples' welfare more important than our quarrel?"

Her cousin, tired and covered in soot, smiled hesitantly. "Absolutely, it is."

"Then waste no time. There's been enough death today and we can make a difference."

So with Tau howling his protest, Lily opened the gates to her magic and let Faith inside her barriers. Together, there was no telling what power they could unleash.

CHAPTER THIRTY-EIGHT

Jack heard the windows in the top storey explode like they'd been shot out. Shielding his head with his arms, he kept running, moving around the side of the asylum towards the rear which he'd so recently escaped from.

The flames had yet to take real hold here, so Jack was able to kick open the door. Ripping off the remains of his stolen shirt, he wrapped it around his nose and mouth and stumbled in. The kitchens and utility areas were deserted. Through the smoke he could see food half chopped on the blocks, and pots still boiling on the stoves.

Down the corridor a bit, he heard screaming. Following it to the source, he found an area locked off by a prison barred door. It made sense that the workers had been too interested in saving their own skins, and had little thought for those behind locked doors.

A crowd of about ten inmates were pressed to the door, eyes wide with fear, their hands shoved between the bars. It looked as though some of them had actually broken their restraints, as several had the remains of straitjackets dangling from their arm. The human body could do remarkable things when in danger.

"Get back," Jack yelled, even as the smoke choked his throat.

Waingaio offered up the little magic to Jack, and he used it to blow the door off. It was a tiny explosion, more a displacement of air than anything else, yet it still smashed open the lock. The door fell to the floor with a harsh screech that made one of the woman howl.

They were so frightened that it had barely finished vibrating on the floor before they were leaping over it towards fresh air. Jack didn't blame them; it was a primitive urge for survival, unfortunately one that he'd somehow managed to overcome.

Waingaio was unhappy as he let them go around him, and very angry when he strode into the room they had just fled. Something lay ahead; seraph and host could feel it. A presence in the flames that drew them like a magnet draws iron. His symbiote wanted to deny that attraction and flee the building, but Jack wouldn't let her choose the easy path. Besides, there were still more in the building. One locked door was not the sum and total of the asylum.

The air was thicker now, choking with smoke. So he ran on, bent over, to get what little good oxygen remained. Ahead he could hear more people, but they weren't screaming; more whispered pleadings.

They were more Awakened, Waingaio felt their presence drowning, dwindling in the smoke. The seraphim were crying too, not for themselves, but for their hosts.

It was suddenly apparent to Jack, right there in the middle of all the chaos, that the symbiotes loved their hosts. He'd never really thought about it before, always assuming that Waingaio was only hanging onto him to see through his eyes. Those seraphim up ahead were dying, yet they were giving what little they had to save their hosts—even if it meant their own destruction. They were fading in order that the humans might live. They loved their hosts more than their own lives.

Jack's eyes filled with tears, and it wasn't all because of the smoke. He could hardly see, but he could feel the flutter of a dozen lives only feet away. The heat here was worse, beating down from above. It couldn't be long until the roof caved in.

Unfortunately, Waingaio had nothing more to offer of herself. Crouching down next to the bars, Jack spluttered what he hoped were calming words to his frightened seraph.

The closest Awakened, a young woman whose hair had been shaved off, stared at him through bleak eyes as her face was pressed to the floor, sucking up the last few gulps of good air. Deep within her, a seraph was slowly dying. Jack could see that, and for the first time in his life he felt sorry for a symbiote.

It was that very creature which he once so disliked that moved the girl's hand. It was soft, and an easy conduit for the seraph to send its last magic to Waingaio, and then the light within the girl was hers alone. A tear coursed down her face, and the expression that came with it was one of the most grief-stricken Jack had ever seen.

"He's gone," she whispered mournfully as if part of her had been cut loose. Jack's fingers tightened on hers, but he knew he had no comfort to offer. What her seraph had given him, he couldn't waste.

The door burst off its hinges easily, and he pointed to the large group where the exit was. Those at the back were lost in the smoke and had been exposed the most. He offered one man, whose face was terribly scarred from some ancient accident, a shoulder out.

It was then that he saw Emma. For a second, the rest of the world became insignificant of his notice. She was just as she remembered, apart from the white hospital gown. And she was standing there staring at him with just as much surprise. Hesitantly, she came over and took the man's other arm over her own slender form. They glanced across at each other almost shyly.

Getting this last lot of people out seemed like a good opportunity for him to gather his thoughts. As he stood coughing with all the rest in the courtyard, he kept his eye on her.

Finally he held out his arms to her, "My God, Emma."

She sobbed and threw herself into his arms. That was when he knew this was finally real. Somehow, he had his wife back. In flames and smoke, his most cherished dream had come true. All other thoughts fled before that one fact. It didn't really matter what happened after that. That woman on the farm had not been his wife. This was her, real, and returned to him.

CHAPTER THIRTY-NINE

Jack was gone. Looking up at the creature of flame, Faith felt his presence disappear from her awareness. It was not death, but something far more calculated, and even in the chaos she felt the pain of the loss. Yet if she didn't concentrate, she would lose more than Jack.

Above, the woman of flame was staring down at them. Both Faith and Hoa were exhausted, and she dared not imagine what the cost for all this power would be on them. Faith's entire body vibrated with magic; it echoed through her bones as if she were holding a powerful horse back from a gallop.

"Faith," Wirimu yelled.

She looked over. His eyes were wide, and he had a tight grip on his wife. Her cousin Lily did not look afraid. Her beautiful face was as calm as it has always been, but through their link Faith could feel that was not entirely true. Her cousin was still wary, still not entirely trusting, but sure that she'd never see her daughter again.

Opening her storm cloud eyes, Faith let the wind howl through her. She gave up her humanity to let it take her.

The woman of fire leapt down, snarling and aiming her wrath at the cousins.

Flames leaped from the burning building towards them. As fiercely as the fire tried to reach Faith, the roaring southerly pushed it back into the asylum.

Hilary fired her pistol at the woman, shouting something that Faith couldn't make out through the screaming wind while the other agents ran again for cover. They usually worked as a tight team, but

Faith hadn't really had time to get her partner up to speed. This was not a situation that had been covered in their training.

The shot actually hit home, knocking the screaming woman off her feet, but one simple bullet wouldn't stop this creature.

Faith didn't have enough time. She spun about, pushing Wirimu and Lily to the ground, and screaming to Hilary to take cover. The final wall of the asylum blew apart, throwing bricks and molten glass over them.

Hilary's pain bloomed in Faith's head.

"No, no, no," she screamed, scrambling to reach her partner. Hilary was thrown on her back, her fingers fluttering at a triangle of metal embedded in her throat. Her eyes were bulging as blood bubbled from the wound and her mouth.

"Wirimu!" Faith howled, clamping her hands against the wound.

He came running, his healer instincts overriding the danger around them. Pressing his hands over Faith's, Wirimu called on his magic, but she knew that he was almost as drained as she was. Healing their wounds from the train had taken him to the edge of death and madness.

Faith watched with held breath, for a minute unable to consider anything apart from the life ebbing out of her partner. Hoa warned her, just as the woman, shaking the remains of the collapsed wall off her back, leapt once again at her.

Yet it was Lily that saved them; pushing with her magic. The compulsion that Faith had feared in her cousin twisted itself around the woman of flame. She stood outlined against the horizon for a second, her hair burning, her body nearly consumed, and then the power of Lily's magic reached her.

She turned and stumbled away down the hill a little as Lily poured her magic into her, willing her to leave the asylum in peace.

Go, go, go!

Wirimu looked up, relief and delight etched on his handsome face as his magic worked on Hilary. "She's going to make it," he gasped out.

His wife's attention wavered, hearing her husband, she turned and smiled. Faith knew that her cousin had no experience in battles, magical or otherwise. She called out a warning, but it was too late.

Their attacker spun about. Her charred flesh cracked and split. Whatever power was using her had very little to play with left. Still, it used what it had.

The instant blossomed into flame. Hoa tried to be everywhere at once; he smothered Faith and her cousin with ice and cool wind and tried to protect the others as well.

That brief moment of panic was where Wirimu chose to put himself in the path of the flame instead of his patient. It was the way of the healer.

The magic that was the last implosion of power from the woman caught him full in the back, surrounding him, drawn into his lungs sheer bloody luck.

He was dead before he hit the ground.

The woman was consumed by the power she'd released, but the toll she'd taken was terrible indeed.

Lily was screaming, and Faith didn't try to stop her going to her man. All she could do while her cousin cried herself raw was hold her. A beautiful, brave and good man was gone from the world and that was worthy of tears.

Hilary was alive, but barely. Through growing darkness, Faith could make out the approaching cautious figures of the surviving Eyes. The consequences of her own magic exertions were about to catch up with her.

As she fell into Shock she could hear a strangers voice, it couldn't be her own, "Look after Lily…"

And then, she and Hoa slipped under the wave of darkness.

In this world of grey, there were words. A subliminal whisper that she'd never heard before. Her battered senses seemed to think they were the call of her seraphim…

We are the earth. We are the food you eat. You inhale us while in your mother's womb. We sleep quiescent and are woken only by pain and loss. Just as you are born with blood and agony, so too are we. Your victories and your despair are ours as well. Like you, we fear being alone, and hunger to be known. Do not cast us out, for our demise would be your loss. Love us.

PART FOUR

The Shaky Isles

New Zealand, 1931

CHAPTER FORTY

Faith pushed one of her blonde curls behind her ear in what she hoped was not a nervous gesture. The warmth of a Napier summer made her feel even more uncomfortable, but she couldn't afford to let it show. She had to assume she was being watched; it was one of the givens while undercover.

Crossing the street, her stylish high heels made a staccato rattle on the hot pavement. Ahead, the park was an oasis in green, a place where children splashed in a leaping fountain, desperate to cool off, and young mothers in large sunhats were walking their dogs and progeny.

Smiling and nodding to her fellow Napier citizens, Faith hoped that she appeared nothing more than another stylish woman out for a stroll on a summer's day; someone who was making the most of her day off.

After making a few sharp turns and wandering down into the sunken garden where she had a good chance to check behind her without it being obvious, Faith made her way to the dead drop.

The rubbish bin was seldom used, tucked in the back of the remembrance garden where the sun beat down without mercy. People avoided it at this time of year for the joys of the fountain and the shade of the palm trees. Pausing and making sure that it looked like she was depositing her ice cream wrapper into the bin, she in fact shoved it into one of the slots at the back of the bin itself.

The signal being given, she moved quickly back to where the Chinese lantern in the corner was slightly loose. She tucked the small roll of paper up and into the stone.

Hilary would wander past in a few hours, as this was the appointed day for any communication. Without such contact, Faith would have been truly on her own. Deep into the organisation as she was, she certainly couldn't risk a phone call.

It had taken nearly eight months to get to this point, and success was so close Faith could taste it on the tip of her tongue.

The fallout from the burning of Shorecliff was still being assessed by the Ministry, but they'd been made painfully aware that they'd missed the real message of the baby farm. The escapee from the breeding facility hidden beneath the main building had told them as much as she could remember. As she'd been kept drugged and humiliated it hadn't been as much as the Ministry might have wanted.

Still, the gist of what someone had been trying to do had been enough to scare the government to action. Lane and two of his superiors had been quietly shuffled off to less 'demanding' roles, and two more vigorous leaders moved in. Captain Lourdes was Faith's sort of commander. Whip smart and yet earthly, she'd taken a rapid assessment of the situation and decided that someone had to try and penetrate the underground organisation immediately.

Finding it had been half the trouble, and Lourdes had insisted that the person who went in had to be a very strong Awakened. Having woken in the hospital five weeks after exhausting her reserves, they still thought Faith a good choice for their next job.

Walking back from the park, she made sure to keep her steps even; it would not do to appear to be running away. Faith relaxed into her cover as best she could. Looking out to her right at the sea, she smiled.

Although she missed the raw blast of Wellington weather, Napier had its joys, too. The warm and flat landscape still took some getting used to. It was a gentler place, and didn't have the frantic pace of the capital. However, it was in this sleepy seaside town that she had finally managed to work her way near the group of people who might well at last know those responsible for the burning.

The grocery shop where Faith, under her cover of Anna Schmidt, had taken a job was quiet in the mid afternoon heat. The housewives tended to come in the cool of the morning, leaving the afternoon to less diligent folk, so when Faith went in to the shop, it was clammy and still. Mrs Allanby was standing behind the counter fanning herself. The little bell over the door rang cheerily but could barely be heard over the jazz coming from the radio.

Fiona Allanby was young, bored, and fond of American music. Mr Allanby on the other hand, was in his seventies and more than happy to let his energetic wife, thirty years his junior, while away her time in one of his shops while he spent his hours on the golf course.

"Anna," Fiona's voice suggested she would be more annoyed if she could be bothered. "Glad to see you back. I've got to go out."

Faith managed to retain her sigh. Clemments, Mr Allanby's accountant, was prone to just drop by, and then she'd be forced to act as cover for the delinquent wife.

So, Faith was left alone in the hot shop, contemplating what on earth she was going to say if that happened. The worst thing, though, she was truly alone.

Hoa had hidden himself down deep at her request; sleeping, waiting for her call. Even though she knew he would come, it didn't feel right. The empty place inside her where he should be ached.

So lost in that painful examination was Faith, that for a moment she didn't even notice that the bell over the door had rung. Spinning around, Faith saw Reggie Clint standing by the door. Without Hoa, she couldn't be sure he was Awakened, but something about the sly smile on his lips made her think he was.

Or perhaps it was only his own assurance in his good looks; those he had plenty of. A tan fedora was tilted over his steel grey eyes, and she would have to have been a statue not to be a little thrilled by the light in them. This was one part of her cover that she didn't have to fake.

Falling into bed with Reggie would have been the easiest thing in the world, but knowing what she knew, it would be impossible to give in totally to pleasure. Part of his attraction had to be related to the danger. It had to be.

"You closing up soon?" He picked up one of the tins and tossed it in the air while shooting her a sideways smile.

It would have been good to have Hoa there to soothe her racing pulse, but if Ray noticed the blush in her cheeks it was all to the good. She nodded.

He pushed back one of her blonde curls and tucked it behind her ear. "You sure look sweet today, Anna. I'm looking forward to showing you off at the club tonight."

The club. Faith's stomach tightened at the word. Ray had hinted that important people went to the Jazz Cat Club. It had taken months of doing the rounds of parties and dances to get to meet the right people and manipulate them into getting her to meet more of the same. Reggie had taken a long time to meet, but not long at all to impress. She'd dyed her hair blonde because the rumour was that was his absolute preference. Now that things were getting closer to some sort of resolution, she wasn't sure that she'd got in a bit too deep.

Hilary and the Ministry were staying well back, and her dead drop had told them to remain so. Covering her concern beneath a shaky smile she hoped he would assume was shyness, Faith asked, "Should I get real dressed up?"

"Your best!" He spun her around as if there was music already in the air. "I want everyone to envy the hell out of me."

Reggie kissed her long and deep, not caring about the people walking past in the street who stared in. Faith kissed him back for a good while too, but then remembering her cover, pushed him off a bit.

"Not here," she whispered in what she hoped was a fair impression of a shy country girl.

It was a little harder to pull off these days, but being Awakened, she still retained most of her youthful looks. Perhaps Reggie thought that meant she was more desperate than most. Women had a harder time finding decent men since the war, and with the way things were shaping up in Europe, Faith had the impression that wasn't about to change.

Dropping her back onto her feet, Reggie sauntered to the door. "I'll pick you up at eight." Then he was gone.

Faith served the few afternoon customers in a fog, arranging in her head what she was going to need that night.

Risking closing early, Faith hurried home, knowing that anyone looking might assume she was just an eager spinster off to hook a man. The little bedsit she had rented was even stuffier than the shop. Taking a cool shower, she tried to get her head in a place where she was only Anna.

The training at the Ministry had been all about keeping the cover to the fore of the brain, while the agent hid beneath. Plenty of Awakened had minor magic that could peer into the upper thoughts of a person, but luckily anything deeper was very rare. Those that could peel back layers that hard to reach were also highly unstable and usually able to be spotted pretty quickly.

Well, that was what the training manual said. After seeing what she'd seen at Newlands and Shorecliff, Faith couldn't be sure of much.

She slipped into the daring red number. With her natural red-brown hair, Faith would never have worn such a colour, but Anna was blonde. Anna was also a lot more desperate than she'd ever been for a man.

Except Jack. Faith flinched upright. If she couldn't control those sort of thoughts, she could be in big trouble. Jack hadn't chosen her. He'd disappeared and the one thing she'd learned in her life was you couldn't make someone love you. He hadn't. End of story.

The little Derringer .22 fitted just right into her sequined purse, not too tight, not too loose. She didn't want to have to fumble around in the bottom of any bag should the situation suddenly turn ugly. Lacing up her shoes and taking her rabbit fur stole out from the wardrobe, she waited by the door until Reggie tooted his car horn from the road.

Her father would have probably gone over and punched a man in the mouth that did such a thing to one of his daughters, but Faith clenched her teeth and went out to meet him.

CHAPTER FORTY-ONE

Life was either unfair or cruel. Standing on the porch looking out over the sunburnt grass, Jack Cunningham contemplated what exactly he was going to do about that.

Emma appeared at the door, leaned around it and smiled at him. "You ready for dinner, darling?"

She always did that, looked absolutely normal. Friends were always telling them what a perfect couple they were, how lucky they'd been to have found each other again, and Jack would agree. He had no choice.

She might be his wife on paper, but over the months and years he had seen through that. So, he was forced to be an actor. "Sure," he replied as he returned her smile. "Smells good."

When she retreated to the kitchen, he went into the house and wandered down the hallway towards the bathroom. The heat in Napier at this time of year was blinding, and a cool flannel over the back of his neck felt like a good idea. Especially when he needed to focus.

He passed the small second bedroom, which should, by rights, have been a child's. It had been Emma's lack of worry about filling it that had first alerted Jack to something not quite right. His wife had always been eager for children, anxious to the point of slight obsession, but this newer version didn't seem bothered.

At first, he'd put it down to whatever horrors she'd seen at the asylum, but it was just the beginning of his suspicions.

The chill water down his back and over his face felt incredibly good. Certainly, these days concentrating on the simple things had become very important; he filled his head with superficial thoughts when Emma was about.

It had taken Jack Cunningham only a few weeks after the chaos of the asylum fire to know that the woman he'd saved was not his wife. Emma looked just the same as she had that last day when he'd left for the shores of Turkey. Exactly the same—which should not have been possible.

No, he couldn't dwell on that. Marshalling his thoughts about the heat of the day and the good smells that reached him from the dining room, he went to meet her with a smile on his face.

"Delicious…" He pulled out his chair, sat down, and began to eat with relish; that, at least, was true.

In the depths of the trenches, in the chill quiet of the asylum, he'd imagined such a scene; laid all his hopes on it. Now that it was real, now that Jack was actually living what he dreamed of, he could only heartily wish it had never come true.

His Emma had not been Awakened. She'd been sweet and naïve in a way that the young Jack had loved. The woman across the table was none of those things.

As he spread mustard on his corned beef and watched her across the table, he felt very alone.

Waingaio had scuttled deep to avoid her notice, doing the only thing she could to protect Jack from his wife's attention. He missed his seraph. The world had certainly changed now that was true, but he would have done anything to feel his seraph once more.

"Are you going out tonight?" Her voice held no ounce of rancour. After all, what self-respecting wife would be bitter about her hard-working husband having a beer with his friends?

His hand was steady as he scooped up the last few forkfuls of peas. "Yes, it's Simon's birthday, so we're all meeting up after dinner. Just for a pint or two."

"Alright then." She kissed the top of his head and bustled into the kitchen. If he was a liar, Emma left him very much in the shade.

Once he was out of the house and walking through the warm Napier evening, Jack let his thoughts run loose. He wanted his seraph back, he wanted to feel the cool coil of her reasoning in the back of his skull, but above all, he wanted not be alone with these nasty vicious thoughts which he had no actual proof of.

The pub was just the same as could be found in every other small town in New Zealand; double doors and frosted windows made it impossible to see into. Menfolk from all around were strolling towards its darkened doorway.

Jack licked his lips, already imagining the taste of a good hoppy beer. It was a pity he couldn't let a drop down his throat.

Inside, the place was all brown calmness. Men leaned on the bar chatting with Norm, the owner, while others were cradling their pints, and chatting around high tables. Everywhere was the smell of smoke, old beer and leather. It was enough to make any woman's lip wrinkle with distain, but to these men it was comforting.

Sometimes Jack did indeed buy a drink just so that the other patrons didn't grow suspicious. It was amazing how if he bought men a bunch of beer, they seldom noticed that he didn't drink in turn.

But today the bar was relatively quiet, so he moved over to where there were three public telephones. One had been broken longer than Jack had been coming here, but the other two worked just fine. He pulled out the tiny fold of paper he'd shoved between the back of the phone and the wall it was attached to.

On it was scrawled two phone numbers. Jack considered for a second and then put money in the slot.

"Number please?" the operator's chirpy voice sounded so normal that he hesitated for a moment to give it to her.

Jack spoke the numbers, and then there was another operator. "Ministry of Awakening. How may I direct your call?"

Clearing his throat, Jack knew this was the tricky part. He'd only caught two names in the mayhem of the asylum fire. Memory of the most important one bloomed in his senses. Trapped in a tiny underground space all those years ago, and yet he could recall the pleasure of her lips on his. With a shake of his head, he addressed the faintly annoyed sounding receptionist, "Do you have an agent there called Faith?"

"Do you have a last name, sir?"

"No, sorry."

He could hear her barely repressed sigh of exasperation and in the background the sound of pages being flicked. "I'm sorry Sir, I can't find any record of there being an active agent with that first name."

It would have been too much to hope for success just like that. "You mean she may have left the Ministry?"

"I couldn't say, Sir."

Jack could tell she was running out of politeness the longer this conversation went on, so he took a gamble. "What about one called Hilary? A Chinese agent." Surely there couldn't be too many Asian agents in Wellington. It had been barely ten years since they'd had the immigration taxed lifted, and some regarded them still as lower class New Zealanders.

It was a good thing agents needed to be contacted, or he got the feeling the receptionist would have hung up long ago. Another furious flicking of papers began in which he could hear the echo of people walking in the hallway and the sound of girlish laughter.

"We do have an Agent Hilary Chen."

Finally. "Then can I speak to her?" he tried to sound as pleasant as possible.

"Agent Chen is on medical leave at this time. Can someone else help you?"

It was tempting to blurt out his fears to this unknown woman. He'd kept them all bottled in, hidden, for so long that it would be good the share them. Unfortunately, they were just that—feelings. These were things that the Ministry would hardly take too seriously. Added to that, he wasn't exactly sure what his status was with them. Jack had not exactly checked out if things were alright to leave the asylum.

"No...no I don't think so." He hung up quickly and shot a look over his shoulder, but no one was listening. It was very tempting to spend his life totally paranoid and when he was around his wife that was probably a good idea. However, he'd not had any evidence that any one else was involved.

The barman scowled as Jack put back the receiver. Jack found it vaguely amusing that once he had been a publican's best friend. Ignoring the angry stare, he considered the remaining change in his pocket; there was one other person that he could call.

Hemi, his old war buddy had moved northwards while he'd been locked away in the asylum. They'd lost touch before that—mostly that hadn't been Hemi's fault either. But shortly after moving to Napier, Jack had run into him on the street. They'd been in touch a couple of times, but he'd never divulged any of his concerns about Emma to his friend. Hemi was married to a lovely young woman from his own tribe, one his mother had introduced him to. They had three children and the kind of happy, calm home Jack had dreamed about. He couldn't bring himself to drop his concerns into that situation like a grenade.

So, Jack dropped his change into the bottom of his pocket and left the pub. Outside the sun had finally slipped beneath the simmering hills, setting the clouds alight. Looking at that fiery cloudscape, he was reminded of the burning asylum.

Jack wiped his brow. Everything had gone wrong in his life, so that even the reunion with his wife had been tainted. It would be nice just to have some moments of real joy.

Deep down, Waingaio stirred. Perhaps she was feeling guilty for leaving him for all this time, or perhaps she, too, was miserable.

Jack heard the car race up the street. It was so quiet that everyone on the street turned and looked. Across the road, the Jazz Cat Club had just turned on its lights. The car screamed to a halt opposite and the door popped open.

Jack, standing among a group of three other men yacking outside the pub, turned to look. He wasn't the only one—everyone on the street watched the woman slide out of the car.

Napier was a small town, and not many women dressed like that. The long bright red dress clung to every dangerous curve on the woman. In the summer heat she wasn't wearing a jacket, so that everyone got a look at the length of her pale back. Jack heard one of the men to his right let out a low whistle. The woman's artfully curled white blonde hair rested lightly on her shoulder.

Jack barely took notice of the burly shouldered man who bent to talk to her, for something in the shape of her face had triggered a cascade of emotion.

Waingaio snapped alert inside him. She filled him with all the heightened seraph senses that he had forgotten the joy of. Scents, colours and sounds threatened to overwhelm him for a moment.

While he struggled to right himself in the flood of sensation, the woman and the man entered the Jazz Cat. The battering of music that poured out from the open doors made him shake his head.

Could he have been wrong? Jack pushed through the little group of men who were still talking about the shot of glamour they'd just seen pull up. Over at the club, it was still early. As pretty much the only hotspot in Napier, Jack had heard that the club could be both bulging and slightly dangerous at the same time.

Half way across the road, he came to a stop. This was foolish; his eyes must have been mistaking him. Faith had always been sombrely dressed, with a mass of dark brown hair shot with red in the light, and even if those things could change, she had been full of seraph magic. The blonde had been empty of any such power; a deadhead, a sleeper, a slumberer.

He must have been mistaken. A car screeched to a halt a bare few inches from his heels.

"Bloody hell!" The driver leaned out and screamed out him, "Get out of the damn road!"

In the glare of the headlights, Jack could make out that the car was packed with men. Most were leaning forward glaring at him, but one in the back was relaxed, leaning into the shadows, hat tipped forward.

His seraph filled him with sudden, undirected anger. His hands clenched at his side and his lip twitched in the snarl of an animal bought to bay. For a minute he stood there twitching in the car headlights, fighting the urge to leap up on the hood and smash his way through the glass. The hatred was that intense.

Eventually he stuffed down Waingaio's emotion and staggered out of the path of the car, turning up his collar against the sudden chill that came in the wake of the rage.

"So, you're back," he muttered to his seraph, keeping his chin low so people wouldn't easily notice that he was talking to himself.

A rush of love flooded him. It felt as though Waingaio was hugging him, so joyful to be back in her place, even more delighted that he had missed her. Jack had a new appreciation of why seraph were labelled 'he' and 'she'. Waingaio was totally female in his mind's eye. He'd never really noticed that in the first years of his Awakening, too occupied with his own misery, most likely.

After a moment of enjoying each other's presence, Jack directed his gaze once more to the door of the Jazz Cat. "So old girl, do I go in?"

Waingaio shared his excitement at the thought of Faith; she had been delighted to share power with the agent's own seraph. Now, however, there was real caution tingeing her thoughts on that matter. In the ether was no hint of Hoa.

Jack started upright. The palette of a seraph's communication was usually only emotion and strange urges, but somehow, just then, Waingaio had told him the name of Faith's seraph. Had he heard the name or had she placed it in among his memories?

Sometimes it could be very confusing sharing a brain and body with another consciousness; hard to tell what was his and what was hers.

Inside the club the band must have finished tuning up, as the car that had nearly hit Jack pulled up, they could be heard belting out 'Come Back Sweet Papa'. The cornet sound rose to toe-tapping heights above the guitar and piano.

Stepping back into the shadows of the haberdashery across the street, Jack watched the men climb out. The broad shouldered man exited first, looking about nervously. Then, after a moment's pause, the man in the back did. Jack only caught the back of the blond man's head as he didn't look about at all, simply entering the club in between the phalanx of what could only be guards.

Once again, Waingaio roused to inexplicable anger. While her host was trying to quell her, the man paused at the door. A chill ran down Jack's spine as he watched the man's shoulders bunch. He still didn't look around, but something was menacing never the less. Waingaio, perhaps even more aware of the dangers, stilled herself deep down, and Jack found he was holding his breath.

The man walked into the club, followed by his heavies. Now, the sensible thing would have been to head home, or back into the pub, anything rather than walk across the street again and try to follow. However, as angry as Waingaio was, she was in no mood to try and stop him.

Pulling his hat down a little more over his eyes, Jack entered the Jazz Cat Club. Inside, the night was just beginning. All the bright young things of the small town were making the most of the band and many were up and already dancing. Jack tried his best not to look out of place, strolling over the bar. Now was not the time to reveal himself as a teetotaller; that would probably result in a quick ejection. So he ordered a single malt whiskey and turned as casually as possible, pretending to take in the twirling skirts and high spirits of those on the dance floor.

The room was even smoker than the pub across the road, but at least the smell of stale booze was missing. The low hanging green lampshades cast the whole place in a very eerie light that did nothing for his nerves. Waingaio had subsided to a dull angry rumble in the corners of his mind, but the effect was still the same; he had a killer headache.

Turning a little to his left, he took in the slightly raised area holding the main cluster of tables. This was where both the cluster of goons and the blonde were. Jack took no notice at all of them as he was totally concentrating on the woman, and from this distance, it was unmistakably Faith.

Dressed slinky, Hoa hidden away, and with her hair dyed an incredibly pale blonde, but still the woman he knew; the Weather Witch. Time had not changed the effect she had on him. The difference was that this time, looking around the room, he could see that he was not the only one.

Jack found he was bristling when the goon in the tan fedora slipped his arm easily around her shoulders. Across the table, the guy that all the other men deferred to was watching her with the eyes of a predator. Somehow, the guy still managed to hug the shadows. Waingaio was practically screaming at him to go over and pull Faith away from whoever these men were. Over there, under that sickly green light, she looked very frail and vulnerable. If somehow she had lost Hoa, then she was exactly that.

For once his and his seraph's thoughts were in line with each other. Tipping back his hat a little, Jack strode over towards the table, determined to rescue Faith from a dangerous situation—whether she wanted him to or not.

CHAPTER FORTY-TWO

Lily waited by the phone, chewing the tips of her fingers. Hilary had said she would call when she'd picked up Faith's dead drop; if there was anything to pick up. The phone was silent.

The churning continued in her stomach. Faith was so close to finding the people responsible for everything; from her original kidnapping to the asylum fire, to Maggie's kidnapping.

Wirimu's death had been terrible, a blow that she might never recover from, but it was returning to find her uncle and cousin in panic. Jean had put Maggie down for her nap, and she simply wasn't there when she went in to get her later. No windows or doors were forced. It was just like when Faith had been taken.

Tau was no use; he had retreated and had barely spoken since the fire. If it hadn't been for Hilary, the agent her husband had died saving, then she might well have walked into the sea in utter misery.

She and Faith had promised to get Maggie back, and while her cousin had gone into deep cover, Hilary had made it her mission to look after Lily.

Looking around the small bungalow they shared, Lily smiled faintly. Hilary had filled it with flowers, her attempt to keep the younger woman's depression at bay. Some days it worked—some days it did not.

Hilary was obviously caught in some Ministry business, and Lily simply could not sit still. Day was grudgingly giving way to night in that long slow way it did at this time of year. It would be nice to get some exercise and not to think for a while.

Putting on her coat, Lily locked the front door and went down to the park. No one bothered locking doors in Napier as a rule, but she'd seen too much of the world not to at least try to keep the bad things out.

Stuffing her hands in her pockets, Lily guessed that a storm was coming. It was too warm, and the stars to the west over the ocean were obscured, yet something dark seemed to be rushing towards them from across the sea. If she had still belief in such things, she might have thought it an omen.

So, Lily increased her pace, walking through the gathering dark head down, towards the park. It was a pleasant spot to stop, next to the duck pond. She had a favourite bench where in daylight she would feed the birds and think of her daughter. How would Maggie have changed, she wondered as she sat down in the gathering darkness.

Quiet and hidden in the deep shadow of the palm tree, Lily noticed two figures walking towards each other from opposite ends of the pond. Quickly, Lily drew up her legs and smothered the chatter of her mind—a skill that she'd retained. One walked right past her and up to the other coming from the direction of town.

"Time's up." The woman's voice hovered on the edge of Lily's recognition.

"It can't be." With a clench of horror Lily did recognise that second voice; it was Hilary. She wondered for a moment if she should rush to help the agent, but something in the tone of her voice didn't communicate surprise.

"You've had all the time we can give." The other woman's form was strangely impossible to make out, even though she was closer than Hilary to the distant street-light.

"We're bringing Faith in and now it is time for you to do the same to Lily. Her daughter is proving rather untalented."

Lily had to jamb her fist into her mouth to avoid squeaking out Maggie's name. Instead, she drew her limbs in closer, trying to become a limpet on the park bench as she strained her ears.

"But her mother isn't any more so," Hilary protested, sounding more beaten than Lily had ever heard.

"We'll be the judge of that. The end game is coming. The ship will be here in a matter of days and we will need all our experiments moved to our base in Fiji."

"But you'll let Joseph go when you do?" Hilary took a hesitant step forward. "You promised, and after all I've done..."

"Don't even think to demand anything from me." The strange woman's voice became sharp. "Your brother is our surety that you will continue to do as we say. You'll have him back when we are done and no sooner."

Hilary took a long shuddering breath, and then her shoulders slumped. "Very well."

Lily waited, choking back her own breath as the two women went their own separate ways. Slowly, she let her legs slide back down off the bench, and clenched her hands around the edge of it tightly. Trying to pull together her scrambled thoughts, she felt tears escape her clenched eyes.

Hilary was her friend, someone that Wirimu had died to save. Lily had thought that meant something, in fact she clutched onto that friendship when everything else seemed so dark and cold without her husband or daughter.

"Oh God," she whispered finally unable to contain her despair. They'd talked about Maggie. That meant they knew where she was. In fact, that meant that they were responsible for her child's disappearance. A chill anger began to build inside her—the primitive rage of a mother denied her offspring.

Deep down she called for Tau, demanded he end his sulk and rise up to help her find Maggie, to do whatever it took.

The seraph stirred within her, unfolding senses so that the world became so much more than any Sleeper could ever imagine. The shadows lightened, the sound of the cicadas in the tree sounded like intricate symphony, and she could smell the complex mingled smells of the ocean and the trees.

Now you see you really need me, Tau hissed in her ear. *Together we will destroy them all.*

Lily would have answered, but the shadows were moving again. With her reawakened senses, they seemed to twist and coil like oil, finally disgorging the female shape she'd just seen bring Hilary to heel.

"There you are." The voice, which had been niggling at the back of her mind, finally dropped into place. It was the woman who had whisked her away to the asylum from the home she shared with Wirimu. Because of her, Maggie had been left vulnerable. Lily had been deceived by this evil creature.

She gave a ragged howl of outrage, and rushed to vent her maternal rage at this creature. Blindly, she ran at the woman, willing to choke out of her where Maggie was, but instead something grabbed her by the throat. She found her cry die into a strangled gasp as her airways were clamped shut.

"Now don't be silly," the woman purred. Her beautiful face was perfectly calm, as she looked up at Lily, dangling uselessly in the shadows. "Don't you want to see your child again?"

Lily, despite the spots dancing in front of her eyes, nodded desperately. She wanted nothing more than that. To know she was safe.

The woman smiled, but there was nothing comforting about it. It was the grin of a confident predator. "Then let us bring this sweet family reunion about as quickly as possible."

And though Lily knew in her heart bad things lay ahead, the thought of seeing Maggie again lightened her heart. Everything would be alright after that. Everything.

CHAPTER FORTY-THREE

So absorbed was she in her acting, that Faith almost missed the approach of the stranger. Her back was mostly to the door, but she caught Reggie's body language; a slight tip of his chin, and a stiffening of his shoulder. Like all animals, Reggie was intensely territorial.

Flicking her head, Faith was stunned by who she saw. Jack Cunningham. Just standing there.

After she'd woken from seraph Shock, she'd returned to the ruins of Shorecliff to search for him, but there had been no sign. Faith had called the wind, and flew over the hills looking for him or a hint of where he had gone. It had all been in vain. Faith could still recall the sharp bite of rocks on her knees as she knelt sobbing in the devastation if the asylum.

Everyone assumed Jack had been killed in the fire; a lot of people had died there and most were burned down to almost nothing. In the aftermath, the confusion, the finger pointing, none of the officials had been too concerned with one more dead patient.

Faith's heart hammered in her chest when she saw him, standing there, smiling with his hands in his pockets. Immediately she saw that he was not the man she'd been trapped in that box with in Newlands, nor the gaunt comatose victim she'd pined over, but something else, something much, much better.

Lily swayed slightly. He was older, having lost that fey handsomeness she'd felt under her fingertips, but age had honed that beauty. A streak of grey glinted in among his hair, but his eyes were unmarred. God, she thought to herself, after everything he's been through how can he look so good?

A tremble of longing ran down Faith's spine; quite ridiculous to be feeling that right now. Yet even in the midst of it, she was aware that Reggie and the people he'd just about been ready to introduce to her were bunching for action.

Before they could move, Faith leapt to her feet and threw her arms around the newcomer. "Cousin Jack, can it be you?" He looked flummoxed for a moment, so she barged on. "It's me Anna, surely you recognise your own cousin?" She giggled and flicked back her bob. "I know the hair has changed a little." With her back turned to their observers she gave him a hard look.

"It sure has," he said catching on quickly and without any dawning realisation being apparent on his face. "You look real different."

Faith spun about just as the band struck up 'I Ain't Got Nobody'. "It's been ages since I've seen my cousin Jack here, Reggie. You mind if we have a quick dance just to catch up? I'm sure you have lots to discuss with your friends."

Reggie was, thankfully, one of those men that believed so totally in their own attraction that they didn't bother with jealousy. Given any half decent explanation, he would always take it, and it certainly didn't hurt that a small town like Napier usually meant everyone was always running into someone or other they knew.

He waved them away and took another sip of his drink. All the men chuckled, but some shot distinctly sharp looks in Faith's direction. The man that she was most interested in meeting, but had yet to get the name of, watched her expressionlessly from under the brim of his hat.

Faith pulled Jack onto the dance floor before they could get in any more trouble. It was to save him from getting killed there and then, but it also had the advantage of getting him close to her.

"Faith," he whispered as his fingers tightened on her waist.

Shooting a smile to Reg over Jack's shoulder, she could only hope that he hadn't heard that. "The name's Anna. Don't forget it."

"Why does everyone change their name?" he muttered, his brow furrowing.

She leaned forward and hissed in his ear, "Because I am undercover, silly."

His shoulder's tensed under her hand, but he drew her into a brisk foxtrot to the lively sounds from the band. Faith was pleased to find out Jack was a tidy dancer.

"What are you up to?" Jack asked softly.

"You don't get to ask that when you left me thinking you were dead." Faith locked her eyes with his, and he was the first to drop away.

Jack spun her away before pulling her in tight. "So where's Hoa?"

His closeness made her blush, but as he turned her about she whispered fiercely into his neck, "He's hiding since my cover is not as an Awakened. Get it?"

She could tell that Jack was examining the men at the table each time he turned in the right direction. Soon Reggie would begin to get restless.

"I think you better go soon," she whispered.

The look that she recognised passed over his face; it meant they were consulting their inner symbiote. It was too much to hope that anyone with a seraph in the room would avoid being able to feel Waingaio, because such a powerful entity could not be concealed for long. Already the men were turning their chairs, and she caught the tail end of the head man's gaze. It was directed not at her, but at her dancing partner.

At any other time Faith would have embraced Jack, exclaimed at the miracle of his survival and thanked God for it. However, right now he was quickly getting in the way of her cracking this case. "Let me be, Jack. I've nearly found the people who've been pulling the strings all this time. The people responsible for what happened to you."

His hand tightened on her waist. "I have so much to tell you. My—"

Before Jack could get her into trouble, she spun free with as much elegance as possible. "Now there, cousin Jack, it was grand to catch up. Say hello to Aunt Ida." Faith walked quickly off the floor just as the band leapt into a swinging rendition of 'Them There Eyes'.

She kept her breathing even, smiled at Reggie, and only turned about once to wave at Jack. Thank goodness he took the hint and melted back into the club's shadows. Dropping into her chair, Faith took a big gulp of her gin and tonic. "That Jack, he sure is a laugh. Haven't seen him for an age," she managed to squeeze out.

Reg didn't make a comment; he had his girl back, and surrounded by his cronies, he felt secure. Faith knocked back her drink in a desperate manner and returned to the demand they had flung at her just before Jack arrived. "What did you need me to get again?"

The man at the end of the table finally tipped back his hat and looked at her directly. His face was unnaturally smooth looking for someone who appeared to be in his late forties, and the eyes gleamed for a second in the light like a cat's. No Awakened would have ever caused such an effect…well, as far as Faith was aware. Unable to test Hoa's reaction, Faith could only stumble on, and stumble she did. It was not put on, but also not out of character for Anna.

"I mean," she said clearing her throat, "anyone can walk in and just buy what they like at the shop. We haven't been rationed since the war."

Even without her seraph, Faith could see they all slightly tensed, and it confirmed what she guessed. It was the nineteenth century all over again. New Zealand had already fended off at least two attempts by foreign nations to enslave its Awakened people. Perhaps they had been foolish to think it would never happen again, perhaps their triumph in Europe had made them cocky; whatever the reason, Faith was surely not going to allow that to happen. Smothering awareness from her expression, she tucked one of her bleached curls behind her ears.

"There are certain things that we need, more than just flour…" The man's voice was soft, but tinged with more than a little disdain.

"The Allanby's sell dynamite to the miners," the man called Tuesday said, taking off his hat and dropping it onto the table. Faith felt her jaw drop.

Concealed under the hat, the top half of his skull was horrifically marked. Half a dozen finger-width shiny scars fanned upwards from his eyebrows into his hair as if some terrible creature had raked him. Faith thought of the creature wreathed in flame she confronted on the train and later at the asylum.

"Oh these," the man said as his fingertips lightly traced the terrible and unusual marks, "were given to me in the union riots in Auckland."

Faith would have asked how on earth he expected her to believe that, but Anna just nodded and made a sympathetic noise.

Tuesday leaned across and laid the tip of one finger on the back of her hand. "You are important. You can help."

Her throat grew dry, but she managed to squeak out, "Me? I don't have access to the dynamite or anything. Mr Allanby sells all that and is very particular."

"But you've got him around you're little finger," the nameless man at the end of the table whispered. "You're very good at that sort of thing—aren't you, Faith?"

It was then that she realised just how deep she was—and it was so far down even the Ministry might not be able to help. The circle of men tightened around her and the Jazz Cat went instantly from comfortable to terrifying. She reached for her power and Hoa, but they were quicker still.

Faith heard the squeal of a trumpet as the band reached the end of its song, and then the world sparked white before falling into darkness.

CHAPTER FORTY-FOUR

Jack watched from the shadows, poised for a moment, and holding Waingaio back from doing something that would get all of them killed. In the trenches of France, he'd learned that a mad rush seldom solved anything.

As much as it hurt to have left Faith in the club, Jack instead watched the entrance from a shop doorway across. When he saw the huddle of men bundling a slumped woman that could only be Faith into their car, a hot rage washed over him.

All but two of the men piled into the car behind the woman, and the car peeled away from the pavement with a squeal. The remaining men, including Faith's presumed boyfriend, clambered into the remaining vehicle and followed after at a slower speed. Waingaio was filled with dreaded certainty and Jack shared it. He knew if he lost sight of Faith now, he'd never see her again.

So, just as the last car got ready to turn, he made his decision. Crouching low in the shadows, Jack ran after it, and just before the driver put his foot down he stepped up onto the back running board. Folding himself against the wheel, he ducked down to keep himself from being seen, and hopefully the slight pressure on the suspension wouldn't be noticed by two drunk men intent on keeping up with their boss.

The truth struck him though; no one knew where he was. He and Faith could be swallowed up by whatever this thing was that they had fallen into, and they would barely be missed.

With his fingers white around the edge of the spare tyre, Jack knew that there was only one person that he could possibly find in this moment. He still had a link that had been forged in the trenches of Turkey and France. Hammered by war, it was still there, still powerful.

Blindly Waingaio reached out across the distance, which had always meant far less to seraph, and touched Hemi's symbiote. Just for a second, Jack caught a flash of his old war buddy's life; his beautiful young wife's laughing face as she stood by flapping washing out to dry by their house, a baby balanced on her hip.

Ahua. Waingaio leapt with delight to find her sister seraph again, and for a second Jack was almost knocked off his tenuous perch by the flood of emotion. That was the thing with the symbiotes; it was always emotion all the time.

However, with the two seraphim holding open the channel, Jack could communicate with Hemi directly. It was a strange kind of communication; not as limited as that with a seraph, but still not as easy as speaking to one another.

Never the less, Jack was able to get across that he could do with some backup post haste. Hemi's voice rattled through Jack's brain, *Tell me where you are when you get there. I'll find you.*

That settled, Jack was able to concentrate on hanging on and not ending up as a nasty smear on the road, because the driver was really pushing his car to keep up with the one containing Faith. They passed quickly out of the town and began to climb into the hills surrounding Napier, their headlights carving tiny slices into the utter darkness of the countryside.

Finally, the cars passed through a pair of iron gates, though he saw no sign of guards. Another odd thing in a very odd day.

They rumbled up a gravel driveway, the stones spitting and chattering up against Jack's legs. Peeping around the corner he saw the long, low black shape of a building against the half-eaten moon. For a second he imagined that it looked a little like Shorecliff. The mere thought made him shudder. This building was considerably smaller, had no looming tower overhead, and the lights were on in every window.

When the vehicles drew up in front of the house, Jack dropped quickly to the path and ran to the dark corner of the building. Waingaio smothered him in silence and darkness as he went.

Jack watched intently as all the men got out, one with Faith carried over one shoulder like a bag of wheat. Waingaio slid deep into Jack's consciousness again, as the boss man strode sharply towards the large front door. Whatever the seraph feared, she was unable to express.

When all of them were in, she appeared again, pushing out the boundaries of his awareness tentatively into the house itself. The place was buzzing with Awakened presences; yet not the usual ones that Jack was used to feeling. These had all the magical strength of the seraphim, but there was no welcoming thrust of the symbiotes. The house in front of them was curiously soulless, empty of the joyful clamour that usually surrounded them. In fact, he was fairly certain that the only creatures in the house were human.

Jack could never have imagined a moment in his life where he'd find that such a terrible thing. If he could go back in time and tell that tormented younger self that he would ever feel comfortable in his skin, even if there was an extra person in it, that Jack would never have believed him.

Tucking that realisation away for later examination, he followed the wall around the back of the house. If they were up to nefarious deeds here, then the blazing lights said they were unconcerned if anyone saw. Such blatant disregard made Jack's pulse race and he instructed Waingaio to send a message to Hemi immediately, just in case they dropped off the face of the earth in the next few minutes. There was no way he wanted to find himself back in an asylum situation.

Jack reached the first of the large illuminated windows. Inches away from the truth, he took a deep breath and hazarded a quick glance in. Leaning back against the cool brick building afterwards, Jack clenched his teeth to keep a wail from escaping him. It was as if all of his past was wrapping him up and choking him; the people tied with green cord, the dead-eyed children on the farm, and the terrible prisoners in Shorecliff. What he'd seen in that room was another in the line of darkness; people in hospital beds, perhaps only teenagers, all lying still with a menacing matron figure seated just as still by the door. Perhaps a dozen, perhaps more, he hadn't seen the full extent of the room in one glance.

How many of these goddamn people were there in his country? Waingaio was, for once, a tumult of emotions; she was terrified for him, terribly angry and deeply sad for those people inside. Jack couldn't make any decisions based on her tumbling emotional state. So, he would have to go on his instinct.

He dearly wished for a weapon; preferably a gun, but in this situation even a knife would have done. Waingaio warmed him, reminding Jack that together they were a weapon, more powerful than anything made by man. Like her host, his seraph could be a little cocky, but it made him smile in what was a fairly dire situation.

Yet he didn't want another Trocadero Hotel or Shorecliff. If he went in there with his power, those people could be dead. The memory of the trapped patients' screams in the asylum was one Jack was sure he would never shake. He wouldn't create a situation where such a thing might happen again, and Waingaio was in agreement.

He followed the building further round, hoping to find a way in by more conventional means so he wouldn't have to rip a hole in the wall. Having worked his way round to the back door, he reached out, ready to give the handle a subtle testing. Jack didn't really think it would be that easy, but neither was he expecting the door to suddenly swing open.

Waingaio leapt to open up all paths to his magic, ready to allow her host to defend himself. But it was just the slim form of a woman standing outlined in the bright light of the hallway beyond.

Jack might have expected Faith, or even in the back of his brain maybe his wife, but it took him a long moment to recognise who it was. That strange lady he'd talked to briefly on the hill just before the asylum caught fire. He'd never suspected she'd had anything to do with it; yet here she was looking at him with something he would classify as a feral gaze. It was not her physical presence, which was definitely slight, but the power behind her eyes. They were not human eyes, they were golden as if seraph possessed her.

Yet Waingaio knew there was nothing of her kind behind those eyes. The wave of fear she communicated to Jack flooded his body with adrenalin, enough so that he could run. He should run.

Too late. It was far too late for him to escape that gaze. Whatever it was that lurked behind those terrible eyes reached out for him, and Jack could actually feel its fingers in his brain, even though the woman had not moved. The grip was icy, numbing his senses and choking shut his throat. His muscles failed him, shutting down under the assault of this creature.

Jack realised his knees were folding and he was falling, yet he couldn't find the will to bring his hands up to catch himself. He fell forward onto his face, something that should have meant instant unconsciousness. However, terribly, it did not.

He couldn't feel Waingaio, as his thoughts chased themselves around his skull. Where was his seraph? It wasn't just like the times when she hid; then he still knew somewhere deep down, or even when the asylum had shut her down. Then he had known she was there, just that he couldn't reach her. This time it was utter silence and loneliness.

The woman's eyes, gold and terrible, focused on him until the world narrowed to her. Jack felt the weight of them pinning him and realised he was drowning in them. It was like being trapped between sleeping and awaking; unable to move but screaming inside his head.

CHAPTER FORTY-FIVE

Faith jumped as the door to her cell swung open. Without Hoa, everything made her jump. Those gold eyes set in the face of her cousin had robbed her of the one person she'd been able to trust. Hoa. She wrapped her arms around her knees and held back her tears as two men came in dragging a third. One of the men doing the carrying was Reggie, and the person he was helping to drag into the room was Jack.

She'd been planning to feign disinterest, yet could not on seeing their prisoner.

"What the hell have you done?" she screamed, but they ignored her as if she were nothing more important than a barking dog. Without Hoa perhaps they were right and that was all she was.

As the door slammed behind Reggie, Faith turned all of her attention to Jack. It had to be whatever the terrible thing was behind Lily's eyes that had done this—just as she had done to Faith when she arrived. With a shake of her head she loosened Jack's shirt collar. That look Lily had worn was burned into her mind—the woman who had attacked Shorecliff was the same.

"Come on, Jack, wake up. I can't be down here alone." Her voice cracked with exhaustion and fear. All Awakened had existed before the arrival of their seraph; it was possible to survive without the symbiote, at least she kept reminding herself that. "I know it hurts, Jack," she whispered into his ear, "but you lived before Waingaio— come back to me."

For a few moments, Faith could feel her throat tighten and her stomach clench. Then Jack gave out a great gasp, as if he'd been punched in the gut. He pulled himself upright, and mercifully, there was no gold in his eyes. They were as green as she recalled.

For a moment they stared at each other, years and disasters falling away.

"Hello," Jack said with an off-centre grin, "so, are you ready to go now?"

"Go?" Faith blinked once.

"Yes, don't you know a rescue when you see one?"

"I think I would, but," she pointed out his chained leg, "practicality says you wouldn't get far with that."

"Perhaps so." Jack rubbed his head, and she recognised the flicker of despair crossing his face.

Lightly, she touched the back of his hand, uncertain what words could describe her longing.

Jack took her offered hand and gave it a little squeeze. "I am sorry, Faith—leaving after Shorecliff like that…but you see I found my wife…"

She yanked back her hand. "Wife?"

He ducked his head. "Well, I thought it was my wife, but she—well she isn't the same person I married. Literally. Changed her name and everything. She's no longer Alice, she's this twisted Emma person."

Faith wasn't sure if this some sort of play for her affections in the face of death. "What do you mean?"

"At first I thought it was trauma, but after a while…" He paused and would not meet her gaze. "I saw the thing behind her eyes."

Faith shuddered. Without their seraphim, they were stumbling towards understanding, she knew that—but she also knew Jack, more intimately than any man—thanks to their time underground in Newlands.

"Now," he said leaning back against the wall, "I think I know why she insisted we come to Napier. I saw the same expression in that woman that did this to me."

The pieces were falling into place. She drew in a long breath. It was always Jack and her—a constant dance that flung them away from each other, yet drew them back into each other's orbit. They both had their loved ones caught up in this.

So she whispered the truth to him. "That's my cousin Lily. Whatever has happened, it isn't her fault. She's a lovely person, really."

"Was lovely." Jack shuffled closer and put his arm around her. "She's gone now, like my Alice."

Faith leaned into his embrace. "There is something in there—but it is not seraphim. Not from Hoa's reaction—he was so angry, so afraid."

"You mean he recognised it?"

"Oh yes, definitely. But he couldn't give it a name."

Therein lay the problem; no one could say what exactly a seraph was, so hard to quantify what it was not. They were silent a moment, and Faith knew they were thinking that very same thing.

Finally she cleared her throat. "Whatever it is, it seems they are working with foreigners. I heard German, Russian, even American accents..."

"Bloody hell," Jack swore, "I thought it was the government—our government."

"Definitely not," Faith said emphatically. "The Ministry put me undercover to find out who it was. And I'm sure it's just like the nineteenth century, when they tried to make slaves of the Awakened. Magic makes us valuable commodities; I think they learned that from the war."

In the early days of the nation, there had been dark times indeed, and every New Zealand child was still taught about them. To even imagine that they could be repeated in the modern day was a terrible thing.

"We've got to get out of here to make sure that doesn't happen." Jack tugged on his chain experimentally. Unfortunately, it was not some old relic; it and the rest of them were bright and shiny under the one swinging bare bulb. Obviously their jailers were prepared for prisoners.

"How do we get our seraphim back?" Jack asked, and his voice conveyed his loneliness and frustration. Much had changed with him, indeed.

Faith shifted uncomfortably, not willing to tell him the one way she knew of for sure. He'd been there when she'd last used this method.

Seraphim were deeply seated in the physical—odd for a creature that didn't have any body of its own. The only possible way to bring them back from there was to call on very physical, very primitive experiences. Starvation, pain or sex, were all known to drive out a seraph.

He came to the same conclusion. Jack tilted her head up to his gaze, "We haven't got time to wait for starvation, and I suppose I could let you try and beat me to death with your handbag…"

Faith didn't want it to just be sex. The attraction she'd always felt for Jack Cunningham was not based just on his physical beauty, but something much more. They'd been twined together in a way that no Sleeper could understand. She wanted him. All of him and for longer than just now, yet if they didn't awaken their seraphim, there would be no tomorrows.

No human had the real words to express such things, there were only actions. She needed Hoa and Waingaio to bridge that gap, yet without her symbiote, she was hesitant. Faith slid her fingers up against Jack's neck, feeling the moment as vividly as his skin.

They kissed as they had under the earth, pressed as close as clothes would allow. Jack's stubble bruised her skin but she accepted whatever the experience would give.

She was burning and aware of her body in a way she had forgotten. Jack's hands cupped her face while he proceeded to kiss her thoroughly. It felt so good that the rest of the world seemed to become irrelevant, and finally pleasure overwhelmed her fear and loneliness.

Though Faith was wearing only her slinky red dress it seemed too much, and Jack was definitely overdressed. Her desire to feel more of his flesh made her fingers fumble on his rough jacket, tugging on his shirt buttons to get her hands against his chest.

She was reduced indeed to a primal creature. It felt so sweet to be touching him, kissing him, letting him do whatever he wanted with her. Abandonment and passion tumbled together.

His lips travelled along the line of her neck, and his slight muffled sigh let her know that the joy was not hers alone. The sharp impact of his teeth on her shoulder punctuated desire down to her core. The demure and shy Faith was gone, washed away by longing. Instead, the new animal writhed against Jack, heedless of her dress riding up or falling down.

Letting go of that last trace of inhibition broke down the final barrier. Faith and Jack were wide open to the world, more accepting and ready than ever before. The seraphim rushed upwards, free of the places they'd been forced to. Hoa and Waingaio twined and curled upon each other as they leapt upward, revelling in the passion their hosts had let loose, like creatures born to it.

This was why many Awakened preferred to find lovers among the Sleepers. No secrets were possible when seraphim took to each other and danced like fire through the veins of their hosts.

It would be easy to fall into pleasure and never want to come away from it; spiral down into delight and end up useless to reality. Finally, it was Jack that pulled back. They held each other's gaze, breathing raggedly, clothes askew, and the faintest tint of gold disappearing in their irises.

Faith had never felt such desire before in her life. It was hard not to give way to such a thing. She'd never thought of her attraction to Jack Cunningham dangerous before, but she might have to reconsider, given what had just happened.

Hoa and Waingaio's emotions were so tangled. If the seraphim had their way, the humans would be on the floor giving in to it at this point. Luckily the symbiotes always gave their hosts the choice— unlike whatever had Lily in its claws.

Careful, God we have to be careful. Want her so much right now.

Jack's thoughts were bleeding into hers, making it even more difficult. She folded her hands over Jack's so that they couldn't go where they really wanted to. "We have to be careful," she said as evenly as possible.

"You can hear what I'm thinking?" Jack was embarrassed and horrified.

"It's just part of the being...close," Faith assured him. "It will let us use each other's power and control. That's good."

Their seraphim were smugly glad.

"Sure." Jack reached out and laid his finger on the restraint around his ankle, too worried about his control to try it on hers. A muffled pop rattled the steel. It was the smallest, most contained explosion he'd ever managed. With a slightly surprised grunt, he made short work of hers as well.

Standing next to the door, they listened with all their heightened seraph senses. She was worried, too. Hoa was already ranging far ahead of them, cautiously searching for Lily. He did not want to touch whatever lurked inside her head.

"Good thinking," Jack said over his shoulder as he began examining the lock on the door. "We'll have to deal with her before we can stop all these people."

She nodded shortly, aware that he spoke the ultimate truth. She'd been hiding from doing this for years—time for kin to take care of kin.

CHAPTER FORTY-SIX

Lily now knew the answers. Standing in the middle of a personal maelstrom, she could see far more than any other Awakened could have imagined. Scholars and scientists had sought what she could now see laid out before her in all its terrifying glory. She walked in alien worlds, heard the cry of the pursued and the hunters. They fled—the others followed.

Trapped in the flames, she wished she could have cried. It was every nightmare she'd suffered since her mother's death. Yet she had managed one tiny success, one chance of redemption. She had told the men to put Jack Cunningham in with her cousin. Together maybe they could reverse what Tau had made her do to them.

Yet where was Maggie? Where was her daughter?

It doesn't matter. Tau hissed, and the flames flared to life once more in her nerves.

Unable to scream or writhe in agony, Lily's body sung with unshed agony.

You don't matter.

Tau was no seraph—that was the truth. The Craven Man had not Awakened her to a partnership of magic where she would never be alone. That would have been too wonderful. No, she had been made into a vessel for something that only needed a body, not co-operation.

Now Lily knew the horrible truth because she was living it. This was an incubus inside her. She'd heard the name from Emma's lips, said with a laugh that was both bitter and condescending.

The image from Tau was even worse; to him she was merely a fruit that had finally come ripe. An incubus was birthed even harder into this world than a seraph, and the one she carried was the most important of all.

Beyond the flames, Lily's streaming eyes could make out shapes moving. Emma talking to a tall man in a fedora, and beyond, huddled forms that she'd caught glimpses of before the flame claimed her. The incubus had some powers of their own, but most they stole from seraphim. The poor unfortunates were Awakened kept for this purpose, chained both in body and in mind.

Lily could feel Tau drawing from them. Their symbiotes were poor, small things, but the incubus drained them like they were dairy cows hooked up in the milking shed. The image was terrible to contemplate yet accurate, and yet Lily herself was no better off.

Maggie was close, that much Tau allowed her to comprehend. She could feel her tiny fluttering power, and knew that they had taken her for a reason, but as yet the incubus would not reveal.

Just let it be over soon. It had to be over soon.

CHAPTER FORTY-SEVEN

Jack was glad of Faith's hand in his. It was the only reassuring thing in the darkness. Hoa and Waingaio were just as entwined, delighting in their nearness, and communicating something that might have been determination.

They would meet guards; Jack knew that. In a place this size they would encounter resistance, but he'd seen what the woman at his side was capable of so he wasn't afraid for himself. He was afraid for the helpless prisoners he had seen on his way in.

Yet there wasn't a choice.

"I'll be careful," Faith whispered into his ear as they crouched in the corridor. The single light bulb hanging at the corner illuminated her face in stark, beautiful planes. The determination written there was as powerful as any soldier.

Pushing away the remains of his desire and ducking low, he shot a glance around the corner and up the stairwell. They could both hear people moving about and the shuffle of many feet, but Jack could only see a broad door with a huge, thick lock on it.

They moved as quietly as possible up to it. Faith's expression was an open question; who would open this door and how? Jack smiled and then pressed his palm against the wood.

It was easy, so easy that he had to bite back an exclamation of surprise. Waingaio and Hoa seemed to be feeding each other a lot of power, like a serpent biting its tail. His own magic had never been so calm. Focusing, Jack could push his awareness through the door and onto the other side with no effort at all.

The tang of metal filled his mouth and he felt the cold stillness of magic bound prisoners. So there were guards, at least three, and maybe twenty-five prisoners. If they blew the door open, people would be injured. Jack felt utterly helpless.

Faith twined her fingers in Jack's and he felt her trust flood over him like balm. A memory flashed from his coma; her voice, low and beautiful speaking words that she probably thought had no meaning, yet had reached him.

Hastily Jack pressed his lips to hers, an unspoken thank-you, before he asked Waingaio to let him have the power.

Stay close, Faith. This will get very, very loud.

Putting aside his own fears as best he could, Jack stood up and let the magic flow through him. The explosion was the perfect size to rip the door off, blowing it off its hinges in an impressive but controlled manner.

Leaping through the noise and dust, Waingaio's alertness prevented him from having his hand smashed in by the rifle butt of the nearest guard. Swaying aside, Jack retaliated with a right hook. He'd never been a great boxer, even in the war, so when his opponent crashed to the floor as if felled, he was a little surprised. No time to ponder that one. He leapt over the body, while catching out of the corner of his eye Faith picking up the fallen guard's pistol. Certainly she could not summon the storm in such close confines, but she wasn't a shrinking violet without it. As Jack charged the remaining guard, to the right he heard her shoot through the cloud of dust. Waingaio let him feel Faith's chilled determination; however, Jack's blood was up. Frustration and rage fuelled his attack.

The guard was bringing up his rifle. Reflexively, Jack threw an implosion at the danger. It was deadly accurate. The rifle blew up in the man's face, and he went down screaming and clutching his head.

Jack spun about as another guard raised his pistol to fire, but a slender Chinese Awakened, apparently released at least slightly from the miasma, threw himself sideways at the man. The gun went off, but thankfully into the roof and Jack was again able to knock him cold.

Breathing heavily, he and his clear-eyed rescuer stared at each other for an instant. Then Jack spun about, worried that Faith was in danger, but he needn't have worried. As an agent, she had more experience in these things than his now distant military training. She was standing there, looking back towards him, a slight gleam of satisfaction in her eyes.

"Joseph Young," the man said, his eyes still slightly shadowed, as the Geas faded from him. He was very pale and thin, like the rest of the prisoners, but Jack recognised that focused determination he'd seen in men just as starved on the beaches of Gallipoli.

"Jack Cunningham. Got any experience with a gun?" When the man nodded, he threw him a spare pistol.

Faith was busy rounding up the Awakened, gently guiding them up the corridor. When she had them in a huddle and they didn't look like they would run off, she strode up to Jack. "Lily isn't here, or her daughter Maggie."

"A little dark-haired woman?" Chen asked.

"Yes—have you seen her?"

The man nodded. "We're the last lot; they're loading the rest onto boats. I think she was with them."

Jack exchanged a concerned look with Faith; he could see this wasn't the end of his rescue mission. "Get these people out of here," he commanded as he slapped the young man on the back. "There are two cars outside, enough to get you all back to the town. We'll need some help quick smart." Jack paused, looking once more at Faith, seeing her pale determination and feeling the depth of the power she had tapped. "Get as many police and ambulances as you can," he told Joseph quietly.

Then, sure that the man would do his best, Jack held out his hand to Faith, "Let's go get your cousin."

CHAPTER FORTY-EIGHT

Like any other fairy tale, there was always a catch, a price that had to be paid. Faith knew it but was not sure Jack did.

The truth was that if they summoned the storm, the kind that was needed to bring this event to a conclusion, then they risked a great deal. Following Jack as quietly as she could, Faith studied that cold hard reality.

Seraphim were not fragile creatures, but there were limits, and channelling the might of the weather was not something she ever did without thought. Every time was dangerous. If she did as Jack asked, and she didn't doubt the necessity of it, then she was risking her life and that of Hoa. A rush of affection from the seraph was followed by a feeling of such trust that she had to blink back tears.

Faith wiped them quickly away as she and Jack reached the cover of a mass of toi toi grass. This close to the beach, the tang of the sea was invigorating, knocking out the final fuzziness that had come with her abduction. The thick mass of thin sword-like leaves hid them well, but the sharp edges cut Faith's bare shoulders.

Jack peeled off his jacket and passed it to her wordlessly, all the time peering around the side and down to the sweep of the beach. In the sliver of moonlight, Faith smiled as she draped herself with his offering.

On hands and knees she too crawled through the dubious protection of the cutting grass to see what lay below.

Down on the foreshore, eight boats were pulled up and a handful of guards were organising the shambling Awakened into them. Her jaw tightened to see that more than half were children. So engrossed was Faith in this spectacle, that Jack had to point to a place closer where another knot of people were conversing. They were only about twenty yards away, but the sound of the wind and the splash of the waves would have made the conversation impossible to overhear, were not Jack and Faith's seraphim helping.

One was Emma, Jack's wife, though Waingaio comforted Faith, conveying that this was only by legality. Emma was talking to Lily. Her cousin's tiny frame seemed bowed as the breeze blew her dark hair over her face. Only Hoa's caution prevented her from starting up from their hiding place.

Jack grabbed her hand. "You see it, right?"

In fact, there was nothing to see, but Faith understood what he meant. The scene was tinged by their seraphim's anger and horror, and she was suddenly absolutely certain that though she could sense a seraph down there, it was something far worse.

Pressing his lips against her ear, Jack whispered words that froze her to the spot. "Have you ever wondered if there are any evil seraphim?"

It had been questioned before; theologians and university professors had wrestled with that one, and she'd even read a paper on that very question in her early days in the Ministry. The conclusion had been that the seraphim never showed any sign of attempting domination of the country. They might have strange emotions, but their only concern being their host.

Yet she could not forget the look in the eyes of the attacker on the train—or indeed in her own cousin. Though she ached for Lily, she couldn't let the creature inside her take all these Awakened away.

Faith jumped when Jack touched her hand again. "I'll keep that lot busy," he whispered, jerking his head towards the small knot of people, including Lily. "You stop those boats from pushing off."

It was a kindness, a chance that she would not have to hurt her own cousin. She grasped the opportunity to avoid that. Neither would she let him go off into such peril without some sort of thanks. Thrusting her fingers into his hair, Faith pulled him close and kissed him, desperately and deeply. The flow of magic between them and the danger of the moment added spice to it and she didn't want to pull away, or stop, or face reality.

Jack did though, tracing her lips with his fingertips and pushing hair from her fancy style back behind her ear. "Be strong, beautiful.

Let me see everything you have." And then he was up and into the darkness without a goodbye, wending his way towards the knot of people that included Lily.

Faith straightened behind the toi toi, clutching at the grass with both hands. It cut deep. The sting and shock was a reminder of other pains, other losses. She travelled back to the moment on the kitchen table of her parent's house where the doctor had cut free her smallest finger; no pain relief, only the look of horror in her father's eyes.

Hoa and she recalled that memory and that moment, like whales taking a gulp of oxygen before the great dive; the moment when they had become one creature. Then, in unison, they let the magic take them.

Her feet might be walking on the sand, the wind buffeting her skin, but Faith could no longer feel it, wrapped in a cocoon of power that had almost disengaged her bodily sensation completely. Only Hoa kept Faith in one piece, holding her to her goal as the storm filled her up. The tang of lightning was in her mouth, the strength of the wind ran in her veins, her eyes blazed with the white of the sun and her skin ran cold as ice. Only a thin strand of conscience remained; the thinnest strands of Hoa and Faith clinging together as the magic roared around them.

Dimly, they were aware of the people down there on the beach, shouting and pointing. The Awakened were, to her strained perception, like bottled glow worms, creatures not meant to be constrained. In the mind of the guards she could see how she appeared now; hair ripped loose and whirling in a mad wind and eyes shining like beacons in the darkness. But these were people used to magic; they did not throw down their guns and run off in fear. The six of them raised their rifles and shot. The bullets were caught by the maelstrom that was birthing around her, whirled away into nothing, and onwards she walked towards where the sea thrashed against the shore.

We are the sky father's revenge. They sang. *Rangi-nui flows through us.* And in their minds bloomed remembrances of alien skies filled with lightning and the roar of winds greater than anything earth could birth.

One guard, grasping his bravery, leapt at her with a knife. The sky spat lightning. It entered the man's body through his head and leapt out through his pointed elbow, piercing him through in an instant.

The distant portion of Faith that remained human felt sorry for him, caught in the powers he did not understand.

People out in the boats also began shooting, but the sea was her instrument. The wind rolled it like ball of wool, smashing huge waves over the boats, breaking and destroying those that would take seraphim from their country.

The blond man, the one Reggie had deferred to, came at her, pushing out of the mass of confused Awakened. He was armed with no physical weapon, but Faith and Hoa immediately identified the greater threat. Her seraph filled her, motivated by some primeval hatred that had to be given its head. One word filled her head, the very first word she'd ever had from her symbiote. It roared through her head for a second, blanking out even the sound of the magic. *Incubus.*

It felt very, very good to give a name to the creature that had been haunting her sleep for so long, and to face an opponent she could unleash her fury on. He wore no familiar face, and while she could feel a wash of despair from Jack, she had yet to hear any pain. So, she let the storm have its way with her.

The man, throwing off his hat, seemed to also let his basic magic take him. The shadow coalesced around him, shrouding his body in darkness until he became a man-shaped pit of nothingness. Then he leapt at her, slicing through the protective layer of whirling wind as if it simply wasn't there. The lightning struck him over and over again, yet was just absorbed by his cloak of darkness.

Faith felt his hands wrap around her throat, so cold that they burned on her skin. This was the creature that wanted her people, desired them, not just for what they could do for foreign nations—but a far more ancient enmity. As the chill invaded her body, draining the magic so that she had to feel her body, she could also feel the incubus.

The humans might have plans for the Awakened, but the other creature needed them. They were like the seraphim in that respect, but no other; they needed a host. Whatever knowledge Faith might have winkled from their connection was suddenly impossible as the blackness began to stuff her throat. She was choking, dying, and worse, she could feel the enemy ripping into Hoa. Abruptly, he that had no body was in pain as well.

In panic Faith called out to Jack, but Waingaio was occupied; something terrible was happening around Lily. Without his magic,

Faith could feel herself going under. Out of the corner of one eye, she saw something moving up on the ridge above the beach, near the toi toi as she had been. Seraph sight helped her recognise it. Hilary. What was she doing here, had she come to save Lily?

Hilary had always been a giver, an enabler of the powers of others, like a battery to the rest of the Ministry agents. Where many might have resented this role, Hilary had always seemed to be content, so it was no surprise to Faith when she felt the familiar coils of linkage between them spring up. It was so easy after years as partners, and all that had happened since then streamed across the connection.

In an instant, Faith understood, knew why the other agent was here. Her brother was now safe, and she'd come to make amends for betraying Lily, her charge. Hilary gave all she had to give...too much. Guilt was a powerful emotion that often drove people to do crazy things, but Faith had no words to stop her friend. The link was made and she had no way to undo it.

The flow of magic through her was utterly complete and, with horror, Faith knew that Hilary was literally giving her all that she was. There was nothing she could do about. Tears sprang from her eyes and were swiftly whipped away.

Sacrifice, as it had always been, was the ultimate power, one that not even the darkness could touch. It was Hilary's revenge.

Bursting out of Faith, the wind of the South cut through all before it, blasting the Craven Man and the creature within him away. It was not just her enemy that was damaged. Faith and Hoa screamed together as they were flayed by so much magic passing through them. Their howls reverberated together like two instruments being driven beyond the limits of their range.

When it was past, the woman's body sagged, the storm dropping away from her, and the wind releasing her.

The world swelled and see-sawed before her eyes while the waves lapped over her. Far off, there was the murmur of people, but it seemed very inconsequential. Her body, oddly, was still doing what it needed to be doing, gasping for breath, twitching to keep her from drowning. *Why is it bothering?* Faith wondered, because she could feel nothing inside. Panic welled up in her, a terrible realisation that she was alone. Hoa was gone. Her emotions were all her own. She was now a Sleeper. Alone.

Someone was sobbing, a ragged voice kept repeating, "Oh God, oh God no!" Only when people took her by the arms and pulled her from the surf did she realise it was hers. Blinking sand out of her eyes, Faith opened them to see a small child with Wirimu's eyes looking at her. She was incredibly beautiful under curling dark hair, and she was staring at Faith with openness and curiosity. This was what Hilary and Hoa had given themselves to save.

They weren't safe, yet. Brushing her tears back and clenching herself over the hollow portion where her seraphim had been, Faith staggered to her feet. Up the beach, Lily was burning and she could see Jack struggling with one of the men. If things went badly...

So, she grabbed up Maggie, her cousin's daughter, and struggled to her feet. She had to get the Awakened out of here—even if she was no longer one of them. The connection to Jack was gone, along with Hoa. Instead, she clenched the pistol that had miraculously remained tucked in her dress and turned to get the people to safety.

CHAPTER FORTY-NINE

Jack wouldn't allow himself to feel sorry about killing the foreigners. They were soldiers from other countries come to steal what was most precious to New Zealand. It should have shocked him how easy it was to step back into habits he'd thought he'd left in Europe.

Jack felt the storm at his back, but could not turn and look because he had his own problem. It was his wife.

Emma stood between him and Faith's cousin. While the frail looking girl hung in the strange pillar of fire, Emma's slender form seemed oddly sinister.

Looking into those eyes of darkness, Jack felt the last remains of the illusion drop away from her. Indeed, she was not his wife. The last time he'd seen his Alice had been on the wharf, waving him off to war. This creature was only wearing her skin. That slow rage he'd been feeling for the last few months, that he'd taken so much care to conceal, abruptly caught light.

He had no chance to voice it though, because Emma spoke first, her eyes darting past him, "Now you have both pushed me too far."

Jack dared to follow her gaze, to see Faith shepherding the Awakened away up the beach. She had the attitude of someone bent, but not broken. He caught her anxious glance over her shoulder, but Waingaio could not find Hoa at all. The seraph wailed inside him.

"You see, Jack," Emma said with a haunting smile, "you are quite alone."

The thing inside her moved behind those eyes he'd once loved. Jack decided that perhaps the only useful thing he could do was to play for time; Faith had to get those people away.

"Not as alone as you are." He took a step closer, the hand in his pocket holding tight to his stolen pistol. The early morning sun seemed incongruous with the darkness that seemed to surround Emma. It was not merely a physical shadow, but something much deeper. The air itself bent around her.

Her beautiful face was folded into a frown. The Alice he remembered had seldom frowned. "When did you know, Jack?"

The hitch in his voice made him stop. Perhaps he'd been wrong, maybe his wife was still in there. He tried to act nonchalant. "I guess it was only the last few months. I wanted it not to be true. I wanted you to be Alice."

Looking down at the sand, he noticed something very odd about the shadow on the sand. It was not that of a woman alone. It blurred and twisted, a chaotic form that never seemed to settle on anyone thing. Pieces fell into place in his head.

"It was you all along," Jack said with a ragged gasp. It stretched out on the broken ground before them both like a representation of everything they'd suffered. He looked up at his wife's eyes. They were pits of reflective madness, like a cat caught in the headlights of a car. Only this onrushing vehicle was the realisation that he was right. "You are the Craven Man, Emma."

She took a step back as if Jack was offering up violence rather than truth. Gaining strength from her confusion, he took another step forward. It fell into place neatly. The news of his death, the one that the foolish bureaucracy had sent after the push at the Somme, had destroyed Alice.

"You don't know," she whispered as her hands clenched at her side. "You don't know what I did, but it was your fault. I wanted to let the loss out, but I let something in instead. I had our child, I had to get rid of it. Get rid of me and it together."

She paused while Jack choked on what she was saying. A child. She'd tried to kill herself even though she was pregnant. Somehow in the Awakening, the death, the child's death—somehow the darkness had found a way in.

Whatever Alice had become, it wasn't her fault. He tried to remind himself of that as the torment on her face was replaced with a slow smile. "You left," she whispered, "but he came instead. He found me, not just one silent seraph…no, because two had Awakened. The incubus followed."

The way she said that made Jack horribly cold. "And the child?"

Her lips twisted in a sneer. "He could not survive Awakening so early, but his death sealed the deal."

The thin female form twisted and Jack caught a glimpse of the Craven Man that had terrified Lily; it was the male shape had even ravaged and raped her, forcing her to become host to an incubus as well.

Jack could feel tears in his eyes as he raised the pistol. Emma's form flickered, beautiful as ever, and she looked so like Alice.

"Shoot," she whispered, staring down the barrel. "The incubus cannot be removed from me."

It had been hard enough to kill strangers, but now here was the woman he'd married asking him to do the same thing. Jack couldn't. He knew he should, but his hand was trembling, unable to tighten his finger on the trigger.

Too late, the darkness swept back and her soft blue eyes filled with it. Waingaio howled a warning but it was the burning woman that acted. She reached out from the fire, and for a second managed to hold back the magic that threatened to choke Jack.

He was caught by surprise and his finger spasmed on the trigger. Emma fell to the ground, her hands going to her throat as blood gushed over her breasts. He'd shot her, just like that.

"Alice?!" God, was that his voice? He ran to her, finding his own breath choking him.

Like the seraphim, the incubus' greatest weakness was their host, and that much blood could only mean one thing. No dark power could save that body.

Jack dropped to his knees next to Emma. She couldn't talk, but she grabbed his hand. Whatever darkness had taken her was still in her eyes, but also the faintest glimmer of Alice-past. He'd left her when he'd known how fragile she was. This was his fault, too. It didn't make any difference—she was mortal and there was nothing to be done. Her mouth worked but no sound came out. Darkness finally took all of her.

But there was no time for mourning, for the woman in the fire howled. "Get Faith. Get my cousin, this end is coming." Her voice was broken, wrecked, but he didn't doubt her for an instant.

CHAPTER FIFTY

The incubus in Lily's head did not care that its own kind were being killed all around. It had no feelings of comradeship with them, any more than it did with her. So, Lily's surge of delight at watching her cousin defeat those that had put her through that was only short-lived. She heard Jack's conversation with Emma, and realised the truth of the matter. The woman had also been possessed of an incubus, but had not had enough power to open the way for more of its kind. It had needed someone with more potential.

Apparently that was what the young Lily had once had.

Bright mind indeed, perfect for us.

The voice that she had once wept with joy to hear now made her quake with horror.

Had to be broken though, for me to enter. Tau went on, enjoying the effect he was having on his host. *So much was needed to do that wasn't it, little gem. Our pact was sealed when you were given to us.*

Lily thought of her mother's death, recalling the small girl who had once been so full of hope and sunlight. It seemed like a long time ago and very unfair that someone had forced her onto that path. Her seraph had been beaten down just as it entered the world, and the incubus brought through instead. Lily felt such sorrow that her potential had always been chained, as her seraph had been. She'd never known it.

Looking out through the flames, Lily saw her cousin running back through the dunes. She had Maggie! In Faith's arms was her child, tousled, with wide brown eyes, but alive and with her kin. Lily could see Wirimu in that beautiful, tiny face and smiled even while in pain.

"It's too late…" Lily felt the fire burning through her bones. The magic had already begun. Indeed, beyond the flames she could see that the sea was already quietly withdrawing from the land, leaving a broad strip of wet sand flicking with abandoned sea-life.

The place of landing shall not be compromised. I shall destroy the people with fire and earth and then we will come—come to hunt the seraphim wherever they hide. Look on your kin for the last time and weep.

And she did. Faith was arguing with Jack while the power of her incubus began to flow into the earth at their feet. She had the same choice as Emma, but Jack's bullet would not reach her, could not reach her.

Lily looked down into herself, to the tiny ember of the nameless seraph that remained; a poor creature that had been nearly consumed by the incubus Emma had placed in there with him. It was no wonder she had been mad for so long.

Help me, Lily asked the creature, even as the earth began to move under her feet. If the invader succeeded, the devastation would be terrible, and she was very, very tired of fighting. Yet she could save those that she still loved—Faith and Maggie.

It cannot be, she spoke to the seraph, *we will not let it be. Together, as it was supposed to be.* As the focus of the magic, she couldn't allow herself be used, so together she and the injured seraph inside Lily turned the power inward.

It hurt—it hurt through every fibre of her body and every strand of her soul. The alien power, from whatever place the seraph and the incubus came from, poured through her. It was too much for a mortal body to contain, too deep and too wild.

Looking out from the flame, Lily saw Faith one last time, and her beloved daughter. She smiled to them, raising her hand so they would know she was not afraid. *Dear family, you were the only thing that gave my life any purpose. I love you so very much, my darling Maggie. Be well, grow up happy.*

Then she turned her face to the brightness and let it take her away.

CHAPTER FIFTY-ONE

"Get down." Faith felt Jack drag her to the ground just as the light flared as bright as the sun come to earth. He wrapped his body around her and Maggie's and held them tight. The backlash she was unable to comprehend, except on a physical level, but that was more than enough.

The earth buckled and thrust upward, a rolling, sickening motion that a human brain could barely comprehend. Beyond Jack's protective arm, Faith caught glimpses of the dunes and the hills beyond, shaking until huge columns of dust rose up. The toi toi grasses and the ranks of cabbage trees lurched like drunks after a night on the town. This made her magic of the storm appear puny by comparison. What would have happened if Lily had let the incubus have its way?

The Awakened hiding up in the dunes broke for cover, screaming. They didn't get far, knocked off their feet as the ground continued to roll. The quake lasted for a very long couple of minutes.

Faith and Jack and Maggie lay on the ground for an instant. When it passed, the only sound seemed to be the little girl snuffling into her jacket. Cautiously, Jack helped them climb to their feet. They stood in a half crouch, as the earth twitched and shuddered.

"Lily," Faith whispered, numb with grief and horror. Her cousin had given her life right before her. She held tight onto Maggie, burying her face in the little girl's sweet smelling hair.

Jack rubbed her back, kissed her, held her. It made no difference. She was hollow and broken. The rescued Awakened huddled around them, as if the two of them had answers.

"Come on." Jack was guiding her, though she was aware of nothing but his voice. The others followed, lonely, uncertain, scared.

So, in a shuffle, they headed towards town, Faith lost her in own broken world. Yet she saw smoke rising from Napier city—there would be devastation there too. Jack held her hand, and they both flinched as the earth repeated a shudder.

"Look," Jack called out pointing to the horizon. "It's my mate, Hemi!"

A group of Māori men were striding towards the survivors along the beach, even as the earth gave another shake. They didn't seem at all bothered by the shuddering of the earth beneath them. Faith could feel their seraphim questing ahead, tasting the incubi influence on them.

Lily had saved them from the worst. These little shrugs of the earth's crust were nothing compared to the destruction the incubus would have wrought without her sacrifice. Her poor cousin never had a chance. Faith found herself hoping fervently that those years with Wirimu had been good to Lily.

Maggie squawked and grabbed Faith's nose. She was reminded that something remained of Lily.

"I'll tell you all about her," she whispered into the little girl's warm ear, "You'll know all about how much your Mummy loved you, how brave she was and how she saved us all."

Yet she could not shake the vast emptiness of losing Hoa. It was so painful that she didn't want to touch it. Then, something bubbled up from that place, and tears overflowed from her eyes.

You haven't lost me. Just the magic. The voice was unfamiliar, but she knew it never the less. It was her seraph. It was Hoa. He had a voice.

For a minute she stood there gaping, and squeezing Maggie. She'd thought him gone, and yet their merged senses were back, bringing beauty even to this scene of devastation.

She watched the group of Awakened struggle up the broken landscape of toppled trees and cracked road, and revelled in the joy of hearing that voice inside her head.

"Am I mad?" she wondered aloud, "No seraph ever speak."

We always wanted to, the sweet, dark voice seemed to bring her insides alive. *It is the magic that prevents it. It is our gift to you, but it drowns out our voices. Now that your magic is burnt so low, you can hear me. I am sorry for your loss. Lily was a bright light—one that the incubus used to try and reach us seraphim. He and his kin are mortal enemies to us, but we thought we had left them behind us.*

Tears leapt to her eyes. "I don't regret the loss of the storm, Hoa, but I am glad I have not lost you."

He was happy with that, glad to be loved and needed, like all living things.

Up ahead, Jack waved to his friend who was at the head of the group of rescuers. The rest of the survivors were running to them, but Jack had turned back to wait for her, and with Hoa back, she could feel every one of his emotions. That too was a gift.

She trotted towards him, and took his outstretched hand while readjusting Maggie on her other hip. The little girl was sucking on her fingertips and giggling. It was a simple gesture that reminded Faith of Lily.

"I think it's going to rain," Jack said looking up at the gathering clouds, before turning and grasping both child and woman to him as if he would shelter them from everything to come.

Looking around at what remained to be done, Faith wished she could banish those oncoming storms. Perhaps it was only temporary, perhaps one day she would wake to feel the rumble of thunder in her veins again. It wasn't as important as Faith had feared, and what she'd told Hoa was true. He was more important than the storm to her.

For right now, there was plenty of work to be done by all of them.

"It's just weather," she replied to the man at her side, feeling a strange lightness begin in her chest. "It will pass."

ABOUT THE AUTHOR

Born in Wellington, New Zealand, Philippa has always had her head in a book. For this she blames her father who thought Lord of the Rings was suitable bedtime reading for an eight year old. At the age of thirteen she began writing fantasy stories for herself.

Philippa is the author of the Books of the Order series with Ace (Geist, Spectyr, Wrayth and Harbinger), and the Shifted World series with Pyr Books (Hunter and Fox, and Kindred and Wings).

As a hybrid author, she has also independently published her novels, Chasing the Bard, Digital Magic, and her novel set in New Zealand, Weather Child.

She is also the co-author of the Ministry of Peculiar Occurrences series with Tee Morris, (Phoenix Rising and The Janus Affair). Phoenix Rising won the Airship Award for best written steampunk, and was the number eight best Science Fiction book of 2011 according to Goodreads.com. The Janus Affair was the seventh most popular science fiction book of 2012 on Goodreads.com, and won the Steampunk Chronicles Reader's Choice Award for Best Fiction. The series continues with Dawn's Early Light in 2014.

When not writing or podcasting, Philippa loves reading, gardening, and whenever possible traveling. With her husband Tee and her daughter, she is looked after by a mighty clowder of cats in Manassas, Virginia.

CPSIA information can be obtained at www.ICGtesting.com
Printed in the USA
LVOW11s1719300715

448252LV00021B/1032/P